T0082621

FIGHT

Other Books by W.R. Blocher

The Dead Side
The Dead Side: Flight
Holocaust's Child
Something About Kate

FIGHT

THE DEAD SIDE

W.R. BLOCHER

iUniverse

FIGHT
THE DEAD SIDE

Copyright © 2023 W.R. Blocher.

*All rights reserved. No part of this book may be used or reproduced by any means,
graphic, electronic, or mechanical, including photocopying, recording, taping or by
any information storage retrieval system without the written permission of the author
except in the case of brief quotations embodied in critical articles and reviews.*

*This is a work of fiction. All of the characters, names, incidents, organizations, and dialogue
in this novel are either the products of the author's imagination or are used fictitiously.*

iUniverse books may be ordered through booksellers or by contacting:

*iUniverse
1663 Liberty Drive
Bloomington, IN 47403
www.iuniverse.com
844-349-9409*

*Because of the dynamic nature of the Internet, any web addresses or links contained in
this book may have changed since publication and may no longer be valid. The views
expressed in this work are solely those of the author and do not necessarily reflect the
views of the publisher, and the publisher hereby disclaims any responsibility for them.*

*Any people depicted in stock imagery provided by Getty Images are models,
and such images are being used for illustrative purposes only.
Certain stock imagery © Getty Images.*

*ISBN: 978-1-6632-5245-6 (sc)
ISBN: 978-1-6632-5244-9 (e)*

Library of Congress Control Number: 2023907017

Print information available on the last page.

iUniverse rev. date: 05/09/2023

CHAPTER 1

Sam and Sarah Hope stand in a light rain, an umbrella over their heads, looking at the headstone of the grave tucked under a large oak tree, the branches blowing slightly in the wind in the cool May air. Sam's right arm is wrapped protectively around his wife's shoulders as she cries softly looking at the grave of their second child, Frank. He was serving in the British Royal Army when he died in France, fighting an Enemy that had nearly taken their lives and the life of their oldest child, Judy.

Both now retired from military service, they make it a practice to visit this military cemetery once a week. It is their way of paying penance for not being able to be there for his funeral. They and Judy were fighting the very Enemy who killed him.

Sam's mind wanders back to when Frank was born, when he was growing up, the fun times they had as a family, and all the things he had missed serving as a Royal Marine while his four children were growing up.

Finally, his memories lock onto the start of the events that have brought them to this point in their lives, and an end to their part in the battle to restore the world.

⟩⟩⟨⟨⟩⟨⟨⟩⟨○⟩⟨⟨⟩⟨⟨⟩⟨⟨

"Brigadier, the new Second Leftenants are here," Color Sergeant Claude Lempriere sitting outside the commanding officer's office says into the receiver.

"Have them wait five minutes," Sam Hope replies.

"Yes, sir," the Color Sergeant says, putting down the receiver. Looking up at the twelve newly minted Royal Marine officers who have just finished a brutal sixty-week training course, he says, "If you ladies and gentlemen will please have a seat, the Brigadier will be ready in five minutes."

Instead of sitting, though, the twelve, who arrived singly and in small groups over the last twenty minutes, just mill around the large off-white waiting room, looking at each other, and out the windows that line both walls, having quiet conversations, and wondering what an interview with the legendary Brigade commander will be like. One of them, Judy Hope, a five-foot-six muscular woman with her long dark hair pulled back in a regulation bun, is particularly concerned—that her father will not understand her choice to go into a combat unit.

In his office at the Stonehouse Barracks in southern England, Sam sits back in his chair, looking out the large window behind his desk, seeing nothing in particular. Thinking back over the last twenty-six years, he contemplates what his life has become. He bears both the physical and emotional scars from battles he has fought, from people he has lost. The only comfort he can draw is that his family, and the other people he is protecting, are still safe. But for how long? That is the fear that nags at him all the time. And now his daughter, the oldest of his four children, is about to join the fight. With the expansion of the military, plans are in the works to invade the Continent.

Perhaps the war will finally be over.

Sometime.

But when that invasion will take place, and the role the Royal Marines will play, is still a mystery to him. All he can do is train and conduct raids to gather intelligence and provide his Marines with combat experience, accepting the deaths and maiming that brings.

His mind wanders back to when he regained consciousness in a graveyard somewhere in what he later learned was America. How he got caught up in a brutal military force run by Sergeants who beat, tortured and killed at a whim. How he and Sarah, along with five others, escaped from the camp after he, Sarah, and George killed the four Sergeants who were trying to rape Mary, who was also in their eight-member squad. How three of their number died fighting The Enemy who kept pursuing them, until they were rescued by a brother and sister, Josh and Debbie McFarland. How they built a ship to flee from the implacable enemy who only sought to destroy.

By then, Sarah and Sam had a daughter, Judy, and were expecting a second child.

After nearly dying in a storm at sea, they were rescued by an armed British fishing trawler. Sam joined the Royal Marines, while Sarah became a civil engineer and a reserve officer in the Royal Army Engineers. Now Judy is a Marine officer and Frank, their second child, is in the Royal Army Reserves while at university. Emily, their other daughter, is in medical school, while Samuel, the youngest, has just started university, not sure about his major yet, though he is leaning toward engineering.

Now, with Judy about to come in as a new Second Lieutenant, he is feeling the weight of all those years, his whole body slumping down in the chair.

Sam glances at the clock, realizing it has been more than five minutes. Straightening up in his chair, he buzzes the Color Sergeant, who then ushers the twelve through the door, closing it behind them. The new Second Lieutenants arrange themselves in front of the desk, behind which sits the Brigadier, watching them closely. All are standing at attention. Sam's eyes come to rest on the one on the far right.

Shifting to the Second Lieutenant on the left, the Brigadier says, "Rest. Name and posting."

Shifting his gaze down the line, each comes to attention, sounds off, looking straight ahead, not daring to make eye contact, then returns to parade rest. When he gets to the final one, he hears, "Second Leftenant Hope. A Company, Four Two Commando."

The Brigadier digests that for a moment. Then, without shifting his gaze from Hope, issues an order: "Second Leftenant Hope, stand fast. The rest, give us the room."

When the door has closed behind the other eleven, the Brigadier keeps Judy locked in his stare. "Sit down," he orders, his angry blue eyes flashing.

"Sir, if you'll let me explain," Judy says, going to attention, her gaze fixed firmly ahead.

"Don't give me that 'sir' shit. This isn't Brigadier to Second Leftenant. This is father to daughter, and you better bloody well have a good explanation. Now plant your ass in that chair!" he says, using his right hand to emphasize he order.

"Yes, sir, I mean Dad," Judy says, sitting down, speaking as calmly as she can. "Now if you'll just…"

"Your mother is going to kill me," he says, the frustration evident in his voice. "Do you know that? What do you have to say for yourself young lady?"

"I just …."

"And when she's done with me, she'll slaughter you! So, why did you break your word?" he demands, his eyes drilling into her.

"Let me…" she tries to say, forcing herself to return his stern look.

"She is going to be furious with me. She'll want to know why I didn't get you assigned to a non-combat unit."

"Dad, that was my…"

"You know I can't intervene in your posting. How do I explain that to her?"

"Dad, I…"

"You know she won't accept any explanation," Sam says, looking at the ceiling. "She won't care about morale, about how it will affect my ability to command, or even your ability to serve."

"I know, Dad, but…"

"She'll just have my hide," he says, throwing up his hands. "And it will be all your fault. You do know that?" he says, looking at Judy.

"Yes, Dad, but…" she says, starting to get exasperated about his not listening to her explanation.

"Oh, God, I can just see her now. How can I go home and tell her this?"

"Sorry, Dad, but…"

"Why did you break your promise to her?"

"Dad, I…"

"How could you do that to her?"

"Dad! Dad!" Judy says, raising her voice to break into her father's diatribe and waving her arms to help the effort. "Will you please let me get a word in? Please!"

Sam clamps his mouth shut, just waving a hand at her as he looks away.

Judy takes a deep breath. "Look, I want to make this a career. If I am going to do that, I have to have combat experience. You know that. And if I start out in some staff job, people will think I am taking advantage of the fact you're my father. I can't bloody well have that. Now can I?"

Sam just shakes his head. "What about the promise you made to your mum not to take a posting to a combat unit?"

Judy looks down at her hands. "I know. I am sorry. But when it came right down to it, I had to do what I wanted, where I would be most effective. And that's in a combat unit."

"What am I supposed to tell your mum?"

"Oh, I don't know. Tell her what I just told you."

"That won't bloody wash. But should I survive, then you will come home at your next liberty, and sit down and talk to your mother," he says emphatically, leaving his elbows on the desk, one finger pointing at her.

"Dad, did I do the right thing?" she answers, deflated, sitting back in her chair, staring at the floor.

"If this is the way you want to live your life, then yes."

"So, you're not worried about me?"

"That is the most bloody idiotic thing that has come out of your mouth in a long time," he snaps. "I love you. You're my daughter. Of course, I worry about you. I worry about all my children. I want you at my funeral. I don't want to go to yours."

"Why is Mum so much worse?"

"Why?" Sam says, leaning forward, staring directly into his daughter's eyes. "She carried you in her womb for nine months. She breastfed you and kept you safe during a time when we didn't know if any of us was going to survive. She has earned the right to worry about you any way she wants."

"Oh."

"Right," he says, a note of triumph in his voice, sitting back in his chair. "Second Leftenant, bring the others back in."

"Yes, sir," she says, getting to her feet.

As Judy goes to get the others, Sam gets to his feet. Standing with his hands clasped behind him, his feet apart, he watches as the new officers march in and come to attention in front of him. He looks them over slowly going down the line from right to left.

"Rest," he says, pausing again. "Now hear this, you new officers may have been certified by your trainers, but that does not mean I will trust my Marines to your charge until your Commando and Company

5

commanders are satisfied you will not get anyone killed unnecessarily. Including yourselves. You will suffer casualties. That is unavoidable in combat. But you are all, all, responsible for the Marines under your command. Is that clear?"

"Yes, sir!" comes the chorus of replies.

Sam looks at them again, "You will keep training and training hard until you are ready for combat. Your senior officers and senior NCOs all have combat experience. You will listen to them and learn from them. Is that clear?"

"Yes, sir!" in unison.

"For those of you who are going to non-combat units, you will train just as hard as the others until you, too, are certified to lead my Marines in combat. In this Corps, every officer is a combat officer as the need arises. Is that clear?"

"Yes, sir!" they say together.

"And remember this, burn it into your brain: The Enemy you will be facing does not take prisoners," he says, speaking slowly and emphasizing each word. "It will always be a fight to the death. Is that clear? We do not know and we may never know how this started; where the hordes who overran most of the world came from, slaughtering everything in their path, human and animal; how their command and control function works; who is behind these atrocities and what their motives and goals are.

"What we do know is that it is now within our grasp to strike back and strike hard. We have intelligence The Enemy is weakening. Food has become a problem. Starvation is stalking The Enemy's ranks. That can lead to a breakdown of discipline, especially when that discipline is enforced by fear and brutality." Sam pauses for a moment to let that sink in.

"Someday, perhaps soon, we will not just raid but invade. We must be ready for that. And that is the responsibility of all the officers and NCOs of this Corps. And that," he says, looking up and down the line to impress the importance of what he's saying, "means you. And remember this, burn it into your brain: The Enemy you will be facing does not take prisoners. It will be a fight to the death. Is that clear?"

"Yes, sir!" the twelve-member chorus barks out.

Sam looks them over again. "Dismissed."

"Yes, sir!" they all say in unison, coming to attention, saluting and marching out.

When the door closes, Sam sits back down and picks up the phone. "Get me commander Four Two. I'll hold."

"Yes, sir," the Color Sergeant says.

Sam listens to the silence for a few minutes, his mind wandering to what he fears will be an unpleasant conversation with his wife.

"Sir, I have Leftenant Colonel McBride on the line."

"Very good," Sam says as he hears the click connecting him to Geoffrey McBride.

"Leftenant Colonel," Sam says.

"Sir."

"I assume you know Second Leftenant Hope is my daughter."

"Yes, sir, I do."

"Good. I want to make something crystal clear: She is to receive no special privileges or treatment. Train her hard, train all your people hard. I know you'll do that, Geoffrey, but I just had to say it."

"Yes, sir. I understand."

"I know you do. Do you need anything?"

"Not at the moment, sir. Unless, of course, you know when our next op will be?"

"That I don't know. I'll give you a ring as soon as I do."

"Thank you, sir."

"Right, goodbye," Sam says, hanging up. He sits back in his chair, looking out a window, wondering, fearing, his conversation with Sarah.

><del>+<del>◆><del>○><del>◆>+><

"What did the Brigadier say to you?" one of the Second Lieutenants asks Judy as five of them head back to the parking lot. "Is he going to pull you out of Four Two?"

"What!" she says, outraged by the suggestion, stopping and turning on the other officer. "He would never do that! He respects my choice!"

"Then what?" another asks.

"If you must know, he's terrified about telling Mum."

"The Brigadier? Terrified?" a third one blurts out as they form a rough circle around Judy.

"That's about it," Judy admits, calming herself and starting to walk again. "I promised her, well, she kind of demanded that I promise, I would not take a combat posting. Now I've bloody well broken that promise and now Dad, the Brigadier, will have to tell her tonight."

"Brilliant. You want us to believe the guy who has led more ops on the Continent, has more medals than God is scared of his wife? This is the guy," the first Second Lieutenant rushes on, dancing in front of Judy and walking backwards as he speaks, "who held off The Enemy by himself so his Troop could escape, who everyone thought dead until a patrol boat picked him up in the Channel floating on a raft? That's the Marine who's terrified of your mum?"

"She is his wife, you know," Judy says matter-of-factly, brushing past him.

"Wait a minute," another says, "I haven't heard about that, about the Channel thing."

"The word," the storyteller goes on, "is that when he was a Leftenant, his Troop was trapped during an operation two klicks from the coast. The commander of the Four Two choked and refused to support his Troop even though they were heavily engaged. Every time they pulled back, the attacks just increased. The Brigadier ordered his Colors to lead the Troop back to the beach, while he held off The Enemy with a machine gun. The Troop reached the coast, but the Brigadier never showed. They waited as long as they could, but The Enemy spotted them and were massing for an attack so they had to leave. Everyone thought he was dead. A month later, a Navy patrol boat spots this guy paddling a door across the Channel toward Merry Ol' England. It was the Brigadier. He was still alive, although a bit worse for wear."

"He was a lot worse for wear," Judy throws in. "Dad was hit in the head by a glancing round, just breaking the skin, but it knocked him out. When he came to, only The Enemy dead and dying were around him. He patched himself up, and managed to evade Enemy patrols, and picked up two deserters. When he reached the coast, Dad took a door off a barn and used it as a raft. He and the other two were floating in the Channel when a patrol boat picked them up. Dad said he was never happier to see the Royal

Navy, and to this day will not allow anyone to say anything derogatory about them," Judy says, prompting the others to laugh.

"They fished him out and brought him to shore. They made him go to hospital straight away, although he wanted nothing more than to go home. Mum was both overjoyed to see him and ready to kill him for scaring her so badly. They had wanted to declare him dead the week before and had even scheduled his funeral with full military honors. I remember the two officers who came to our home to give Mum the news. They barely escaped with their lives. I have never seen her so mad or raise her voice so loud. The Corps decided to hold off on the funeral.

"After he landed, the Corps arranged for a helicopter to take her to him. When he walks out of hospital, Mum first slaps him for scaring her so badly, then throws herself on him with a big hug. Now he hadn't really eaten much in four weeks and was drifting around the Channel for like four days, so when he walks in the door, we kids pile right on him with such force it knocks him onto his back. Mum had to dig him out. On top of that, the doctors ordered him to rest and regain his strength. Mum made sure he stayed down for a while. That, I can tell you, was a real battle. It is the only time I have heard her raise her voice to him."

"Did he yell back at her?" one of them asked.

"Only in fun," Judy says.

"You've never heard him yell at anyone?"

"The only time was when my brother Frank was six. He was riding his bike down a hill when he lost control and was heading straight for a pond. Dad didn't so much yell as bellow at this bloke near the bottom to catch him. Which he did. The bike went into the pond, but Frank stayed dry."

"Bloody weird."

"You can say that again."

"Well, we all have to get back," another says.

The group splits up to go to their buses.

<hr/>

Sam decides that he can't avoid the inevitable forever. And he won't get any work done until he has what he has begun to think of as The

Conversation. He picks up the phone, holds it in his hand for a moment, then pushes the button that connects him to his Color Sergeant.

"Have my car brought around," he says, waits until he hears the affirmation, then puts the phone back down. He goes back to staring out the window, thinking about his little girl going into harm's way, and what Sarah and he had endured to bring her to safety. A few minutes later, the phone rings again, and he's told his car is waiting for him.

Sighing, he heaves his six-foot broad frame out of his chair, puts his cover under his arm, and marches out, putting his hat squarely on his head as he walks out the HQ door. The Color Sergeant knows something's wrong when he walks by without saying anything. The Colors has been with the Brigadier for ten years, since the Brigadier was a Lieutenant Colonel and the Colors was a Corporal.

Sam sits in the car's back seat, staring out the window, until they reach his home outside of Plymouth on the coast of Devon in southern England where his headquarters is located. He gets out, not waiting for the driver to open his door, which is protocol, and walks toward the front door. Sarah's car is not in the driveway of his official residence, so he knows he has time to dread The Conversation some more.

Once inside, he puts his hat up, then pours himself a stiff scotch. A lot of things are in short supply—coffee, tea, cane sugar. Bourbon he's read about but never tasted. Happily, the Scots and the Irish still brew their whiskeys, and gin is available, as is beer and wine of questionable quality. He sits in a living room chair which gives him a view of the front door.

And waits.

The wait seems like an eternity but is really only about twenty minutes. He hears the key in the lock, and sees the front door swing open. Sarah comes in, carrying the mail and her keys in one hand, her briefcase in the other, her purse slung over her shoulder. She puts the brown leather briefcase down next to the small table in the foyer. As she walks into the house, looking at the mail, she glances up, and comes to a sudden stop.

"You're home!" she says to Sam, surprised.

He waves his glass at her in reply.

"What's wrong?" she asks suspiciously, walking into the room and putting the mail on a small table by the couch. "You're never home this early! What happened? Are the kids alright? Is anyone hurt? What's wrong?!" The worry is growing in her voice.

"The children are all fine," Sam assures her. The problem is he never calls them "the children" unless something is wrong.

"You bloody well better stop this evasive tactic. What's the matter?"

"Sit down," he says, patting the seat on the sofa next to his chair. "We need to talk. Have a drink," he says, handing her the scotch he has poured for her.

Sarah walks over, keeping her gaze fixed on him. Taking the offered glass, her eyes narrowed in suspicion, she sits down on the couch, angling her body toward him, as he swivels around to face her.

"What is wrong?" she demands.

"Have a sip. It's good scotch."

"What is wrong?" she asks more emphatically, putting the glass down on the small table next to the couch, hard enough that some of the scotch spills out.

Sam gently takes her hands in his. "It's Judy."

"She's been injured. I knew she would get hurt in training. I just knew it."

"No, no, she's not injured at all. She's, in fact, the picture of health."

"Then what?" Sarah demands, panic rising in her.

Sam takes a deep breath. "I saw her today."

"And?" Sarah prompts when he pauses.

"She got her posting," Sam says slowly.

"And?"

"A Company, Four Two Commando," Sam says, the words pouring out of his mouth, his eyes avoiding hers.

"What?" Sarah nearly screams, jumping to her feet, pulling her hands from Sam's.

"She'll be a Troop leader when she is cleared for operations," Sam says quietly, avoiding looking at her as he takes a big swig of his drink. "You know," he says, looking at his wife, "a lot of people think you two are sisters when they first meet you. You don't look like someone in her forties. And you're only an inch shorter with the same hair and brown eyes."

"What?" Sarah barks out, incredulous at his attempt to change the subject. "Stop that! You are not going to divert me! How could you? How can you let that happen to our daughter?" comes the outraged response as she takes a step forward, her five-foot-five slender frame seeming to grow as she towers above him.

"I had no say in it," Sam says, defensively, shrinking back into his chair.

"What do you mean you had no say? You're the goddamned Brigadier. A legend in your own time," she announces, sarcasm dripping on every word, while her expression shows her disdain for him at this moment. "You could order her to another posting, where she won't get shot at, where she won't have to face what we did. Get her out of there!"

"I can't," he says quietly, avoiding looking at her.

"What do you mean you can't?" she demands. "This better be good, mister!"

Sam swallows hard, then takes a deep breath. "Two reasons," he says, pausing to collect his thoughts. "Please sit down," he says, pleadingly, patting the seat of the sofa she had vacated.

"Reason one?" Sarah demands, pausing a moment before sitting.

Sam looks at her, smiling weakly, taking another swig of scotch. "She graduated at the top of her class. That means she has her choice of postings. She chose this. It's what she wants."

"Talk her out of it."

"I already tried. It didn't work."

"Try harder."

"Sarah, sweetheart," Sam pleads, reaching for her hands, which she reluctantly gives him, "I can't. That's sort of the second reason. If I transfer her, it will taint her for the rest of her career. Other officers will resent her, and me, and the ranks will not respect her. And I will lose my ability to command effectively. I might as well retire."

"Maybe you should," Sarah says defiantly, looking away from him, her anger ebbing. "You've shed enough blood in this war. It's time for someone else to step up."

"You know I can't do that," Sam says, as Sarah deflates a bit more. "Judy wants to make the Marines her career. To do that, she needs combat experience. This will give it to her. And she'll show she is not trying to hide behind her dad. That will give her credibility. I can't take that away from her. I can't crush her dreams just because you and I are frightened for her. Can I?"

Sarah slumps back on the sofa, her head down as tears flow down her cheeks. Sam moves beside her, and takes her into his arms, pulling her head onto his chest, stroking her hair.

"Haven't we gone through enough?" she says between sobs. "Don't we deserve peace? Safety for our children?"

"I don't know. Maybe someday," Sam answers softly, kissing her lightly on her head.

CHAPTER 2

"Sir, GHQ is on the line," Color Sergeant Lempriere tells Sam as he walks into the office about the call from General Headquarters.

"Brilliant," Sam says, a bit sarcastically, suspecting this can only mean problems. "Give me a bit to get settled and then put them through."

"Sir," comes the reply.

Sam walks quickly into his office, throws his coat over a chair, and picks up the phone as he settles himself in his chair. "Right, Claude, let me have them."

"Right away, sir."

"Brigadier Hope here," Sam says as he hears the line click.

"One moment for General Alexander," a voice on the other end says. Then Sam hears, "Ma'am, I have Brigadier Hope on the line."

"Put him through," comes the terse reply.

"Ma'am."

"Sam?" the General says.

"Yes, ma'am."

"I need you straight away at the Defense Ministry."

"Ma'am? What's doing?"

"You need to be here. It's a show-and-tell thing."

"Yes, ma'am. Let me collect my Chief and we'll be right there."

"Leave your Chief of Staff. We may need someone on the ground straight away."

"That sounds like an emergency, ma'am."

"No, Brigadier, but we may be in a position to take action on the Continent, and we may have to move fast."

"Yes, ma'am. I'm on my way."

"Right," the General says and hangs up.

14

Sam sits for a second digesting what he has just heard. He can't help wondering if five months has been enough time for his daughter and the other new officers and ranks to get ready. He springs from his chair, grabs his coat, and walks quickly to the outer office. "Colors, have my car brought around immediately. And have a 'copter ready. I'm off to Defense Ministry."

"Yes, sir," Lempriere says as he picks up the phone.

Sam quickly walks to the office next door. "Sergeant," he says as he enters the outer office, "is he in?"

"Yes, sir. He's alone."

Sam just nods as he quickly goes into his Chief of Staff's office, which is a bit smaller than his but has windows stretching across the outside wall.

"Sorry to barge in like this," Sam says to Colonel Tom Codrington as he takes a padded chair facing the desk, "but I've been called to Defense Ministry. Something is brewing, but Alexander won't tell me over the phone. She wants you to stay here in case we need to get things organized to move fast. And that is the extent of my knowledge. Sorry."

"Yes, sir. Is this something that is coming at us?"

"Apparently not. She indicated it's on the Continent," Sam says, adding a bit sheepishly, "I guess I did know a bit more than I said. But now that's really all I know."

"Right. Should I alert the command?"

"Hmmm, what do you think?" he asks the slightly smaller man who has become his alter ego. "Get them to pull all their people in, and get their kit in proper order?"

"Yes, sir. That's my thought."

"Brilliant, Tom. Do that, while I find out what the devil is going on," Sam says, as he propels himself up from the chair, and heads out the door.

⬗~⬗~⬗~◯~⬖~⬖~⬖

Twenty minutes later he's in the air on the hour-long flight to the Ministry of Defense in London. He keeps going over all the possible scenarios of what is going on. The latest intelligence reports have indicated a sharp drop in the number of Enemy soldiers along the coast, and what appear to be large numbers of bodies scattered around. There has also been a sharp drop in radio traffic, which could go along with the declining numbers of soldiers. But it also could signify a trap being laid for them. He would like to dismiss the trap idea because he doesn't believe The Enemy is that cunning, but he can't afford to, just on the off chance they have become just that. He's determined not to send his people into a trap.

When the helicopter lands, a staff car is waiting. Sam is driven to the four-story light stone main headquarters building, where he is ushered into a huge rectangular conference room already crowded with officers from every branch of the military. He knows most of the senior officers and a few of the junior ones, greeting as many as he can, chatting briefly with a few. A map of the Continent's Atlantic coast covers one long wall.

"Stand!" someone orders as General Alexander and the Royal Army's top commander enter the room, followed by the commanders of the Royal Air Force and Royal Navy. All the officers snap to attention.

"Take a seat," the Army's commanding Field Marshal says. The senior officers take seats around the large conference table, while the junior officers sit, or stand, along the wall.

"Ladies and gentlemen," the Field Marshal begins, taking his position at the head of the table next to Alexander, "I trust you have all seen the latest intel." His statement is greeted with a general assent around the room. "Good," he continues, "then you know we have what appears to be an opening to return to the Continent. We would like to exploit that opening. Brigadier," he says, turning to his chief of intelligence who is standing just behind and to the right of him.

"Sir," he replies, picking up a long pointer as the Field Marshal moves his chair so he can see the presentation. "Ladies and gentlemen," the Brigadier says, "as you have seen from our satellite photos and other reconnaissance, there are what appear to be a large number of bodies scattered around the coastal region and well inland." He sweeps across the map of France and Belgium with his pointer as he talks. "In addition," he says, moving his pointer well into Germany, "there don't seem to be any large, organized Troop concentrations west of the Rhine. In fact, we have to go to the south of France and Italy, and the vicinity of Berlin and Vienna to find any large numbers."

"What of Spain?" someone down the table asks.

"Ah, yes, our Spanish friends. Well, there, too, The Enemy concentrations seem to have evaporated. Now, if I may continue, our plan is to land around Calais and secure the port. That, Brigadier Hope, will be the job of your Royal Marines," he says, looking at Sam. "After the port is secure, the Army will land in force."

"Then what?" Sam asks.

"Then, you will proceed to secure the coastal area in preparation of moving against The Enemy's troop concentrations," General Alexander says, joining the briefing.

"Ma'am," the Army Chief of Staff asserts, "our forces are not large enough to secure the Continent. We would need millions of troops for that."

"I am aware," she replies. "Our strategy will be to attack Enemy troop concentrations in France and the Low Countries up to the Rhine River, securing air bases along the way for resupply and staging for attack aircraft. After the large concentrations have been destroyed, we will turn to mop-up operations. We believe many Enemy soldiers may be willing to surrender without a fight."

"Yes, ma'am," he replies.

"Very good. Now," she says turning to Sam, "do you have any thoughts on the matter Brigadier Hope?"

Sam stays quiet for a moment, staring at the map. His mind has been churning rapidly since the intelligence chief said his Marines would be the first to land. "Two things, ma'am," he finally says, leaning forward in his chair. "I would prefer to put my Marines ashore at Cherbourg. Calais is in open country which means our flanks would be open or we would be stretched so thin it would be difficult to carry out the mission in any timely fashion. But if we go ashore at Cherbourg, it's on a peninsula, so we can land on either side of it, securing our flanks as we clear the harbor."

"And the other thing?" the General asks.

"Yes, ma'am. I think almost everyone here knows my history. I have a unique perspective on our Enemy. If their command structure is actually breaking down…"

"It is," the Army Brigadier interjects, "we are confident of that."

"Brilliant," Sam says as he glances at the man standing pompously before the map, skepticism still in his voice, "their common Soldiers may be quite willing to switch sides."

"Are you saying we should arm them?" an Army Lieutenant General says, alarm in her voice.

"Not immediately," Sam replies. "They are poorly trained. The Enemy has won simply by using overwhelming numbers with no regard for casualties. We would need to train them properly, and make sure they are reliable. I believe many of them will jump at the chance to fight against their former masters. They have been treated viciously."

"And why would we do this?" an Army Major General asks.

"It will help give us the forces we need to take the Continent back," Sam says, sitting back in his chair, looking around the table.

"That," the Army Field Marshal says, considering the notion, "is something to take under advisement. Since your people are the ones going in, I will let you pick the point of attack, with the proviso that you can secure the roads we will need to quickly strike out across France. Normandy is hedge-row country. We picked Calais because it is open country from which we can quickly launch our invasion."

"Yes, sir, I understand. But what if this is a trap? My Marines would be walking into a slaughterhouse. With Cherbourg, we could defend ourselves easily."

"Are you afraid of a fight?" another Army Major General challenges him.

"No!" Sam snaps back, sitting ramrod straight in his chair, his eyes blazing. "I'm concerned about a slaughter. I would prefer to make sure our attack will be successful with minimal casualties. I don't know about you, sir," he says staring the other down, "but I value the lives of my people!"

"Gentlemen," Alexander interjects, "that is enough. Brigadier Hope," she says, turning back to Sam, "your point is well taken. Prepare a plan for an attack on Cherbourg. Include in that plan ways to egress from the peninsula onto the French plain. Coordinate with the Air Force and Navy."

"Yes, ma'am."

"The attack," the Army intelligence Brigadier says, "will take place two months from today." His comment creates a stir in the room, as the officers look at each other.

"I know that is an ambitious timetable," Alexander says, "but we must take advantage of the opening. Brigadier," she says, turning back to Sam, "I would like you to dispatch your recon people within a week."

"Yes, ma'am."

"Very good," the Field Marshal says, looking around the room. "We have a monumental job ahead of us, so I suggest we all get cracking," he says, rising from her chair along with Alexander, with everyone else in the room following his example. The four commanders leave behind a stunned group, who soon break into excited conversations. Sam says little, quickly leaving the room to head back to his headquarters to get things going.

⊳━┤━◈━━○━◈━┤━⊲

"Chief, I'll be in my office in ten. Please be there," Sam tells Codrington on a mobile phone call as soon as he is in the staff car on his way back to HQ.

"Yes, sir," comes the crisp reply.

As Sam puts the phone in his pocket, he stares out the window not really seeing anything. His mind is racing about how to accomplish the job he's been given. And he's second guessing himself. His request to move the invasion to the Cotentin Peninsula was based more on gut reaction than anything else. Just looking at the map told him Cherbourg was better than Calais if the goal was to secure an area for a buildup. It would be easier to take and defend. But it would also be more difficult to break out. He and his staff would have to work all that out, with the help of Corps intelligence.

Has he made the right decision? That's the question he hopes he will be able to answer in the affirmative. Not that it really matters now. The decision is made, and he has to make it work.

"Sir," the Color Sergeant says as Sam walks into the outer office, "the Chief is waiting for you."

"Very good," Sam responds as he strides to his office door. "Chief," he says as walks through the door.

"Sir," Codrington replies, nodding casually to Sam.

"We're invading the Continent in sixty days," Sam says as he rounds his desk and sits down.

"What?" the Colonel replies, confusion and surprise in his voice.

"That's right," Sam says, shaking his head. "This is no raid. The powers-that-be think we can retake the Continent, or at least a chunk of it. And they want us to go ashore in eight weeks."

"Sir," Codrington protests, "that's not enough time to plan and organize an operation of this scale."

"Perhaps, but it's all the time we've got, so let's get cracking. You've alerted the Commandos?"

"Yes, sir. All leaves have been canceled, and kit is being brought up to battle standards."

"Lovely," Sam says. "We need to get the planning staff going right away. I expect logistics will be the biggest headache, so Supply will need to jump on that ASAP. Accelerate recruit training so everyone can be at full strength and replacements will be available as needed."

"Yes, sir. Are we going ashore with armor and artillery?"

"Definitely. I'm not having our guys' butts hanging out in the breeze. We are also going to insist on Royal Navy and Air Force support on as large a scale as possible. And we will insist on having Royal Engineers come in on the second landing."

"Good idea, sir. I'll call the staff together right now. Will you be joining us?"

"Of course," Sam says, smiling at the man who has become his best friend and most trusted adviser. "Did you think I would let you have all the fun, Tom?"

"I should be so lucky," comes the humorous response.

"Here's the bad news: All the prelim plans must be done in a week."

"That is an extremely tight time frame and could create problems. What if in the rush to finish we miss something?"

"This whole thing is rushed. But that is out of our hands. What we can do," Sam says, leaning forward, "is have the preliminary plans done in a week so we can get logistics and everyone else moving, and coordinate with the other branches. Then we will have a bit better than six weeks to flesh things out and fix any mistakes. But the key is getting the initial work done quickly."

"Yes, sir," Codrington says with a shrug. "I'll tell the staff to move onto base and plan on working twenty hours a day."

"Just twenty?"

Codrington just gives Sam a look of 'I know you're kidding', then says, "Is that all, sir?"

Sam nods, then says, "Staff meeting in fifteen?"

The Colonel looks at his watch, "Make it twenty."

"Right," Sam says as his Chief of Staff gets up and leaves the office.

Sam looks out the window as he pulls out his mobile phone and calls Sarah.

"Hi, Sweetie," he says.

"What's up?" she demands, responding to the tone she hears in his voice.

"We have to plan an operation. I'm afraid I won't be home for a while."

"How long is a while?" she asks suspiciously.

"At least a week." The line goes silent. "Sarah?"

"Are you going?" she asks finally, worry in her voice.

"I can't talk about that. Security and all, you know."

"You're going." It's a statement, not a question.

"Sweetheart, you know I can't talk about it."

"Don't 'Sweetheart' me. What about Judy?"

"Sarah, enough. We'll talk about this later."

"You're a jackass. I love you. But you're a jackass."

"I love you, too," Sam says, with a sigh. "I'll call you when I can."

"Don't you dare get dead," she warns him. "And don't you let Judy get hurt."

"I'll do my best."

"Do better."

"Love you."

"Love you, too."

The line goes dead as Sam puts his phone down. He stares out the window, wondering about the similar conversations his officers and ranks will be having with their spouses, significant others, parents … The ringing of his office phone interrupts his thoughts. "Yes?" he says, picking up the receiver.

"Sir, they're ready in the conference room."

"Thank you. And, Claude, please join us. You will be part of all this."

"Yes, sir," Lempriere says, wondering about the Brigadier's informality, something that happens only on rare occasions, and only when the news is really good or especially terrible. The Color Sergeant decides it must be bad news. He rises and follows behind Sam as they leave the office and head for the conference room down the hall.

CHAPTER 3

S tand!" comes the command as Sam strides into the auditorium filled
with officers from across his command—all five Commandos, Logistics
and Intelligence, as well as his staff just one week before the invasion.
Codrington and the main command staff are on the stage, a large map of
the invasion area behind them.

Sam marches to the front, climbing the stairs onto the stage. "Sit," he
says, allowing the officers to take their seats.

He surveys the packed room for a moment. "Ladies and gentlemen,"
he says, his tone serious, "you have had your assignments for five weeks
now. We go in a week." He pauses, allowing that to sink in, although
they have all known the time frame. "This is a rushed operation. But it
is an operation we can accomplish." He pauses again. "This is what all
our training and experience have prepared us for. We are going to be the
tip of the spear. We, ladies and gentlemen, are going to lead the way to
liberating Europe."

He pauses again. "This meeting will be devoted to providing you with
the overall picture of what is to come. While you have your individual
assignments, you need to understand what we, the Royal Marines, are
going to do and how your part fits into the whole."

He turns to Codrington. "Colonel, they're all yours."

"Sir," the Chief of Staff says. "Ladies and gentlemen, as you know, 30
Commando has conducted a series of patrols of the target area. No, I repeat,
no large-scale organized enemy forces have been discovered, although a
large number of enemy soldiers are milling about apparently without
direction or minimal direction. Also, a large number of bodies, unburied,
are lying about. They seem to have died of starvation or other non-combat
causes. In short, we expect to land unopposed or face minimal opposition."

Codrington stops and looks around the room. "I must emphasize this intelligence could be wrong, the situation could change, so we must stay vigilant."

The Colonel then goes on to explain that Commando Forty will land to the left of Cherbourg, while Four Two lands to the right. The two Commandos will clear the harbor area, while Four Five and Four Six Commandos will be held in reserve to provide reinforcements as needed. Once the harbor is secure, Four Five and Four Six will come ashore, if they haven't landed already. With them will be a battalion of Royal Engineers.

"The Army?" someone calls out, disdain in his voice.

The Colonel smiles a bit. "You will be thankful for their presence should you run into mines, booby traps, blocked roads, fallen bridges, or anything else like that. We don't have enough of our own engineers to do the job," he says of the small detachment of Royal Marine Engineers that will be attached to the Brigade. "I suggest you take good care of them, especially as the Brigadier has promised to return them undamaged." That provokes general laughter. "Just remember, these engineers are not trained for combat in the same way we are. So, do be careful with them."

A chorus of "Yes, sir," is the response, accompanied by laughter and chuckles.

"Now, since this is an invasion and not a raid, we are going in with all our armor and artillery from the jump. We also will have the full support of the Navy and Air Force. That means you will be able to call in naval gunfire and air strikes as needed. To do that, you will have Navy and Air Force liaison officers with you." He pauses a moment. "Take care of them as well, they may save your butts." That comment draws knowing laughter.

"As for communications," the Colonel says, "we'll be using our standard headgear amongst ourselves. The command staff, plus the Commando commanders will also be utilizing more powerful radios to ensure communications between the two invasion beaches, and that net will also be looped in with the Navy, Air Force, and Army—yes, the Army. Be nice, guys," he says as derisive comments begin to circulate among the officers. "Those blokes will be taking over once we have given them a good start."

The Colonel and other staff members then go into the details of the invasion. When they are done, Sam goes back to center stage.

"So, that's the plan," Sam says. "The Chief will land with Four Two, while I will go ashore with Forty. We will not be there to exercise tactical control, that will be up to the Commandos' individual commanders. What we will be doing is making sure the two Commandos stay coordinated, and we will be able to bring in reinforcements and other support more quickly than if we were offshore. Once the harbor has been secured, we will move inland, clearing a route for the Army, which will begin to land in force behind us. They will come into line beside us as we push inland, lengthening the line."

Sam surveys the room. "Any questions?"

"Sir," Lieutenant Colonel McBride says, standing, "our flanks will be in the air until the Army catches up."

"Yes, they will," Sam responds. "That's where the Navy and Air Force, and our own assault helicopters, come into play. We will use their firepower to cover our flanks. You will keep patrols active. Any movement by The Enemy will draw an immediate response from either naval guns or airstrikes, or both."

"Thank you, sir."

Sam nods. "Anyone else?"

"Sir, why don't we just land in the harbor with all four Commandos?" a Major in the back of the room asks.

"The problem is that we don't know what we will find in the city," Sam replies. "We know the countryside is clear of any large concentration of enemy soldiers. But we are not so sure about the city. They could be taking cover in buildings. We don't think that is the case, but we cannot rule out the possibility. We don't want to walk into a trap where we have a few Marines ashore who then get slaughtered. And we can't land all four Commandos across the beach in a timely manner because we simply do not have the landing craft. We are counting on the element of surprise to enable us to move quickly to secure the harbor so the following landings can be made in safety. Does that answer your question?"

"Yes, sir. Thank you, sir."

After a few more questions, Sam says, "If you meet Enemy soldiers willing to surrender, take them prisoner. We will set up POW cages to house and evaluate them. But if they show the slightest resistance, crush them with all the force at your disposal. Watch for ambushes. Watch for flanking movement. Use your training. Use your brains. I want to do this with as few casualties as possible. To do that, I expect you all to act aggressively but with prudence. Understood?"

"Sir," an officer says, raising his hand.

"Yes?"

"Sir, can you explain what you mean by 'acting aggressively but with prudence'?"

Sam looks at the man for a moment. "Anyone else need that explanation?" Sam looks around the room. When no one else says anything, he turns to the Chief of Staff. "I want that officer and his commander in my office now."

"Yes, sir," Codrington says.

Sam nods, then indicates to Lempriere to follow him as he leaves the stage.

"Stand!" Codrington orders, bringing everyone to their feet as Sam strides down the middle aisle and out the door.

Half an hour later, he is standing behind his desk when Codrington comes in, followed by Lieutenant Colonel Clyde Lee, commander of Commando Four Six, and Captain Frank Herbe, commander of D Company of the Four Six.

"Gentlemen," Sam says, which is responded to by a chorus of "Sir."

"Rest," he says. He then gives his attention to Herbe. "Captain, you will report to Supply in the morning."

"Sir?" both Lee and Herbe respond, both caught by surprise.

"Captain, if you have to ask what being 'prudent' and 'aggressive' mean, I question whether you can safely lead my Marines into battle. I could be wrong, but I am not willing to risk the lives of my Marines."

"Sir, I…" Herbe begins to say, pleading in his voice, his face looking stricken.

"This is not a debate," Sam says sharply. "You will report to Supply in the morning. Dismissed."

"Sir," Herbe says, coming briefly to attention, confusion and dismay playing across his face. He salutes and leaves the office.

"Clyde," Sam says turning to Lee, "I apologize for pulling that on you at the last minute, but it had to be done."

"Yes, sir," he says, his mind working quickly with how to fill the vital command slot that has just opened.

"You have someone who can replace him?" Sam asks.

"Yes, sir, I do," Lee says, his decision being made quickly.

"Who?"

"Leftenant Harry St. George, sir."

"How much experience does he have?"

"She, sir. Harry is a woman."

"Excuse me?"

"Her proper name is Harriette, but everyone calls her Harry."

"Right. That's right. I remember her now. Didn't know about the name thing, though. How much experience does she have?"

"She's commanded a Troop, been a Company exec. For the past year, she's been on my staff. I have been grooming her for Company command, sir. She's excellent."

"Good," Sam says, then turns to the Chief. "Brevet her captain. If she does well, we'll make it permanent."

"Right," Codrington says.

"Good," Sam says, ending the meeting. "We all have a lot to do, so let's get cracking."

"Sir," both men say, as they come to attention and leave.

Sam watches them leave, then sits down and starts making calls, tying up loose ends to make sure the Navy and Air Force are nearing completion of their plans, and the Army has chosen an Engineering Regiment to accompany his Marines. After talking to Navy and Air Force commanders, he's about to call the Royal Engineers' commander, when the Color Sergeant buzzes in.

"Yes, Colors," he says.

"Sir, two Royal Engineer officers from Five Regiment are here."

"Lovely. Send them in."

"Sir," the Color Sergeant says, then hangs up. The door opens almost immediately as the two officers come in.

"What the bloody hell!" Sam exclaims jumping to his feet. "What the bloody hell are you doing here?"

"Nice to see you, too, dear," Sarah says, a smile broadening across her face.

"I should have guessed," the Colonel with her quips. "Same last names. Not a coincidence."

"No, sir, the Brigadier is my husband."

"I see," Colonel Jack Bosquet says. "Will this be a problem, Brigadier?"

"Definitely not," Lieutenant Colonel Sarah Hope says before Sam has a chance to respond.

"What? No. No problem," he says, his attention fixed on Sarah. "Why the bloody hell didn't you tell me?"

"I haven't seen you in four weeks, you know," she responds, indignantly. "You've been cloistered here."

"Hmmmph," he responds, a sour look on his face because he knows she's right.

"Besides, you know this is maximum effort. The reserves were bound to be called up."

"What about Jack?" Sam asks about their second child.

"He's been called up as well," she says about their son who was at university, but is now with his Army infantry unit.

"Bloody Christ," Sam says, sitting down. "Take a chair, please," he tells the two others.

"If I may sir," Bosquet says, sitting down, "we have received the plans and have a few questions."

"Yes, of course," Sam says, "let me get my Chief of Staff in here."

When Codrington arrives, the four dive into the plans.

"Well, if that's everything, my Chief will arrange a meeting for you with commanders for Four Five and Four Six so you can get to know who you will be going in with. Later, you can touch base with the commanders of Forty and Four Two."

"Thank you, sir," Bosquet says, getting up.

"Colonel," Sam says, "would you mind if I borrowed your Executive Officer for the evening?"

"No, not at all, sir," he says.

"Is this an order?" Sarah says in mock outrage.

"I can make it one if you like," Sam replies, smiling. "I don't believe you can make a case for harassment."

"I just hope your mess is better than ours," she says.

"Don't hold your breath. We Marines always seem to manage to be at the end of the supply line, but I think we can manage a decent meal."

"You better."

"Leftenant Colonel," Bosquet says, smiling at the exchange. "I will see you in the morning."

"Yes, sir. Thank you, sir," Sarah says reverting to formality.

Sam and Sarah are soon left alone in the office, locked in a passionate embrace.

CHAPTER 4

From the flying bridge of the command ship, Sam scans the shoreline with powerful binoculars. His Marines will be going ashore in thirty minutes, and he still hasn't heard from Thirty Commando, which is collecting information about what to expect.

"What the bloody hell is that stench?" asks a Navy officer standing near Sam.

"Bodies. Lots and lots of dead, rotting bodies," Sam says in a flat tone without interrupting his attempt to pierce the diminishing darkness as dawn slowly creeps across the landscape.

"It's a right bloody hell of a stench, sir, and we're two kilometers from shore," the officer says, then disappears inside the bridge.

"It's the way the wind is blowing," says Sam to no one in particular, who just smiles to himself. He can't help but enjoy the stench in a way—the more dead Enemy there are, the safer his people will be.

"Sir," Codrington says, coming out of the ship's Combat Information Center, "just heard from Jack Griffith."

"And?"

"The coast is clear to within a klick."

"Lovely. Tell the Leftenant Colonel to push on further if he thinks it's safe."

"Will do, sir."

"And Tom, tell Jack to be careful."

"Yes, sir."

"Pass the word to Staffero and McBride," Sam says, referring to Lieutenant Colonels Michelle Staffero, commander of Forty Commando, and Geoffrey McBride, who commands Four Two.

"Will do," Codrington says. "Oh, one of our blokes is a history buff. It seems that in World War II, the Yanks put a kind of battering ram on front of their tanks. They used them to cut through the hedgerows. McBride thought it brilliant, so a number of tanks have been fitted with them. They'll go ashore with both Forty and Four Two."

"Let's hope we won't need them," Sam says, putting down the binoculars but keeping his eyes focused on the shore.

"They are detachable."

Sam just shakes his head, smiling. "We better get to our boats if we're going ashore."

"By the way," Codrington says, "Color Sergeant Lampriere seems to be among the missing."

"He's fluent in French. He's landing with Four Two."

"Right," Codrington replies. "We will probably need all the French speakers we can find."

The two senior Marine officers make their way to the port side where a gangway has been lowered to the calm English Channel waters and the two boats waiting for them. They climb into the boats, Sam off to join Forty's first wave, while Codrington's boat takes him to the Four Two rendezvous area.

Overhead, Royal Air Force jet fighters and Marine attack helicopters sweep across the coast, the planes heading inland looking for targets, especially large camps or concentrations of soldiers, while the copters stay with the first wave to provide fire support. The naval guns are silent. With no reports of landing opposition, the Marines don't need them—yet. They will be there to provide fire support with both gunnery and missiles, if called upon. Their presence eases a bit of Sam's concerns.

Sam's boat is at the tail end of the first wave as he watches the shore rapidly near. He scans the beach repeatedly with binoculars, looking for trouble. Despite the good intelligence reports, and the fact that he does trust his Commando Thirty to do the job, he can't relax until the first wave is safely ashore. And even then, only a little.

He watches as his Marines and the tanks land and rapidly move inland, fanning out to protect their flanks. A few minutes later, a green flare goes up from off the beach, indicating an unopposed landing.

"Lovely," Sam mutters to himself. "Okay, boys and girls," he says to the Marines and sailors in his boat which is about to beach, "time to land."

"Sir," the Coxswain says, gunning the engine as he heads the craft toward shore ahead of the landing craft carrying the rest of Commando Forty, and most of the armor.

The hover landing crafts skim across the surface, allowing the Marines to land above the waterline. Sam and his staff aren't that lucky. They are not in a hovercraft. Their boat grounds in nearly half a meter of water. Sam leads the way, jumping into the surf.

As he wades ashore, he watches his Marines race across the beach.

He finds the lack of gunfire reassuring.

"Find us a ride," Sam tells one of his aides, Lieutenant Timothy Gowing.

"Yes, sir," he replies and heads off looking for the command vehicles that are to come ashore with the second wave.

"Radio," Sam says, prompting a Corporal carrying a portable set to come running up.

"Sir," the corporal says, handing Sam the receiver.

"Big Bear to Forty Alfa." Sam calls, keying the hand-held combination microphone and receiver, and wondering again what joker came up with these call signs.

"Forty Alfa," Staffero replies.

"Status."

"More than two klicks in. Pushing on. No resistance, yet."

"Any POWs?"

"None. No sightings of any live Enemy yet, but plenty of bodies. Looks like they starved to death."

"Right. Out." Sam pauses for a moment as Gowing returns with two staff vehicles and three trucks loaded with command center gear, some of the first vehicles off the second wave which had followed closely behind the first.

"Big Bear to Little Bear." Sam says, calling Codrington.

"Little Bear."

"Report."

"Pushing inland. No resistance. No POWs. Flanks secure."

"Same here. Out." Sam hands the handset back to the Corporal, then turns to his staff. "Let's mount up. It looks like we can head for the villa," he says, referring to a large house about three kilometers off the beach that was preselected for the HQ.

Sam gets into the front seat of the lead vehicle, while his staff and security detail climb into the backseat, the other vehicle, and the trucks. Sam looks around. When he's satisfied everyone is aboard, he tells the driver to head off.

The five vehicles move slowly up the beach. When they reach a paved road, or what used to be a paved road, their speed picks up to less than fifteen kilometers an hour over the rough and broken road. A pace Sam finds irritating. They pass Marines making their way inland on foot to support the first wave since not enough vehicles could be loaded onto the landing craft to give everyone a ride at this point. The first wave and the members of the second wave who could get rides, some on tanks, will halt at the six-kilometer mark until the rest catch up. With the speed the Marines are walking at, Sam doesn't expect that to take long.

The little convoy takes about half an hour to cover the three kilometers, pulling in through what used to be a gate to the villa. The vehicles move up the driveway, stopping in front of the dilapidated building. The stench from rotting flesh is almost overpowering. As Sam gets out, he glances back in time to see one of his staff officers vomiting. He shakes his head and surveys the poor condition of the building's exterior as members of his security team head inside to secure the place.

"Captain," Sam says, looking around at the bodies strewn across the lawn, "get a detail to clean this mess up. Burn them if you must."

"Yes, sir," Captain Leon Failly responds, quickly turning and calling a Sergeant to put together a detail to collect the bodies on the grounds and carry others out of the building as soon as it is secure. Just as he finishes, Lieutenant Cliff Pelissier comes out of the main door.

"All clear!" he calls.

Sam nods in response. "What's it like in there?"

"A mess, sir. Must be sixty bodies lying around."

"How did they die?" Sam says as he joins Pelissier on the top step.

"Looks like the poor buggers starved to death, sir. I didn't see any wounds or blood."

"Very good," Sam says.

"Sir," Pelissier says as members of his team come out of the building. He leads them across the property to join the rest of the team securing the perimeter.

"Sir," Failly says, coming up.

"Yes?"

"We should have the bodies cleared out in hour. We're collecting them near the south wall and will burn the lot. With all the windows broken, airing out the building should not be a huge problem."

"Captain," Sam says, nodding in acknowledgement, "have the temporary POW enclosure set up over there," pointing to the northside of the property. "And let Leftenant Colonel Staffero know."

"Sir," Failly says, saluting and heading off.

"Gowing," Sam says.

"Sir."

"Find out where Forty's HQ is. We're going to pay them a visit."

"Sir."

"Radio," Sam says, prompting the Corporal to come up and give him the handset.

"Big Bear to Little Bear." Sam says. He waits a few seconds and then repeats the call, fear popping into him that something bad has happened.

"Little Bear."

"We're home." Sam says, using the prearranged signal that his HQ is in the pre-selected location, and relieved Codrington's voice sounds relaxed.

"Same here."

"Brilliant. Out." Sam gives the handset back to the Corporal who is shadowing him with the radio. "What the bloody hell is that?" Sam blurts out.

"It's a tank, sir," Major Pierre Dessairt says matter of factly.

"I can bloody well see that, Major. But what is it doing here?"

"Leftenant Colonel Staffero thought we should have more security," Dessairt replies. "Just in case we are attacked. She's worried about our right flank, sir. It is in the air."

"Really?" Sam says about the end of the line not having any protection against attack from that direction, sarcasm dripping from his voice. He pauses a moment, thinking about this new event. "Right, the tank can lead HQ down to the city when it's time to move."

"Move, sir?" Dessairt asks. "I thought we are establishing HQ here. I came down to tell you that we have found you a lovely office. Well, it will be when we cure its faults."

"Thank you, Major, but we'll be moving on with our Marines."

"Then why…"

Sam cuts him off with a laugh. "We are cleaning this place up for the Army."

"Sir?" The Major is really confused now.

Sam chuckles. "We will be dependent on the Army for our supplies. I want them in our debt."

"I see, sir. Then how much would you like us to do here?"

"Get rid of the bodies and trash from the building and grounds. You'll have to burn them since we have no way of burying. As soon as the place is in order, follow me down to the city. That bloody thing," Sam says, gesturing at the tank, "can lead the way."

"Sir," the Major says and heads off.

"Sir," Failly says, "I've located Forty HQ."

"Brilliant. Let's go."

CHAPTER 5

B ig Bear. This is Little Bear," Codrington says into the handset.

"Big Bear." Sam replies.

"Four Two in place."

"Forty is almost there. We'll go in thirty mikes."

"Roger." Codrington turns to McBride, Four Two's commander. "Leftenant Colonel, we go at fourteen hundred. Everyone know their mission?" He knows he doesn't really have to ask, but he can't help himself.

"Right, sir," McBride nodding as he replies and turns to issue orders. He has set up his command post on a hill overlooking the city. From that vantage point, they can see Cherbourg laid out before them. The plan is to move through the suburbs and outskirts as quickly as possible, then secure the harbor area so the rest of the Marines, and then the Army, can land.

McBride's not happy about it. His left flank is in the air. He has patrols out scouting in that direction but the area is too large to patrol properly, and he worries about Enemy Soldiers slipping in behind his command.

As he gazes out at the city, a burst of rifle fire breaks out to the rear. Taking most of his HQ security guard and his aides, McBride heads toward the sound of the fight on the run.

The firing dies down quickly. When he reaches the kitchen area about four hundred meters away, he comes across a scene of kitchen staff, many still wearing their aprons, checking about twenty dead Enemy.

"Colors, report," McBride says to the Color Sergeant in charge of this kitchen.

"Well, sir, they came upon us sudden like, but we heard them off a bit because they were yelling, some kind of war cry, I guess. Anyway, that gave us time to grab our weapons. As you can see, sir, we made quick work of them."

"Any casualties?"

"Just one, sir."

"Serious?"

"No, sir. Private Galev was in such a hurry to grab his rifle he knocked a pot of hot oil down his trouser leg. You should have seen him, sir. It was kind of comic. He was firing with one hand and trying to take his trousers off with the other. Comic, it was, sir."

McBride just shakes his head. "Is he being treated?"

"Medical is with him now, sir."

"Right. Colors, post guards around the perimeter. If you're attacked again, you may not have this kind of warning."

"Right, sir."

"And Colors, we'll be moving out shortly, so you best pack up."

"But, sir," he protests, "the lads and lassies need a hot meal."

"That they do, but it will have to wait 'til we get to the port. Now get cracking, Colors."

"Yes, sir," comes the reluctant reply.

"And Colors, fall in behind D Company."

"Right, sir."

McBride takes a quick look around, then, motioning those with him, heads back to his HQ. When he gets back, the attack will now launch in twenty minutes.

"We set?" he asks his executive officer.

"Yes, sir."

"Brilliant. Be prepared to move in after the attack. We'll reestablish HQ at the port."

"Yes, sir," his exec replies, and heads off.

McBride then turns to Codrington, who has been quietly watching the proceedings. "Colonel, I'm going to check with my Company COs," he says about talking to Company commanders.

"Very good. Just be careful, Geoffrey. Can't afford to lose you now," Codrington says.

"Wouldn't think of it, sir," he says as he heads off, a radio operator and four Marine guards with him.

He works his way from right to left, the flank that is in the air, the most vulnerable place in the line. He has placed A Company there, his best one commanded by his best commander, Captain Lewis Johnston-Stone.

"Well, Lewis," McBride says as he reaches Company HQ, "ready to go?"

"Five minutes and then we're off," Johnston-Stone says, a determined smile on his face.

"Excellent. Good hunting."

"Yes, sir," Johnston-Stone says. "All right, guys," he says, turning to the HQ staff, "we're about to step off. He keys his radio headset, "Big A to all Little As."

Each Troop commander acknowledges to call.

"We go in," he looks at his watch, "thirty seconds. ... Twenty seconds ... Ten ... Go! Go! Go!"

"We're off!" Second Lieutenant Judy Hope says as she gives the handset back to her radio operator. She steps out in front of her forty Marines as they head toward the outskirts of Cherbourg. She has told her Color Sergeant, Anne Mayran, to deploy a Section on the left to guard that open flank, since they are on the extreme left of the Commando. Their right flank is protected by the Troop on that side. Johnston-Stone has repeatedly warned her of the consequences if she fails to protect that open flank. Judy had been on raids, but this is her first major action. She's nervous about making mistakes but hides the fear from the Marines depending on her to keep them alive.

Since her Troop is on the most vulnerable flank, five tanks move out with them. She's happy to have them, especially since The Enemy is not believed to have any effective anti-tank weapons. Two tanks are in the lead with a Section of Marines walking alongside, while two others pay attention to the vulnerable flank, their turrets sweeping to the left periodically. The fifth is on the left tail of the Troop, its turret pointing to the rear, eight Marines walking with it. Attack helicopters patrol overhead about a hundred meters up, watching the left flank and peeking down among the buildings for trouble as they move into the suburbs, passing houses and business ranging from poor repair to nearly collapsed.

Like Forty Commando on the other side of the city, the companies of Four Two move in a choreographed manner down four parallel suburban streets, checking at each intersection to ensure they are staying abreast. B Company on the right flank has three tanks with it. The other two companies each have two tanks. The Marines hug the walls as they work their way through the city. They soon enter the urban area. No more detached houses, just dilapidated building after dilapidated building, broken up by the occasional alley and cross streets.

"Contact forward!" is called over the radio. Judy doesn't know which Troop or Company made contact or what kind of contact it is, especially since there is no firing. She halts her Troop, while they all await the order to resume the advance. Most of the Marines take advantage of the stop to sit down, but they stay alert.

"Hey, Boss," a Private asks Judy as she walks by, "what do you think's going on?"

"If I had X-ray vision I could tell you," she replies, "but no firing, so it can't be too serious."

"Yes, Boss."

Mayran walks up to Judy. "You really think it's nothing?"

Judy just gives her a funny look, shaking her head and looking at the sky. Mayran gives a short laugh.

"Move out!" McBride orders over the radio, and the advance resumes.

Four Two is less than two kilometers from the harbor when several hundred uniformed but unarmed people come staggering down the street toward them. Many are already in the street, but others are coming out of the buildings on either side.

"Contact forward!" Judy says over her shoulder to her radio operator, as she also keys her radio connecting her to the rest of the Commando.

"Contact forward! Contact forward!" the radio operator says into the handset, urgency in his voice.

"Hold your fire!" Judy orders her Marines. The lead tank won't shoot unless the Marines open up or they start taking hostile fire. Mayran has one of the tanks blocking the last intersection on their left with a Section around it. Another Section is with the rear tank, while several Marines are watching the street on their right flank, just in case. That is a delicate spot since any firing could hit the Marines on the next street.

Judy trusts her Color Sergeant to guard their left flank, so she concentrates on the disorganized mob of walking skeletons stumbling toward them. Their clothes are in tatters. They all look as if they hadn't eaten in weeks. Many stumble and fall, rising painfully from the pavement to continue approaching. Weak, pathetic pleas for food and help, along with the foul stench of unwashed bodies, flow over Judy as she steps out in front of the tank.

"Careful, Boss," one of her Marines tells her.

Judy replies with a nod as she scans for danger.

"What's up?" Johnston-Stone asks as he comes around the tank. The A Company commander had been with the Three Troop two streets over.

"That," Judy says flatly. "Halt! Stop! Halt! Stop!" she yells down the street, stopping the crowd about twenty meters in front of them. "I said stop!" she orders, raising her rifle, as three resume their advance. They stop abruptly, two dropping to the street.

"Well, sir," she says over her shoulder, "what do we do now?"

Before Johnston-Stone can respond, rifle and machine gun fire break out behind them. That prompts the gunner in the tank behind Judy to open fire, a machine gun raking the crowd in front of them.

"Stop shooting! Stop shooting!" Judy screams in her radio while pounding on the driver's hatch.

As abruptly as the shooting begins, it stops. But the damage is done. Too weak to move quickly, many of the people in front of the tank have been hit. Blood is everywhere.

"Bloody hell!" Johnston-Stone exclaims as Judy just stands there in stunned silence.

"Sir, will you watch here? I need to check on …" before she can finish, one of her Marines comes running up.

"Boss, Colors has everything under control. About twenty of The Enemy attacked, but we made short work of them."

"Any casualties?"

"Not for us, Boss."

"Very good. Tell Colors to keep a tight perimeter."

"Yes, Boss," the Private says as he pivots to head back.

Judy turns to talk to Johnston-Stone, but finds he is on the radio with McBride.

"Right, sir. Out," the Captain says, giving the hand set back to his radio operator who had followed him. "Well, Hope, we keep moving."

"The wounded, sir?"

"Leave them. Our primary concern is reaching the harbor. These poor devils will just have to wait for medical. Have your blokes move those still breathing off to the side so the tanks don't run over them."

"What about those who aren't wounded?"

"Leave them, too. These sods don't look like they will be any trouble."

"Yes, sir," Judy says, turning to issue orders. Johnston-Stone watches for a few moments as the Marines move the wounded not too gently from the street next to the buildings. They are nothing but skin and bones.

"When you've cleared a path, give the word to move out," Johnston-Stone tells Judy as he turns to leave.

"Sir," she says.

"Boss," Mayran says as she walks up. "We wasted the entire lot. They look well fed, if not well led," she says of the group who attacked as she surveys the carnage in the street before them.

"The tank started shooting when you did," Judy says, shaking her head. "We have orders to move the wounded and prisoners out of the way and then move out."

Mayran looks at her questioningly.

Judy just shrugs. "I suppose someone will come back to collect this lot after we secure the harbor."

"If any of those poor devils are still alive," Mayran says.

"That's a big if," Judy says, looking down the street as about fifty of the skeletons get to their feet.

"What of those?" Color asks.

Judy just shrugs. "We leave them, too." She watches as the last of the wounded and the feeble are moved onto the sidewalk. "Right, Colors, let's go." Taking the handset, she keys the other radio, "Move out."

The lead tank starts rumbling down the street, smashing bodies into the pavement. The Marines do their best to avoid the blood, brains and guts being spilled into the street while also watching the buildings and the street in front. Judy walks up some steps in front of a building to get a better view of the street. She watches as the lead tank clears the next intersection. Glancing back she sees the rear tank picking up some speed to close with the column, while the accompanying Marines do a bit of a dance around the mess in the street.

Satisfied her Troop is back on track, Judy walks quickly forward to catch up to the advance.

Just as she gets there, the voice of one of her Sergeants comes over the radio.

"Boss, some of these buggers are following us."

"Say again?" she says, a bit perplexed.

"Boss, I ain't kidding. Looks like about thirty of them are coming after us. At least trying to."

"On the way," she says as she heads back to the rear at a fast clip. When she gets there, she joins Sergeant Andre Dumas, who is walking backward while keeping an eye on the group stumbling after them. Two of his Marines have mounted the tank, their weapons pointing down the street, along with the tank's turret which has been reversed.

"They don't look threatening," Judy comments. The Soldiers are slowly walking after the column, some apparently too weak to walk on their own are supported by others.

"Boss, they don't look much like the living. Walking skeletons, if you ask me."

"Well, let them follow us, assuming they can keep up. When we form a perimeter, we can take them prisoner, and deal with them then."

"Yes, Boss," Dumas says.

"You speak French, don't you?" she asks.

"That I do, Boss. My family was from France originally."

"Good. You can talk to them if they get that far."

The rest of the trip is made without another halt, although occasional rifle and tank fire breaks out when someone spots a possible threat. Everyone is nervous and watchful. The Enemy Soldiers stumbling after Judy's Troop fall further and further behind until they are several blocks back.

"Halt!" comes across the Commando radio. "Form your perimeter," McBride orders.

Each Commando has a designated zone, and each Company a zone inside that, and each Troop a particular street to guard.

The rear tank with Judy's Troop pivots in the intersection, and back to one side of the street, going up on the sidewalk. Soon another tank pulls up beside it. A Section of Marines joins them. Judy orders the other Marines to start clearing the buildings on either side. The buildings at the end of the block are cleared first. Marines then occupy those buildings, setting up firing positions. Once the block is cleared, Judy leads the rest of her Marines through clearing the buildings down to the harbor, with trips down the side streets until they meet members of a Troop from Four Six coming their way. The last two Commandos land in the harbor after a company from Thirty Commando determined they would meet no initial resistance.

"Boss! You have to see this!" one of the Marines calls down the street to her. She's standing at the top of some steps leading into an apartment building.

"On the way!" Judy calls, hurrying toward her. "What's up?" she asks as she bounds up the steps.

"In there," the Marine says, motioning through the door.

Judy goes into the dimly lit hallway. The stench of unwashed bodies and unflushed toilets is overpowering. Three Marines are standing near the door, their weapons at the ready. All three look uncomfortable. One looks as if he is about to vomit. In front of them, crowded shoulder to shoulder, are Enemy soldiers, hundreds of them by the looks of it, filling the hallway and staircase. She looks up the stairs, seeing more huddled there.

"Does anyone speak English?" she calls.

No response.

"Get Sergeant Dumas," she orders one of the Marines.

"Right away, Boss," he says and hurries out.

"Boss, can we rotate guards?" another asks, his face a light shade of green.

Judy looks at him, and almost laughs. "Not at the moment. I don't think this lot poses a danger, but changing right now could give an opening to some of them. Besides, if I can stand it, you can, too."

"If you say so, Boss," the Marine says, not at all happy with the response.

The wait seems interminable. Finally, Dumas arrives.

"Boss, you wanted ..." he starts to say. "Oh, my sweet Jesus, the stench!"

Judy just smiles at him. "See if any of these poor sods speak French."

Dumas starts talking to some of the huddled masses. In as loud a voice as he can manage, he explains they are now prisoners of the British Royal Marines, and they will be treated well. They will be fed and receive medical attention if they don't resist and don't carry weapons. Any resistance, he explains, will be met with deadly force. The babble of voices goes up the stairs and through the throngs, the volume and excitement growing.

"I think they got the message, Boss," the Sergeant tells Judy.

"You think?" she responds, her humor overriding her sarcasm at the obvious statement. "Tell them to start filing out into the street. Set up an area we can collect them in before moving them to the POW cages."

"Do you know where those are?" Dumas asks.

"I should be so lucky," she replies. "I'll find out while you organize this lot."

"Yes, Boss," he says, as Judy heads out.

As she comes out of the building, she runs into Codrington and McBride, who are touring the operation with Johnston-Stone.

"Sirs!" she calls.

The trio stops. "What is it, Second Leftenant?" Johnston-Stone asks as she comes hurrying up.

"Sir, we have come across a large patch of Enemy Soldiers in one of the buildings. They are surrendering. What do we do with them?"

"How many?" McBride asks.

"I'm not sure yet. We just discovered them in that one," she says, gesturing behind her just as Dumas begins to lead the first group outside, a Section of Marines gathered to guard them as they are directed to line up against the building. "They are coming out now, but there were so many of them crammed in there that we couldn't get a count."

"Are you certain they are all willing to surrender?" Codrington asks.

"No, sir," Judy replies. "That's why we're bringing up a tank," she says, as one rolls up from the other end of the street, "and my blokes are on alert. We are checking each prisoner for weapons as they come out the door."

"Very good," Codrington says.

"Yes, sir," she says, a bit of frustration entering her voice, "but what do we do with them?"

"A warehouse down by the harbor has been designated as the POW cage, but we haven't gotten it set up quite yet," the Chief of Staff says. "Take them down there," he says, pointing down the street to the harbor. "Just follow this street. You'll see a big sign 'POW CAGE.' If the Major in charge gives you any grief, tell him I sent you."

"Yes, sir. Thank you, sir."

"Good God!" Johnston-Stone exclaims as he sees the mass of humanity come stumbling out of the building. "How many of those poor devils were in there?"

The others turn around. The prisoners are stretched over fifty meters, six ranks deep, with more still coming out. Few look healthy. Some can stand only with the help of others. They all look as if they haven't eaten in days, if not weeks.

"Boss," a Private says, coming up to Judy.

"Yes?"

"The Sergeant says the building is clear except for the bodies."

"Bodies?" McBride asks.

"Ah, yes, sir," the Private says, realizing for the first time he is in the presence of senior officers. "Bodies are all over the place, sir. We haven't taken a count, but there must be more than a hundred. Looks like they starved to death."

"Right," Judy says. "Tell Dumas to seal the building. We'll have to deal with that later."

"Yes, Boss," the Private says, hurrying off.

"If you'll excuse me, sirs," Judy says, "I have work to do."

"Will you need any help?" Johnston-Stone asks.

"Well, sir, I could use another Section. It will take at least two Sections to move this lot, since we haven't cleared any of the buildings to the harbor."

"I'll send over an MP Section," McBride says.

"Thank you, sir," Judy says, as she pivots to go.

"Dumas!" she calls as she nears the Sergeant.

"Yes, Boss?"

"Get a Section organized to provide security while this lot is taken to the POW cage in the harbor. And I want two tanks to go along since we haven't cleared all the way to the harbor yet."

"Right. Do you know how far they've cleared toward us?" Dumas asks about the units who landed at the harbor.

"No. All I know for sure is that they've secured the area right around the harbor and are setting up the POW cage."

"Right, Boss," he says as he heads off to get organized.

A few minutes later, a Color Sergeant leads up a Section of MPs. "Second Leftenant Hope?" he asks.

"Ah, you must be the blokes who are going to accompany this lot to the harbor," she says, waving a hand toward the mass of POWs.

"Yes, ma'am," he says slowly. "That's a bloody hell of a lot."

"True," she responds. "One of my Sections will provide security, and you'll have a tank in front and another in the rear. Besides, this lot is in such poor shape, I suspect that about all they're capable of doing is walking."

"Have they been checked for weapons?"

"Yes, they have."

"Very good, ma'am. When do we move out?"

"A tic," she says, keying her mic, "Dumas."

"On the way, Boss," comes the reply.

"Colors," she says, "this is Sergeant Dumas. He'll be leading the Section providing your security. And he speaks French, should you need that."

"That's good, ma'am. None of my lot do."

"Right, then move these poor sods. I leave it to you two to coordinate."

"Yes, Boss;" "Yes, ma'am," come the replies.

Judy heads off to check on how the rest of her Troop is doing clearing the buildings.

Dumas and the MP Color Sergeant soon have the POWs moving toward the harbor, trailing a tank. As they walk the four blocks to the harbor, more emaciated Enemy Soldiers come stumbling out of buildings. Several are shot when they come out carrying weapons. The word must have spread quickly because more than three hundred emerge with their hands up if they can walk well enough. The rest support each other or lean on makeshift canes.

The column moves so slowly that it does not have to stop as the new prisoners are checked for weapons and then added to the end.

⊱❖⊱⊷◇⊶❖⊰

Major Seldon Pelissier is not a happy Marine.

The Brigade supply officer is setting up the POW collection center. He has his people cleaning the floor and walls of an old, deserted warehouse, and securing the doors and windows to prevent escapes. Entrance and exit will be through a closely guarded truck entrance. Cots, bunkbeds, mattresses, sheets, blankets and pillows are piled in the center of the cavernous room.

The work is going nicely, but too slowly for Pelissier's taste.

Then, Doctor Suzette Egerton arrives.

"Major Pelissier?" she asks as she leads her Royal Navy medical team into the dimly lit interior.

"Ah, yes?" he replies, tearing his attention from the work.

"I'm Dr. Egerton. Where would you like us to set up?"

"Excuse me?" the perplexed supply officer responds. "Set up for what?"

"You didn't receive notice?"

"About what?" he responds, his irritation growing.

"Two to three hundred POWs, possibly many more, are on their way here. Colonel Codrington ordered my unit here to tend to them. We also have water and rations on trucks outside."

"Colonel Codrington what?" comes the outraged reply as Pelissier raises up on the balls of his feet, stretching his five-foot-seven frame. "I'm not ready for that. I can't possibly handle that many. Look at this place," he says, his right arm sweeping around the cavernous room. "I am just getting started organizing this place. We won't be ready for hours. What does the Colonel expect me to do? I am not a miracle worker!"

The doctor looks down at the concrete floor to hide the smile she can't suppress. Regaining her self-control, she looks back up. "Well, Major, what can I tell you? The Colonel says we are to take care of this lot when they arrive."

"How am I supposed to guard them? All my blokes are hard at work still getting this place set up."

"An MP Section is with them. They are to stay and provide security. The Colonel's orders, should anyone ask."

"I don't have any say in this, do I?" the exasperated Pelissier says.

"Afraid not. Now, where should we set up?"

"Give me a moment," he replies, rearranging the room in his mind to accommodate the medical team and the incoming guests. "Leftenant Hanson!" he calls.

"Sir!" Hanson replies as he quickly crosses the room.

"We will receive up to four hundred POWs shortly."

"Yes, sir."

"Line them up across that wall," he says, indicating the wall nearest the entrance. "They can sit there and wait. Doctor Egerton here has water and rations outside. They will be distributed once the POWs are in place."

"One of my doctors will supervise the food distribution," Egerton, a Navy Commander, interjects. "We have to be careful. These poor buggers are starving. If they eat too much too fast, it will kill them."

"Yes, quite," Pelissier says, shaking off the distraction. "Commander, your medical station will be set up there," he says indicating the back wall near where the POWs will be. "Will that be satisfactory?" he asks.

"Very," she replies.

"Good," he says. Turning back to Hanson, he waves his arm to the other side of the room and says, "The sleeping area will be over there. We'll deal with setting up a mess later."

"Yes, sir," Hanson says.

"Now get cracking, Leftenant. We don't have much time."

"Sir," Hanson says crisply, then turns to get his people moving faster.

"We'll help set up our station," Egerton says. "I already have my people unloading the rations and water. We'll stack them near our station for distribution."

The next few hours pass in a haze for the Marines trying to deal with the flood of prisoners. They are lined up ten deep along the sixty-foot wall. After rations and water have been passed out—and quickly consumed, with MPs having to intervene several times to prevent prisoners from stealing each other's food—the three doctors start examining the POWs. Those who are seriously ill are immediately sent to a section of cots set up as a clinic, with medics bedding their patients down.

"How are things progressing?" the voice behind Pelissier asks.

"It's a proper cock up, if you ask me!" the Major blurts out as he turns around, to come face-to-face with Sam. "Brigadier!" the horrified Pelissier stammers out. "Sorry, sir! I didn't know it was you!"

"No worries, Major. It looks like you have everything well in hand. At least, as well in hand as can be expected given the time you had to prepare."

"Yes, sir. Thank you, sir. Sir, as you have probably noticed, the stench is nearly overpowering. Would it be possible to hose the prisoners down. Just as a temporary measure, you understand."

"No," Sam says, shaking his head, "hoses are out. I'll see about getting showers. Is there anything more you need?"

Pelissier looks around for a moment, exasperation evident in his expression. "The Army, sir. I could use the Army to assume responsibility for this…place."

"Yes, well," Sam says with a laugh. "They'll be along in a couple of days. I'm afraid you'll just have to muddle through until then."

"Yes, sir," comes the dejected reply.

Sam gives Pelissier's arm a reassuring squeeze, then walks over to the medical area.

"Commander Egerton?" he says, walking up to where the Royal Navy doctor is examining one of the prisoners.

"Yes, sir?" she says looking up. "One moment." Finishing with the patient, she turns her attention to Sam. "Now, sir, what may I do for you?"

"You have that backward, doctor. What may I do for you?"

"Well, sir, we could do with fewer patients," she says, laughing a bit, "but I don't suppose you can do anything about that."

"I'm afraid not," he says, smiling. "How are they?" he asks, looking over at the crowd of humanity.

"Not very well, I'm afraid. They are all starving and dehydrated. Seven died already."

"Died?"

"Yes, sir. They were just too weak to continue. I suspect the walk here did them in. They just sat down and died," she says with a shrug. "We have the worst cases over there," she says, indicating the area with cots and medics going around the beds. The rest we will get bedded down as soon as we can. They need time to heal and regain their strength. What we could use right now are showers and new clothes. They are all filthy and in rags. And we need more portable toilets. Lots of them."

"Very good. I can organize the showers and latrines. Clothing is another matter. I can't issue them our uniforms. We'll see what we can scrounge up for you."

"Thank you, sir," she replies. "Now, if you'll excuse me, I have patients to tend to."

"Carry on," Sam says. He gives the room a final look, then heads for the door. The air outside smells fresh and sweet after the rank air inside the POW facility. He's relieved he doesn't have to stay in there, then feels guilty for having that thought. *'I wonder if we have a medal for surviving working in a place like that? Probably not, but we should.'* He makes a mental note to write commendations for the Marines and Navy medical people working there.

He walks quickly the two blocks to where Brigade headquarters has been established. Inside, he heads to the supply office, issuing orders for portable showers and latrines to be sent over to the POW facility immediately. To the objection that portable toilets do not exist, Sam orders latrines to be built. Pelissier will decide where to put them. He also orders a search for clothing of any type and size to be sent over there.

Sam then goes up to the next floor to the Brigade command center. He updates Codrington on his inspection tour. The Colonel in turn updates his Brigadier on their progress. With all four Commandos now operational, they have cleared the area between the front line and the harbor.

Thirty Commando is sending patrols as far as three kilometers outside the city. So far, contact has been light and sporadic. No casualties. What the reconnaissance has discovered are masses of bodies, most seemingly having starved to death, and a large number of the starving Enemy Soldiers trying to surrender.

"Jack Griffith wants to know what they should do with them," Codrington tells Sam, referring to the Lieutenant Colonel who runs Thirty Commando.

"Hmmm, not much we can do at the moment. Tell him to disarm them and leave them in place. He can tell them to try to make it to our lines, but only approach in daylight with their hands raised. If they do that, we will take care of them."

"Will do. Do we send lorries out for them when we have an opportunity?"

"Good idea. Any sign of organized resistance?" Sam asks.

"Air Force has spotted three largish concentrations," Codrington says, indicating three places from fifteen to twenty kilometers away on the map in front of them. "They estimate five thousand to ten thousand in each."

"That's quite a range."

"Yes, it is. They are under the trees so it is hard to get a firm grasp of their numbers. The fighter-bombers attacked them. No large explosions, so results are not known. I suspect we scattered them if nothing else."

"I suppose disrupting their plans is the best we can hope for at this point," Sam says, frustration in his voice. "Have Jack pull his people back to our lines before sunset."

"He's not going to like that," the Colonel observes.

"Too bad. Until we get a better idea of what's out there, I am going to play this cautiously. We've been lucky so far. I don't want to push it. I really, really hate surprises."

CHAPTER 6

H ere they come again, Boss," Private Jimmy Alexander says in a low voice to Judy, who is taking a nap next to him by the barricade made up of old vehicles and some heavy furniture they found in the buildings around them and set up at intersections to tunnel any attack between buildings. A tank is on either side, so close to the buildings that a person could not squeeze past.

Judy is immediately awake. Flipping down her night vision gear, she peers down the street. She can see a mass of figures creeping as silently as possible.

"Make sure everyone is awake," she quietly orders Alexander.

"Right, Boss," he says as he heads off to alert the rest of the Troop.

Judy then notifies Johnston-Stone of the impending attack.

"Schwartzee, are you ready?" Judy asks quietly in her radio. The response is two clicks, followed by another two, meaning both tank crews are ready. The Schwartzee call sign has become a joke among her Marines and the two tank crews. When Sergeant Hiram Schwartz introduced himself, his driver piped up with "Just call him Schwartzee. Everyone does."

"All ready, Boss," Alexander says as he returns and other Marines join them at the barricade, some lying on the tanks' decks, others are in the lower and upper floors of the buildings on either side.

"Lovely," Judy says, keeping focused on the approaching mass. The Marine line stretches in a horseshoe shape with both flanks anchored on the harbor. Barricades have been set up to block the intersections. Some Marines are on the rooftops to prevent The Enemy coming that way, even though the five previous attacks that night all have come on the ground.

The Enemy apparently only knows how to attack straight at them in mass waves. Not an effective tactic in confined spaces against the massed firepower of a Troop of Marines and two tanks. While the carnage makes her uneasy, knowing it's more a slaughter than a fight, she is happy her Marines have only suffered three casualties, none life threatening, or even serious.

Judy glances up quickly, looking for some sign of dawn. *'It has to be close,'* she thinks. She looks back down the street. The mass of Enemy soldiers is about halfway down the block.

"Fire! Fire! Fire!" she orders over the radio. A fusillade of machine gun and semi-automatic weapon fire pours bullets into the packed mass. Like the other attacks, The Enemy soldiers start screaming and break into a run toward the Marines, firing as they come. Those in front are torn apart, their bodies falling in heaps onto those who were shot down in the earlier attacks. The attack lasts no more than five minutes, although to Judy it seems like an eternity.

Unable to stand the withering fire, the survivors take cover behind their fallen comrades. Some just hide, but many use the bodies as barricades, firing over them. The Marines on the ground do not have clear shots, but those on the upper floors and on the roofs do. They put down a murderous fire on the street, joined by the tanks firing their 120-milimeter main guns.

"Cease fire! Cease fire! Cease fire, damn it!" Judy orders after another few minutes.

Silence descends on the street. The Marines listen intently for any sound or movement. All they hear is the groaning of the wounded.

"Amazing any of those sods lived through that," Alexander says, as he relaxes a bit.

"Boss, what do you think?" Color Sergeant Mayran says as she comes up.

"I think those bleeding incompetent bastards are sending their blokes to the slaughter. And, God help me, I am happy they are."

"Maybe God is helping us," Mayran replies.

"Helping with a slaughter?" she says skeptically. "Well, perhaps. Any casualties?" Judy asks, happy to change the subject.

"Just a few nicks. Mostly from pieces of masonry sent flying. Nothing serious enough to take anyone out of the line. The worst is Nichols. She's flushing out her eyes after some brick chips hit her face."

"How about ammunition?"

"That's being distributed now, and I sent two back to secure some more."

"Colors, I don't know what I would do without you."

"Let's not find out, shall we, Boss?"

"Brilliant idea."

About twenty minutes later, the sky begins to lighten. It's another hour before the canyon created by the buildings on either side of the street becomes light enough to see. And then Judy wishes she didn't have to look. Bodies and body parts are piled up, in some places four and five deep. The only gaps are where cannon shells struck. The street is awash in blood, which is flowing into storm drains. Judy scans the street, looking for movement. She sees a bit here and there, but nothing to indicate a threat.

She scans the roofline, seeing her Marines looking down into the street, weapons at the ready.

"Hold fire unless you see a threat," she says over the Troop's net. She watches as the Marines on the roofs relax.

"Colors," Judy says as Mayran comes up. "Have everyone break out rations. They need to eat before we see what's out there."

"Yes, Boss," she says, then goes to get it done.

Judy takes a ration packet out, and starts eating as she resumes scanning the street, looking for a threat.

"Good morning, Leftenant," Johnston-Stone says as he comes up behind her.

"Sir," she says, holding the ready-to-eat ration in one hand and a fork in the other as she turns slightly around, swallowing her mouthful, so she can see him and watch the street as well. She is preoccupied so she doesn't catch that he called her Leftenant and not Second Leftenant. The Captain comes up next to her, and they both stare at the carnage stretching out before them.

"Casualties?"

"Just minor. No one off the line."

"Survivors?" the captain asks, nodding his approval about the casualties.

"Don't know yet, sir. I'm having everyone breakfast before we go out there."

"Right. I'll have hot meals sent up for lunch and dinner."

"Thank you, sir," she replies.

"Just so you know, your lot took the brunt of the attacks. What was it? Four?"

"Six." Her voice is flat and emotionless.

"Right. Your Troop did an excellent job holding the line. You should be proud."

"With all due respect, sir, it wasn't a battle. It was a slaughter. They just kept coming at us. They didn't stand a chance."

"All that said, you held the line. Not everyone could have done that in the face of repeated human-wave attacks. By the way, you are now Leftenant by order of Colonel Codrington. Apparently, he thinks your action was brilliant. Leftenant Colonel McBride and I agree. Here, you'll be needing these," he said, handing her the pips of her new rank.

"Thank you, sir," she says, tentatively, not sure she deserves the honor.

"Leftenant, trust me, your leadership of your Troop was nothing if not outstanding."

"Yes, sir. Thank you, sir," she says, more firmly this time.

"You be careful out there," Johnston-Stone says, indicating the other side of the barricade.

"Yes, sir."

The Captain hands her the new pips for her new rank, turns and heads off without another word.

"Well, Boss," Mayran says, who has been standing nearby listening. "May I have the honor of putting those on for you?"

"Yes, please," Judy says, still a bit shocked with what just happened, handing the Color Sergeant the pips.

"There," Mayran says, standing back to admire her handiwork.

"Hey, guys!" someone yells, "the Boss just got bumped to Leftenant!"

When a cheer goes up, Judy keys the radio. "Knock it off! We still have to check that mess out there." She turns to Mayran, all business now, "Colors, get a Section and let's go."

"Yes, Boss," she says.

Soon Judy is leading a Section out among the dead, looking for survivors and collecting weapons for destruction. They are guarded by the Marines on the rooftops and from windows on the higher floors.

"Boss! I have a live one!" a Marine calls.

"Right," she says, working her way over the piles of dead. "What condition?"

"Not good," comes the reply. "His guts are spilled all over the street."

When Judy gets there, she looks down at the pitiful mess. The Soldier is looking up at her with silently pleading eyes. His stomach is torn open, his intestines lying outside. "Do you have fentanyl?"

"Right here," the Marine says, pulling out his first-aid kit.

"Give him a shot. We may not be able to save the poor bugger, but at least we can let him die without pain."

"Yes, Boss," the Marine says as he gives the man a shot, and then moves on.

"Got a live one!" another Marine calls.

As Judy moves up the street, the Marine kneels beside the injured soldier. "Leg and shoulder wounds," the Marine says, looking up at her, then going back to applying a bandage to the leg wound.

"Colors," Judy says over the radio, "we need a medic and a stretcher up here."

"On the way," comes the reply.

"Stay with her until the medic arrives," Judy tells the Marine.

"Right," comes the reply.

"Boss!" The alarmed cry catches Judy's immediate attention. As she looks down the street, several dozen enemy soldiers start to stand up. One holding a weapon is immediately shot by two Marines. All the others who are able raise their empty hands above their heads. Some wounded are just kneeling, raising their hands as much as they can.

"Bloody hell," Judy says to herself. "Colors, I need another Section out here now, and as many medics and stretchers as we can find. Is Dumas back?"

"Yes, Boss."

"Get him up here fast."

"Right away."

Judy contacts Johnston-Stone to let him know what is going on and to ask for more medical personnel to be sent. The next two hours are spent sending the uninjured and walking wounded back to the POW cage, while those too wounded to walk receive battlefield care, then are carried there by Marines and Navy medical people because the other POWs do not have the strength.

While all that is going on, Marines finish collecting the rifles that are just as numerous as the bodies, cursing as they slip and slide in blood that is fifteen centimeters deep in places.

As for the dead, two bulldozers push the bodies down the street to where a large pit has been dug. They are dumped in and covered. Hoses and pumps are rigged to wash the blood off the street with water from the harbor.

"Booty, you're a royal bloody mess," she tells one of her Marines.

"So are you, Boss," he replies with a big grin. Both are soaked in blood to their waist and have blood on their shirts and splattered up to and in their hair. "You're not going to spring a spot inspection on us, are you?"

"Dismissed, you silly sod," she says laughing.

Standing in the middle of the now deserted street, she wonders what will happen next when her Company commander comes up.

"Brilliant job," Johnston-Stone says.

"Thank you, sir. Any chance my blokes can get a shower and clean uniforms?"

"That's why I came. The Army has finally arrived. A Battalion is moving in on our right, so we are moving everyone. I'm pulling your Troop off the line. You can get some hot food, as well as those showers and uniforms."

"Brilliant, sir. Thank you."

"Don't mention it. B Troop should be here in fifteen minutes to relieve you. You can take your Troop down to the harbor. Showers have been set up, and the mess is right near them."

"Yes, sir."

"Again, Leftentant, brilliant job," he says, turning to walk off. "Oh," he says, turning back around, "don't get too comfortable. You're Company reserve."

"Sir." Judy feels like a great weight has just been lifted from her, trying to be confident her Troop will at least have the rest of today and tonight off. She heads back to the barricade to find Mayran to get things organized for their relief.

CHAPTER 7

Tom," Sam says as he walks up to Codrington in Brigade HQ, "change of plans. We are not going off the line as we expected."

"That is not really a surprise," the Colonel says, who has been sitting at his desk doing paper work.

"No, I suppose it isn't," Sam says, sitting down in a chair in front of Codrington's desk. "In any case, the plan is for us to stay in the fight until we reach the open country. The Army will feed Regiments on both our flanks to keep us anchored on the shores as they build up behind us. When we get out of the bocage, the plan is for the Army to break out, taking northern France and Belgium up to the Rhine, while we and some Army units will be strung along the Loire River from the coast to the Rhone to guard the southern flank."

"How many Army units?"

"I don't know," Sam says, spitting out the answer in disgust. "But whatever it is, we will be obliged to do it."

"So, we're being hung out to dry by some wanker," Codrington says in anger. "I suppose the Army will take the right flank?"

"Good guess."

"And we get to take a long stretch down the Loire River into the mountains and then establish a line between the Loire and the Rhone. Is that about right?"

"The Swiss have promised to join us once we reach their border, so we may be able to count on some help from them. They have said they will send forces down the Rhone to Lyon, if we can supply weapons and ammunition, especially heavy weapons. If they actually do that, it should help."

"Do they have heavy weapons?"

"Mostly just rifles and machine guns, with some artillery. But no transport, and not much ammunition."

"We don't have much transport, and ammo, especially for the artillery. Those will quickly become issues," Codington points out.

"The Army is fat. They will have to provide for everyone."

"And the chances of that happening?"

Sam just looks at his Number Two, then continues. "Once the Rhone line is secure, the Army will shift most of its forces down here to clear southern France to the Italian and Spanish borders. Then, garrisons will be established at the mountain passes, and everybody heads back north for the drive up through Holland and across the German plain."

"All this," Codrington remarks, "is based on the assumption intelligence knows what it's talking about. What if enemy strength is stronger than we think down south?"

"Then, Colonel, we will be in for one hell of a fight."

"Marvelous. Simply, marvelous."

"Speaking of intelligence, have you seen any reports about survivors to the south or east?" Sam asks as first he and then Codrington walk over to a large table with a map of Western Europe on it.

"Not really," Codrington says, shaking his head. "We know about pockets in Scandinavia, especially northern Norway, and, of course, the Swiss. Intelligence says there are indications of pockets in the Carpathian Mountains and the Alps. Possibly some in Basque country. But nothing definite, no, nothing definite."

Sam nods, thinking wistfully of finding allies, as he and Codrington continue to study the map on the table in front of them. It will be months, probably a year, before any of the POWs who volunteer to fight will be ready. And the forces available now are "adequate"—a term often used by the British military, which Sam finds irritating and somewhat misleading—for the conquering of a continent, regardless of how depleted, badly led, and poorly equipped The Enemy forces are.

Intelligence reports put Enemy strength at nearly two hundred thousand around Berlin and further east, with scattered units ranging from ten thousand down to a few hundred between there and the Rhone, and weak enemy units in France. Enemy strength in Italy is estimated at the tens of thousands, though no one is really sure. What bothers Sam is that he could never get a definition of how many Soldiers are in a "weak" unit.

"Supply?" Sam finally asks.

"It seems your appeal worked. Major Pelissier says we've received even more than we requisitioned."

"The Army sent us more than we asked for?" Sam asks, sounding skeptical. "Someone over there must have screwed up."

"If they did, we'll take it. Right now, we have enough rations for sixty days, and enough ammunition and medical supplies for a three-week high intensity fight."

Sam just shakes his head, wondering what is going on.

He doesn't have long to wait.

"Sir," an aide says, "Leftenant General Drinkwater is on the line demanding to speak with you."

"He is, is he?" Sam says, giving Codrington a knowing look. The Colonel shrugs in reply. "I'll take it in my office."

"Yes, sir," the aide says, heading off to arrange the transfer of the call.

"I wonder what the Leftenant General wants," Sam says, smiling as he heads to his office to face what he expects will be the angry Army Quartermaster who is in charge of supply for everyone.

"Brigadier Hope, here," Sam says when he picks up the phone.

"What the bloody hell are you people doing?" Drinkwater shouts into the phone.

"Sir?" Sam responds, keeping his voice calm and innocent sounding. "May I ask what you are talking about?"

"You know bloody hell what I am talking about, Brigadier," he yells. Sam has a mental image of the veins standing out in the Lieutenant General's neck. "I want the officer responsible for this outrage court martialed and I want the supplies he stole, stole I say, returned immediately!"

"Sir, this is the first I've heard of this," Sam says, sounding as placating as he can. "I will launch an immediate investigation." His voice gaining a hard edge. "What is the name of the officer in question, sir?"

"That man is not only a thief, but a scoundrel as well! He used a fake name! He called himself Leftenant Colonel Johnathan Drinkwater! My son's name! He had the audacity to use my son's name! I want him caught! Do you hear me, Brigadier?"

"That is certainly outrageous," Sam says, sounding as outraged as he can, all the while suppressing a laugh. "I will certainly look into it immediately. And I give you my word, sir, the offending officer will be brought up on charges."

"Good. Do that," the upset Drinkwater says, slamming down the phone so hard Sam wonders whether he broke the receiver.

Sam sits back in his chair thinking about how best to proceed. The problem his Brigade faces is that all its supplies come through the Army. And the Army has not been forthcoming in resupply. He had talked to Drinkwater a week ago about the resupply and had been promised large quantities of everything they needed. The Marines had landed with minimal stores of food, ammunition, and medical supplies, counting on promises by the Army of being resupplied immediately. The resupply that materialized was woefully short of everything. Sam assumes a frustrated Marine decided to take matters into his own hands. And he knows who that is.

He smiles to himself as he summons his supply officer.

"Sir, you wanted to see me?" Pelissier says, entering the crammed office that holds a desk, four chairs, and a cot.

"Yes, Major," Sam says, motioning him to sit down. "I just received an angry call from Leftenant General Drinkwater. It seems one of our officers used his son's name to make off with truckloads of supplies."

"Sir, if you will allow me…"

Sam holds up a hand, cutting Pelissier off. "I want you to find this officer, and immediately draw up court martial charges…"

"But, sir…"

Sam holds up his hand again. "I promised the Leftenant General the offending officer would be brought up on charges. I intend to keep my promise."

"If I may…"

Sam holds up his hand a third time. "Please allow me to finish, Major."

"Yes, sir," the dejected Major says.

"I will be extremely disappointed if I ever see those charges on my desk. Are we clear?"

"Sir, yes, sir," Pelissier says, perking up.

"And, Major, make sure those supplies are, shall we say, stored safely. We will have to return them, should we ever have available transport."

"Yes, sir!"

"Thank you, Major."

"Thank you, sir," Pelissier, leaving the office, a smile spreading across his face.

Sam sits back in his chair, thinking about the two-front war he is waging: The Enemy in front of him, and the Army supply system behind him. Life was simpler, if much less safe, in North America. There, all they had to do was stay alive.

CHAPTER 8

T hat didn't take very long," Codrington observes as he and Sam survey the comparatively open country in front of them. Thirty Commando, reinforced by other Commandos, have pushed out into the open country on reconnaissance missions, pushing out five kilometers. The two senior Brigade officers are standing in the shade of trees in front of Four Six Commando whose Marines are busily preparing to move again. The British forces needed just two weeks to clear the hedgerow country in Normandy, and now stand on the doorstep of the open country that leads across France to the mountains and the Rhine River.

"We could've done it a lot quicker if the Army hadn't been dragging its feet," Sam says, sounding a bit exasperated.

Enemy opposition had been light and sporadic, but because of how thick and overgrown the hedgerows were and the poor conditions of the roads, the Army had insisted on moving slowly and cautiously, sometimes covering just a few kilometers in a day even when they faced no opposition.

"They are an overly cautious lot," the Colonel says. "Besides, we were able to rest our guys, and get organized for the drive south."

"Always have to look on the bright side, hey?" Sam says, humor in his voice. Then he turns serious. "Are we going to have enough trucks?"

"Only if nothing breaks down."

"Brilliant," he says sarcastically. "Any static from Drinkwater?"

"Not recently."

"I thought he'd eventually get tired of asking about the court martial."

"You never did tell me what you said to fob him off."

"Oh, just that we were too busy pushing through the bocage to put together a proper court."

"And he believed that?"

Sam shrugs. "He didn't have much of a choice."

"I suppose not," Codrington says, then goes back to business. "We'll be ready to move south as soon as the Army heads east."

"Right. I want Jack Griffith to take his Thirty Commando further out now. I want to know what we are running into."

"I'll let him know."

"No, Tom, I'll give him the good news. You come, too, though. The three of us can determine, or guess, at the best routes for his recon Booties to take. I want them to fan out, but not to the point that they can't manage any trouble they run into."

"Right. I'll fetch him and meet you at HQ."

"Good," Sam replies. Codrington heads off to find the Lieutenant Colonel, who runs Thirty Commando, the Brigade's reconnaissance force. Sam spends the next few minutes studying the open ground in front of him and contemplating what lies ahead. His Marines will be responsible for hundreds of kilometers of river front, not to mention the open ground between the Loire and the Rhone rivers. Army intelligence has assured him only minimal Enemy forces are in the region. What worries him is he has received no numbers with that "minimal" assessment. The best he can do is patrol the banks aggressively and establish quick reaction teams to deal with any threats coming from the other side of the river.

And if major threats are on his side of river? He involuntarily shudders. He knows the kind of mass wave attacks The Enemy uses, heedless of the lives of their Soldiers. He experienced that both in North America and here on the Continent. He fears a bloodbath—among his Marines. He's thankful that Marines from outside the Brigade have been assigned to his Commandos, bringing them up to and even past full strength. He just hopes the Air Force and Marine air, along with armor and artillery can deal with what his Marine infantry can't. Combined arms, they call it. It will take combined courage to deal with a major attack. Sam sighs, resigned to fate and following orders, then heads for HQ.

Codrington and Griffith are already there when he arrives. He greets the two officers, and they gather around the large tabletop map.

"Starting tomorrow," Sam says to Griffith, "I want you to push out ten to fifteen kilometers at Troop strength on each these roads." Sam points out the routes on the map as he talks. "Keep your guys from getting strung out. This will be our major axis of advance," he says, drawing his finger along a path, "so those two roads are a given. And I think you need to take a look at the roads on either side."

"Yes, sir," Griffith says, his eyes fixed on the map. "One problem I see is that this road," he says, indicating the side road on the south of the advance, "diverges what looks like three klicks on. If that Troop runs into trouble after that, I will be hard pressed to support them."

"What if you patrol down to the point where the road turns south," Codrington offers, "then have that Troop hold position until the others have completed their sweeps. You can push a patrol a bit further down to ensure no surprises on the flank of the main advance."

"Yes, sir," Griffith says, "we can do that. Another thing, I would like to push out twenty klicks. I think that will give us a better feel for any possible trouble, and enough warning if there is. My blokes will set up there and await the main body. After that, we can stay two or three klicks ahead of the advance."

"Ten, fifteen if everything is clear," Sam says, contemplatively. "It will be hard to support you quickly if you run into trouble."

"Oh, don't fret, sir," Griffith says. "If we run into trouble, we'll come tumbling back in a hurry. My guys know they're there to look and report only."

"Except the last time you were on the Continent, your guys got into a major blow up, as I recall."

"Yes, sir," Griffith replies, smiling, "but we were just testing their weapons and The Enemy's tactics so we could make a comprehensive report."

Sam just looks at his recon commander, not sure whether to laugh or chew him out. "You leave at first light," he finally says, his voice flat. "The rest of us head out the day after."

"Yes, sir. Ten to fifteen klicks it is then," Griffith says, assuming his Brigadier has agreed.

"Just be careful, Leftenant Colonel. This is too early in the campaign for me to lose my eyes and ears."

"Sir, I am the picture of prudent aggressiveness."

"Get out of here!" Sam says, half in jest, half in annoyance at having his words thrown back at him.

"Sir!" Griffith says, throwing a salute, turning on his heel and heading out, not waiting for Sam to return the salute.

Sam and Codrington watch him leave.

"He'll be alright," the Colonel says.

"He bloody well better be," Sam responds. "Now, let's make sure everyone else is ready."

CHAPTER 9

Let's go," Judy tells her driver as she gets into the cab of the armored personnel vehicle at the tail end of Four Two Commando, which is at the tail end of the Marine Brigade's column, with Four Five in the lead. Her Troop will provide the rear guard as the Brigade moves into position along the Loire River.

The other Commandos will take positions along the eastern end of the river, starting with Four Five Commando. Commando Forty will then take up positions from the Loire along the River Lot toward the River Dordogne, where they are to link up with the Royal Army units which will carry the line to Bordeaux and the Atlantic Coast. Four Six will be the Brigade's reserve.

Four Two Commando will guard the gap between the Loire and Rhone rivers on the extreme east end of the line. And since Judy's Marines are at the end of the column, One Troop will be on the left of her Commando with its flank resting on the banks of the Rhone, as far away from help as it is possible to be. Most of Thirty Commando will watch the Rhone, too thin a line to do any more than sound the alarm, until the Swiss arrive.

If they arrive.

Judy has learned not to depend on help outside the Brigade. The Air Force, the Navy, and the Royal Engineers are the exceptions. Her brother Frank is a Staff Sergeant with a Royal Army Reserve unit, which has been called up for the invasion. He is the only reason she tolerates the Army at all. The most common way to refer to that branch is the "bloody wanker Army." Especially the supply operation. The Marines always seem to be at the tail end, getting the leftovers after the Army has stuffed itself.

Judy settles back into her seat, staring out the window at the trees and open fields. In a few days, if all goes well, they will be climbing up the northern edge of the rugged Massif Central in southeastern France on their way to Avignon, more than nine hundred kilometers to the southeast. Judy has never been this far from the sea, and it makes her a little uneasy. The sea has always provided that cushion of safety against The Enemy. And now she won't even have a river.

"Hey, Boss, look at that," her driver calls out, breaking into her thoughts. She glances up to see hundreds of Enemy Soldiers slowly trudging in the opposite direction. She looks back, seeing the line stretch far behind them. She realizes she has been so lost in thought that she wasn't seeing what was right in front of her.

"Prisoners?" she says, snapping back into the here-and-now.

"There must be a thousand or more," the driver says. "They look like they're in pretty bad shape."

"Yeah, but better off than the lot we first ran into," she observes. "At least they don't look like skeletons."

"And best yet, we don't have to fight those wankers," the driver says, his voice exultant.

"Don't let your guard down. There still may be some with fight left in them."

"Thanks, Boss, I didn't really need to hear that. And I was in such a bloody good mood," the driver says, dejection in his voice.

"Just trying to keep it real and keep us alive," she says, watching the passing ragamuffin Enemy Soldiers slowly walking along the side of the road, guarded by a handful of Marine MPs.

Over the next few days, the column is halted several times. Small arm and cannon fire from the front signal contact with Enemy still ready to fight. But the stops last no more than a hour, indicating that no serious opposition has been met. Overhead, Air Force jets and Marine attack helicopters patrol steadily. Sometimes the sound of bombs and rockets can be hears at the end of the column.

The longest stops come when the Royal Engineers have to replace or repair a bridge that has deteriorated through neglect. No evidence of sabotage is ever found.

As they head south, Four Five Commando is the first to peel off, starting the Brigade's occupation of more than 300 kilometers along the River Lot. Next, Forty Commando takes its stretch of the line. Four Six forms up behind those two commandos, with the bulk of its forces behind Forty, and one company sent as reserve to Four Two.

Finally, Four Two Commando reaches its main campsite, from where it will be responsible for guarding the more than seventy kilometers between the Loire and Rhone rivers. Commando HQ is set up midway between the rivers, with each of the five companies given a sector to patrol. Each company HQ is in the approximate mid-point of its sector, with its Marines arranged to guard the routes through the mountains. Judy's company guards the most obvious route of attack—the Rhone River valley. Consequently, Company A's sector is the smallest of the five.

As soon as they arrive, Judy has her Marines start digging defensive positions.

"What do you think?" Johnston-Stone asks her as he tours his Company's positions.

"I think we are buggered if they come through here in strength, sir," she replies, keeping her voice low so her guys don't hear her pessimistic appraisal.

"Hmmm," the Captain replies. "On the bright side, we have a good portion of the Brigade's artillery supporting us, and the Air Force and our attack helicopters will be on patrol. And don't forget the tanks. We have good armor support."

"Yes, sir. And if they hit us on a narrow front, we will slaughter them. But if they come at us on a broad front, we just won't have the firepower to stop them. And if they come at night, the jets and 'copters won't be much help."

"Have you been talking to the Brigadier?"

"Sir?"

"I heard from McBride that is what worries him."

"No, sir," Judy answers, trying to avoid any implication that she has special access because the Brigadier is her father. "I haven't spoken to the Brigadier for several months."

"Great minds, I guess," the Captain comments, laughing a bit. "Well, keep a sharp eye out. Keep your patrols active. And tell your Booties not to get trigger happy. Thirty Commando will have guys going out on deep patrol."

"Yes, sir."

"Very good. Carry on," Johnston-Stone says as he walks back to his vehicle.

Judy watches him leave, then turns back to her guys working hard on their defensive positions.

Soon, the entire Commando settles into a boring routine of endlessly patrolling their sectors and establishing listening posts on their flanks and in front of their main position. Aircraft patrols run constantly during the day.

Unlike the other Troops, Judy has her Marines patrolling at night as well as during the day. She can't shake the feeling that something is out there. And that something won't come when they expect it.

CHAPTER 10

"Tom, I'm worried about Four Two," Sam tells Codrington, who has just come into HQ, now housed in a dilapidated stone building in the remains of a small village about five hundred meters behind Forty Commando's main line of resistance.

"I was just down there today," the Chief of Staff replies as he joins the Brigadier at the large map spread on an even larger table and indicates an area in front of Four Two and Forty, "and all is quiet."

"I know. That's what worries me. It's too quiet. I don't like it."

"Have you been talking to your daughter?" Codrington asks, a smile growing across his face.

"What? What are you talking about?"

"According to her CO, she has the same worries. She's worried about a night attack."

"Yes, yes. They've never done that before, but it doesn't mean they won't now that their backs are to the wall."

"Perhaps. What can we do about it?"

"Just what I was thinking. I want you to take another Company from Four Six, along with some additional armor, along with the reserve company that is already there, and establish a flying force, say, about here," Sam says, indicating a point on the map about one kilometer behind Four Two's right. "I also want more artillery over there."

"And if they hit us along the rest of the line?"

"Then I've buggered us. But we have the river as a barrier and can hit them hard with air. We'll see them coming a lot more easily than if they come up the valley, or over the mountain passes."

"It's a gamble," Codrington says dryly.

"Yes, well, life's a bleeding gamble. And maybe I'm just being paranoid. We've been collecting thousands of POWs. Perhaps The Enemy has finally collapsed. But I'd rather be prepared."

"Right. I'll get on it. We should have everything set up on the morrow. Also, we have just received about five thousand of those new land mines, the ones that can be radio controlled. I'll have several thousand sown before Four Two. That should make everyone feel more secure," he says, a little smile crossing his face as he looks sideways. Sam is so engrossed in the map he fails to notice the look, or the hint of humor in Codrington's voice."

"Good. Thanks, Tom," comes the distracted reply as Sam leans further over the map, his eyes boring through it as if he is trying to find The Enemy on the march.

"Sir," Codrington says, and goes to issue the orders.

Studying the map, Sam wonders why he can't shake the feeling of impending doom.

"Sir?" an orderly says, coming up politely behind him.

"Yes?" Sam says, his attention still on the map.

"Sir, an Army Brigadier is here to see you."

"A what? An Army Brigadier? What does he want?" Sam says, wrenching his attention away from the map.

"I don't know, sir. He just asked to see you."

"Then, I guess you'll need to show him in, Lance Corporal."

"Yes, sir," the orderly says, pivots and goes out of the office, quickly returning with the Army Brigadier.

"Brigadier Hope? I'm Brigadier Octave Cullet."

"Yes, Brigadier. What may I do for you?"

"I'm afraid I have some unpleasant news."

"And what may that be?"

"It's about Staff Sergeant Frank Hope."

The mention of his son's name, staggers Sam. He leans back against the table, his hands on the edge, propping him up. "Yes?" he manages to say.

"I'm afraid I must report that Staff Sergeant Hope was killed in action two days ago."

Sam suppresses an almost overwhelming urge to scream in rage. Collecting himself, he asks, "What happened?"

"His Regiment was hit by a massive frontal assault. The Company on his Company's left gave way, opening a gap in the line. The Companies on either side of the gap closed it with the help of the reserve Battalion and defeated the attack. Unfortunately, Staff Sergeant Hope's company suffered more than sixty percent casualties. At the moment, that's all I know."

"Where was the attack?"

"About twenty kilometers west of the Rhine near Nancy."

"Yes, thank you for telling me," Sam manages to choke out.

"Staff Sergeant Hope will be returned to Britain for burial with full honors. Would you like to attend?"

"What?" Sam nearly yells out, "and leave my Brigade at a time like this? I have no right! My grief is private. My responsibility is to my Brigade and keeping them alive."

"Right you are," Cullet says, somewhat taken aback.

"Have you told his mother?"

"We have not located Leftenant Colonel Hope yet."

"Brilliant," Sam says, looking at the floor. "Her Battalion has been on secondment to us. I will tell her."

"Thank you," Cullet says, the relief obvious in his voice.

"Well, thank you, Brigadier, for coming all this way to let me know. And I apologize for the outburst."

"It's the least we could do."

"Yes, well, thank you again," Sam says, reaching out to shake the other man's hand. Cullet then hurries out of the office. Sam watches him go. Collecting himself, he calls on his orderly to get his vehicle.

"Where are our engineers?" Sam asks as he walks into the main room at HQ.

"They are building fall-back defensive positions for Four Two in a mountain pass here," Failly says, pointing to the location on the map.

"Right. Please let the Colonel know I'm going down there."

"Yes, sir."

Sam gets into his vehicle, tells the driver where to go, and then uncomfortably settles back into the seat, his mind wondering about the past. The birth of Frank, and his other children, the games they used to play, how Frank grew up, his independent streak, his determination to make his own way, to become an expert on soil management and crop production. Tears slowly roll down Sam's cheeks. He's glad no one is here to see him in this state. Not the image a Brigadier wants to display.

The two-hour ride–a ride filled with memories of Frank as an infant, a young boy, a university student, a soldier as Sam sits immobile in the back seat staring out the window, not seeing anything–finally ends at the engineers' HQ. Sam gets out of the car and finds Colonel Bosquet, Sarah's boss.

"Colonel," Sam says, coming up and shaking the officer's hand.

"Brigadier?" Bosquet says, somewhat surprised to have Sam show up unannounced.

"Would it be alright if I had a word with Leftenant Colonel Hope?"

"Well, of course. She's out supervising some work on the line at the moment. I will take you out there."

"That's quite alright. I don't want to take you away from what you're doing. If you just have someone take me out there, that would be fine."

"Yes, of course," comes the reply. Bosquet, resisting the urge to ask what this is about, even though he can see the distress written on Sam's face, calls one of his aides, who then climbs into Sam's vehicle with him and takes him to where Sarah is working.

When they arrive, Sam gets out, telling his driver and the aide to stay with the vehicle. He walks slowly up the incline to where Sarah is directing her Engineers in building an obstruction. He walks up quietly behind her, standing a foot away, watching for a moment, collecting his thoughts.

"Sarah," he says softly, reaching out to touch her shoulder. The voice and the touch make her jump. She wheels around quickly.

"Sam? What ar…" she says, stopping when she sees the stricken look on her husband's face. "Oh, my God! Which one? Which one!" Fear spreads across her face.

"Frank," Sam manages to say.

"How bad?" Sarah says, shrinking away from him. Sam reaches out and pulls her back, hugging her.

"We lost him," Sam says softly. He feels Sarah sag against him as the strength leaves her body. She begins to sob, holding tightly to him.

"How? Why?" she cries, softly, her tears dampening his shirt. Sam remains silent, knowing those are not real questions. Not yet, anyway.

Sam leads his wife off to the side to some camp chairs. He waves away the Army Engineers in the area. They give him quizzical looks but leave. He sits Sarah down, then positions a chair next to her, sitting down and taking her hand. "He's being taken back to England for burial," Sam says. "I can't go, but I can arrange for you to."

"No, no," Sarah says through her tears. "I have work to do here. We have to be ready if they come at us. Judy has to be ready."

"Yes," Sam says, soothingly.

"Does Judy know? What about the other kids?"

Sam sighs heavily. "I'm going to tell her after I leave here. As for the others, I'll call them tonight. At least we can have some family at the funeral."

"Yes. That's good. That's good," Sarah says distractedly, her eyes fixed on the ground. "Why?" The cry escapes from her involuntarily. All Sam can do is shake his head. There is no good answer. "I must have my Engineers keep cracking on," Sarah says, shaking herself and standing up. She wipes her face against Sam's shirt. "I've made you soggy."

"No worries," he says. "I need a bath anyway."

Sarah lightly punches him in the chest. "Back to work."

Sam kisses her forehead.

"Go see Judy now," she tells him.

"Right. Will you be alright?"

"Eventually. I have work to do. Those people out there," she says, waving at her Engineers, "are my kids, too. I have to take care of them."

"I understand," Sam says, kissing her again, then slowly leaving, looking back at his wife as he heads to the vehicle. As he leaves, she sighs, collects herself, wipes her face with her hands, then goes back to work.

An hour later, Sam has visited Judy and is heading back to his HQ.

Judy watches her father leave, tears welling up. She suppresses the tears, and collects herself, so she can go back to work. She immerses herself in her job, spending more time with her Marines, making sure they are ready for what she fears is coming. She has no proof. She only has a gut instinct that trouble is on the way. She puts her Troop on four-hour watches at night, with patrols going out constantly, setting up listening posts. Either she or her Color Sergeant are on watch twenty-four/seven. Her guys think she's crazy, but they follow orders.

The constant activity can't stop her mind from wandering, and wondering about life without her brother.

✥⊱⋯⦾⋯⊰✥

"Leftenant Hope."

The voice behind her makes Judy stand up straight and whirl around. "Mum… Leftenant Colonel Hope," she says, catching herself as she comes face to face with her mother.

Sarah grins broadly and holds out her arms. "I think the discipline of our blokes will survive an unregulation hug."

Without a word, Judy wraps her arms around her mother, squeezing tightly and feeling her mother's strong arms around her.

"You've heard about Frank?" Sarah asks.

"Yes, Dad was here."

"And how have you been?"

"Keeping busy. You?"

"Same. Now, down to business. I've brought along two companies of my Engineers to lay mines. About two thousand, I believe."

"Two thousand?"

"Yes. I trust that will be enough."

"Brilliant. It should be. But how long will that take? I'm not sure how much time we have until they hit us in force."

"Oh, it won't take long. These mines aren't live until you arm them with this," Sarah says showing Judy a small touch pad. "Turn the device on, push the arm button twice, and boom. The slightest pressure will set a mine off. Push the off button three times and the mines are no longer armed."

"This will work for all the mines?" Judy asks. "Is there a way to turn on or off just some of them?"

"In a way. I can have my guys set some up so it will take four pushes to arm and five to disarm," Sarah answers. "Do you see these switch?" she says pointing to a small push button on the left side of the pad. "Push it up to arm the majority of the mines and down to arm the others."

"Why have a different number of pushes then?"

"A fail safe in case some wanker isn't paying attention."

"Brilliant. I need some of those running along the east side of the road forming a path about three meters wide."

"We can do that. May I ask why?"

"So my blokes will have a safe path to come through should we need it."

"Very good. Now, where do you want us to lay the mines?"

"Here, I'll show you on the map," she says, leading her mother to a small table under a shelter half that holds a detail map of the Commando's sector.

"They have hung you out to dry!" Sarah gasps as she looks at the map showing the positions of each Troop in the Commando. "Your father did this? You'll get hit the hardest! If they come in strength, they'll roll right over you. You're buggered."

"Take it easy, Mum. We have a plan to deal with that," she says, starting to trace a line on the map. "My Troop is anchored on the river, and we've been reinforced by the some of the Company Weapons Section, two Mortar Sections, as well as Two Troop. The Swiss line hooks up with us there," she says pointing to the river, "and runs to their border. It's thin but it's there. And do remember we do have our armor and artillery for fire support and to help with a withdrawal."

"But look at the gap between your Troop and the rest of the Commando. The Enemy will just pour through there."

"We're counting on that."

"What?"

"We'll inflict as much damage as we can, and then fall back with the Swiss about a kilometer to the new positions, which your blokes have been building. Reinforcements and more armor will be there, and we will have more artillery support. It will also mean that when they reach that position, it will be daylight, so all our air assets can be brought in."

"And what about your right flank?"

"Depending on how wide the attack is, the rest of the Commando will hit them there, along with a flying force of two Companies from Four Six and armor."

"And if it's too wide?"

"Then the other Troops will withdraw to the new line as well and we'll have both our flanks anchored on the rivers."

Sarah looks at the map, a look of horror and worry on her face. "That is a bloody awful plan. If they come on a front from river to river, none of you will stand a chance."

"It will be difficult for them to do that," she says confidently. "The mountains and lack of roads will get in the way. The only practical way is to come up the Rhone valley. You and Dad have both said they keep tight control of their Soldiers. That would mitigate against a broad front, especially in this terrain."

"They're coming right at you." Sarah's voice is flat, resigned.

"Right at me," Judy acknowledges.

"Brilliant."

"That's where your mines come in. I need them from the river to about three hundred meters to our right, and then curl them back about two hundred meters. Sow them in the meadow in front of our position. That will be our killing field," Judy says of the four-hundred-meter wide grass area between the Marines' lines that gently slopes down to the forest The Enemy will come through.

"Yes," Sarah says thoughtfully. "We can do that. Just one thing."

"And that is?"

"Don't get yourself killed. I can't afford to lose both of you."

"Mum, you better get cracking."

"Leftenant Colonel Mum to you," she says, forcing a smile.

"Yes, ma'am," Judy says, coming to attention and throwing a salute.

"Knock it off, Leftnant," Sarah says as she turns to leave. "And congratulations on the promotion."

"When do I get the buttons?" Judy calls after her.

"When we're done," Sarah calls over her shoulder. "I bloody well don't want you to blow us up playing with this thing."

Judy laughs to herself and goes back to work.

CHAPTER 11

oss! Boss! They're coming in force!" The Lance Corporal's voice cuts through Judy's dreams of playing with her brother Frank. She quickly swings into a sitting position on her cot under a shelter half, shaking her head a bit and rubbing her eyes to wake herself up. She has taken to sleeping fully clothed, even with her boots on.

"Have Colors get the guys up and in position," Judy says as she reaches for her kit.

"She's already doing that, Boss. And she's alerted Company, and pulled in the listening posts and patrols," the Lance Corporal says, a bit of pride evident his voice.

"Right," Judy says, standing up, putting on her kit, and picking up her rifle. "Let's get cracking then."

She follows the Lance Corporal out into the dark, sending him to get the Two Troop commander, Lieutenant Henry Clifford. She glances at her watch as she walks over quickly to the tent half that serves as Troop HQ. Zero three thirteen a.m. No moon. Not that it would really matter because the attack is coming out of the forest.

"Report, Colors," she says as she reaches Mayran.

"Looks like you were right to be paranoid, Boss."

"Somehow that does not make me feel any better."

"Right. Some Thirty blokes are hidden about four klicks south of us. They report a large number of Enemy soldiers coming this way in march formation. At least two columns are approaching along these roads," she says, indicating them on the map lit by a small hooded light. One of the roads is leading right to their Troop. The other leads to the other end of the Company line.

"Any estimate on strength?"

"Just an estimate. The one coming at us apparently has at least several thousand."

"At least? What's that estimate based on?"

"They're marching four abreast, which I understand is their standard formation. The recon guys counted the number of ranks that passed. They didn't see any heavy equipment, really. Some trucks with machine guns mounted on them, but that's about the extent of it."

"Right. Have you sent a patrol down the road?"

"About a klick. My guess is that is about where they'll shake out into attack formation. No idea how broad a front they will come in on."

"Damn the dark," Clifford says as he comes stumbling through the night, his Troop immediately to the right of Judy's.

"Hello to you, too, Cliff," Judy says, the humor coming through her voice if not her facial expression hidden by the night.

"Yes, well, this is all bollocks. They couldn't come at a more convenient hour?"

"Like never?" Judy says, now laughing a bit.

"That would have suited just fine," he replies. "But back to business. I heard what Colors said. Any idea on the how wide their front will be?"

"Probably not too broad," Judy says, contemplating what they know about The Enemy and what her father and mother have told her about their experiences with them. "They'll want to keep tight control of their Soldiers. The problem is that it won't take a very wide front to flank us on the right. And they may try to overrun us on the left to push us away from the river."

"What are your orders?" Mayran asks.

"Let's assume they will flank us," she tells Mayran and Clifford. "We've got machine guns on both flanks. Have the mortars ready to fire three hundred and sixty degrees. But above all, we have to keep a path open for withdrawal."

"Retreat?" Shock and some outrage in Mayran's voice.

"No, just attacking in another direction," Judy responds, some humor in her voice. "Look, Anne, if we get cut off, this will turn into a blood bath. We'll be outnumbered ten-to-one, or worse. I'm not going to let our Marines be slaughtered when we can keep them alive to fight another day. If we have to abandon this position, we'll stage a fighting withdrawal.

Command has created a second line of resistance about here," she says, pointing to the position on the map. "We should find reinforcements there. And the rest of the company is ready to hit them in the flank."

"Right, boss," Mayran says, still somewhat dubious.

"The Brigade has been preparing for something like this. They expect us to hold as long as we can, to inflict as much damage as we can, but not to sacrifice ourselves needlessly. Are you with me?"

"Yes, Boss," Mayran replies, reassured this can work.

"You know," Clifford says, "I would be much more comfortable with this plan if they wait to daylight so we can see what we, and they, are doing."

"That would be brilliant, but I don't think those sods will give us the luxury," Judy says. "We'll just have to deal with it."

"Yes, I suppose you're right," Clifford says with a sigh. "At least they are not Marines."

"Right. Let's get cracking, make sure everyone is set," Judy says as they head out in the thick darkness. The work is slow because no one can see much and they can't use any light to avoid giving their position away to The Enemy.

"Damn this darkness!" Johnston-Stone's voice comes out of the black.

"Here, sir!" Judy calls to her company commander as she checks her Troops fighting positions.

"Ah, there you are, Hope. I had just about despaired finding you in this bloody damnable stuff."

"Yes, sir. It is bad."

"How are you doing?" he asks, urgency in his voice.

"We are making sure everyone's in position. Latest intel has a column of at least several thousand coming down that road," pointing in the direction of the road coming out of the woods, both of which are hidden in the dark. "We have a patrol out about a klick out to give us warning. It's now zero four hundred. I expect the attack to come about daylight, but it could come a bit earlier."

"Right. I've brought along an artillery liaison. His secondment is for the duration of the battle."

"Thank you, sir. What about the other column?"

"It does not appear to be as strong as this one. Not more than five hundred. And given the terrain over there, they will play the devil forming for a coherent attack."

"Reinforcements, sir?"

"Until we know their intentions, I am keeping everyone in place at the moment, although C and D Troops are getting organized to hit their flank. The flying column will form along their left flank to the north as needed."

"Thank you, sir."

"Right. Do remember, you are in command of more than just your own Troop as senior Leftenant. You have to stay in overall command. Colors Mayran is quite capable of taking command of the Troop during this fight."

"Yes, sir, she is. Do we have any intel of total enemy strength?"

"Nothing I would put a lot of stock in. Air has been hitting them as much as possible as they moved north and west. The best guess seems to be they are emptying Italy out, so there could be tens of thousands for all we know. But we haven't seen any heavy weapons or armored vehicles. And they seem to be dribbling bodies along the road, in addition to the damage our air strikes are doing."

"Comforting, sir," Judy says, her voice ripe with sarcasm.

"Yes, right. In any case, this is Leftenant Oxendine. He'll coordinate artillery for you." A tall, lean man steps out of the gloom.

"Good to meet you," Judy says, holding out a hand to shake his.

"Same here, Leftenant," comes the reply. "Where shall I set up?"

"Did you see the shelter half over there?" Judy says, waving in the direction they came from.

Oxendine turns to look into the gloom. "No, can't say I did."

"Right," she says, turning to one of her Marines. "Private Scott, show the Leftenant to Troop HQ."

"Yes, Boss," he says, climbing out of his fighting hole. "This way, sir," he says, leading Oxendine off.

"I'd better get cracking, sir," Judy tells her Captain.

"Yes. Stay in constant contact. I can't help you if I don't know what's going on. And, by the by, the Thirty guys have pulled out to clear the field of fire for the air blokes."

"Yes, sir. That's good to know, and I certainly will stay in contact."

"Good," he says starting to turn away, "and Judy? Do take care of yourself. Good Troop commanders are hard to come by."

"Yes, sir, thank you, sir," she says, the dark hiding the ironic smile crossing her face.

"Boss?" The voice coming over her headset is low and soft.

"Report," she replies.

"The Enemy has already deployed. They're coming along slowly and making a lot of noise doing it. They don't seem to care about giving themselves away. It's too dark to see how wide their front is."

"Good enough. Pull back half a klick."

"Yes, Boss. Out."

"Colors!" Judy calls.

"Yes, Boss," comes the reply.

"Expect the attack about zero five hundred," she says, loud enough so that most of the Troop hears her. Those who don't will soon be told by the others.

"Yes, Boss," Mayran replies.

"Take charge of the Troop," Judy says, lowering her voice.

"Boss?"

"I have to watch over this whole lot, so you'll have to watch over ours."

"Yes, Boss."

At four-thirty, Judy gets another call from the outpost. "Boss, they're here."

"Right. Pull back to the main line. Make sure you stay on the path through the mine field."

The Enemy is right on schedule.

Unfortunately.

Dawn won't come until shortly after zero six thirty. They will have to fight essentially blind for about an hour and a half. No air support. Artillery also will be firing blind for the most part. They will have to depend on the mines between their lines and the tree line. Night-vision goggles will have limited use because once the shooting starts, especially the artillery, they could prove more hinderance then help. The flares set to trip wires won't help in that regard, either, but they will give the artillery and mortars the ranges needed to hit the attackers.

Judy radios Johnston-Stone about the situation. No contact has been made on the other flank yet, either. Her left flank worries her. Her line stretches to within ten meters of the river and then curves in the woods toward the north. If The Enemy gets around that flank, the Troop could be cut off. She has a couple of her best Marines out there watching. If that begins to happen, all the Marines and the Swiss will pull back, regardless of how well the main line is doing.

Soon, the patrol is back. The Troop is dug in on the far side of a meadow with clear fields of fire across to the woods on the other side. She's not too worried about a frontal assault. That they can beat off. But she doesn't have enough Marines to cover a wide enough front to keep from being flanked. And if they have to withdraw, she will not leave any wounded behind, complicating that maneuver.

The noise pouring out of the woods in front shakes her out of her reverie. It is the unmistakable sound of thousands of feet tramping through the forest.

"Oxendine," she says to the artillery liaison standing near her. "As soon as they hit the trip wires have the artillery come down on them hard."

"Will do. You do realize it will be tree bursts."

"Wood splinters can take them out as well."

"Brilliant."

"Everyone stand to!" she calls out over the radio link. "Do not shoot, until ordered." Judy assumes The Enemy doesn't know their position, or at least, their exact position, and she wants to surprise the attackers as much as possible.

Through night-vision glasses, she sees a skirmish line of soldiers emerge from the trees, hesitant at first at being out in the open, before advancing cautiously. "They must have missed the trip wires," she says quietly to herself. Just as the words leave her mouth, a series of explosions go off in the woods—the main line has hit the wires. Oxendine keys his radio to have the artillery open fire on pre-designated areas, as do the mortars. Shells start screaming overhead, exploding in the trees beyond the meadow.

The skirmishers hesitate again, stopping about ten meters from the tree line. They are being pushed to keep moving by men she assumes are the Sergeants her parents have described to her.

"Machine guns, prepare to fire! Fire!" Judy calls. All the machine guns that can be brought to bear open on the skirmishers who are quickly shot down or dive for cover. One of the Sergeants tries to get the Soldiers back on their feet, until he is nearly cut in half by bullets.

"Cease fire! Cease fire!" Judy calls. The line goes silent, but the crash of artillery is nearly deafening. Part of her shudders at the thought of what the people on the receiving end are suffering. Most of her wants revenge for her brother, for Frank.

Scanning the tree line, she sees The Enemy's main line emerge from the woods, the lines being closed as they emerge from the trees onto the meadow. It looks like a nineteenth century infantry attack described in the books she'd read. She watches as they form up.

"Steady!" she calls out. "Hold your fire!" She has a lot of faith in her Marines and their discipline, but none of them, including herself and Mayran, have ever been in a situation like this.

The Enemy line starts running toward them across the field, firing as they come. Judy yelling "Steady!" as much for her own benefit as for her guys. She has to push the button on the mine pad just once more to arm the mines.

Two pickup trucks come roaring out of the woods, machine guns blazing in their direction. When the trucks are halfway across the field, she arms the mines. Explosions blossom across the field, destroying the two trucks and many of the attackers. The line staggers to a stop, then resumes the charge as more mines go off.

"Fire! Fire at will!" Judy yells into her headset to be heard above the noise. Her order is repeated by Clifford and the Sergeants of both Troops.

The whole line spits fire, semi-automatic rifles as well as the machine guns. The attackers in front are shot to pieces but those behind keep coming in wave after wave, the bodies piling up as new lines climb over them, exploding more mines as they charge.

"Oxendine!" Judy calls as she scans the front through night-vision glasses. "Have the artillery drop fire 50 meters in front of us!"

"That's too close!" he protests.

"They'll overrun us if we don't," she says, dropping the glasses and looking at him, urgency in her stare.

"Your call."

"Yes, my call."

Oxendine nods and picks up his handset.

"Artillery coming in danger close," Judy says through the coms, hoping all her Marines make themselves as small as possible as the shells explode near them.

Artillery stops firing for a brief moment and then resumes, the shells landing between fifty meters and a hundred meters in front of the Marines' line. The shells are armed with proximate fuses, exploding about three meters before they hit the ground, spreading explosive force and shrapnel around them. Through the flashes of explosions, Judy can see bodies being torn apart and thrown into the air. But The Enemy soldiers keep coming. She doesn't understand what propels them toward certain death, she just hopes the Marines' ammunition outlasts the attack.

"Boss," a quiet voice comes over the radio channel Judy has reserved for the patrol out past their left flank. "They're coming round us."

"Right," she replies. "Any estimate on their strength?"

"No, the woods are too thick to see much of anything even with the night-vision glasses."

"Keep track of them as well as you can. See if you can establish how far north they go, but don't let yourself be cut off."

"Yes, Boss. Out."

Judy keys the command circuit to her Color Sergeant and Clifford. "We're being flanked on the left," she tells them. "Be ready to pull back."

"We're being overrun!" The urgent call comes from Sergeant Tony Galev, whose Section is on the river bank on A Troop's extreme left.

"Bosquet, move immediately to support," Mayran orders the Sergeant in command of the reserve Section.

"On the way," he replies.

Judy listens intently as the firing on her left increases in volume and then falls off, then rises again. She scans the front. The attack along the rest of the line has stopped. The Enemy must be concentrating forces on the left. She has to suppress her instinct to rush over to the breach where her Marines are fighting for their lives. Her mind races to something she can do. The artillery fire has stopped, and the firing along the rest of line has died down.

"Colors!" she says over the radio, "pull everyone back now. Send in another Section to help on the left. We'll withdraw under the cover of the artillery fire."

"Yes, Boss," comes the reply.

"Cliff, start falling back now, now," she says.

"Understood," he replies.

Judy calls Johnston-Stone to alert him to what is happening.

She pulls her small command staff back to where the tanks and armored personnel vehicles are waiting. Soon, all of Two Troop's personnel are gathered there, and some of One Troop's.

"Cliff, take your guys with half the tanks up the road. Hold it open for us. We'll be right behind you. Load your casualties in the APVs and take them with."

"How far up are they?"

"I'm not sure. I have some guys trying to figure that out but, right now, all I know is that they are north of us and moving west."

"Right," Clifford says, as he organizes his Troop to move out.

Judy has her guys form a perimeter around their APVs and the remaining tanks.

"Oxendine, be ready to have the artillery come down further toward us."

"Right."

"I have to see what's going on," Judy says, no longer able to restrain herself. "Leftenant," she says to Oxendine, "you're the senior officer right now. Take command until I get back."

"But …"

"No, buts," she says as she heads off toward the sound of the fighting. As she goes, she takes another Section with her as well as two machine guns.

As Judy nears the battle, the light of dawn finally filters through the trees on the west side of the river. She can see her Marines drawn in a tight semi-circle, their backs to the river as they battle The Enemy's wave attacks. The Enemy seems intent on destroying those two Sections of Marines before moving on. The Enemy is breaking into the new line, with hand-to-hand fighting going on. Judy quickly deploys the Marines and machine guns to take The Enemy in the flank.

When they open fire, The Enemy line recoils in surprise. The trapped Marines quickly take advantage of the break in The Enemy's line to pull out toward Judy's line. Those Marines adjust their fire to keep from hitting their comrades.

"Brilliant," Judy says as the trapped Marines reach her line, the wounded being carried by the others. "You have everyone?" she asks Galey.

"All the wounded. We lost five."

"Right. Can't be helped. Get everyone back to the APVs. Two Troop is holding the road open but I don't know how long they can do that. We're being flanked. Leave me six guys and two machine guns for a rear guard."

"Boss."

"Move! Now!" Judy barks, then turns to the position.

Galey quickly details six Marines to join Judy, then organizes the rest and leads them back to the APVs.

The Enemy soldiers don't take long to get reorganized, forming quickly to resume the attack.

Judy gets Oxendine on the command circuit. "I need a concentration of HP at grid A14. Give me a ranging shot."

"Where are you?" comes the reply. Oxendine knows Judy is willing to have artillery drop dangerously close to her position.

"Just do it." she barks.

"We can't drop it in if you are too close."

"We'll be dead if you don't. Now do it."

After a brief pause. "Stand by."

"Guys," Judy turns to the six Marines, "you two on that gun, you two on that one. Stay small. Artillery is on the way." After detailing the machine gun positions, she splits the other two up on the outside to guard the flanks.

Just as everyone gets in position, the machine guns come to life as The Enemy resumes the attack. A second later, two shells explode in their midst throwing them into disarray.

"On target. Pour it on!" she radios Oxendine.

"Keep your head down. Out."

The shells start dropping in a constant stream just behind the front ranks of the attackers. About one hundred Enemy Soldiers are still able to assault the Marines. The two machine guns and three semiautomatic rifles deal with them, although a few reach the line. They are shot down before they can do any damage. Judy is firing from a kneeling position just behind the firing line when a round glances off her helmet, knocking it off and her to the ground. She is dazed for a moment, then, collecting her wits, grabs her helmet and swivels around to resume the fight from a prone position.

With the artillery shells pouring in and no attackers left in front of them, she decides it's time to leave.

"Right, guys," she yells above the sounds of explosions, "let's go!"

The Marines scramble up, heading for the APVs. Judy brings up the rear, but just as she starts moving away, the artillery fire stops.

"What the bloody hell!" She quickly calls Oxendine. "Why did the artillery stop? We need the cover to make our withdrawal!"

"They're low on shells. They have to resupply. They can resume in fifteen."

"Crap!" Judy exclaims. "McDonnel!" she yells at the Corporal among the six Marines. "Drop a machine gun and all the ammo."

"Boss?"

"Do it! Then get your guys back to APVs!"

"I'll stay with you, Boss," he says.

"That's an order! Now do it! I'll be right behind you!"

"Boss," he says challenging the order.

"Do it now or face court martial!"

"Yes, Boss," he says, having one of the Marines put a machine gun on the ground, and two others drop their ammunition.

"Move it!" Judy barks.

As the six Marines run back to the APVs, they hear the machine gun open fire behind them. A Lance Corporal starts to turn back, but the Corporal pushes him around. "Move!"

They soon reach the four APVs. The wounded have been loaded on two, and the other two are holding all the Marines they can carry.

"Where's the Boss?" Maynard asks McDonnel.

"Back there," he says, motioning toward the sound of the machine gun chatter.

"You left the Boss alone?" she asks incredulously as she looks in that direction.

"Colors, she ordered us back."

"And you followed that order?"

"Colors…"

"Never bloody mind," Mayran said. "Get your guys with the others. Franklin!" she yells to the senior Sergeant.

"Yes, Colors?"

"Get this lot and the two APVs with wounded moving as fast you can! I'm going after the Boss."

"Right, Colors," Franklin says.

As the Sergeant starts two APVs and the Marines on foot heading toward the road to the rear, Mayran leads two tanks and APVs with Marines on board toward the sound of firing. As she runs forward, a dozen Marines run up next to her.

"Where the bloody hell do you think you're going?" she asks them without breaking stride.

"You're not going alone," one of them says.

"Bloody hell!" Mayran picks up the pace. They are most of the way there when the machine gun stops firing.

"Bloody hell!" Mayran says again. Up ahead she sees Judy on the ground, staging a last ditch fight with her sidearm against about twenty enemy soldiers, who apparently are out of ammunition. They are not firing at her but trying to get close enough to club her with their weapons.

"Halt! Fire waist high! Fire!" Mayran orders. All the Marines open fire, as do the machine guns on the APVs and tanks, quickly cutting down the attackers, as the Marines on board pour out of the rear doors and come around.

"Cease fire! Cease fire!" Mayran orders, as she runs forward to check on Judy. "Boss! Boss!"

Judy raises her right arm, waving it to show she is still alive.

When Mayran and the other Marines reach her, they find Judy covered in blood. She has a head wound and her left arm has been hit. She has blood coming from her right side, and what looks like a knife wound on her left leg.

"Medic! Medic!" Mayran yells.

"Knock it off," Judy says. "I just had the wind knocked out of me."

"Sod off, Boss. You've been wounded."

"Just a scratch. Let me get up," she says, struggling to her feet as a Medic runs up.

"Boss, lay back down!" the Medic orders.

"Not here. We have to get moving," Judy orders. "They'll be back soon. We have to collect our KIA and get to the new positions before they close the road. Now move!"

A group of Marines with both tanks and an APV recover the five bodies. Everyone scrambles back to the APVs, except for Mayran and the Medic who are on either side of Judy.

"Colors, Doc, let's go!" she orders.

As they begin to move, the twenty-millimeter turret guns on the APVs open fire. A dozen Marines run up behind the trio making their way to the APVs. The Marines fire as they withdraw. Several are hit by return fire and are dragged back to safety by others. The tanks and other Marines open on the new attackers, making short work of them, the 120-millimeter cannons firing as fast as they can. Judy tries to break away from her minders to resume command.

"Boss!" Mayran says sharply, "You're in no condition. I got this."

"Right, Colors," Judy says as she feels her legs become wobbly.

`Mayran turns back, joining the firing line and speeding up their withdrawal. As soon as the Marines come even with the APVs, the hull machine guns start firing bursts to discourage pursuit.

Then the artillery resumes firing, dropping shells at the old coordinates. Mayran gets the fire shifted closer to them. Some of the Marines clamber back into the APVs manning the firing slits, while others climb on top, lying flat so they can find targets. The APVs reverse out of the area, the drivers getting directions from Marines looking out the back. When they are clear of The Enemy, the APVs turn around and with the tanks join the withdrawal.

The road out is hemmed in by trees on either side. Some on the roof swivel toward the east – the side from which small arms fire is coming – others turn to the west to guard that flank. The rear tank has reversed its turret, its machine gun and main gun defending the rear, with Marines on its deck and beside it in support. As they move up, they come up to other Marines who are in a running fight.

As casualties mount, the wounded are loaded into the still moving APVs, while uninjured Marines take their place, some from inside the APVs and others who had been sheltering on the westside of the APVs when they couldn't find good firing positions. Machine gun fire from the tanks and APVs help hold The Enemy at bay, while artillery shells pour into the forest on both flanks well away from the road, the barrage moving along with the column.

Eventually, the column breaks out of the woods. Nearly a kilometer ahead, the Marines can see the new line, already manned by their comrades. They are dug into a ridge stretching several kilometers from the river to a mountain. As the last tank clears the forest, fighter jets drop napalm along the tree line, then the artillery resumes shelling further into the forest.

As they move through the new line, Captain Johnston-Stone finds Mayran, who is coming in with the last APV.

"Colors, where's your Leftenant?"

"In that APV, sir," she says, indicating the second from the end. "She's been hit."

"How bad?"

"She's lost blood. I think they're all flesh wounds."

"All?"

"Yes, sir. As far as I can tell, she was hit at least four times."

"My God!" The Captain pauses for a moment. "Colors, take charge of the Troop. Get your guys sorted and rested. See to your wounded. Did you get everyone?"

"Yes, sir, we went back for the KIA. Our left flank was overrun."

"Yes, yes, I know. Well, good job. Now get cracking. You lot will be in reserve for now."

"Yes, sir. Thank you, sir." Mayran, her shoulders sagging with fatigue, slogs after her Troop. The APVs stop by the medical tent where the wounded and then the dead are unloaded. The walking wounded also queue up there.

Judy, now weakened by the loss of blood, is helped into the tent.

"Leftenant," Johnston-Stone says when he finds her lying on a cot, "I thought I told you not to go into combat."

"Sorry, sir," she replies, looking up at him. "You can court martial me later. Right now, I have to get back to my guys."

"Stand fast!" the Captain orders. "The docs have to get you patched up and you have to get some rest. You'll stay here until the docs clear you. And that's an order. Violate that one, and I'll throw you in the brig. Understand?"

"Yes, sir, but my guys ..."

"Color Sergeant Mayran can fill in for you for now."

"Yes, sir."

"Now rest. I need you healthy."

"Sir."

"Judy," Johnston-Stone says, his voice dropping low and gentle as be bends down to her, "you do what you're told. Get healthy. Get better."

"Yes, sir."

Johnston-Stone straightens up, looking down at his officer who has now closed her eyes. Her breathing becoming slow and regular as she drifts off into unconsciousness.

CHAPTER 12

Well, Major," Sam says to the head of his Intelligence Section as he lowers his binoculars from surveying the area in front of the Brigade's new line, "what should we expect from our friends over there?" Sam waves his hand toward the woods in the distance. Engineers are finishing laying a dense minefield from the forest to within twenty meters of the Marines' lines. The Army has added Troops to its southern deployment and extended its lines east and south along the river, allowing the Marines to concentrate more Troops along the threatened portion of their lines.

"We expect an attack in strength within the next three days, sir," Major Pierre de Castellane replies. "They are moving their Soldiers up and spreading them out over what we expect to be a two-kilometer front."

"What did you say their strength was?"

"We estimate between ten and fifteen thousand."

"That is kind of a broad estimate, isn't it?" Codrington asks.

"Right, well, several things hamper nailing down a better number," De Castellane says. "First, that forest is hard to get good numbers in, even with heat-sensitive equipment. On top of that, we have managed to degrade their forces with air strikes, and we do know they are dribbling a constant stream of Soldiers who can't keep up. We suspect that many of them are dying of starvation. They have very limited motor transport, and no animals, so the bulk of their equipment is being moved in handcarts. Not exactly an efficient mode of transport. Their whole supply infrastructure seems to be breaking down."

"Yes, we've already seen examples of that," Codrington says.

"Exactly," De Castellane responds. "We have been heavily bombing any troop concentrations we find either here, to our west, and in Germany.

Actually, our attacks have now stretched into Poland and other places in Eastern Europe."

"Has anyone figured out how their command-and-control system works?" Sam asks.

"That's still a puzzle, sir. We think we find a center and knock it out, but nothing changes. So the Air Force decided attacking troop concentrations and any supply dumps we can identify would have to do."

"Brilliant," Sam says. He pauses for a moment, then says, "I never understood why they attack on such a constricted front? I know they need to keep tight control of their Soldiers, but still."

"It's the way they hit us near the Rhone," De Castellane says. "They concentrated an overwhelming force along a narrow front."

"We'll make sure that won't work here," Codrington chimes in.

"Hmmm, let's not get overconfident," Sam replies.

"By the way, sir," De Castellane says, "we have confirmation The Enemy has nearly emptied out not only Italy but also Spain and Portugal of all able-bodied Soldiers. The Iberian contingent is headed toward the Army's lines to the west of us."

"How did we confirm that?"

"In Italy, it came courtesy of the Sicilians."

"The Sicilians?" both Sam and Codrington reply in surprise.

"When they found out about our landing in France, they decided to give us a call. They also decided to send people to Italy. They found the same thing we found when we landed: Thousands of starving people and thousands of dead. They've asked for our help in feeding and taking care of these people."

"Were they like the ones we found here? Soldiers?"

"So I've been told, sir. The question is whether we will be able to help them in any meaningful way."

"That is above our pay grades," Sam says with a rueful smile.

"Yes, sir," De Castellane says. "The Sicilians also put us in touch with the Maltese, who have managed to survive, and the people on Crete, Cypress, Corsica, and Sardinia. It seems that the islands were not taken over by The Enemy and have formed sort of a mutual aid society."

"Brilliant."

"In the Pacific," De Castellane hurries on, "Japan has sent some Troops to Korea to see what's going on. And the Filipinos, Tawainese, and Indonesians have sent parties to China, Southeast Asia and India. We have no reports yet about what they've found. Oh, yes, and the Australians and New Zealanders are helping them."

"Is that all?" Sam says, a bit overwhelmed by all this news.

"Not quite, sir. The Russians holed up in the Urals are beginning to tentatively push out, as are the Chinese from the northwest of China. And there are reports that different nationalities have survived in the remote areas of the Himalayas, though none of that is confirmed."

"What about the Americas?"

"Nothing on that yet, sir, outside of Long Island off the coast of New York and, of course, the Canadians on Prince Edward Island and the other Atlantic islands. And, of course, you know about Iceland and Greenland, that they are free."

"Well, thank you, Major," Sam says, looking over at Codrington who is talking softly with an aide who has just come up, "keep me posted on any changes, and even if nothing changes."

"Sir?"

"If I don't hear from you periodically, I'll begin to worry I've missed something."

"Yes, sir," De Castellane says, smiling. "I'll be sure to do that."

As De Castellane leaves, Codrington comes up to Sam looking serious.

"Sam, it's about your daughter," he says.

"What about her?" Sam says sharply, fear and worry in his voice.

"She's in hospital. No catastrophic injury, no vital organs hit. The doctors say she will make a full recovery. She has soft-tissue wounds."

"Thank God," Sam says, relaxing a bit. "Which hospital?"

"The Eighty-Seventh Field Hospital. Apparently, her injuries were not judged serious enough to ship her out," Codrington says. "And…"

"And what?" Sam says, suspicion in her voice.

"I am told she threatened to shoot anyone who tried to move her any further away from the front."

"She did, did she," Sam replies, shaking his head.

"So I am told. Anyway, I have ordered your vehicle."

"Thank you," Sam says, and starts to walk away. Then he stops and turns around. "Tom, I expect them to attack before dawn tomorrow. Have everyone sleep in their fighting holes and by the artillery."

"Sir? Are you sure?"

"No, it's just a feeling."

"Yes, sir, I'll take care of that."

"I'll be back before dark," Sam says as he hurries away to HQ and his ride to hospital. On the way, he contacts Johnston-Stone to get briefed on what happened.

Twenty minutes later, Sam is at the field hospital and has been told where to find his daughter in the sprawling tent complex. He locates the large ward tent she is in and, ducking through the flap, walks down an outside aisle toward her bed. Two women are standing there, their shoulders touching. He recognizes one as Sarah but can't tell who the Marine is.

He walks up quietly behind them. Sarah jumps as he puts his arms on her shoulders and pulls her toward him.

"How is she?" he says quietly in her ear.

"She'll be alright. Our baby will be alright," Sarah says, wheeling around and holding Sam in a tight embrace, crying softly on his shoulder.

"I was told no bones or vital organs were hit, just flesh and a little muscle damage," Sam says, looking over Sarah's shoulder at their sleeping daughter.

"Yes, yes, quite right," Sarah agrees, pushing back from him and looking down at Judy. "She suffered a lot of blood loss and will need time to heal. You'll make sure she does what the doctors tell her to?"

"I'll do my best."

"Do better," Sarah insists.

"This is Judy we're talking about," Sam says. "Have you ever known me to be able to talk her out of anything?"

"Make it an order. You can do that."

"I can't give her special treatment. I have to treat her the way I would any of my officers. Although," he says, half-jokingly, "I suppose I could court martial her for failure to follow orders."

"Good," Sarah says sternly.

"Good?" Sam asks quizzically.

"Yes, good. By the way," Sarah says, changing the subject, "this is Judy's Color Sergeant, Anne Mayran."

As Sam turns toward her, Mayran comes stiffly to attention.

"Don't," Sam says kindly, "not here, not now." He holds out a hand. Mayran relaxes, looking a bit confused. Finally, she reaches out to take Sam's hand. "I want to thank you for saving my daughter. Your Company commander told me what you did."

"Just doing my job, sir," Mayran says.

"Bollocks," Sam replies, smiling. "You did more than that, and, as a father, I thank you for that. But as your Brigadier ..."

"Don't you dare!" Sarah says, cutting him off.

Sam looks at her and smiles. "Well, Colors," he says turning back to Mayran, "it looks like I've been outranked."

"Yes, sir," Mayran replies, smiling in turn.

"I understand you are in charge of the Troop now," Sam says.

"Yes, sir, just until the Leftenant recovers."

"I am told you are doing an outstanding job."

"Thank you, sir."

"Any interest in getting your own Troop?" Sam asks. "You are qualified."

"Thank you, sir," Mayran replies hesitantly. "But, in all due respect, I like it just where I am. The Leftenant and I make a great team. We get the job done and keep our blokes alive, as many as we can."

"So I've been told. If you change your mind, let me know."

"I will, sir."

"By the way, I expect an attack before dawn tomorrow," he tells Mayran, his voice serious and official.

"Yes, sir," Mayran says, returning to her Marine form.

"Sam," Sarah says a bit alarmed, "you have solid intelligence on that?"

"Just a gut feeling, I'm afraid."

"Oh," Sarah says, a bit skeptical.

"Sir," Mayran says, "now I know where the Leftenant gets that from."

"Her what?" Sarah asks.

"Her gut feelings. Ma'am," Mayran says turning to Sarah, "I've learned to pay close attention to her gut feelings. They're usually spot on."

"I see," Sarah replies.

"If you'll excuse me, sir," Mayran says to Sam, coming to attention, "I'll go make sure my guys are ready."

"Carry on, Colors," Sam says. "And thanks again."

"Sir," she says and turns to go. But Sarah grabs her and swivels her back around, giving her a big hug.

"Thank you for saving our daughter," Sarah says, hugging her.

"Yes, ma'am," Mayran says, a bit strangled by Sarah's tight embrace, and completely embarrassed. Sarah finally lets her go.

Mayran comes to attention again. "Brigadier. Leftenant Colonel." And turns and walks swiftly away, anxious to get back to her Troop.

The couple briefly watch her go and then turn back to their sleeping daughter. Sam slips his arm around Sarah's shoulder, pulling her close. She in turn wraps an arm around his waist.

"You should give that girl a medal," she tells Sam about Mayran.

"Not my call, given who is involved. That's up to Codrington. He's the one who suggested giving her a battlefield commission."

"I didn't think the Marines did that."

"We don't. But we have suffered the loss of a number of junior officers. Times change."

"Yes, they do," Sarah says as they look down at Judy, she moves a bit, then opens her eyes and looks up at them. A weak smile crosses her face.

"Hi," she says.

"Hi back at you," Sam says.

"You, young lady, are to stay in bed until you are completely healed," Sarah says, her voice stern. "That's an order."

"Mum," Judy says, her voice tired, "you're Army; you can't give me orders even if you are a Leftenant Colonel."

"I'm giving you the order as your mother and you bloody well better follow it."

"Yes, ma'am," Judy says, giving her father a knowing look. "I think I'll go to sleep now."

"And I have to get back," Sam says, bending down to kiss his daughter on the forehead but anxious to escape getting caught in the middle of this mother-daughter dispute.

"I'm staying a bit," Sarah says, pulling a chair over that was near another bed.

CHAPTER 13

Mayran surveys the forest a kilometer away, downhill from the Marines' positions, through night-vision binoculars. It's three in the morning. The noise of masses of soldiers moving toward the Marine line is unmistakable. But so far, nothing is visible. Not even scouts. She wishes the artillery would open up, even if they're firing blindly. The noise of the exploding shells would be comforting. But she knows it's impractical and not part of the plan.

"How are you doing, Colors?"

The Captain's voice startles the Color Sergeant. "Fine, sir," she replies. "The Troop is on alert, every other Trooper is awake, and all are at their firing positions. We are ready for them, sir."

"Brilliant," Johnston-Stone replies. "Sorry I couldn't leave you in reserve, you took quite a beating the other day, but yours is the best Troop I've got."

"Not a problem, sir. We owe those bloody sods."

"Right. Make sure you hold fire until after they are clear of the minefield. Let that do its work. Artillery and air will also be hammering them at the tree line."

"Yes, sir. And, sir, thank you for not putting us on the flank. We seem to always be there. It's nice to be in the middle of the line for a change."

"Don't mention it, Colors," Johnston-Stone says. "Crack on," are his parting words as he disappears in the dark.

Mayran takes a tour of her line to make sure everyone who is supposed to be awake is. Each fighting hole has two Marines. At least one has to be awake in each one. In most, both are awake, too keyed up to sleep. She returns to the Troop command post. The Corporal there gives her some hot coffee to drink. She welcomes the help in keeping her alert; she just hopes she doesn't have to pee in the middle of the attack.

"Colors," the Corporal says quietly.

"Hmmm, what?" comes the distracted reply.

"The Boss is here."

"What!" she exclaims, wheeling around, some of the coffee spilling on her hand, to see Judy walking slowly toward them, looking like a ghost in the pale moonlight.

"Good morning, Colors, Corporal," Judy says as she comes up.

"Boss, what are you doing here?" the irritation and worry are clear in Mayran's voice as she shakes the hand the hot coffee is on.

"Don't worry, Colors. I'm not here to take command. I am in no condition for that. Besides, everyone says you are doing a brilliant job."

"You should be in hospital! You're in no condition to be running around!" Mayran protests.

"I don't plan on running around," Judy replies, a weak smile that can barely be seen in the night. "I can, however, still use a rifle. I want to join the firing line. I want a piece of those sods."

"But Boss…"

"Not buts, just point me to a fighting hole I can inhabit," she says, unslinging her semi-automatic rifle.

Mayran contemplates Judy for a moment. "Four Section is short. Join them."

"Brilliant," she says, looking around. "Where are they?"

"Corporal, show the Boss to Sergeant Franks."

"Yes, Colors. This way, Boss," the Corporal says, trying to hide the bemusement he feels.

"Thanks, Anne," Judy says as she starts to hobble off.

"Don't thank me yet. We have no idea if we can hold these sods."

"We will, we will," she says and disappears into the night.

Mayran watches her go. *'We better,' she says to herself, 'you can't pull back quickly.'* Shaking her head, she goes back to scanning the forest. She looks at her watch. Zero three thirty-seven. Time drags. The noise of moving masses in the forest grows. She finds comfort in knowing The Enemy is not smart enough, or careful enough, to try to hide their movements. Or maybe they just don't care. Perhaps this is part of a psychological game. If it is, it won't work, she thinks.

There, just coming out of the woods, Mayran sees four figures emerge from the shadows of the forest. Spaced about twenty meters apart, they creep up the gentle sloop. When they are about two hundred fifty meters from the Marines, they stop, apparently studying the crest. Mayran watches them closely, praying that no one gets jumpy and opens fire.

After pausing for what seems an eternity, but in reality is just a few minutes, the four figures creep back down the hill and back into the forest. Shortly after they reenter, the sound of thousands of people moving stops.

"They're ready," Mayran says to no one in particular. She goes along the line, making sure everyone is awake and alert, warning them the attack could come any time and to hold fire until ordered.

Half an hour ticks off the clock, passing zero five hundred.

Screams and shots come pouring out of the forest as a mass of soldiers come charging up the slope.

Mayran runs along her line, encouraging her Marines and reminding them to hold fire. She stops at Judy's fighting hole.

"You alright, Boss?"

"Couldn't be better, Colors. Couldn't be better," Judy says, grimly, her weapon pointing toward The Enemy. Waiting for the word.

When the mass of soldiers is halfway to the Marine lines, the thick field of mines is activated. The field suddenly blossoms in explosions, ripping apart bodies, throwing the attack into disarray. Artillery opens fire, blasting the woods and the area just in front of the trees.

"Don't see how anyone can live through that," Franks says, looking up from his weapon's sites.

"We're about to find out if they can," Judy replies grimly, her hand tightening around her rifle's pistol grip.

"Right, Boss."

As the smoke and dirt from the explosions clear, the Marines can see the wreckage in the light of the partial moon that has risen high in the sky. Of the thousand or so who attacked, a few hundred are left milling around in confusion and shock. Wounded are screaming in pain, their cries pitiful. Those who are lightly wounded or uninjured stumble back toward the forest as the artillery fire is lifted. Few of the badly wounded are picked up by their comrades.

And still the Marines hold their fire.

"Good job, guys," Mayran says as she works her way down the line. "They'll be back and there'll be no minefield to stop them this time, so stay frosty."

When she gets to Judy, she stops. "Boss, will you please go back to hospital now."

"Colors, you said it: They'll be back. And when that happens, you'll need every rifle you can get. I'm staying."

"Yes, ma'am. But just remember this: If the Captain, the Leftenant Colonel, or the Brigadier find out, it won't be just you who is in for it."

"Well, Colors, then I suggest we don't let them find out, especially my mum. They won't be looking for me here," she says, referring to the fighting hole she's in.

Mayran just shakes her head and moves on.

⤐⋯⟡⟩⋯⟡⋯◯⋯⟨⟡⋯⟨⟡⋯⟵

"They did exactly what you expected. Attacked on a broad front," Codrington says to Sam as the two officers scan the tree line after the attack subsides. They are just behind the lines on the highest point available where a makeshift forward HQ has been set up under a canopy. "Do you think they'll do it again?"

"Let's hope so," he replies. "The Enemy has always used human-wave tactics. I don't think they'll change that. My only fear is that they come on a narrow front. That could overwhelm the units in their path. We must be ready for that."

"We are. The tanks and APVs have all been alerted to be ready to move immediately. Artillery is also on notice to be able to shift fire. We can concentrate all our artillery in one area in a matter of minutes."

"Brilliant. I hope it's enough."

"Add in air power and we should be able to hold."

"The problem is numbers. I have read about nineteenth century infantry tactics, which those people mimic," Sam says, nodding toward the woods. "Massed attacks on a narrow front have a good chance of succeeding if you're willing to accept horrendous casualties. And those people are willing to do just that."

"Brigadier, we'll hold."

"I hope so. You better get back to HQ. Keep your finger on things. I'm going to stay here. I can see our whole line, so I can help coordinate the response."

"Yes, sir," Codrington says.

Sam is left alone with his thoughts and fears, except for an aide and radio operator, both of whom keep a discreet distance. He wishes he could do something proactive. That would be easier than waiting to be attacked.

"Sam! Sam!!" Sarah's panicked voice cuts through his thoughts. He wheels around to see his wife running toward him. "It's Judy! She's gone!"

"What do mean gone?" he asks, fearing the worst, as Sarah runs up to him.

"She's not in hospital! I went to see her and she's gone. Nobody knows when she left or where she went."

"Oh." Sam's relief is obvious in his voice, the tension leaving his body.

"You're good with that?" comes the accusation.

"No, of course, not. I just thought ...." He leaves the words unspoken.

"Thought what?"

"That she was…"

"No, of course not. How could you think that?" The words come pouring out of Sarah. "But you have to find her and get her back to hospital!" she says, grabbing her husband's upper arms in a grip so tight it hurts. "She's not strong enough yet! You have to get her back there!"

Sam puts his hands on Sarah's shoulders, feeling her sobs, seeing the distress on her face. "My love, I can't do that."

"Why not?" comes the challenge as Sarah pushes herself back from him.

"Two reasons," Sam says patiently. "I don't know where she is…"

"You know exactly where she went! Back to her Troop!"

"Probably," Sam concedes, knowing good and well that is where their daughter would go. "But then we have this second problem. If I find her, I will have to have her court-martialed as an example. Officers are not allowed to break orders, including staying in hospital. If they can do it, the ranks will believe they can. And that will be the end of discipline."

"That's crap! And you know it!"

"Not really," he replies, although he really does know it. "I can't show favortism to my daughter. I would not embarrass any of my officers by doing that."

Sarah looks hard and long at him, tears running down her face.

"Leftenant Colonel," Sam says, "you need to return to your unit. The attack could start at any moment."

Sarah turns without a word and stomps off, the anger evident in the tightness of her shoulders.

Sam sighs as he watches her go. He can see the anger and fear in her. He swallows hard, and says a quick prayer for his daughter. Then he turns back to the forest.

⊱───⊰◇⊱───⊰

The attack bursts from the woods. Solid ranks of soldiers charge up the hill in a front half a kilometer wide.

Judy swallows hard as the mass of enemy soldiers comes directly at her. She wants to pull the trigger but makes herself wait for Mayran's orders. She has to remind herself that today she's just one of the ranks on the line.

"Shit, there a lot of them," the Sergeant next to her says.

"At least that makes an easy target," Judy says, without taking her eyes off the attacking soldiers. "We won't even have to aim. Just point and shoot."

"Thanks, Boss," comes the sarcastic reply from the Lance Corporal who is sharing the fighting hole with them.

Judy just grins to herself as the artillery shells scream overhead. Fighter-bombers fly over the woods, dropping napalm along the entire length of the front about a kilometer into the forest.

The artillery shells seem to cover the entire width of the attack and then some in a steady stream. The Marines can't see anything through smoke and dirt that is thrown up. The continuous noise of the explosions is deafening. If an order to open fire is given, Judy fears she may not hear it even through her earphone. She decides to open up when the Sergeant does. Then the thought strikes her, he may wait for her to start firing. If that happens, they're screwed. Perhaps none of The Enemy will make it through the curtain of fire.

Suddenly some of the artillery lifts, its fire shifting toward the river. Judy quickly glances in that direction. Another attack has just burst from the woods along a half-kilometer front.

"Clever sods," she says under her breath.

With half the artillery gone, Enemy soldiers begin to emerge from the smoke and haze, charging toward the Marines, firing as they come.

"Come on, Colors. Give the order," the Sergeant says to no one in particular.

"Steady. Steady." Mayran's voice comes through the earpiece as if in response, calm and reassuring. "Wait for the order."

First the tanks and APVs open fire, followed by the machine guns. The attackers are cut down by their hundreds, but they still keep coming.

"Prepare to fire," Mayran orders. "Fire!"

Judy squeezes the trigger as do the two Marines in the fighting hole with her. As she finishes a magazine, she hits the eject lever and slams another in its place, with hardly a break in her firing. Most of the human wave breaks against the Marines' line, but in places it breaks through. Hand-to-hand fighting rages along some segments. Mayran brings up the reserve Section to seal a breach in her line, leading the Marines in a charge that rocks The Enemy back on their heels, and then kills all within the Marine lines.

As The Enemy wave begins to recede, Judy is able to catch her breath. Around her feet are spent magazines and casings. She can hear the thunder of the artillery and tanks again, along with the chatter of the heavy machine guns. Off to her left, the attack is still going on. The artillery is shifted over to that threatened area. Attack helicopters come in, along with fighter bombers, to hammer the area in front of Judy and along the threatened line. She can see smoke rising up deep into the woods where napalm has been dropped. Further back, massive explosions are going off. She realizes high-flying bombers are carpet bombing the forest.

Around her, Marines are cheering. Judy feels drained, her strength ebbing away. But staying in hospital was not an option.

"Boss."

Judy turns around to find Mayran, the grime of battle covering her.

"You need to return to hospital," the Color Sergeant says, standing on the lip of the fighting hole, looking down at Judy, her weapon slung over her shoulder. "You're not in any condition to join the attack."

"Yes, Colors, you're right."

"Sergeant," Mayran says, "help the Boss back to hospital."

"I don't need help!" Judy protests.

"Boss," comes the sharp reply, "don't argue with me about this, please."

"Fine," she says petulantly. "Let's go, Sergeant."

Judy starts to climb out of the hole, almost slipping back in. Mayran and the Sergeant catch her, helping her out. Judy feels wobbly. She fights to regain her balance, shrugging off the proffered help.

Slowly she starts the journey back to hospital.

Down the line, the other attack is finally beaten back. As the Marines care for their wounded and clear the dead, Sam walks along the line talking to his men and women, helping here and there. He stops when reaches Mayran.

"Colors, glad to see you made it."

"Thank you, sir."

"Casualties?"

"Three dead. Seven wounded."

"I understand they broke through here."

"We plugged the hole and drove them back."

Sam nods and starts to ask a question. Thinks the better of it, resuming his walk.

"Brigadier?" Mayran says.

"Yes, Colors," Sam replies as he turns back to her.

"The Leftenant is back in hospital."

Sam shakes his head and smiles. "Thank you, Colors."

"Yes, sir."

Sam continues his journey, thinking he will have to call Sarah ASAP.

><>——<◊>——<◊>——<◊><

"Get Leftenant Colonel Hope of the Royal Engineers on the phone," Sam orders an aide as he enters the HQ tent.

"We stopped them. We stopped those wankers cold," Codrington exalts as Sam walks up to him at the map table.

"Yes, but we still need to finish them off," Sam replies, looking down at the map showing the Brigade's disposition.

"Sir," the aide says coming up, "the Leftenant Colonel is in a meeting."

Sam just looks at the young Lieutenant.

"Yes, sir, I'll get the Leftenant Colonel on the phone immediately."

"Thank you," Sam says, turning back to the map table. "Do we have an estimate of the number of casualties we inflicted?"

"Nothing solid," the Colonel replies. "We estimate about six to seven thousand in the attacks against us. It's hard to be sure. The artillery didn't leave a lot of bodies intact. Further back, there is no way of telling. We can't even be sure the heavy bombers hit anything at all."

"We'll find that out when we attack."

"Sir, the Leftenant Colonel is on the line," the aide calls from a desk about three meters off.

"Thank you," Sam says. "Give me a minute, Tom."

"Yes, sir."

Sam crosses the tent to where the aide is holding the phone. "Sarah?"

"How is she?"

"Back in hospital."

"That's a relief. Do you know where she was?"

"I can guess. She must have joined her Troop for the attack. Her Colors is the one who told me she was in hospital."

"What? She was in no condition to command her Troop!"

"She didn't. Her company CO is praising Mayran for the leadership she provided. I am willing to bet Judy joined the line."

"Like one of the ranks?"

"Exactly."

There is a pause as Sarah gets her emotions under control. "I don't know whether to hug her or kill her."

"Hug her. She's had enough violence for the day."

"Will there be repercussions?"

Sam laughs at that.

"What is so bloody funny?" Sarah says, now confused.

"If Johnston-Stone finds out, he'll give her an oral dressing down. But no Marine anywhere has ever faced formal discipline for joining a fight."

"Oh."

"Anyway, I can't get away. If you can, give her a hug for me."

"I will. By the way, we're working out a plan to set up a secure mobile phone system, so we can do away with this antiquated crap."

"That will be nice. Any idea when?"

"Within a month. Another bit of news, I'm being promoted to Colonel in two days and put in charge of this regiment. My boss is being moved to HQ."

"Congratulations, Colonel-to-be," Sam says jokingly.

"Thanks. In a bit, I expect to catch up to you."

"Two Brigadiers in one family. That will be interesting. But I'll still be your senior."

"Goodbye, sweetheart," Sarah says, her voice tinged with sarcasm.

"Bye," and Sam hangs up, going back to where Codrington is waiting for him.

"Some of the Commando commanders have suggested delaying our attack until the morrow," he tells Sam matter-of-factly.

"Heavy casualties?"

"Actually, lighter than we expected. No, they say their blokes are tired and could use a rest."

"I'm sure they could. So could The Enemy. We've knocked them back on their heels. Now is not the time to let them rest and regroup. No, the order stands. The entire Brigade will advance in," he looks at his watch, "two hours. How is resupply going?"

"Very well. We're nearly done."

"Brilliant. I'm going on a tour of the Troops. Keep me posted."

"I will."

Sam nods and leaves. He spends the next two hours talking to his commanders, explaining the reasons for attacking today, answering their questions. He also touches base with his Marines, thanking them for their work and assuring them today's attack is vital, that it will reduce casualties and, hopefully, shorten the war.

Ten minutes before the attack is to commence, Sam returns to his observation spot to watch.

At eleven hundred on the dot, the artillery opens on the tree line. With tanks and APVs mixed in with the leading infantry elements, the Marines come warily down the hill. As they approach the tree line, the artillery barrage lifts and moves further into the forest.

The Marines enter a world of shattered trees and blasted bodies. The armor rolls over the trees in their path. Periodically, they halt to allow the barrage to move forward.

About a kilometer in, the artillery stops as they come across a belt of utter devastation. Not a tree is left standing. A few bodies are around. And some body parts. The one thousand- and two thousand-kilogram bombs the Air Force dropped didn't leave anything standing. The remains of several pickup trucks are scattered about what was once a road. They have been shattered and thrown around like flimsy plastic toys.

The devastation extends nearly half a kilometer. On the other side, the forest starts gradually thickening again. The Marine line halts as patrols are sent to probe for ambushes. After a half-hour stop, the Marine line starts advancing again, but more slowly this time. And as the land begins to climb, the line starts to fragment in the hilly terrain.

Just before dark, a halt is called. The Brigade digs in for the night. As they prepare their defenses, hot food and water are brought forward.

The Marines spend the night on edge now that they know The Enemy will attack in the dark. Listening posts are put out to guard against a strike, and the members of Thirty Commando probe ahead in the dark.

<hr/>

As the dawn light filters through the trees, the Marines relax a bit. The night was quiet. Breakfast is prepackaged rations. Each package has a chemical heating element and either tea or coffee. Both are nearly impossible to get at the front, so the Marines enjoy the treat.

When it is light enough to see a few yards into the dense foliage, the advance resumes. The tanks and APVs are forced to stay on the roads, reducing their support for the infantry.

Away from the roads, the Marines start running into scattered resistance, usually launched from ambush. As casualties mount, the advance slows as the Marines carefully probe ahead. Occasionally, The Enemy sets up roadblocks. The tanks make short work of those.

As they push further into the woods, the Marines start coming across Soldiers who want to surrender. Sometimes they are still carrying their weapons, or their hands are not raised above their heads. Many of those are killed by Marines thinking only about protecting themselves and their comrades. Others, who come out with their hands above their heads usually succeed in surrendering. Word must have gotten around, because enemy soldiers start coming in droves, their hands high above their heads.

As the Marines move south, several Army divisions keep pace on their right flank, sweeping through southern France. As they reach the Mediterranean coast, the mountain passes to Italy and Spain are sealed off. The remnants of The Enemy's combat strength is squeezed into the ruins of Marseille, Cannes, and Nice.

The Marines get the job of clearing the Cannes and Nice area, while Marseille falls to the Army.

⧓⧓⧓⧓⧓⧓⧓

"Thanks," Judy says as she gets out of the truck's cab.

"Ma'am," the driver replies.

Judy shoulders her kit and sets off to find A Company headquarters. The company is camped in a wooded area several kilometers from Nice.

"Back on the flank again," she thinks to herself. After asking directions, she finds her way to HQ. Walking in, she puts her kit down. An orderly tells her where to find Johnston-Stone, so she sets off. Soon, she sees him talking to a supply officer. She stands quietly a couple of meters behind him, waiting patiently for him to finish.

"Hope!" Johnston-Stone says as he turns around. "I didn't expect you until next week."

"I left early, sir," she says, coming to attention.

"Stand easy," he says, looking intently at her. "As I understand it, you tried to leave early any number of times."

Judy suppresses the urge to roll her eyes and, instead, shrugs at her commander. "I wanted to be here."

"Yes,, well, we want you completely healthy. You're no good to us otherwise."

"Yes, sir."

"Walk with me," he says as he starts back to HQ.

Judy falls in beside him, waiting for him to resume the conversation.

"We've had some changes here, mainly because of casualties. The exec is KIA, as is our company's other senior Leftenant. That leaves you."

"Sir?" she says, not sure of what is going on.

"You are to take command of the company."

"Sir?" she protests, nearly stopping in her tracks.

"I'm moving to Forty Two exec. You are being breveted captain."

"Sir, I ..."

"Colonel Codrington issued the orders. He and I, as well as Leftenant Colonel McBride, have complete confidence in your ability to do the job."

Judy swallows hard. "What of my Troop?"

"Mayran has done an excellent job. Which brings me to another topic. I want you to convince her to take a battlefield commission. She refused before because she didn't want to break up the team or take your place, but now that you're moving to company, she may accept. Especially if the request comes from you. Think you can sell her on it?"

"I'll do my best, sir."

"Do better than that. Once this unpleasantness is over, she can go through the formal officer training, though God knows she doesn't need it."

"Sir, I didn't think battlefield commissions were allowed."

"Times change, Captain Hope, times change. By the way, I've been breveted Major."

"Congratulations, sir."

"Yes, quite," he says, as they enter the HQ tent. The Major proceeds to show Judy the Company's dispositions on a map and to explain the plan for the attack on the Nice-Cannes area after the Brigade has cleared the rest of the ground outside the city.

"Any questions?" he asks as he finishes.

"Thousands, sir, but I need to get settled in, talk to the Troop commanders, see how everyone is doing."

"Brilliant, then I'll be off to Commando. Call me anytime you have a question."

"Thank you, sir," she says, still somewhat in shock over this promotion. She watches Johnston-Stone leave, then looks around the tent, talking to the ranks who staff HQ. Then she heads off to talk to the Troop commanders, all of whom have heard of her promotion. A couple of them are replacements. She misses her friends but swallows her sorrow and puts on a stern face.

She saves Mayran for last.

"Boss!" Mayran calls when she sees Judy walking toward her.

"Colors, it's really good to see you."

The rest of the Troop quickly gathers around her, welcoming her back. She sees a number of new faces and is introduced to them.

"Guys, if you'll excuse us, Colors and I have some things to discuss," Judy announces. She watches them leave, and then leads Mayran away from the camp a bit, out of earshot of those who would want to listen. "Anne, I can't tell you how much I've missed you."

"Boss, the feeling is mutual, but you've been moved up to company. Who's going to take over the Troop?"

"You," Judy says forcefully.

"I'm no officer," Mayran protests.

"That can be fixed. I want you to accept a battlefield commission. You're more than qualified to lead a Troop, and I can't think of anyone I would rather have taking care of these blokes."

"But …"

"No, buts. I don't want some boot second leftenant doing something stupid and getting my guys killed."

"Are you sure? I never went through officer training. I have no college degree."

"I'm here to tell you that there is nothing in that officers' course you don't already know. And you have combat experience that cannot be taught. As for college, we'll work that out when, as Major Johnston-Stone put it, this unpleasentness is over."

"You really think I can do this?" Mayran says, doubt and a bit of fear in her voice.

"No, I know you can do this. Now let's go see McBride."

"Okay, Boss," Mayran says, doubt still in her voice.

"Here, you'll be needing these," Judy says, handing her old Second Lieutenant pips to Mayran. She had been carrying them around in her kit, and never knew why. Now she does.

CHAPTER 14

In many ways, this is going to be a repeat of our attack on Cherbourg," Judy tells her Troop commanders during a meeting in Company HQ tent after the Brigade has cleared the area up to one kilometer of Nice. "The main difference is that we are not driving to the harbor and then turning around and clearing the city. There will be no sea-borne landings."

"But we're still on the flank," Lieutenant Henry Clifford comments dryly, looking down at the map spread on a large table they all gathered around.

"I wouldn't have it any other way," the new breveted Second Lieutenant Mayran says in an upbeat tone tinged with sarcasm.

Judy just smiles and shakes her head. "We will have more armor support than we did at Cherbourg. Cliff, since you are so keen about being on the flank, why don't you take the Company's left flank."

"Leaving me out in the rain are you now?" he replies, a big smile on his face. "Love it. How much armor?"

"Your Troop will have five tanks and four APVs. And Cliff," she says, returning his smile, "the APVs are for fire support, not taxis."

"Bollocks, and here I was looking forward to riding in comfort."

Judy gives a short sharp laugh. "One Troop will be next in line. Mayran, be ready to support Two Troop if he runs into trouble."

"Yes, ma'am."

"Good. Four will be next with Third in reserve. Avigliano," Judy says, turning to the Three Troop commander, Lieutenant Keith Avigliano, "keep a Section as flying reserve. Your guys will have to move fast to wherever they're need."

"Yes, ma'am."

"Cullet," she says turning to the Four Troop commander, Second Lieutenant Amanda Cullet, "you hold on tight to C Company on our right. I don't want a gap opening up. And if it does, I want to know about it yesterday. Clear?"

"Yes, ma'am. Ma'am, may we hold one Section as Troop reserve?"

"That would be brilliant, but we have a lot of front to cover. We're going to be stretched, but then we are always stretched."

"That we are," Cullet replies.

"Ma'am," Avigliano asks, "will we have more than armor support?"

"We'll have attack choppers as well as some artillery. Keep in close contact with me. Our artillery liaison will call it. Any other questions?"

"When do we step off?" Mayran asks.

"Zero six hundred tomorrow. Make sure your guys get well fed, have plenty of ammo and water, and get as much rest as possible. But stay alert. We don't want any surprises tonight. For you new officers, listen to your NCOs," she says with a wink at Mayran. "They fought their way through Cherbourg. They know what to expect. This is no time to pull rank. I want to move fast, hit hard, and keep casualties down."

They all acknowledge her orders and disperse to their Troops. Judy looks at her watch and realizes she has to be at Commando HQ in twenty minutes. She touches base with her HQ staff, and then heads off.

She reaches Commando HQ just ahead of the other Company commanders.

"How are things going?" Johnston-Stone asks her.

"Brilliant, sir. We are primed and ready for the morrow."

"Good. But I meant how are things going with you?"

Judy pauses at that question. "I have settled in. The last week has helped a great deal."

"What do you mean?"

"I've become more comfortable maneuvering the Company. And I'm not too worried about going into Nice."

"Good. I think Cherbourg was a lesson for us all," Johnston-Stone says. He looks around. "The other Company commanders are here," he says. "Attention," he calls as McBride walks in.

"Stand easy," the Four Two Commando commander says. "Ladies and gentlemen, I just want to make sure we are all on the same page of this script." He briefly goes over the plan of attack, and what each Company is expected to do.

"As for intelligence, we still don't know what we will be facing. There have been no reports of large enemy movements. Thirty has been poking around inside the city and has not run into anything major. Lots of bodies and starving Soldiers. So that is a good sign," he says, before continuing with a bit of a sigh, "but they have not been more than two hundred meters in. So what lies beyond that…"

"Sir," Captain Marty Bosquet of C Company says, "my concern is that when we go in, one of us may get bogged down in heavy fighting, holding up the whole Commando."

"Actually, it will hold up the whole Brigade. The key to this operation is no one gets ahead, or behind, anyone else. No exposed flanks. If you do run into trouble, bring down the hammer. We're not here to preserve buildings. Use air, armor, and artillery as much as you can get. Snuff out opposition as quickly as possible. If you need help from a neighbor, you will get it. Understood?"

"Yes, sir."

"Brilliant. Now if there are no more questions, return to your Companies, and try to get some rest. Tomorrow will be a busy day, as I expect each day will be until we complete this operation. Dismissed."

When Judy gets back to her HQ, she has a bite to eat, then goes to check in with her Troop commanders as the light rapidly fades. She wants to make sure listening posts are out far enough to give a good warning of trouble, and that patrols will be active all night on the left flank to guard against any surprises from that direction.

Tired, she finally lays down on her cot, fully clothed, and quickly falls asleep.

⊱────❖──❀──○──❀──❖────⊰

"Captain! Captain!" The urgency in the sentry's quiet voice brings Judy to full awake instantly.

"What?"

"Movement in the left rear."

"Who's over there?"

"Leftenant Clifford and Second Leftenant Mayran."

"Take me to them."

"Yes, ma'am."

Judy grabs her weapon and the rest of her kit, putting it on as she heads off into the dark. She finds Clifford first. He's crouched down, scanning the woods with night-vision glasses. The sound of slow movement in the forest can be clearly heard.

"Report," Judy says in a whisper, kneeling down beside him.

"We have a lot of movement over there," he whispers back, indicating off to their left. "I have three Sections strung along here. Mayran has another two on my left. She also has a patrol out further to the left."

"Any idea of numbers?"

"No, outside of the fact they are making a lot of noise."

"So I hear," she says, listening to the sounds moving cautiously toward them.

"Right."

"Boss," one of the ranks hisses, "to the right."

Through their night-vision, they can see crouched figures moving slowly toward their line.

"Prepare to fire," Clifford says quietly into his radio. "Fire."

The Section of his line opposite the approaching Soldiers opens up. All the figures go to ground, either hit or trying to avoid the low fire coming in from the Marines.

"Cease fire! Cease fire!" he calls.

In the ensuing quiet, only the cries of the wounded can be heard. Then voices cry out in French: "Ne tirez pas! Ne tirez pas!" one calls. "Nous nous rendons!" another cries out.

"They're trying to surrender," Judy says. "Do you have anyone who speaks French?"

"Yes," Clifford says. He calls over a Corporal.

"Corporal," Judy says, "tell them to come in four at a time, walking slowly with their hands over their heads and no weapons."

"Yes, ma'am," she says. After she calls out, a few shadowy figures tentatively rise from the forest floor and carefully come forward. Judy has stood up and collected several of the ranks with her to greet their new arrivals. The Marines are tense and ready for an ambush. She realizes the slightest misstep could lead to a blood bath.

"Everyone stay calm and watchful," she says through the Company radio. "Don't fire unless they attack."

In the dim light, five scarecrows come stumbling into the Marine lines. Judy has them checked for weapons of any kind. Two have knives, which the Marines throw away. The Corporal then calls for a few more to come in. The rest don't need to be told. Soon hundreds of starving Enemy are coming into their lines. Judy has more of the Marines processing and guarding their captives.

"Captain, we have Enemy Soldiers coming into our lines to surrender," Mayran says quietly over the radio.

"Be careful but let them come if they are not a threat," Judy tells Mayran, whose voice she recognizes. "Have them brought down here so we can collect them all together."

"Right."

Judy then contacts Commando to report what is going on. Soon McBride is on the radio.

"How many?" he asks.

"Close to two hundred and they are still coming in."

"Any have weapons?"

"No, sir, except for a few knives. Most of them can barely walk. They're starving. They're clothes are in tatters."

"Brilliant," he says, sarcasm in his voice. Then a pause. "I'll send over some help. I'll contact Brigade to find out what they want us to do with these people."

Judy goes back to managing the growing number of prisoners while maintaining as much security as possible, mindful of the possibility The Enemy could launch an attack under cover of this mass surrender. She worries that it is just a distraction. It's now four in the morning. Two hours before the attack is to be launched. How all this is going to work, she has no idea. She can only deal with what is in front of her.

Soon, Bosquet arrives with two of his Troops. She has him guard the prisoners while she redeploys her guys back on the line, guarding against an attack and checking the POWs.

McBride comes back on the line with word that the attack is being delayed until this situation is resolved.

"Once they stop coming in, push out to the left. Find out what's going on," he tells her.

"I'd like to wait for light before doing that."

"Agreed. Once it's light have the prisoners escorted to Brigade HQ. They are preparing facilities."

As dawn breaks, Judy can see more of the slow-moving figures coming in.

"God bloody damn, Captain," Clifford says. "Are they ever going to stop coming?"

"Leftenant," she says dryly, "the more that come in, the fewer we'll have to fight. I say, keep them coming."

"Yes, ma'am," he says with some exasperation in his voice and walks back to his guys to keep an eye on things.

Judy heads north to find Mayran.

"Well, Second Leftenant, a busy night," she says when she finds her.

"That it is. We must have had nearly a thousand come in. And my patrol is bringing in more they found wandering around over there."

"Stay on your toes. The Enemy may use this as a smokescreen to launch an attack."

"Will do, Boss," she says.

"Good. Stay in touch," Judy says and goes back to the Four Troop.

When she gets there, Bosquet finds her. "What do you say we start sending some of these people to Brigade?"

"Can you spare the guards?"

"I'm pulling in a Section from Eight Troop," he says. "I think we can send them back safely in groups of five hundred. These poor sods are in no condition to put up much resistance. My guys are passing out what water and rations they have but it's not nearly enough."

"Lovely. Do it," she says, calling it in to Commando so they know what's going on.

By zero eight hundred, the flood has dropped to a trickle. The final count is just more than eight thousand POWs. Judy has the two Troops push slowly out to the left in search of more. Those who were wounded in the initial contact and are still alive are brought in for medical treatment. The dead are left where they fell, for now.

The sweep goes out half a kilometer, finding a few more who were unable to walk further. They are helped into the Marines' lines and sent to Brigade.

Judy sends patrols out three kilometers. When they no longer find any enemy, she calls them back in. As the last of the POWs are dispatched to Brigade, some on trucks because they can't walk, McBride and Johnston-Stone arrive.

"Sirs," Judy says, coming to attention and saluting when she sees them.

"Stand easy," McBride says. "You've had a busy night."

"Yes, sir, but I'll take a night like that over an attack," she replies.

McBride nods in agreement.

"The assault has been rescheduled for zero six hundred tomorrow," Johnston-Stone says. "Same plan."

"Sir," Judy says in acknowledgment. "Has anyone else had anything like this happen."

"On the right flank," McBride says, "Four Five has about eight thousand. They're in about the same condition as this lot. A few thousand more have come in along the rest of the front."

"Intelligence is reporting a breakdown in command," Johnston-Stone says. "POWs are reporting even their commanders, who seem to be all Sergeants, are dying of starvation or even deserting. Obviously, their supply system has collapsed."

"Opposition should be minimal, if at all," McBride adds.

"You'll pardon me if I approach that with some skepticism," Judy comments.

"Exactly," her Commando chief responds.

"Well, get things reorganized here," Johnston-Stone says. "And keep your patrols out."

"Will do, sir."

"Hope, you did an excellent job last night," McBride says.

"Thank you, sir, but it was Clifford and Mayran who deserve the credit. They had things well in hand when I arrived."

"Yes, excellent. Pass along my compliments to them," McBride says, then heads off with Johnston-Stone.

〜〜〜〜〜◯〜〜〜〜

Zero six hundred. Judy moves out with her old Troop so she can keep an eye on her vulnerable left flank, while also being able to watch the front as her company moves into Nice's suburbs.

They find a few more starving enemy Soldiers, who are more than willing to surrender. They collect them, turning them over to the Military Police following behind who take them to the POW stockade. They meet a few of The Enemy who are still armed, but most drop their weapons before the Marines can fire. Those who don't are shot.

As they advance, they move into more built-up areas, collecting more POWs. Movement is slow as the Brigade keeps a continuous front while each building is cleared. Some Troops can move faster than others. They wait for the others to catch up, pausing at intersections. Most of the buildings are falling apart. Few have intact windows. Dead power lines are scattered around. Many of the poles are broken and on the ground. Streets are in bad shape. In some places, they have disappeared altogether, overgrown with grass and weeds.

"This is spooky," Judy's HQ Sergeant, JoAnn Eyre, comments as they move into the more built-up areas. "This is like being in ancient ruins that are haunted."

"Except these ruins may be haunted by a living enemy intent on killing us," Judy says, scanning the buildings.

"Yes, ma'am."

An eerie quiet grips the area. No animals, not even birds. The only sounds come from the engines and treads as the tanks and APVs move forward and the bangs as Marines kick in doors checking the buildings. Occasionally, a helicopter flies past. The only voices come over the radios as Marines stay in touch with each other, and the quiet conversations and orders among themselves.

The advance slows to nearly a crawl as the Marines start to clear multi-story buildings densely packed together. Occasional alleys separating them must be cleared as well. They start finding starving, terrified Enemy

Soldiers huddled in rooms. What weapons they have are scattered on the floor. Once they realize they are not going to be killed, they are anxious to surrender, complying with every order as they hobble out into the sunlight to be collected by MPs.

Once in a while, an Enemy soldier refuses to put down a weapon or raises it toward them. A fatal mistake.

The first night, the Brigade halts along as continuous a line as can be managed. When they stop for the night, the tanks are used to form roadblocks with Marine sentries around them. In the quiet, movement can be heard but no attacks come. Night-vision reveals a few figures flitting about several streets ahead. None are coming toward the Marine lines.

In the pre-dawn light, Judy gathers her Troop and armor commanders. "We are in prime territory for ambushes. Make sure you are covering the rooftops and high windows as well as those lower down. Watch the basements as well."

"In other words," Avigliano says, joking in his voice, "watch everything simultaneously."

"Exactly," Judy says. "You know how to do it. At the first sign of trouble, shoot. I'd rather have a few dead Enemy who may or may not have been trying to surrender than dead Marines."

"Yes, ma'am," comes the chorus of replies.

"Get cracking. We move at zero six hundred."

Judy watches her officers disperse.

"Here, ma'am," Corporal John Padolov says, handing her a steaming cup of tea.

"Thank you," she says, taking the cup and sipping the hot liquid, enjoying its warmth as it flows down her throat.

Just more than an hour later, the radio crackles as the order from Brigade comes down and everyone starts moving forward again. Judy goes over to the right flank to make sure the Troop there is staying in contact with the neighboring company.

Small arms fire, followed quickly by cannon, machine gun, and more small arms fire breaks out from Three Troop in the next street.

"Contact forward! Contact forward!" Avigliano calls over the company radio.

Judy immediately starts running, calling Commando to let them know as she goes. By the time she reaches the scene, the firing has stopped, except for one tank throwing HP shells into a building two blocks down. It ceases fire when the building collapses after the fourth round.

"Report," Judy orders as she reaches Avigliano.

"We took fire from there," he replies, pointing to the rubble a few buildings down. "The tanks made short work of it."

"Casualties?"

"Outside of one of the new guys having the wits scared out of him, none."

"How heavy was the attack?"

"Machine gun and maybe half a dozen rifles. They were scattered from the first floor to the fifth."

"What happened down there?" Judy asks, indicating a building across the street from the one that was just demolished.

"Some machine gun fire came from there. Our tanker mates took care of that as well."

"Brilliant. Let's get moving again," Judy orders as she passes word onto Commando. Soon, Brigade orders the advance to resume.

The rest of the day is a reprise of Three Troop's experience as other Troops and sometimes Companies find themselves under attack, all of which are quickly suppressed. Casualties are few. Hope's company does not meet any more resistance. Most of the time is spent clearing buildings and gathering POWs by the hundreds.

As night falls, the Marines hunker down, staying on guard while trying to get some sleep. Hot food is brought forward, as are resupplies of ammo, rations, and water.

⊱────────◯────────⊰

"Good morning, Captain." Her mother's voice startles Judy, who turns around to find Sarah coming out of the pre-dawn darkness.

"Mu .. Colonel," she stammers out. "To what do I owe the honor?"

"You've probably heard about the building collapse that killed one Marine and injured seven others."

"I did, ma'am."

124

"I've detailed my Engineers to every Troop to check out the buildings to avoid a repeat of that."

"What? Your Engineers will be going on patrols with my Marines?"

"Exactly. We are Combat Engineers, you know."

"I can't guarantee their safety."

"No one is asking you to."

"Does Brigade know about this?"

"Of course. They think it's a brilliant idea."

"Lovely," Judy says sarcastically. "Who is going with my Company?"

"Me and three of my Engineers."

"You! Impossible! Does Dad … does the Brigadier know about this?"

"I don't discuss Engineer assignments with Brigade. That is my responsibility alone. And I am not going to put my people at risk without sharing that risk."

"Does Da… the Brigadier know about this?" Judy repeats.

Sarah just shrugs. "It doesn't matter one way or another. As I said, how I assign my people is strictly up to me. Besides, your father has no room to criticize. Nearly every time I go see him, he's somewhere along the front line."

Judy just sighs. She knows her mother is right.

"Oh, by the way," Sarah says, "Colonel Codrington asked me to give you these." She hands Judy shiny new captain's pips.

"I already have a set," she says.

"Yes, but the Colonel thought you could use a new set since you are no longer brevit Captain, but a full Captain."

"Thanks," Judy says, satisfaction in her voice. "Why…"

"He thought," Sarah says, cutting her off, "that I would enjoy being the one to tell you. And he was right."

"Thanks, Mum," she says, giving Sarah a hug.

"Enough of that, Captain," Sarah says, stepping back in mock sternness. "We have work to do."

"Yes, Colonel," Judy replies, a smile spreading across her face.

CHAPTER 15

Hey, Brigadier! Come on in! The water is lovely!" a Marine wearing a bathing suit yells to Sam, who is standing just above the surf line on the Mediterranean beach.

"Not today!" he yells back, smiling. "I have work to do!"

The Marine waves at him and dives into the water again to join his mates. Hundreds of Marines have been given permission to take a swim, partially to wash off the grime of weeks of fighting and marching, partially as a reward for their accomplishment clearing Nice and then Cannes, and partially as a way for the young men and women to let off steam. One Commando at a time is freed to spend a day at the beach, along with barbecue and beer. Music is provided by the Marine band.

"I wonder how many pregnancies we'll get out of this?" Codrington says quietly to Sam as he comes up.

Sam glances at him. "They're young and have been under intense pressure for months. As long as the fathers step up, I have no problem with that."

"Oh, they'll step up," the Colonel says, a veiled threat in his voice.

"Yes, I am sure they will," Sam says with a laugh. "As for us old timers, we need to get back to work."

The two top Brigade officers walk quickly to the building that has become their headquarters. The Royal Engineers checked it out and ruled it habitable, one of the minority of structures in Nice to get that seal of approval. Brigade HQ is in an old shop with a glassless storefront overlooking the sea. As they enter, an Army Colonel comes to attention and holds a salute. "Sir, I would like to report the Royal Engineers have completed the initial survey of structures in the city of Nice."

Sam just stares at Sarah for a moment. "Really? You're really going to do the formal bit?"

"Sir, the proper forms must be observed if we are to maintain discipline," she replies, still holding the salute.

"Really?" he says as he quickly crosses the room, wraps his arms around his wife and kisses her passionately on the mouth.

Sarah returns the kiss, then pushes him away, laughing. "Sir, really, I must protest," she says half mockingly. "What will your staff think?"

"They'll think what I tell them to think. Besides, they don't think much of Army officers."

"Why, you old sod ..."

"Now, now, proper form must be kept, don't you know."

Sarah glares at him for a moment before both break into laughter.

"How long has it been?" Sam asks. "A fortnight?"

"More like a week and a half," Sarah says. "I see more of Judy than I do of you."

Sam sighs. "I don't see much of either of you. Now, down to business. Get with my supply officer to see where we can billet the guys."

"Already done," she replies, inserting haughtiness into her voice.

"Brilliant. How about the POWs?"

"We found a football stadium in reasonably good shape. We've set up tents, kitchens, showers, and toilets," she says. "Your medical staff is tending them."

"They're in poor shape," Codrington adds. "Some of the buggers have died from malnutrition and a variety of health issues. We are still trying to organize new clothes for them."

"What's the final count?" Sam asks.

"Approximately thirty-four thousand," Codrington says.

"And they fit comfortably in a football stadium?" Sam asks, skepticism in his voice.

"Did I say comfortably?" Sarah says. "Right now, it is the only secure place we have to put them. We are looking for more accommodations, but those are not plentiful. There is some park land we may be able to use; however, security is an issue."

"Right," Sam says. "Keep me posted."

"Are you going to stay with us in Italy?" Codrington asks Sarah.

"I have not received any orders to the contrary. Why?"

"We are going back to being Marines," Sam says.

"Meaning?"

"Meaning we will be landing on the coast ahead of the Army to secure supply depots and to probe for opposition," Sam says. "Two Commandos will be landing on the west coast, while the other two will land on the east coast. I'm taking the west. Tom is taking the east. I'll be landing in the Pisa-Livorno area, while Tom will come ashore in the Ravenna-Rimini area. From there, we will be flexible. We will deal with any resistance we meet, but if it's significant, we'll dig in and wait for the Army coming down from the north. We'll have gunnery and air support from the Navy, and air support from the Air Force and our Marine choppers."

"And if there is no resistance?" Sarah asks.

"We'll push inland as far as we can safely. If all goes well, we'll meet up east of Florence, or possibly in Florence itself."

Codrington adds, "We will also have medical teams and several freighters of rations if we find the conditions warrant them landing."

"Something we'll need from your Engineers," Sam goes on. "As we push inland, we would like to establish bases for our attack and transport choppers."

"Right. I'll split my Regiment. We will land with you on both coasts, Brigadier."

"Excellent. Your Engineers have performed brilliantly. I thank you, and them, for that."

"Thank you. And, by the way, I understand from my command, that you requested my Regiment."

"That I did," Sam says, with a big smile on his face. "Have to keep the family together."

Sarah stares at him for a moment, then shakes her head. "Anything else?"

"That will be all, Colonel. Dismissed," Sam says brusquely.

Sarah looks shocked, then slaps Sam on the arm, before reaching in and kissing him. She steps back and salutes. "Very good, sir."

"Come by for dinner tonight?" he asks as she turns to leave.

"Eight o'clock?"

"Yes, that sounds lovely."

"Lovely," she repeats as she turns to leave, casting a glance over her shoulder as she walks out the door.

"I wish my wife could be here," Codrington says wistfully.

"Yes," Sam says. "On the other hand, you wife isn't in danger of being shot, blown up, or having a building fall on her head."

"Lovely thought. But that," Codrington says, "is a good point. By the way, Army command promises to send trucks to start carting the POWs to northern France in a few days. They are also working on restoring the railroads. And the airport here is nearly in condition to start receiving planes."

"Brilliant," Sam says. "Speaking of the Army, any word when they'll be moving down here? We can't go into Italy alone."

"A month or so," Codrington says. "The plan is to stockpile supplies first. The trucks that bring in those supplies will take POWs back with them."

"What about the freighters? The port is in good enough shape to receive them, and that would be a lot more efficient than trucks."

Codrington just shrugs. "The Navy is being noncommittal on that right now. Seems our sailor friends are concentrating their shipping on the buildup for crossing into Germany first. We, I am afraid, are a sideshow."

Sam looks disgusted. "I should have known. Can't be helped, I guess. At least the Swiss are dependable. I talked to their CO this morning. They have the Italian passes properly bottled up. So we don't have to worry about that. And our patrols are finding nothing out there on either flank. The Army says it has the passes to Spain blocked, as well. The Sicilians, by the way, have taken Italy as far north as Naples, but they aren't willing to go any farther until we come in from the north."

"When we do that," Codrington asks. "What about the passes from Austria and the Balkans?"

"The Army will plug those, or so I'm told," Sam says. "The Swiss want to go home and tend to the passes into Austria and Germany from there."

"They can certainly be of help. What about the Rhine? When does the Army cross it?"

"From what Command tells me," Sam says, "in about six months, if not sooner. It seems many of the POWs are more than willing to join the Army. Good food, good treatment, pay, and the promise of revenge seem to be highly motivating. The Army expects to be able to equip ten new infantry divisions in a few months."

"Really? Will they be reliable?"

"So I'm told. I do know from personal experience the thought of sticking it to these bloody bastards is highly motivating. I think they will be, if properly trained and led. And I think even the Army is capable of that."

CHAPTER 16

Sam scans the coast from the command ship as the morning sun slowly drives back the darkness. He envies the east coast force with the sun to their backs and no mountains to prolong the darkness. On the upside, the members of Thirty Commando who have already landed are reporting no opposition. They found a scattering of starving people and an even larger number of corpses in various stages of decomposition.

They also report that it appears some of the dead were used for food. The thought of cannibalism makes Sam shudder. While it is revolting, he can't dismiss the idea he might be driven to that extreme if his death was imminent. He might be able to do it. As long as the meal was already dead.

He looks at his watch: zero six zero two, thirteen minutes after sunrise. But the light hadn't reached the shore. On the east coast, Forty and Four Five Commandos have landed. With no opposition, they have already started pushing inland. Commandos Four Two and Four Six are loaded and ready to go—as soon as it is light enough.

"Damn it, Tom," he thinks to himself, "you have an unfair advantage." With the head start, Codrington might win their bet on who reaches Florence first. A bottle of eighteen-year-old single-malt scotch is at stake. Sam sighs, realizing this was his own fault since he didn't pull rank on his Chief of Staff. One the other hand, Florence is closer to the west coast, so he has that going for him.

"Brigadier," an aide says, breaking into his thoughts, "Captain Duberly believes it is light enough to send in the landing craft."

"Thank you, Failly. My compliments to the Captain. Ask him to proceed."

"Yes, sir," the aide says and heads back into the bridge.

A few minutes later, Sam sees the hover landing craft head for the beach. With no competition from the Army this time, the Marines have all the landing craft they need. Both Four Two and Four Six Commandos will land together, along with the armor, as was done on the east coast. Artillery and supply will land soon after them.

Passing the landing craft, transport helicopters guarded by attack copters head for the beach. Given the reports from his scouts, Sam is confident it is safe for the airborne contingent to land first.

"Gowing," Sam calls to another aide.

"Sir," the Lieutenant responds, stepping forward to just behind Sam.

"Time for us to go."

"Yes, sir. Your helicopter is ready."

"Lovely. Lead on." Sam follows the Lieutenant to the cruiser's flight deck where a helicopter is ready for takeoff. He and about half of his HQ staff fit aboard. Soon, they are on their way to the beach. Sam's staff want him to wait until the seaborne Marines land, but he's having none of that. He told his Marines opposition would be light at most. He's determined to show them he has faith in that evaluation. And if he's wrong, he is prepared to pay the consequences with them.

The flight takes less than fifteen minutes. Sam jumps out of the helicopter as soon as it touches down, followed by his staff. His communications people immediately establish contact with the command ship and Codrington, as well as air support. The helicopter returns to the ship for the rest of the staff.

Sam strolls over to talk to McBride, who is in charge of the airborne landing. Sam waits patiently as the Lieutenant Colonel finishes issuing orders.

"Leftenant Colonel, are things going as expected?"

"Better, I should say, Brigadier. My forward element is already half a klick inland. We've made contact with Thirty Commando and will push out another klick. We'll hold there until everyone is ashore."

"Brilliant," Sam says. "Carry on."

"Sir," McBride says and goes back to work.

Sam walks down toward the beach to greet the first of the seaborne Marines who are about to land. To his pleasant surprise, Judy is the first Marine out of the first landing craft by perhaps fifteen seconds as craft after craft beaches, their forward doors dropping as ramps. Marines and tanks come pouring out.

"Well, Captain," Sam says to her, "I did not expect to see you this soon."

"Expect the unexpected, sir. That's what we were taught," she replies lightly.

"So it is. Carry on."

"Sir," she replies as she goes past, leading her Marines up and off the beach.

Sam watches as the Marines swarm inland. When he sees the new commander of Four Six land, he goes over to her. "Leftenant Colonel," he calls to Mary Raglin.

"Sir," she responds, turning to face him.

"So far, no opposition. McBride is over there," he says, indicating the small cluster of Marines just off the beach.

"Yes, sir."

"You know the plan. If you need anything, call."

"Sir," she replies and heads off, issuing orders to her Company commanders as she searches for McBride to coordinate with him. Sam isn't happy about replacing the Four Six commander at the last moment, but Sean Polasky suffered a serious head trauma and lost a leg, among other injuries, when his vehicle went off the road and crashed two weeks before this operation started.

On the good side, Raglin was the Commando Four Six's XO. She was fully briefed on the plan and has his confidence. He breveted her Lieutenant Colonel, something that could become permanent. Best of all, her spirit and attitude remind him of Sarah.

As the landing craft pullback to sea for another run, Sam walks over to where his two commanders were conferring.

"Report," he says as he comes up.

"Four Two is forming on the right, Four Six on the left," McBride, the senior of the two, responds. "We should be ready to move in forty-five minutes," he says, almost as a question as he looks at Raglin for confirmation. She nods.

"Brilliant," Sam says. "You're each holding a Company in reserve?"

"Yes, sir," comes the joint the reply, which is nearly drowned out as six attack choppers swoop low overhead. Sam glances up at them as they pass.

"My HQ will follow as you move inland. Supply is being set up on the beach and as soon as transport lands, it will be ready to follow you. If you run into trouble or need anything, I want to know yesterday."

"Yes, sir," comes the joint reply again.

"Crack on," Sam says as he turns to head back to where his staff is waiting for him. He needs to make sure the Marine MPs and Royal Engineers will be landing with the second wave, ready to set up a POW stockade, as well as anything else that is needed.

⟫⟩⟩⟩⦾⟨⟨⟨⟪

"This stench is incredible," Mayran says as she and Judy go with the Troop up a hill and off the beach. "Two of my guys have puked, and the rest of us are green. Looks like you are, too," she comments after a glance at the Captain.

"Just keep on moving," Judy says, feeling queasy. "With any luck, we'll be out of this soon."

"How are we going to dispose of all these bodies?" Mayran asks, looking around at the rotting corpses.

"Not our problem. At the moment," Judy responds, leaving an opening just in case higher command makes it their problem. "We need to keep pushing inland until we meet resistance."

"Right, Boss, but gas masks wouldn't hurt."

"Nice thought, but it isn't going to happen. Now keep your guys moving," Judy says as she goes to check on her other Troops.

Half an hour later, Johnston-Stone finds her as she surveys the road ahead of another Troop.

"Captain Hope," he calls, his voice muffled by the scarf he is holding over his nose and mouth.

"Sir," she says turning around.

"How are things here?"

"No opposition, Major, but lots of dead. We haven't come across one living person yet. And some of these corpses show signs of being partially eaten. Since there're no animals around, that can only mean one thing."

"Yes, yes," he says, cutting her off before she can go any further. "That is being reported along the entire line. The Colonel is reporting the same conditions over there," he says waving toward the east.

"What happened?"

"As near as we can tell, The Enemy's whole supply system collapsed. I would like to say we had something to do with that, but we didn't. And we don't know why. Right now, finding out is not our major concern."

"Captain," Clifford calls over the company net at that moment, "we've found some live ones."

"How many?" Judy says, holding up a finger to pause her conversation with the Major.

"A dozen. They're not armed and they're in no condition to fight. They look like skeletons with some skin stretched over them."

"Any hostile moves at all?" she asks.

"No, ma'am," he replies. "Some of them keep trying to hug us. I think they are thanking us for saving them. I can't be completely sure. I think they're speaking Italian. My guys are passing out some rations and water."

"Put a guard over them and keep moving."

"Right."

<hr />

"Sir, my guys have found about a dozen Enemy, unarmed and starving," Judy tells McBride about one hour later as he visits his Companies. "The report is they are not hostile. What do we do with them?"

"Keep them in place. Brigade will send medical to help them."

"Yes, sir."

"Keep us updated on your progress and if you find more survivors."

"Survivors?"

"Yes, survivors. These poor wankers have been left to die," the Leftenant Colonel says. "It seems all the ones fit for combat were marched over the mountains. Those are the sods who attacked us. We hear from the Army the roads and passes are strewn with bodies in various stages of decay."

"Are we going to try to save these people?" Judy asks, looking at some rotting corpses a few meters away.

"That is the plan. Save them if they surrender. Kill them if not," he replies matter-of-factly. "By the way, the Army is meeting the same kind of conditions we are. They are already over the mountains and moving across northern Italy. Once they hit the Adriatic, they'll turn south toward us."

"What about this?" Judy asks, waving an arm toward the corpses.

"For the time being, we leave them. Clearing the country is more than cleaning up this mess," he says. "I am told eventually we will get used to the smell and it won't bother us anymore."

"I hope you're right, sir."

"So do I, Captain. So do I." With that McBride heads off to finish his rounds of the Commando's companies.

Judy shakes her head and goes back to keeping her people moving. She walks to where the prisoners are. What she finds horrifies her. She just stares at the figures of what used to be men and women, now clothed in tatters, their eyes as hollow as their cheeks. Some of them look at her with hope in their eyes as she comes up.

"Help is on the way," she finally manages to stammer out, not sure they understand her, before walking quickly away before she starts to cry.

⁂

That evening she meets with her Troop commanders after the Company commanders have been briefed at Commando HQ and given their orders and routes of advance for the next day.

"Right guys," she tells her Troop leaders, "we made excellent progress today. Nearly fifteen kilometers."

"Against no opposition," Clifford observes dryly.

Judy shoots him a look that lets him know further such comments would not be appreciated.

"Sorry, Captain," he contritely says in a low voice.

"Anyway, we are being told to expect more of the same. We handle any prisoners the same way as today. Our Company picked up one hundred fifty-seven. The entire Brigade brought in more than three thousand."

"All in the same condition as ours?" Mayran asks.

"Yes. And no one met any opposition."

"Those poor sods are incapable of mounting opposition," Clifford says, unable to keep his mouth shut, "even if they wanted to."

"Quite," Judy says. "Another thing we are to watch out for is food. The way things are going, Brigade doesn't believe we'll have enough rations for these poor devils. Anything we can find will help. Assuming they haven't eaten it all already, which is a big assumption. Any questions?"

After discussing the details of the next day's march, all of them gathered around a camp table with a map, Judy dismisses her Troop commanders. She goes to her desk to deal with all the paperwork she never realized a Company commander faced—strength reports, ammunition, supplies, rations, water, fuel for vehicles, and on and on. At about midnight she is finally finishes and crawls into her cot for a few hours' sleep.

⟫⊶⊷⊶⊷⊶⊶❰⊱⊶⊷⊶❰⊱⊷⊷⊱

"Captain," the sentry says quietly, "zero four hundred."

"What?" she says sleepily.

"Zero four hundred," the sentry repeats.

"Brilliant, thanks." Judy swings into a sitting position on her bed, slipping her feet into her boots, as the sentry leaves. Yawning, she stands and puts on her kit. Picking up her rifle, she walks out of her tent. In another hour, the Company will be awakened. In the intervening hour, she makes sure a hot breakfast is ready, as well as the supplies needed for that day. She had made sure of that last night but wants to double check everything. As she makes her rounds, she meets her Troop commanders who are also up before their Marines.

"Halt! Who goes there!" a sentry calls in a loud voice. Judy heads in that direction as the call awakens every Marine nearby. They all come pouring out of their tents ready to fight, some of them not quite dressed.

As she trots toward the sentry, she hears a Marine cry out in pain. Automatically she turns in that direction looking for a threat. What she sees is a Marine carrying a rifle and dressed only in underwear hopping around on one foot.

"Put your boots on, you silly wanker," another Marine says as he runs past.

"Who's there?" the sentry calls again, drawing Judy's attention back to a possible threat.

Several weak voices respond in a language none of them know. But from the tone of voice, it sounds like they want to surrender.

"Torches!" Clifford orders.

The light of multiple flashlights shows the emaciated faces and bodies of perhaps twenty people. Clifford orders them brought in. Judy orders them fed.

"Ma'am, if we feed them, we won't have enough for our guys," the Mess Sergeant objects.

"It can't be helped," she says. "Short rations all around. Our guys can have some cold rations if they're still hungry."

"Yes, ma'am," she responds, not at all happy about the situation.

Judy informs Commando HQ what just happened.

"What brought them in?" McBride asks, his voice still sounding sleepy.

"I suppose the smell of breakfast cooking," she replies.

"Right. I'll pass the info up to Brigade. Out."

<hr />

As the light grows, Judy orders her Company to move out. Today starts as a repeat of yesterday. More bodies. More starving people. Some die just after her Company finds them. Some die waiting for medical help, which can be long in coming. Some die on their way to hospital. Some die after getting there, victims of starvation and disease ravaging their bodies. No one was prepared for this level of disaster.

"Captain, you have to come to see this," Clifford calls over the company net.

"What's going on?"

"We have a locked building complex with survivors and bodies scattered all around," the Lieutenant says. "There must be several thousands of them. Living and dead."

"On my way." Judy runs the nearly half kilometer to the site, her radio operator, carrying all his kit and the heavy radio, panting behind her.

"Report," she orders Clifford as she comes up.

The Lieutenant just gestures toward the heavy three-meter fence topped by razor wire. The dead and dying lie thickly on the ground.

"Any idea on what's in there?" Judy asks, indicating the building.

"No. We might if we could understand what these people are trying to tell us. That guy over there," he says, pointing to one of the living who doesn't look as close to death as some of the others, "keeps making an eating motion. Maybe there's food in there."

"Right. Let's go in," Judy says. "Carefully, Cliff. There may be boobytraps. There may be defenders waiting for us to breach. We approach it as a hostile situation. I'm going to bring in a couple of Sections to bolster you."

"Yes, ma'am." Clifford heads off to get his people organized,

Judy briefs Commando HQ on the situation and has another of her Troops send over two Sections as reinforcements. When everything is ready, she orders Clifford to commence the attack.

A five-meter Section of fence that has been cleared of the living and does not face any doors—the buildings have no windows—is blown and four Sections go pouring in, ready for trouble.

They don't find any.

What they do find is a deserted complex. The heavy steel doors on what appear to be six large warehouses are locked by huge padlocks.

Judy has the lock of one blown off. The doors are opened just wide enough for two Marines to enter at a time. Soon two Sections are inside. The Marines fan out, searching the building that has only one small room in addition to the large storage room filled with sacks.

Judy enters with the first Section. As her Marines search, she inspects one pile of sacks. They are fifty-kilogram bags filled with some small grain. She cuts a slit in one, holding her hand under the slit.

Wheat spills into and over her hand.

"Food. Millions of kilograms of food," she says in wonder. "I have to report this." Then she stops herself, realizing she has to find out what the other warehouses contain. "Cliff," she says, urgency in her voice, "check out the other buildings. I need to know what they hold."

"Yes, Boss." The Lieutenant runs off, calling on his guys to come with him. Soon the big doors on all the warehouses are open.

They are all filled with thousands of sacks of wheat.

"I have to phone this in," Judy says, more to herself than anyone. "Clifford!" she calls. "Search the rest of this area. I want to know what else is in this compound!"

"Yes, ma'am."

Judy has two of her Troops set up perimeter security. "Callet," she tells the commander of her Four Troop, "you draw the dirty job. I want the road cleared."

The Second Lieutenant looks at the area strewn with the living and the dead. "Where do we put them?"

"Move the living to that grassy area," she says pointing to a place with thick grass about twenty meters from the road. "I don't care where you put the bodies, provided they are nowhere near those poor sods."

"Will do."

That taken care of, she contacts McBride, letting him know what they have found.

"Right," he replies. "Keep me apprised. I will get onto Brigade and organize a medical team."

That done, Judy makes sure everything is being taken care of, and starts trying to figure what to do with all that wheat. Then she realizes that is above her pay grade. Besides, without some way to grind it and to turn it into bread or something edible, there isn't much she can do, although she has heard of roasting wheat kernels and eating them that way. She is wondering whether that would work when Clifford intrudes on her thoughts.

"Captain, we found what looks like a mill and a bakery on the northwest perimeter," he says over the Company net.

"On my way," Judy says.

When she gets there, she finds two buildings, both with windows, doors, and loading docks. One is about one hundred by two hundred meters, while the other is about half that size. The larger building houses what looks like milling equipment. The other, ovens, mixing equipment, and tables, along with a variety of loaf pans. Power lines from both buildings lead to a small windowless structure. Inside are half a dozen generators.

Judy calls this in, too.

McBride, for his part, relays all this information to Brigade.

◦━━◦━━◦━━◦━━◦

Sam puts down the radio receiver, digesting what his Four Two commander has just told him.

"Major," he says to Pierre Dessairt, who is acting as his Chief of Staff, "have Major Pelissier report to me immediately. Have Leftenant Colonel Raglan and Colonel Hope meet me at these coordinates immediately," he says, handing Dessairt the location. "And have Leftenant Colonel McBride meet me there as well."

"Yes, sir. Should I tell them what this is in reference to?" Dessairt asks, as much for his own information as for theirs.

"It's about saving lives. Now move!"

"Sir."

"McFarland!" Sam calls. "Get my detail, we're going on a road trip."

"Yes, Sir," the Lieutenant says.

Sam walks out of the headquarters tent toward his vehicle.

"Sir, you wanted to see me?" Pelissier says coming up.

"Yes, Supply, we're taking a road trip. I'll brief you on the way."

"Sir."

Sam and Pelissier are soon in the second vehicle of the four-vehicle convoy. Although the area is considered secure, the Marines still treat it as potentially hostile. As they drive, Sam fills his supply officer in. It distracts him from the bodies scattered along the road, although the overwhelming stench of human rot can't be ignored. Only tolerated.

As they drive up to the complex, Sam is happy to see the road has been cleared of bodies. The potholes and other damage the pavement has suffered is tolerable. Driving over corpses is disgusting.

As they drive through the main gates, they are directed to the front of one of the large warehouses where they find McBride and Judy just emerging from the building.

"Report," Sam says as he gets out of the vehicle before it comes to a full stop.

"Six buildings filled with grain. Some of it appears to have rotted but most appears good," McBride says.

"You've inspected all of this?" he asks Judy.

"Not personally, sir. Ten of my blokes grew up on grain farms, so I had them check out the wheat."

"Very good. What is this I hear about a mill and a bakery?"

"Yes, sir," Judy says. "I was about to take the Leftenant Colonel there."

"Crack on. I'll follow."

Judy leads them to the back of the property, and on a tour of the buildings. As they are standing in the bakery, Sarah walks in, followed by Raglan.

"Brigadier," Sarah says, "you called."

"Yes, Colonel, I did. I need your Engineers to get this place working again. There is a generator building there," he says, leading the party outside. "That building houses milling equipment."

"To what purpose?" she asks, a bit perplexed.

"Those six warehouses you passed coming in are filled with wheat. I want to turn that into bread."

"Understood. We'll get on it immediately."

"Whatever you need let us know. Supply," he says to Pelissier, "your number one priority is to get the Engineers whatever they need. I don't care how you do it. If you run into any problems, call me. I want hourly reports on the progress."

"Sir," Pelissier says.

"Raglan, McBride, on me," Sam says, ending that conversation. He leads the two Commando commanders off to the side. "I want all POWs and anyone else found alive transported to Brigade ASAP. We'll be better able to care for these poor sods if they are all in one place."

"Ah, sir," McBride says, "that will slow our advance down."

"So?"

"Your bet, sir?"

A small smile crosses Sam's face. "The Colonel and I were always going to split that bottle anyhow. It was just a question of who provides it. Speaking of the Colonel," Sam says, a broader smile on his face now, "I'm going to spoil his day."

"Sir?" Raglan says, intrigued.

"I'm going to pull his baker," he says, thinking about all that needs to get done.

As much as the two Lieutenant Colonels would love to press the subject, they know better. They salute and head back to their commands.

Sam walks around the area, inspecting the warehouses and talking to the Marines. Then he goes off by himself, contemplating how best to dispose of the bodies, and whether the stench will affect the taste of the bread, although he doesn't think starving people would notice much.

"Sam." Sarah's quiet voice behind him brings him back to reality. He turns around to her, and smiles.

"One of my electrical guys thinks she can get at least four of the generators running. The other two may be shot. But we won't know for sure until we get some diesel here. Your supply officer is working on that now. As for the milling and baking equipment, a cursory look shows them to be in good shape, if in badly need of cleaning. But again, we won't know for sure until the power is restored."

"Thanks. Let's do it as quickly as possible. I don't want to lose any more POWs than we have to."

"Yes," she responds quietly. "Judy looks good."

"Yes," he says, smiling at the change of subject. "She seems to be in her element. A natural leader."

"She gets that from you."

"She gets that from both of us." Sam pauses a moment. "Do you think you could get some bulldozers up here?"

Sarah looks around for a moment. "For the bodies?"

"Yes. We need to bury them."

"I should be able to do something about that. I can divert at least one from the airstrip work for a day or so."

"Thanks."

"No worries, sweetheart. I better get cracking. I have a lot to do."

"Yes," Sam says, a sadness in his voice. "Don't we all." He watches her leave, then heads back to his vehicle. He'd like to see Judy, but that could be construed as favoritism.

⤚⦿⤚⦾⤚⦿⤚

"What do you think? Will they keep running?" Sarah asks Major Harmon Podpalor, her senior electrical engineer, about the generators.

"I think so, with a lot of tender loving care. They are not in the best of shape," comes the reply.

"Do your best. We have a lot of starving people depending on us."

"That's what I like: No pressure," he replies wryly.

"Yes, exactly," Sarah says. "Let's see if the other stuff works."

"Nothing will work if we don't get more diesel," Podpalor says.

"Pelissier is working on that," Judy replies, then sees the look of question on Podpalor's face. "Major Pelissier. He's the Brigade supply officer."

"Is he any good?"

"The Brigadier thinks so," she says as they walk to the milling building where some Engineers are at work on the equipment, making adjustments and some repairs. Work is also in progress in the bakery building, where Marine cooks are also busy cleaning.

Having inspected the work, Sarah heads off for Brigade HQ to report progress, and to find out about fuel.

As she nears the HQ which is housed in a dilapidated barn, she spots Pelissier coming out. "Major!" she calls.

He looks in her direction, waves, and alters course toward her.

"Fuel?" she asks, ignoring all the usual military courtesies.

"Interesting problem," he begins to say.

"I'm only really interested in the solution," she replies, cutting off any description of what he has been up to.

"Yes, lovely, right," he stammers out, disappointed about not being able to brag about his accomplishment. "I have one hundred sixty thousand liters ready to roll. I was just getting clearance to send them off. The Brigadier, you know, still doesn't want our supply columns rolling out without escort."

"Yes, of course," Sarah starts to say. Then it hits her: "Did you say one hundred sixty thousand liters?"

"Quite. I should have another two hundred thousand or so ready to go tomorrow."

"Where on earth did you get all that fuel?"

"Let's just say the Royal Navy will not be overly fond of me when they find out."

"Brilliant. Thank you, Major."

"Any time, Colonel. I'm here to serve. And by the by, it's Leftenant Colonel now. The Brigadier was good enough to promote me."

"You obviously deserve it," Sarah says, "and I apologize for not noticing your new rank insignia. I have to check in with the Brigadier now."

"No apology needed, ma'am. And I must get that convoy moving."

"Have whoever is in charge see Major Podpolar when they arrive. He's leading the Engineer contingent there," she says. "They should have the fuel tanks read when the convoy arrives. How we'll store the rest ..."

"No worries, Colonel. I will be there and I'm sure the two of us can work it out."

"Yes, thank you," Sarah says as they head off in different directions.

As Sarah enters HQ, she looks around in the dim light for Sam. She finally spots him at a desk off to one side, talking to someone over a radio phone. She goes over and sits down in a chair in front of the desk.

Sam glances up at her and smiles, then goes back to his conversation. "I'm sorry, Tom, but in this instance, I'm pulling rank. Send him over by copter ASAP. .... Understood, this is under protest. Bye, Tom." Sam hangs up, a big smirk on his face.

"What are you doing to that poor man?" Sarah asks.

"Stealing the best baker in the Brigade," he replies. "Stan Mercer's a Color Sergeant with Forty. Tom doesn't want to give him up, and I wouldn't either in his place. But I need him running that bakery your Engineers are getting in shape. They will get it running, won't they?"

"We'll find out if the generators and equipment will keep running once the diesel is here," she replies. "That equipment is in poor shape and starting it is just part of the battle. But I think this will be a go."

"Brilliant. Pelissier is organizing the potable water and salt Mercer will need. He even says he can probably organize some yeast so proper bread can be made," he observes. "If not, it will be flat bread, which is still edible."

"That is one amazing supply officer. He deserved the promotion."

"That he did," Sam agrees. "Then again, we Marines are always at the end of the line when it comes to supplies, so supply officers frequently have to get creative."

"I've noticed."

"By the by," Sam says, looking at his watch, "care for some lunch?"

"That would be lovely. I haven't eaten today," Sarah says as they both get up and head out. "I didn't see Judy at the site this morning."

"Her Commando has moved east. My MPs, cooks, and other personnel can handle security."

"You expect cooks to handle security?"

"This, my love, is the Marines, not the Army. Every Marine is trained to be in combat. We have no rear area types like the Army."

`"My, you are a proud one."

"And with cause," he says laughing as they enter the officer mess tent. They go through line with trays, getting their meal, then sit at an open table."

"I must say, I'm looking forward to having fresh bread," Sam says. "I will send a share over to Tom's guys."

"That should make him feel better."

"Not that he'll ever admit it." They fall silent for a few minutes as they eat.

"Any word from up north?" Sarah asks.

"Funny you should ask. I just received a command-wide status report. The Army launched its attack across the Rhine earlier than expected because reconnaissance found only a thin crust of defense. They hammered several areas with artillery and air, then infantry crossed in force. They threw up some bridges and the armor went in. Opposition lasted about two days and then crumbled. Right now, they are advancing east into Germany and Austria."

"What are they finding?"

"Pretty much what we are finding here," Sam replies: "Lots of dead and dying. They're mounting a rescue operation to save as many as they can, but it doesn't look promising. We got lucky here, finding all that wheat. Without that, we would not have the resources to save many. We can only hope the Army runs across the same kind of supplies."

"I've been told by Engineers up north that they are making good progress repairing rail lines," Sarah says, "but it will probably be a couple of years before many trains are running again. There are years of neglect that have to be repaired. The roads are an easier matter, but still a task. Apparently, many of the survivors are quite willing to work at those and other jobs. All we can do is feed and house them, but that seems more than enough for now."

"We both know how that goes, and we didn't suffer the way these poor bastards did."

"No, we didn't," she replies reflectively.

"By the by, the first plane landed this morning at our new airport. Pelissier seemed particularly excited about that. I'm not sure why, and I probably don't want to know. Deniability and all that."

Sarah just laughs at that, then looks at her watch. "I have to run. See you tonight?"

"I hope so, assuming neither of us is pulled away."

"Such is the life we've chosen," Sarah says as she leaves the table and heads out.

CHAPTER 17

aptain, you have to see this," Avigliano calls over the company net.
"On my way," Judy replies, who was at Company HQ. The calm in the Lieutenant's voice tells her it is not an emergency. But obviously he has something interesting to show her.

Fifteen minutes later, Judy finds her Troop commander and several of his Marines lying prone on the crest of a large forested ridge, all staring intently down into the valley.

"What's so interesting?" Judy asks as she lays down next to them.

"Down there," Avigliano says, gesturing into the valley.

Judy raises the binoculars she wears on a strap around her neck. What she sees makes her freeze in astonishment. "Have they spotted us?"

"Not yet," Avigliano says. "But they probably will shortly. Since we've been watching, several patrols have gone out."

"Incredible. My parents have told me about the area where I was born, but I never dreamed there would be anything like that here," she says, her eyes fixed on the village where life is going on normally. Fields have been planted with grain, large gardens abound on the edges of the village, where the houses are in good repair. Children are playing in the streets and yards. The adults are dressed simply but in what looks like well-made clothing. As she shifts her gaze, she spots animals: chickens, pigs, dairy and beef cattle, and horses. She sees plows and other farm equipment that are horse-drawn. The sounds of birds near where they are lying start filtering in.

"Over there," Avigliano says, pointing down to the foot of the hill where a five-member patrol is approaching.

"We have to phone this in," Judy says. She quickly gets McBride on the Commando net, telling him what they see. "Yes, sir, we'll do that."

Avigliano looks at her quizzically.

"We are to make contact with the patrol if it comes up here. Otherwise, we wait for orders and just observe."

As they watch, the patrol goes up another portion of the ridge, where they study the area below. What they see alarms them. They turn and hurriedly go back to the village, calling out what sounds like a warning.

"They must have seen our guys," Avigliano says.

"We weren't trying to hide," Judy responds, looking back over her shoulder. She sees the Commando HQ tents set up in the valley below. "And they certainly don't know who we are. I'm just surprised air hasn't spotted them."

"And a good thing," Avigliano says. "They would have bombed them out of existence, no questions asked."

"You're probably right," Judy responds, watching intently as the patrol runs back into the village, shouting and gesturing wildly.

Judy and the others watch as the people in the village stare up at the ridge, then pandemonium breaks out. Most of the adults emerge from their homes carrying rifles and pistols, while the children are herded into a stone structure that looks like a fort with firing slits in the walls. Fighting pits along the village's perimeter are uncovered, with people getting into position.

"They're ready for a fight," Avigliano's Color Sergeant comments dryly.

"Indeed they are," Judy replies. "Look over there," she says pointing to their right. Another patrol is heading up the same path followed by the first one.

"Probably want to keep an eye on us," Avigliano says.

"Only they don't know it's us," Judy replies, worry in her voice. She gets back on the radio to Commando to update HQ. "Yes, sir, we'll do that now."

"What's up?" the Lieutenant asks.

"We are to make contact with those folks," she replies, gesturing down to the village.

"Want me to?" Avigliano offers, excitement in his voice.

Judy stays silent for a moment, forming a plan in her mind. "No, Leftenant," she finally says. "I want you to organize an infiltration party in case anything goes wrong. Send them about a hundred meters from the trenches. If something happens, they can give us covering fire."

"Yes, ma'am. Who's going?"

"I need to find someone who speaks Italian."

"Cliff has at least one guy who does."

"Good," Judy says and gets Clifford on the radio. "Leftenant, I understand you have someone who speaks Italian."

"Two actually. Both fluent."

"Send the one who is most proficient."

"They both are. They both grew up in the Italian colony on Blighty. Speak Italian like a native, or so I'm told."

"Then send over the one who is most reliable."

"They both are."

"Cliff, send one over now. Out," Judy says, the exasperation evident in her voice.

Finished with the call, Judy hears Avigliano's quiet laughter next to her.

"Something funny, Leftenant?"

"Just Cliff being Cliff," he replies trying to suppress his laughter. On her other side, Judy hears sniggering.

"Oh, just shut up," she says. "Avigliano, don't you have a party to organize."

"On it, Captain," he says as he slips away.

After about ten minutes, things begin to quiet down in the village as everyone has taken positions.

"Sergeant Maria D'Angelo reporting as ordered, ma'am," a quiet voice behind her says.

Judy swivels around to the Marine crouching down just below the ridge line. "Did any of those people see you coming?" Judy asks, gesturing toward the village patrol now intently watching the Marines in the valley.

"I don't think so, ma'am."

"Brilliant. Sergeant, you are going to be my translator when we make contact with those folks," she says gesturing toward the village.

D'Angelo raises up a bit to peer over the top of the ridge. "Yes, ma'am."

"Captain," Color Sergeant Tommy Hertzog says, "this may come in handy."

Judy takes the proffered British flag from Hertzog. "Where did this come from?"

"Oh, I've been shlepping it around since we landed. Never know when a Union Jack will be needed. We're organizing a staff for it right now." Just as Hertzog finishes speaking, a Lance Corporal comes up with a long thick stick.

"Will this work, Colors?"

"It will do, Beechum," Hertzog says as he pulls out some rope, cuts it in half and affixes the flag to the makeshift staff. "There, that should do the job. Beechum, you will accompany the Captain down to that village."

"Me?"

"Now you don't expect the Captain to carry the flag herself do you?"

"No, Colors."

"And the Sergeant here," Lane says, indicating D'Angelo, "can't because she's the translator and outranks you."

"Yes, Colors," comes the unhappy response.

"Captain, I think you're good to go," Hertzog announces. Just then, Avigliano's voice comes over the radio to report the infiltration party is in place along the tree line closest to the village.

"Brilliant. Right, guys, sling your weapons on your backs. We go in hands free and looking as peaceful as possible. Remember these people have been living with the constant threat of death."

"As if," Beechum mumbles, "I could even hold a weapon with this bloody big flag."

"Don't worry, Lance Corporal," Judy says in a reassuring voice, "what's the worst that can happen?"

"That's what worries me, if you get my meaning, ma'am."

Judy laughs as she stands. "Let's go."

The trio walk down the ridge through the trees toward the valley, Judy and D'Angelo's hands held out slightly to their sides to show they're empty. As they emerge from the trees, the movement catches the attention of the people in the village and the patrol on the ridge. Weapons are pointed at the trio walking slowly down the slope.

"Do you think these blokes know about Britain?" Beechum nervously asks.

"We'll soon find out," Judy says. "But don't worry, Lance Corporal, they'll take out the easiest target first."

"Thank you, ma'am. That's really reassuring, since I'm the poor sod with this big bloody flag."

As they near the trench line, D'Angelo starts calling out in Italian that they come in peace and to liberate Italy, and that they have fought the common Enemy and won. They are nearly to the trench line before someone stands up, followed by two, then three, then four others.

The first one to stand, orders them to stop where they are. Then with the others still training their weapons on the trio, he climbs out of the trench and warily approaches them. He walks up to D'Angelo and studies her for a few moments. He asks her where she learned that odd form of Italian.

The Sergeant takes a bit of offense at being told her Italian is odd. She lectures the man on the Italian colony in England, how they've kept the Italian culture and language alive after the catastrophy which swept the country, and now, after all these years, she and other Italians have come with the British to drive The Enemy out.

The man suspiciously asks her about the large military encampment on the other side of the ridge. D'Angelo explains those are British Royal Marines, and she is one of them. They defeated The Enemy in France and have now come to Italy to do the same.

While this is going on, Judy only has a glimmer of what is being said, but she gets the general drift of the conversation from the gestures and tones of voices. She calls back to her Company HQ. "Ask Commando to get a fly-by of either jets or helicopters or both over this valley. We need a demonstration to show these people we're different from The Enemy," she tells her Executive Officer. "Just make sure the bloody sods don't shoot this place up."

When she finishes, D'Angelo is still working on the man, who still has not given his name.

"Begging your pardon, Captain," Beechum asks, "how is a fly-be going to prove we ain't The Enemy?"

Judy smiles at him. "Did you ever see those guys fly anything?"

"Brilliant, ma'am."

About five minutes later, two fighter jets come roaring down the valley near tree-top level. They are followed by six helicopters flying over the ridge and down to the valley floor. Two of them land behind Judy, their weapons facing away from the village. Judy has a quick conversation over the radio as her XO passes information from Brigade.

The display stops the conversation between D'Angelo and the man.

"Sergeant, ask the gentleman if he has ever known The Enemy to fly planes or helicopters," Judy says.

"No, ma'am, he hasn't," the Sergeant replies after a quick exchange with the man.

"Ask him his name."

"Antonio Guisseppi."

"Right, tell Signori Guisseppi he and any other three people he wants to take can fly to meet the top Marine commander. Beechum and I will stay here to guarantee their safe return."

"Captain?" Beechum sounds worried.

"No fears, Lance Corporal. The only thing we have to worry about is a helicopter crash."

The response prompts Beechum to take a close look at the 'copters. Judy just laughs and shakes her head.

"Captain," D'Angelo says, "he agrees. He'll take two others with him."

"Lovely."

"And, Captain, I should stay here as well. You'll need a translator and there are others who can translate at Brigade."

"Thank you, Sergeant," Judy says.

As Guisseppi goes to get the other two, Judy goes to one of the helicopter pilots to tell her what is going on. "Brigade will be expecting them when you arrive," she assures the pilot. Then she walks away to talk to her HQ to let her XO know its happening.

D'Angelo returns with Guisseppi, another man and a woman. "I told them the helicopter will take them to our top commander and they will be well treated. I also assured them these things are safe. They've never flown, never even seen an aircraft. Just heard about them."

"Very good, Sergeant. Get them aboard." As D'Angelo takes the three to the helicopter to get them seated and strapped in, Judy goes back to the pilot to plead again for a level and easy flight so their passengers won't be too terrified. The pilot and copilot just laugh but agree to take it as easy as they can.

Judy and D'Angelo back away from the helicopters as the two take off and head back over the ridge.

"Well, Sergeant, shall we see if anyone will talk to us?" Judy asks as they turn toward the village. The people who were in the trenches have climbed out and covered them, slinging their weapons. Adults and children are coming out into the open, staring at the newcomers.

"What about me?" Beechum asks.

"Oh, Beechum, just follow us around. Show the colors," Judy says. "And try to look happy," she adds when she sees the sour look on his face.

"Yes, Captain," he says, trying to force a smile. And failing.

The trio is soon surrounded by curious adults and children. Some of the children reach out to touch Judy and her companions. A wife and husband come out to offer them wine, cheese, and bread. Even Beechum begins to relax, especially when he has some wine and fresh bread.

"Don't get carried away," Judy quietly tells him as he gulps down some wine.

"No, ma'am," he replies happily.

D'Angelo relays what she's being told to Judy. The village is one of several along the valley that has managed to survive because for some reason no one understands The Enemy never came across the ridge. As far as they know, the animals they have are the only ones that survived.

Again, they don't know why.

"The same experience my parents had," Judy comments.

In return, D'Angelo, partly on her own and partly translating what Judy says, explains to the villagers who they are, where they come from, and what they are trying to do, not just in Italy but in Europe. That information provokes excitement as the villagers start talking among themselves, hope and relief apparent in their voices.

The sound of a helicopter coming over the ridge disrupts the conversations as everyone turns to watch it.

As it lands, Sarah jumps out and strides over to where everyone is watching.

"Captain," she says to Judy as she comes up.

"Colonel."

"How are things going?"

Judy gives her a quick synopsis as quiet, excited conversations go on among the villagers.

"Thanks," Sarah responds. "The Brigadier is talking to the three you sent to HQ. I decided to come here because he and I are the only two around who can relate to what these people have experienced. Sergeant," she says, turning to D'Angelo, "you are the translator?"

"Yes, Colonel."

"Please translate for me."

"Yes, ma'am."

Sarah then begins relating her history to the villagers. "I came from a situation not unlike this one," she says, nodding to D'Angelo to translate. That one sentence captures everyone's attention. Silence descends on the gathering as parents hush children.

"My husband and I were in America. We had to flee The Enemy who was out to kill us," she says, nodding to D'Angelo to translate. The Sergeant is just staring at her, not having known their history. "Sergeant?" Sarah says, shaking her out of her stunned silence.

"Yes, ma'am," she says and quickly translates.

"My daughter, this Captain, was born there. We found refuge in a valley not unlike this, but eventually we had to flee because The Enemy came for us. We had built a ship and managed to make it to England. We are here to help you. We are here to rebuild our world together. But we need your help as well. We could use any information you have about where The Enemy is."

Sarah goes on to explain what they have found, the starving remnants of Enemy forces, soldiers dying of hunger who are anxious to surrender and escape the captivity they've been held in for so long.

When she is finished, several men and women step forward and, through D'Angelo, start telling her what they know of The Enemy, where the concentrations had been, about the mass of Soldiers marched north, and the disintegration they have seen of the forces left behind.

"Captain," Sarah says, turning to Judy, "you need to relay this information to Brigade."

"Yes, ma'am."

"And may I borrow the Sergeant? I want to tour the village and see what my Engineers can do to help make life better for these people."

"Yes, ma'am. Sergeant," she says looking at D'Angelo.

"Happy to do it, Captain."

"Lovely," Judy says. "Lance Corporal, time for us to go."

"Right off?" Beechum asks, holding a pitcher of wine, the flag propped up against his shoulder.

Judy just looks at him.

"Right away, ma'am," he says, handing the wine back to the man who gave it to him.

As Judy leaves, Sarah and D'Angelo start their tour of the village, with Sarah asking detailed questions about the infrastructure. The village lacks electricity, and Sarah starts thinking about the possibility of putting wind turbines on the ridge to bring power to the village.

CHAPTER 18

With the enthusiastic help of villagers in a string of valleys, Sarah and her Engineers are able to build windmills to bring electricity in. Some of the ancient refrigerators and radios are able to be restarted, and with the arrival of light bulbs, the night is brightened. The electricity isn't dependable yet because the wind isn't constant, but the villagers are just excited to see something they have only heard about.

And the Royal Engineers promise to find a way to build a battery system that can maintain a constant source of power.

The bakery is churning out bread twenty-four hours a day, seven days a week, providing the food that saves thousands of starving former soldiers, who then readily agree to work to rebuild their country.

The Royal Army, along with Divisions formed by surrendering soldiers, is sweeping across Europe. In Italy, Army units meet the forces from Sicily south of Rome. They find a few surviving villages in the mountains. Other units cross the Pyrenees mountains and sweep down Spain and Portugal to the Mediterranean and the Atlantic. There, too, a few surviving settlements are found in the mountains, such as in the Basque region on the coast of northern Spain.

Starvation and death are the most common discoveries across Europe. But here and there, survivors, even some of the former soldiers, have begun farming. Some villages in the mountains still have animals that can be used, such as in and around the Carpathian Mountains in eastern Europe. Some of those people have pushed out into the plains of Hungary and other areas as The Enemy forces receded.

Limited trade and some primitive manufacturing have resumed in some areas. The only danger is from renegade forces that raid villages for food and things such as clothes. The Army and local people work to suppress them. Russians and Ukrainians who have hidden in the Urals make tentative movements, mostly west of the mountains.

The Royal Navy finds a thriving society in Crete and other Greek Islands, and Cyprus. The Greeks are anxious to return to the mainland. With the help of two Royal Marine Commandos and weapons supplied by Britain, they land in Greece, finding conditions there much the same as further north. Food and medical supplies are brought in from Crete.

In Asia, the surviving Chinese are pushing out of the northwest and Indians are coming down the peninsula from the Himalayas. The Australians, New Zealanders and Indonesians are probing the Asian mainland, looking for survivors.

In Africa, survivors are coming out of the jungles, along with the surviving animals, both domestic and wild.

With no real place to hide, the only survivors in the Mideast are the starving soldiers.

"Have we heard anything from the Americas?" Codrington asks Sam as they sit in his office in Florence, sipping the scotch Sam provided after losing their bet.

"Not really," he says. "Just a smattering here and there. Apparently, some communities have survived in the Rocky Mountains and the Amazon. There has been sporadic radio contact with them. All we know for sure is that a group has survived on Long Island just off the coast of what used to be New York. Apparently, we've been doing some trading with them. We provide military hardware and they are providing some kind of technical expertise. There are probably more but we haven't heard anything from anyone else. And then there are the Canadians on the Atlantic islands."

"Think we'll go over there?"

"I don't know. Sarah and I have talked about that. We want to go, but that is above our paygrades. We'll see what the future holds."

"Speaking of the future," Codrington asks, "what's in store for us? Except for Four Two and Forty, we've just been sitting here for three months. When do we get to go home?"

"Yes, well," Sam says slowly, reaching for some papers, "I've been meaning to talk to you about that."

"And?" Codrington asks, his eyebrows raised.

"These came in about an hour ago," Sam replies, pushing the papers across the desk.

The Colonel picks them up, his eyebrows furrowed as he peruses them.

"We are going to Scandinavia by way of Switzerland," Sam says quietly, waiting for a reaction.

"Switzerland?" Codrington asks, looking up.

"Mountain training," Sam says in a dead pan manner.

"Mountain training?" Codrington repeats, incredulously.

"Mountain training," Sam reaffirms.

"The Brigade will love that," exasperation showing in the Colonel's voice.

"I'm not too happy about it either," Sam says with a sigh. "But we'll need the training when we go north to help the Scandinavians clean up the mess up there."

Codrington looks sour as he puts the orders down. "Bloody cold this time of year. And not much daylight."

"Drink up, Tom," Sam says, holding up his glass with scotch in it. "We'll bring this with us to help us warm our insides."

"Brilliant. When do we go?"

"Next month. So it will be even colder and darker," Sam says, with a bit of resignation in his voice, as he drains the rest of his scotch.

"How do you want to break the good news to the Brigade?" Codrington asks.

"What if we brief the officers first," Sam suggests. "Then tell the ranks."

"Sounds good to me," the Colonel responds. "A Commando or Troop at a time?"

"I think a Commando. A Troop at a time is just too many meetings," Sam says as they both laugh.

"Alright you blokes, settle down," McBride tells his Four Two's Marines, who are gathered along the beach facing the city. He is on a one-meter-high speaker's platform equipped with sound equipment that was built for this purpose. The Commando commanders had drawn lots to set the order of the meetings. McBride's got the first slot.

The Marines quiet down, expectations high and rumors about going home running rampant through the ranks.

"Attention!" the Commando staff's Sergeant Major barks, bringing silence as Sam and Codrington stride onto the platform. McBride and the Sergeant Major come to attention and salute.

Sam returns the salute and then steps in front of the microphone.

"Stand easy," he says. "Oh, bloody hell, just take a knee." As the laughter subsides while the Marines all kneel or sit down on the sand, Sam surveys the scene waiting for complete quiet. When he has that, he pulls the microphone off its stand and walks along the platform looking at the men and women in his command, seeing the expectation on their faces—and knowing he is going to disappoint them. He sighs inwardly, then steps back into the middle of the platform.

"You have all heard the rumors about us going home for a well-earned rest," he says, listening to the murmurs of approval sweeping through the people in front of him. "I know I was looking forward to it," he says. "And I have the advantage of seeing my wife occasionally, since her Royal Engineer Regiment is assigned to the Brigade to augment our Engineers. Not that we need it," he hurries on to add, knowing the laughter that would spark.

"Unfortunately, we're not going home." Sam not only hears the grumblings of disappointment but also sees shoulders sag and faces fall. Out of the corner of his eye, he sees McBride step forward, but waves him off.

"We have been given a new assignment before we go home," Sam says forcefully. That focuses the Marines' attention. "We are headed to Scandinavia to help the Norwegians and Swedes liberate their countries." He lets that sink in for a moment.

"But first, we are going to Switzerland where we will train in mountain warfare, courtesy of the Swiss Army. We leave in two weeks for two months' training. You will all be issued cold-weather kit. Take care of it, because where we are going it will be cold. I would like to tell you how long this will be, or that we'll be going home at the end of this mission, but I can't.

"What I can tell you is that the war is going well. The Enemy has fallen apart. The Army is sweeping east with minimal resistance. They are finding conditions pretty much as we found here. Asia and Africa are being reclaimed, not with our forces, but with the help of weapons we are providing. The death and devastation that is being found is catastrophic. Survivors are starving skeletons for the most part. Any pretense of an economy or agriculture is universally absent except in a few cases, like the mountain villages we found here."

Sam pauses for a moment. When he resumes, he speaks slowly and emphatically. "Our job is to make it possible for the survivors to rebuild their lives and their societies. The Royal Engineers, along with some civilians, are already hard at work doing just that. We, the Royal Marines, are the force that clears the way for that to happen. Our sacrifices, the loss of our mates, is in a noble cause. Their sacrifice, our sacrifice, is not in vain."

Sam looks over the members of Four Two Commando. He sees his speech has hit home. The shoulders of most of the Marines square up and they sit up a bit taller.

"Any questions?" Sam asks.

"Sir?" one Marine says, raising his hand.

"Stand when addressing the Brigadier!" the Sergeant Major barks.

"Yes, Sergeant Major," the Marine says standing up.

"Sir …"

"How did you manage to get in the Corps?" Sam asks, unable to stop himself as he stares at the mountain of a man who is well above regulation height. "But more than that, how did they find kit to fit you? What's your name, Lance Corporal?"

"John Trembleton, sir," he responds, somewhat meekly.

"We call him 'Little John'," someone calls out from the crowd as muted laughter ripples through the Troop and then spreads to the rest of the Commando.

"I'm sure you do," Sam says. "And I suppose you have a Robin Hood as well?"

"That's a secret identity," another Marine calls.

"Brilliant," Sam says, smiling. "Whose Troop do you belong to Lance Corporal Trembleton?"

"He's one of mine," Mayran says, standing up.

"Very good, Leftenant," Sam says. "Make sure supply finds cold weather kit for this Marine. And do it quickly."

"Yes, sir," she replies sitting back down, a bit perplexed at not being addressed correctly as Second Lieutenant.

"Excuse me, sir," McBride says quietly, walking up to just behind Sam. "Leftenant Mayran has not been informed of her promotion."

"Really?" Sam says just as quietly. "Thank you, Leftenant Colonel." McBride then steps back as Sam turns his attention back to Trembleton who is still standing. "I apologize for the distraction, Lance Corporal. You had a question?"

"Yes, sir," he says, swallowing hard, provoking light laughter from those around him. "How cold will it get?"

"The highs in November will be right about freezing or below," Sam says. "So, the training the Swiss give us will be vital to our survival."

"Thank you, sir," Trembleton says, sitting back down, anxiety obvious in his voice, while a ripple of negative reaction ripples through the Commando.

"Lance Corporal," Sam says.

"Sir?" he says as he stands back up.

"You are a big target," he says, provoking the laughter he was after to lighten the mood. "So, please, be sure to duck fast if we come under fire."

"Yes, sir," he says, laughing despite himself.

"Any more questions?"

"Sir?" another Marine says as she stands up.

"Yes, Corporal?"

"We won't have much daylight in November, will we?"

"Approximately eight hours, give or take a couple of hours depending on what part of the country we are in and how far into the year we are there."

"Sir, won't that be problem?" she asks.

"We will issue night-vision goggles to all Marines. That should go a long way to solving that problem. Using them will be part of our training in Switzerland."

"Yes, sir," she says, sitting down.

"Sir?" another Marine says, standing up.

"Yes, Private?"

"Sir, we're Marines, not mountain goats," he says, provoking laughter that goes like a wave down the ranks.

"True, Private. But we are Marines. What does our training emphasize?" Sam asks.

"Adapt and overcome, sir."

"Correct. And that is exactly what we will do, adapt and overcome."

"Yes, sir," the disappointed Marine says, sitting down.

Sam surveys the ranks. "If there are no other questions, we have one more order of business to conduct." Sam pauses. "Second Leftenant Mayran, front and center."

"Yes, sir," Mayran says, startled and perplexed, springing to her feet. Medal award ceremonies have already been held, so she has no idea what this is about. She marches out in front of the speaker's stand and comes to attention.

Sam looks down at her for a moment. "Four Two Commando, attention," Sam orders. When everyone is at attention, Sam continues. "Second Leftenant Mayran, you have proven yourself an effective and versatile combat leader. Your Troop has consistently fulfilled its missions with a minimum of casualties. In light of that record, I have the distinct honor of promoting you to Leftenant. Leftenant Colonel McBride, will you do the honors."

"Sir," McBride says. He marches down to stand before Mayran and pins the pips to her uniform and steps back.

"Four Two Commando," Sam says, "salute." Everyone, including Sam, holds the salute until a blushing Mayran returns the salute.

"Four Two Commando," McBride says, "dismissed!"

"Congratulations, Leftenant," he says, shaking her hand.

"Thank you, sir," she replies.

"Leftenant," Sam says, walking up to her, "you've earned this. So be proud. And stay safe."

"Sir," she replies, still taken aback a bit by the public honor.

CHAPTER 19

H ere," Codrington says, handing Sam a steaming mug of tea when he joins him on the bridge level of the HMS Devonshire.

"Thanks," Sam says, taking a sip as the two men watch the French coast slip away. The heavy cruiser is the flagship of the fleet of more than one hundred warships, assault ships, and combat-loaded cargo ships heading for Bergen, Norway. Some of the ships, including those carrying the Brigade, sail from the French port of Brest while the others come from a variety of ports in Britain and Ireland, including two Brigades the Irish Army is contributing to the effort.

"Do you think our guys are ready for this?" Sam asks as he stares out at the sea.

"As ready as intensive training can make them," Codrington says with shake of his head.

"I wish we had more time to train," Sam replies. "This tea is good," he adds after taking another sip.

"The Navy has some advantages," the Colonel observes.

"That they do," Sam agrees.

"As for training, the Swiss did right by us as much as they could," Codrington says.

The Brigade had spent early September into late October training in the Bernese Alps in western Switzerland, learning how to survive in cold weather and operate in mountains. Members of Thirty Commando, as well as some volunteers from other commands, scaled the Finsteraahorn and Jungfrau mountains, both rising above four thousand meters, while the rest of the Brigade settled for climbing lower elevations. They also learned how to cross glaciers safely, and attack and hold mountain passes, practicing in the Gemmi, Lauitor, and Sanetseh passes. A few Marines were injured in climbing accidents or by ignoring advice about avoiding frostbite. But no one died, which Sam considers an accomplishment.

"Hmm, I guess the Swiss did," Sam agrees. "Still, I would feel better about this operation if we had more time to train."

"Look at it this way," Codrington replies, "if we had waited any longer, we'd be even deeper into winter. November is bad enough."

"Always the optimist, Tom, always the optimist."

"It's a fault I learned from you," he replies grinning.

Sam gives him a sour look. "Let's go make sure everyone is where they're supposed to be," he says as he leads the way into the fleet commander's operations center, which is filled with Navy officers and enlisted ratings manning the electronic equipment for communications and radar, along with a computerized plotting table showing the positions of all the ships in the fleet as well as other ships within scanning distance of the electronic warfare plane circling overhead. There is barely enough room for the Marine officers to crowd into the remaining space.

"Brigadier," the duty Navy officer says, "the Admiral will join shortly."

"Thank you, Commander," Sam replies. Then, looking around the room, he tells his gathered Commando leaders and top intelligence officer, "Ladies and gentlemen, thank you for joining us."

"Sir," comes the chorus of replies.

"Have our Irish allies arrived?" Sam asks, referring to the Brigadier Generals in command of the two Irish regiment-sized Brigades.

"Their helicopter just touched down," the duty officer says.

"Thank you," Sam answers.

"Sir," Lieutenant Colonel Lee of Four Six asks, his voice tentative, "what do we know about these Irish Brigades? Can they be trusted?"

Sam gives Lee a withering look. "We'll have no more of that," his voice stern and uncompromising. "It is true these Irish soldiers have not been tested in battle, but Leftenant Colonel de Castellane has inspected their training and readiness and assures me they are up to Royal Army standards." That evaluation is greeted with groans and dismissive snickers, drawing a withering look from Sam.

"That's right, sir," the newly promoted De Castellane says. "Each Brigade is about the size of one of our Army regiments."

"Alright, you lot," Codrington says in mild rebuke, "we need these Irish formations to extend the line. They are good soldiers, so show them respect and make sure everyone in your Commandos treats them well."

"Yes, sir," comes the chorus of replies, although some of the voices show reluctance to agree with the order.

"I am serious about this," Codrington says, looking around the room as the officers look sheepishly away.

Just as he finishes speaking, the hatch to the Combat Command Center opens and two Irish officers are ushered in by a Navy Lieutenant, along with their entourage.

"Brigadier Hope," the Lieutenant says in a formal voice, "I have the honor to present Brigadier General Sean Leary and Brigadier General Ian Gerard of the Army of the Irish Republic."

"Thank you, Leftenant," Sam says formally as well.

"Sir," the Lieutenant says, turning and leaving.

"Gentlemen," Sam says, holding his hand out to shake the others, "welcome. We look forward to working together to liberate Scandinavia."

"As do we," Leary says, shaking Sam's hand.

"It's an honor to meet someone of your reputation," Gerard says as he shakes Sam's hand.

"Ah, yes, well, thank you," Sam stammers out. "May I present my Chief of Staff, Colonel Tom Codrington." The three men exchange greetings as they shake hands.

"This is Leftenant Colonel de Castellane, our chief intelligence officer, whom I believe you have already met," Sam says. The comment is greeted with acknowledgement. He then introduces the other Marine officers. The Irish Brigadier Generals introduce their chiefs of staff and the aides who have accompanied them.

"Admiral on deck!" a Navy officer announces as Sir Harold Nicholson enters the Center where all the officers and ratings not working come to attention.

"As you were," the Admiral says. "Brigadier," he says to Sam, "Good to see you again."

"As it is for me to see you, sir," Sam replies, shaking the proffered hand. "May I present Brigadier Generals Sean Leary and Ian Gerard of the Army of the Irish Republic."

The Admiral exchanges cool greetings with the two Irish officers. "Now, Brigadier," Nicholson says, turning back to Sam, "you may precede with the briefing."

"Sir," Sam says. Then turning to De Castellane, he orders, "You may commence the briefing, Leftenant Colonel."

"Yes, sir," De Castellane says. He pulls down a clear screen from the overhead and turns it on, showing a display of the Scandinavian peninsula. "Ladies and gentlemen," he says, picking up a laser pointer, "our Norwegian and Swedish allies are about here." He then hits a button which displays a line stretching from Trodheim on Norway's west coast to Sundsvall on Sweden's east coast.

"We have been landing military hardware, kit, food, medicine and fuel at Sandessjean," he says, indicating a port in northern Norway, "and here at Ornskoldsvik," indicating another in northern Sweden. "By the way, the Swedes and Norwegians have been paying us in such raw materials as iron ore and phosphate, and rare earth metals as well as quantities of fish and lumber." He looks around the room to make sure what he has said sinks in. He doesn't want anyone to think these two countries are receiving handouts.

"Continue," Sam says quietly.

"Yes, sir," De Castellane says. "The Norwegians and Swedes have cleared everything to the Finnish border and have made contact with surviving Finns. No effort has been made to push south from there because then we are getting into Russia. That must await the arrival of the Army from the west. The Scandinavians met no opposition as they headed north, outside of a few stragglers who readily surrendered. The poor blokes were starving and in danger of freezing to death. It seems they had deserted their units in the southern part of the countries."

"And our part of this operation?" Codrington prompts De Castellane.

"Ah, that, yes, sir," he says, realizing he has gotten off track. "We will be landing at Bergen, here," he says, pointing to the port of the southern coast of Norway, "under the guns of the Royal Navy. The Norwegians have informed us the area is clear of civilians and the Navy and Air Force are free to use their ordinance."

"That doesn't mean," Sam interrupts, "that we are to go in firing indiscriminately. As we found in France and Italy, we can expect any number of Enemy soldiers to surrender. Those who don't," he says pausing for effect, "will be dealt with swiftly. No unnecessary casualties. Clear?"

"Sir," comes the chorus of replies.

"Brigadier," the Admiral says, "will you be wanting a preliminary bombardment?"

"Sir, we are sending in members of our recon Commando. It will depend on what they find. From what Leftenant Colonel de Castellane has been told by our Norwegian friends, they understand our need to avoid casualties but they would appreciate it if we could keep destruction to a minimum. Bearing that in mind, our recon Marines will make an assessment."

"I see," Nicholson replies, nodding his head. "We will be prepared for either eventuality," he says, glancing at an aide scribbling notes.

"Thank you, sir," Sam says, then nods to De Castellane to continue.

"Right," the Lieutenant Colonel says, calling up a detailed map of the Bergan area. "The Marine Brigade will land first and establish a perimeter, sealing off the peninsula. The Irish Brigades will then land, followed by supply."

"Why are we landing after the Marines?" Leary asks.

"Because, Brigadier General," Sam says, "the Marines are battle tested against this Enemy and we have done this before, so we judge the safest and swiftest way is for us to land first. We mean no disrespect and, in fact, value your participation. You make this effort possible."

"I see," he says nodding. "Please continue," he tells De Castellane.

"Yes, sir," he says. "The main landings will start after Thirty Commando gives the word. If they run into opposition, they will withdraw and a naval bombardment will commence. If no opposition, they will hold in place and the Brigade will commence landing. Forty and Four Two land first and will establish a perimeter on either side of the city while Thirty Commando pushes farther out.

"As Four Five and Four Six land, the perimeter will expand, sweeping through the city and countryside until a line is established across the neck of the peninsula. The Brigade will then dig in until a general advance starts. The line will protect the buildup of armory, artillery, supplies and the Irish Brigades. Any questions?" De Castellane looks around.

The Marine officers have already been briefed, so they have no questions. De Castellane had briefed the Irish officers before they sailed so they also just nod in acknowledgement.

"Right," De Castellane says. "Once the general advance starts, Forty and Four Six, along with the One Irish Brigade, will advance to the north, under the command of Brigadier General Leary, while Four Two and Four Five with Two Irish Brigade, under the command of Brigadier Hope, will wheel to the south. The northern force's objective is to link up with the Norwegians and Swedes coming down from the north. Oslo is the southern force's objective. Any questions?"

"What about our flanks?" asks Leary.

"Thirty Commando will not only be screening the advance but also the flanks," Sam says, jumping in. "Griffith," he says, nodding toward Lieutenant Colonel Jack Griffith, "and his blokes will ensure that our flanks are well protected, and if there is any threat, you will have plentiful warning."

"Yes, sir, we will," Griffith says. "My guys are experienced and thorough, Brigadier General," he tells Leary. "In addition, we will have liaison officers with both your Brigades to ensure timely communications."

"Very good," Leary says, satisfied with the answer.

"The order of battle for the northern force," De Castellane says, "will be Forty, One Irish Brigade, then Four Six; the Southern Force will be Forty, Two Brigade, and Four Two."

"You don't trust us to cover the flanks?" Gerard challenges.

"Quite the contrary, General," Sam says, jumping in again, "your Brigades are in the vital center. If they don't hold the line, the whole force faces disaster." Sam gives Codrington a knowing look as he finishes, receiving a nearly imperceptible nod in response, the real reason being the inexperience of the Irish.

Gerard grumbles something under his breath but lets it go.

"Yes, right," De Castellane says. "Once the northern force has linked up with the Scandinavians, it will turn south. With the combined forces of all four national forces, an offensive will be launched from Oslo aimed at mopping up everything from there north to secure our rear from any attack. After that, the peninsula to the south will be cleared. That is where the bulk of Enemy forces are concentrated." Finishing he looks at Sam, "Sir?"

"Thank you, Leftenant Colonel," he says. "After we have cleared the peninsula, our orders are, shall we say, nebulous. The Norwegians and Swedes do not intend to continue the offensive in other countries, with the possible exception of Finland. As for the Irish Brigades," he says, looking at the two generals, "their government has not decided whether they will continue with us or head home."

"It is a political question, as I understand it," Leary says.

"Quite right," Sam agrees. "We will let the politicians hash it out. As for now, we all have jobs to do. Sir Harold," he says, turning to the Admiral, "do you have anything for us?"

"No, I think not. I would just say the Royal Navy will do its part. We will have ships off the east coast ready to provide gunnery support and land supplies when the ground forces have secured the requisite ports."

"Thank you, sir," Sam says. "Then if that is all?" He looks around the room and finds no one who wants to prolong the meeting. "Right. We all have our blokes to get organized and only a few days to make sure the ranks know their jobs." As he finishes, the Admiral, followed by his staff and the Marines, head out of the Center.

"A moment, if you please," Leary tells Sam as he and Gerard come up to him. Gerard indicates to their staffs to leave, so Sam does the same with his.

"Yes, Brigadier General?" Sam says, curious about what is going on.

"Do we have some place private we can talk?" Leary asks.

Sam looks around at the crowded ship's Command Center, realizing a private conversation would be impossible there. "Yes, I think I can find a place." He leads the two Irish Brigadier Generals out of the Center, down to the main deck to the fantail.

"I think, sirs," Sam says turning around, "we can have a private conversation here without fear of being overheard."

The two Irish officers, huddling in their great coats against the cold wind, look around and then at each other as they steady themselves against the roll the ship. The Devonshire is in the middle of the convoy plowing through four-meter seas moving north into a 26 kilometer per hour wind.

"At the stern?" Gerard asks, skeptical.

"Actually, yes," Sam responds, smiling. "The two most private places on a ship are the bow and the fantail. No one goes either place if not in need. And at the bow, everyone on the bridge would see us. In addition, we would have to contend with the spray. And here, the wind will blow away our words. Let's just look out at the ocean. People will think we have just come to admire the view."

"I see," Gerard says, satisfied but skeptical about the excuse given the cold.

"Well, gentlemen," Sam says, watching the sun sinking below the horizon, "what may I do for you?"

"Sir," Leary says, "we just wanted to let you know that you are the primary reason our government agreed to us joining forces."

"Pardon me?" Sam exclaims, not sure where this is going. "I am not THAT good."

"It has more to do with you being an American," Gerard says. "Or shall I say, from America."

"Although your outstanding combat record also played heavily into the decision," Leary adds quickly.

"You do realize," Sam says, somewhat defensively, "I am a British subject and have been a member of the Royal Marines for nearly twenty-seven years."

"Be that as it may," Leary says, "you are not a member of the English aristocracy. Those people always look down on the Irish as if we are lesser human beings."

"And the intelligence we have on you," Gerard adds, "is that you will treat us and our Irish Brigades as equals."

Sam just nods, thinking back to his first command of a Troop and the aristocratic commanding officer who abandoned him and his Marines when they were in heavy combat in France. His Marines were evacuated only because his Color Sergeant defied orders, while he was left for dead. He spent the next month in France before he was able to make it back to England. A Royal Navy patrol boat found him, along with two Enemy deserters, floating on a barn door in the Channel.

"Well, gentlemen," he finally says, "all I can tell you is that all Marines care about is that the Soldiers they are fighting with can do the job. From what Leftenant Colonel de Castellane tells me, your lot will do just fine."

"Thank you, Brigadier," Leary says.

Sam just nods.

"Well, that having been cleared up," Gerard says, "I suppose we should return to our commands and warmer quarters."

"Yes, indeed," Sam replies as the three head toward the cruiser's helipad.

⟫⎯⎯⟩⎯⎯⟨O⟩⎯⎯⟨⎯⎯⟪

"Brigadier," Codrington says in an unusually formal way when the two are alone. Sam has just entered his quarters on the cruiser to find his Chief of Staff waiting for him.

"Colonel," Sam replies equally formally but with a raised eyebrow, wondering what is going on.

"Major Benedict Whitestone would like a word with you."

"He would, would he," Sam says, skepticism in his voice about where this is going. "And what is this about?"

"Sir, I would prefer he tell you in his own words," comes the stiffly formal reply, telling Sam this is not going to make him happy.

Sam nods, thinking a moment. "Alright, Colonel, have him come in. And please be present during the interview."

"Sir," Codrington says, moving toward the door as Sam goes to his desk in the tiny rectangular cabin, sitting down facing the bulkhead with various maps on it, his mind working overtime about what is about to happen. Codrington shuts the door as he leaves.

He doesn't have to wait long.

"Enter," he calls in response to the knock on the door, swiveling in his desk chair to face the cabin door.

Whitestone, dressed in a newly pressed uniform, cap under his left arm, marches in and comes to attention. Codrington walks in behind him, his face a mask.

Sam glances at the Colonel but reads nothing from his expression.

"Stand easy," Sam tells the Major, whose gaze is fixed on the bulkhead above Sam's head. Not a good sign, Sam thinks.

"Sir," Whitestone says, moving his feet apart and putting his hands behind his back, his gaze still fixed on the bulkhead.

"Well, Major, what is it?" Sam says, a bit annoyed by the theatrics.

"Sir," Whitestone says formally, "I and other officers have a concern about going into battle with the Irish Army."

172

Sam looks at him for a long moment before speaking. "And what, may I ask, is that concern?"

"Sir," Whitestone says, staying formal, "we can't trust the Irish to hold the line or to maintain any kind of discipline."

Sam glances at Codrington who just returns the look, his expression blank, his head cocked a bit. "I see," Sam says. "What makes you think that?"

"Sir," the Major says, drawing himself up straighter, "the Irish are scum. Always have been. Always will be. They have no honor. Sir."

Sam almost leaps from his chair, standing a few centimeters from the nose of the slightly taller man, his hands clasped behind his back as he fights to control his anger. "Major, you will be transferred back to Britain, assuming duties in supply."

"Sir!" Whitestone says, horrified, "I am just looking out for the welfare of the Brigade. With all due respect, sir, given your history, you don't know the Irish like we do."

"We?" Sam says, keeping his temper in check, but his words come out biting and hard. "Who is we?"

"We," Whitestone stammers out, his eyes fixed on the bulkhead, "the English who have a long history of dealing with the Irish and their perfidy. Their word can't be trusted."

"Major," Sam says, spitting the words out, "I will not have anyone in this command who will undermine this operation. You obviously cannot work with the Irish Army, your prejudice is too deep. Perhaps I am not 'we.' What I am is the Brigadier and I expect all of my officers to do their duty. You will be transferred tonight. *Dismissed.*" Sam emphasizes the last word.

Whitestone, a look of horror on his face, comes to attention, does a formal aboutface and marches out of the cabin, Codrington stepping out of his way.

"I doubt he expected that," Codrington says, a small smile across his face as he watches Sam regain his composure.

"No, I suppose not," Sam agrees, forcing himself to calm down, his shoulders visibly relaxing as is his face, as he leans against the cabinet that holds his clothes. "Tom, get him off this ship tonight. In fact, get him back to Blighty tonight."

"My pleasure," Codrington says.

"And, Tom," Sam says, "better find a new exec for Four Two."

"Already have one in mind," he replies.

Sam looks at him thoughtfully. "You knew this would happen." It's a statement not a question.

"I suspected as much," he says, turning to leave.

"A moment, Tom," Sam says, prompting the Colonel to turn back into the cabin. "How widespread do you think this attitude is?"

Codrington thinks for moment, looking down at the deck, frowning. "I can't say for sure, but I would suspect a few other officers at least have the same feelings. Maybe," he pauses for a moment looking up at the overhead, "ten percent or so. I can't say for sure. What I can say is that most of them have the same attitude toward the Irish as they do the Royal Army."

"That I would expect," Sam says. "They will get over that as soon as they have experience with the Irish just as they do when they fight alongside our own Army. It's amazing how shared combat experience dispels prejudice."

"All painfully true," Codrington says. "A little nudge in the right direction wouldn't hurt." Flashing a smile, Tom turns and leaves.

Sam shakes his head as he watches his Chief of Staff and friend leave, then sits down at his desk. Opening his laptop, he thinks for a moment before writing an order to all his officers. He knows word of Whitestone's abrupt transfer will run swiftly through the Brigade.

"We are about to enter combat alongside the Republic of Ireland Army. I have full confidence in their combat readiness and their will to fight our common Enemy. I expect all my officers to have that same willingness to serve alongside our Irish brothers and sisters, and to cooperate with them fully and cheerfully.

"Any officer who has reservations about serving alongside the Republic of Ireland Army is directed to apply for a transfer forthwith with the Chief of Staff. Said transfer will be granted immediately. After the combined forces have landed, any officer who shows reservations about serving alongside the Irish Army will face disciplinary action. Signed, Brigadier Samuel Hope, Officer Commanding."

Sam sits back in his chair, looks at the order for a moment, then sends it.

He doesn't expect anyone to follow in Whitestone's footsteps.

They don't.

CHAPTER 20

"Gentlemen, thank you for joining me," Sam says as an aide leads the two Irish Brigadier Generals to the port side railing where Sam is watching the shore.

"Thank you for inviting us," Leary replies as he and Gerard shake hands with Sam.

"Yes, I thought it important that you have real-time intelligence before your Brigades go in," Sam says.

"That's kind of you," Gerard replies as the aide hands each of them a pair of powerful naval binoculars, causing both Brigadier Generals to look quizzically at Sam since it was just after zero seven hundred, more than an hour before the October sunrise this far north. It was too dark to see the Norwegian coast with the fleet more than five kilometers away.

"The binoculars will be of use presently," Sam says, smiling. "Would you like some tea?"

"That would be lovely," Gerard says.

Sam just looks at an orderly who nods and heads off. "Right now," he says, "if it is alright with you, I suggest we stay out of the operations center. It's a bit crowded in there. We will go in presently when things get interesting."

"And now?" Leary asks.

"And now," Sam says as a mess attendant hands the three commanders mugs of steaming tea, "we allow Colonel Codrington the room to handle the initial phase of this invasion. Right now, Leftentant Colonel Griffith is leading Thirty Commando ashore. Two Companies will land at the Bergen port while the other two will land on either side of the city."

"Isn't that chancy?" Gerard asks, shuffling down a bit in his overcoat as the breeze picks up. The sea is calm with waves of less than a third of a meter.

175

"Not as chancy as you might think," Sam replies matter-of-factly. "We did a sweep with heat sensors that picked nothing up along the shore. In addition, they are going ashore in black boats equipped with electric motors that are nearly silent."

"Still," Leary says, doubt in his voice.

Sam's smile is almost invisible in the dark. "Jack's blokes are the best. They have done this kind of operation countless times. They are excellent at concealment and stealth. They won't be seen unless they want to be. And," he says, almost with a bit of a laugh, "should they get into a tight spot, we have the guns of the Royal Navy to help. And when it is light enough, our helicopter gunships."

"I take it," Gerard says, "they will be providing intelligence before the main landing."

"Exactly," Sam says. "How the main body goes in will be determined by what they find. Gentlemen, I know the Royal Marines have a reputation for aggressiveness, which is well earned, but that doesn't mean we are fools. We like to know what we are getting into before we jump."

"Sir," Gerard says, "I meant no disrespect."

"And none is taken," Sam replies quickly. "I suppose I am a bit sensitive about our reputation. Some in the Royal Army seem to think we just go charging heedlessly in."

"The aristocrats, no doubt," Leary says, a bit of bitterness in his voice.

"No doubt," Sam says lightly. "What concerns me is the intelligence from the Norwegians that our opponents have resorted to cannibalism."

"Excuse me!" Leary exclaims, nearly spitting out the sip of tea he had just taken, at this revelation.

"That's the word," Sam replies grimly. "According to the Norwegians, The Enemy has apparently taken to eating their own people. The assumption is that they have exhausted their food supplies. The Norwegians and Swedes also believe that they have turned on each other in warring factions, hunting as it were each other."

"Good God!" Leary says ashen faced.

"You know," Gerard opines, speaking matter of factly, "that should make our job that much easier."

"Indeed," Sam says. "What concerns me is how our blokes are going to react. What the impact will be on them. The trauma of combat is bad enough. But this? I just don't know."

The trio fall silent, not looking at each other as they contemplate what they are sending their Marines and Soldiers in to face.

"Listen," Sam says after a few moments, "as crowded as it is in there, I suppose we should get out of the cold. We just have to stay out of the way."

"Thank you," a relieved Gerard says as the three head toward the hatch into the operations center, handing their now empty mugs to an orderly.

Inside, they find a room crowded with Navy officers controlling the movement of ships as the fleet gets into final positions for the attack. Codrington along with a few staff officers are at a charting table to track Thirty Commando's progress.

"Sir," Codrington says to Sam as the trio walk up, "Griffith is landing at the wharf just about now with A and D Companies. C Company landed five minutes ago north of the city with no opposition and no contact as yet. B Company is about fifteen minutes from the shore south of the city."

"Thank you, Colonel," Sam says formally as he looks at the plotting table showing the respective positions of each company.

"Big Bear, this is Spy Bear," Griffith's voice comes clearly over the headsets that have been handed to the three commanding officers.

"Go ahead, Spy Bear," Codrington responds.

"No opposition. No contact."

"Proceed," the Colonel says. "Out."

⊱────⊰◦⊱────⊰

"Right," Griffith says quietly as he hands the ship-to-shore receiver to his radio operator. He nods to A Company commander, Captain Edward Scanlon, while keying his Commando circuit to let Captain George McHenry know to proceed. Using nightvision glasses, the Marines cautiously fan out, checking the buildings for any sign of movement.

They find none.

"C Bear," Griffith says quietly over the radio, "report."

"All quiet," Captain Scott Bernfall replies. "Moving inland."

"Right," Griffith says. "B Bear, report."

"Just coming ashore," Captain JoAnna Promonte says. "No opposition."

"Right," Griffith says as he follows A Company into town. The Marines in town have cleared the buildings about two hundred meters from the wharf when gunfire breaks out, prompting the Marines outside to freeze. Those inside buildings cautiously move to windows and doorways with a view of the street.

The Marines quickly relax as two things become apparent: The gunfire is more than a kilometer away and it is not moving toward them.

"What the bloody hell?" one of the Marine says, standing up.

"Mind your manners, Bernie. Sound discipline," Color Sergeant Mac Franklin of One Troop says in a low voice.

"Yes, Colors," the Private says, kneeling back down.

"He does have a point," Lieutenant Bev Whitehouse, the One Troop commander, says quietly to Franklin.

"Just don't let him know that," Franklin says, humor in his voice.

"Right, Colors," she replies, smiling in turn.

"Whitehouse," Griffith says, coming up to the pair. "Send out a patrol. We need to find out what's going on."

"Yes, sir," she says.

"And Leftenant," he adds, his voice low but emphatic, "neither you nor your Colors are to lead it. We need to finish clearing enough of this place so the Brigade can land."

"Yes, sir," she replies, disappointment in her voice.

"I have to call this in," Griffith says, heading inside a cleared building so his voice won't be heard. Whitehouse sends a Sergeant leading a six-member patrol, then gets her Troop clearing buildings again, as Griffith tells Scanlon, the Company's commander, what is going on.

"Spy Bear to Big Bear," Griffith says.

"Go," Codrington replies.

"We have small arms fire about a kilometer off. Unclear who is fighting who. Patrol is out," he says.

"Right," comes the reply. "Keep us posted."

"Will do," Griffith says. He walks back outside again, listening to the small arms fire which has become sporadic, punctuated at times in heavy bursts. It seems to be moving to his right. "What the bloody hell is going on?" he asks himself in an undertone.

"Sir," a Lance Corporal says quietly as he comes up to Griffith, "Captain Scanlan says you need to see this."

"See what?" Griffith says, his attention torn away from the battle that has flared up again.

"I can't describe it, sir," the Lance Corporal says, disgust in his voice. "Piles of bones. People. It looks like they've been cooked."

"What?" Griffith says, incredulous. "Lead the way," he says, motioning to be shown where this is. The Marine leads her commander down the block and into the courtyard of what used to be a five-story apartment building, now in disrepair with the roof collapsed and windows gone. Despite the growing light of dawn, the courtyard is still in deep darkness. A group of Marines is standing around shining flashlights onto the ground.

"Do you think torches are a good idea?" Griffith asks Scanlan as he comes up.

"The building has been cleared," he replies. "We found these when one of my guys tripped over them," he says, motioning toward the pile of human bones, skulls included, piled on the ground around what looks like the remains of a fire. Some of the bones are charred. All look gnawed on.

"If I didn't know better," Scanlan says matter-of-factly, "I would say they are eating each other."

"Cannibalism?" Griffith says, disbelief mixed with disgust in his voice.

"Begging your pardon, sir," Two Troop's Color Sergeant, Henry Fielding, says, "but it makes sense, in a way."

"Go on, Colors," Griffith says.

"Sir, we saw they were starving in France and Italy 'cause they were out of food. And we saw discipline was breaking down. Broken, if truth be told. So, I guess here they decided that if they were to have a meal it would be each other. At least, that's how it seems to me. Sir."

Griffith looks at Fielding a moment. Then back at the pile of bones. "Colors, I would have to say that you have in all probability hit on the truth."

"Yes, sir."

"Leave this, this site, as is," Griffith manages to choke out. "I'll call this in. We'll let Brigade handle it."

"Sounds good to me," Scanlan says.

Griffith walks off, shaking his head. He is far enough away from his advancing Marines to feel safe going on the radio outside. He is about to call Brigade when another call interrupts him.

"B Bear to Spy Bear," Promante says.

"Report," Griffith says.

"We're nearly two kilometers in and have discovered a large encampment. Discipline seems to be holding."

Promante stops talking. Griffith has picked up the stress in her voice.

"Go ahead," he says.

"Sir, they are eating people. There is a stockade filled with people. We saw." Griffith can hear her swallowing. "We saw them butchering people like you would a sheep or a pig. We saw them roasting the meat." Disgust and revulsion are in her voice.

"Take it easy, Captain," he says. "We have found evidence of cannibalism here. Can you tell if they are eating each other or civilians?"

"The people in the stockade are in uniforms," she says.

"Right," he replies, pausing a moment to think. "How far are you from the camp?"

"We pulled back half a klick."

"Good. Hold position. Send two patrols around each side the camp. Give it a wide berth," he orders, the idea being to determine the size of the camp and gather any other intelligence they can.

"Understood."

Griffith takes a deep breath, trying to get his mind around what they have found. He looks in the direction of where the small arms fire had been coming from, deciding it must be two groups battling to see who gets to eat. He motions to his radio operator.

"Spy Bear to Big Bear."

"Go ahead," Codrington says.

"Sir," Griffith says, his mind still reeling, "they are eating each other."

"Say again?" comes the incredulous reply.

"The Enemy Soldiers seem to have broken into groups and are eating each other. I assume they have no other source of food." He goes on to relay the details of what they have discovered.

"Standby," Codrington says. The radio goes silent for a few moments.

"Big Bear to Spy Bear." This time it's Sam's voice that comes over the radio.

"Sir," a still stunned Griffith replies.

"Advance with caution. Meet any resistance with deadly force. Stop any cannibalism you discover."

"Yes, sir," he says, pulling himself together. "Landing can commence at your convenience, sir. We are three klicks into the city. C Company is six klicks in with no opposition. B Company is two klicks in and could use reinforcement to attack the camp."

"Right. The Brigade is on the way," Sam says. "We will divert Four Two to back up your B Company."

"Thank you, sir."

"And, Jack, good job. Pass that on to your Marines."

"Yes, sir. Thank you, sir," Griffith hands the hand set back to the operator. He starts to walk out of the courtyard when an angry voice breaks the quiet.

"Holy bloody fucking shit hell!" a Marine yells as he tumbles out of a doorway with an Enemy Soldier not just wrapped around him but biting him, her teeth dug deeply into his neck. "Get this shit off me!" he calls.

Another Marine runs up and fires a rifle round into the Soldier's head, knocking her off as it kills her, spraying blood onto both Marines.

"What a bloody mess!" yells the Marine who was attacked, rolling to his feet as he kicks the corpse away.

"You're welcome," the other Marine says, grinning.

"Bloody hell," the first one says, pulling out a handkerchief to wipe his face. "My ears are still ringing," he complains.

"Next time, I'll let you become dinner," the other says, still grinning, drawing a sour look in response.

Griffith gets on the Thirty Commando net to his Company commanders. "No one is to enter a building alone. Two Marines will be together at all times inside or out. That is an order that will be strictly enforced. We just had a Marine attacked by an Enemy Soldier who was chewing on his neck. We have found evidence of cannibalism. Pass the word to all your guys. Take no chances."

Griffith signs off, shaken by what they have discovered.

Lieutenant Colonel Michelle Staffero is in the first landing craft to beach south of Bergen. She was moved from being commander of Forty to Four Two after McBride was seriously injured during training in Switzerland when the helicopter he was in went down. Her experienced XO took over command of Forty. As for the landing site, 'beach' is a bit of misnomer for the rocky shore leading straight into a forest. As she follows a few Marines onto the shore, she is greeted by Lieutenant Marty Fairfield, CO of Thirty's Five Troop.

"Leftenant Colonel Staffero?" he asks as she climbs up the steep incline into the forest.

"Yes," she replies.

"Captain Promante has asked me to lead you to her command post."

"Right. Give us a minute to sort things out here," she responds as she looks around. "Major Hope," she calls to her new Executive Officer as Judy disembarks from another landing craft.

"Ma'am," comes the brisk reply.

"I'm going to find out what's going on. You get things sorted here."

"Ma'am," Judy replies, then turns her attention to dealing with the looming chaos. Four Two had been scheduled to land on the quay in Bergen, but with the discovery of the large camp—no one knows yet exactly how large—the Commando has been diverted to this rocky shore. And that means no armor support or heavy artillery. No vehicles. Just mortars and heavy machine guns. And everything has to be humped in.

Once the Marines and their portable supplies are landed, the vehicles and artillery will be taken to the port to offload there.

No one in Four Two is happy with the situation. Especially the lower ranks who will have to carry everything first up the incline and then through the forest.

"Crack on," Staffero tells her guide.

Fairfield leads the Lieutenant Colonel in about a kilometer through the forest to where Promante has set up her HQ. Staffero finds the B Company CO talking quietly on her company net to the patrols she sent out and to the observation posts set up to watch The Enemy camp.

"Captain Promante, good to see you again," Staffero says. "What is the situation?"

"Leftenant Colonel," she says, turning around. "Leftenant Colonel Griffith has ordered me to place my company under your command until released."

"Very well. What about The Enemy?" she says, somewhat impatiently.

"There is a large encampment here, about a klick off," she says, kneeling down as she points to a place on the map laid on the ground. "The camp is about half a klick by a klick wide set up among the trees. We estimate about one thousand Enemy. No vehicles. We didn't see any evidence of heavy machine guns but that doesn't mean there aren't any. No fences or fortifications except for a stockade near the south end," she says, indicating the spot. "We believe the prisoners are being used for food. We have seen prisoners slaughtered like livestock, butchered, and cooked. The prisoners are wearing the same uniforms as the captors." Promante swallows hard and then goes on. "We have seen Sergeants patrolling the perimeter and enforcing discipline but not to the extent we saw in France. Perimeter defense is basically nonexistent."

"Discipline has weakened," Staffero comments.

"Yes, ma'am, it appears so," Promante responds.

"Interesting," Staffero responds, her mind exploring the possibilities that presents. "Where are you?"

"Six and Eight Troops are stretched across this line," Promante says tracing her finger across a line about a quarter of a kilometer this side of the camp. "OPs are close to the camp. Five and Seven are along the sides and behind the camp keeping watch. They don't know we are here. In fact, six Soldiers marched a group of fifteen prisoners right by one of the patrols, and by right by, I mean within a meter without noticing them."

"Brilliant," Staffero says, straightening up from looking at the map. "You and your Company have done an excellent job."

"Thank you, ma'am," the Captain says, standing up.

"Keep your people in place until we are ready to strike."

"Yes, ma'am. We'll keep a close watch," Promante says.

"I'm sure you will," Staffero says. "It will be several hours before we can get Four Two in position. We will attack through your lines, but I will want your people close to the camp to pull back just before we do, especially those on the other side. I want no friendly fire casualties."

"Understood," Promante replies.

"I would like two of your Troops to deploy on our flanks."

"Yes, ma'am. Should I deploy the rest of the Company there as well?"

"Excellent, but just after the attack begins."

"Ma'am," Promante says as Staffero turns away and heads back to the beach.

When Staffero gets back to the landing area, she finds most of the supplies have been landed and organized by working parties of Marines who have stripped off their combat kit and weapons. Many have taken off their coats as the work has made them hot.

"Major, how goes it?" she asks Judy.

"Brilliantly, ma'am. We should be finished unloading in about thirty. We can start moving inland immediately if you wish."

"I wish," Staffero responds. "I'll have two Companies start inland. Have all the Company COs report to me. Are the mortar and heavy machine guns ready to move?"

"Yes, ma'am," Judy answers. "They are gathered over there," she says, indicating a group of Marines in the woods, some sitting on ammunition boxes.

"Right," Staffero says. "Have the heavy weapons CO report to me as well."

"Yes, ma'am," comes the reply.

"And Hope, as soon as you have the rest of this mob moving inland, report to me so I can update you on the situation."

"Yes, ma'am," she says as she turns back to making sure everything is running smoothly.

Judy has mixed feelings about her promotion, which came without warning three days ago when Whitestone was sacked for not wanting to serve with the Irish. Judy wasn't given a choice about becoming Four Two's Executive Officer on the eve of battle. Staffero just called her in and told her. The Chief of Staff was there and handed her the Major's insignia. On the one hand, Judy is happy her career is moving forward, but on the other hand, she misses running her company and being in the fight with her Marines.

Most of her duties now involve paperwork. Lots of paperwork. She can do the paperwork. She just doesn't like doing it. She finds it boring and frustrating at the same time. She never realized how many forms and reports a Commando had to file and keep track of. Her head is still spinning at all the various forms for everything from weapons and ammunition to pens and paperclips, from food and uniforms to shoelaces and buttons. But that's the job. And she worries about her Company, now under the command of Brevet Captain Clifford. He is a good, sound officer and tactician, careful with the lives of the people under his command, and respected by other officers and the ranks, despite, or maybe because of, his off-beat sense of humor. She trusts him but can't help but worry.

As the last of the supplies are organized at the edge of the forest, Judy has the two Company commanders organize their Marines to carry them through the forest. As the Troops start moving forward, quietly voiced complaints run up and down the columns, their Sergeants and Corporals hushing them.

Satisfied the Company COs have everything in hand, Judy sets off to find Staffero. She finds her commanding officer talking to the commander of Thirty's B Company.

"Ma'am," Judy says as she comes up to them.

"Ah, Major, there you are. You know Captain Promante?"

"Yes, ma'am," she says. "Nice to see you again, JoAnna."

"It's been too long, Judy," she responds.

"Alright, now that the greetings are over," Staffero says, "please summarize what you have told me for the Major's benefit."

"Yes, ma'am," Promante says. She then explains about the camp and the dispositions of her Company.

"Brilliant," Judy says.

"We will attack," Staffero tells the two officers, "through Thirty's B Company with A, C, and D Companies, in that order from right to left. B will be in reserve in the center. Heavy weapons will be set up at the corners to provide supporting fire. Mortars will stand down. In this forest, they would probably be as much danger to us as The Enemy. After we pass through Thirty's B, they will peel off to provide flank guard. Unfortunately, we will have to go in with no artillery support. That means surprise will be the key. Ensure that everyone maintains noise discipline. Any questions?"

"Do we attack straight through the camp?" Judy asks.

"We will halt just on the other side to reorganize and determine whether to continue the assault. As for the stockade, post a guard to keep the prisoners inside. B Company can handle that if we don't need them for reinforcement. We will sort them out later."

"Surrenders?" Judy asks.

"Follow SOP," Staffero said about the Brigade's standard operating procedures. "For your blokes," she says turning to Promante, "keep me posted about any developments. If you need support, you will get it."

"Thanks, ma'am," Promante says.

"Hope," Staffero says, turning back to Judy, "I want you to take the right flank with Company D and the reserve, as well as the Heavy Weapons Section on that flank."

"Yes, ma'am," Judy says, perking up at the chance to get involved in the fight.

Turning to Promante, Staffero says, "Your first contact on the right flank will be Major Hope."

"Yes, ma'am," the Captain replies.

"Right," Staffero says, rubbing her hands together to warm them, "let's get cracking."

Judy makes sure the Marines of D Company quietly advance just behind the Thirty line, lying down until the attack begins. Everyone is silent. They have left anything that could make noise on the beach, the only metal are their weapons and helmets. As soon as D Company moves forward, the Thirty guys are to pull out to take up positions on the left flank. B Company has Troops in the center of the line, about one hundred meters back, with another Troop behind each flanking company.

Judy is walking back to the left when she gets a call from Staffero.

"Big42 to Little42."

"Little42," Judy responds, keeping her irritation over the call sign out of her voice.

"The Navy is going to hit them with a thirty-minute bombardment. Pull everyone back two hundred meters and make sure all stay undercover, that includes Thirty's blokes. They will commence firing as soon as we give them the signal."

"Yes, ma'am," Judy responds. She quickly has her Marines pull back, then creeps forward to get the recon Marines only to be startled when one of them suddenly appears before her.

"Major," the Corporal whispers, "we've been ordered to fall back."

"Right. Brilliant," she manages to whisper back. "Carry on." She feels a bit embarrassed because she did not know the Marine was there before he appeared, then realizes the Corporal was waiting for her, so she starts moving to the new line as well. When she reaches it, she makes sure all her Marines have pulled back, then radios Staffero.

Ten minutes later—it seems like an eternity to the Marines—the first shells roar overhead. A pause. Then a steady stream of heavy naval gun fire pours into the area of The Enemy's encampment. Even more than two hundred meters away, the roar of exploding ordinance is deafening. Judy, like most of those around her, covers her ears, which helps but only a little. She can feel the ground shake underneath her feet as she walks around checking on her charges, making sure that they will be ready to go as soon as ordered. When the barrage finally lifts, Royal Air Force jets join in, dropping both high-explosive and napalm bombs in an attack that lasts no more than five minutes.

"Little Bear, move," Staffero says over the radio.

Judy acknowledges the order, then gets D Company and the Heavy Machine Gun Section moving up, followed by the B Company Troop and the Mortar Section, which is trailing the Company in case they are needed. The Thirty Marines head off to the right to provide flank guard.

The Marines still maintain noise discipline—The Enemy may know they're coming, but not necessarily the direction the attack will come from. As they move quickly forward, Marine attack helicopters fly overhead, hitting the encampment area with rockets and machine-gun fire.

"They'll know which way we're coming from now," Judy says to no one in particular, although she is happy for the additional fire support.

As the battle line approaches the encampment, the Marines enter a land of blasted trees and turned up earth. Deep holes have been blown out of the ground by the Navy's heavy shells. Many trees have been stripped of their branches, other are mere stumps. In some areas, fires are still burning from the napalm. As they move further in, they find deep bomb craters as well. Body parts and sometimes whole bodies have been blown up into the remnants of shattered trees. The advancing Marines start stepping over and around bodies and parts of bodies scattered on the ground as they sweep through the camp in two staggered lines. Caught unprepared, The

Enemy soldiers had no place to hide from the fury of the naval gunfire and bombing.

"Poor buggers," Judy hears a Marine to her right say with pity in his voice.

"Well, mate," another answers, "better these sods than us."

"Stay sharp," a Sergeant tells both of them. "There may be some fight left in these blokes."

No sooner has she spoken, then a number of Marines open fire on several Enemy soldiers who have turned to them with weapons in their hands. Up and down the line, she hears periodic firing as Marines initiate combat or return fire. The fights are brief. The surviving Enemy soldiers are in a state of shock from the intense shelling and bombing they have undergone. Some of The Enemy are shot before they can even raise the weapons they are holding. Judy wonders if they would have surrendered if given the chance. She dismisses the thought immediately. Better them than one of her Marines. A few of The Enemy not holding weapons are taken prisoner.

A Marine goes down, shot through the leg, his attacker immediately gunned down by other Marines. Judy watches as a Navy corpsman rushes to his aid, and with the help of another Marine, evacuates the casualty to the dressing station near the edge of the camp.

When the Commando reaches the far edge of the camp, Stafferro has the line advance another five meters and then dig in, giving the Marines a reasonably clear field of fire for another thirty meters thanks to the shelling and bombing. She has been ordered to hold her position until the rest of the Brigade comes up. Clearing the city is slow work and may take more than a day, despite the lack of opposition, since each building has to be cleared.

Once her line is secure, Staffero sends out patrols to probe for The Enemy as well as sweeping the camp for any Enemy who were overlooked.

The shelling shattered the stockade where the future meals were kept. Any prisoners who survived have fled. All that remains inside the shattered barbed wire are bodies and body parts. The Marines step gingerly around the remains, looking for survivors. None are found.

"Leftenant Colonel," Sam says as he comes up behind Staffero, startling her, "how are things?"

"Brilliant, sir," she says, turning around to face the Brigadier who has a couple of aides with him.

"Casualties?"

"Six wounded. No fatalities," she reports.

Sam just nods, a satisfied look on his face. "You have everything sorted here?"

"Yes, sir," she says, somewhat tentatively.

"But?" Sam says, picking up on her reservation.

"Sir, Sergeant Major Haroldson has found something," she says, swallowing hard, "somewhat disgusting. Well, extremely disgusting, if you'll pardon the expression."

"Go on," Sam says, curiosity and impatience in his voice.

"Yes, sir," she says. "Apparently he's come across a butcher shop on the north side of the encampment. I haven't had time to inspect it yet."

"A butcher shop?" Sam responds, now confused.

"For humans, sir. Humans." The disgust is evident in her voice.

"I suppose I better have a look," Sam says. "Would you provide a guide?"

"Yes, sir," she responds crisply. "Corporal!" she says, turning to one of the headquarters personnel, "show the Brigadier to Sergeant Major Haroldson."

"Yes, ma'am," the Corporal responds. "This way, Brigadier, sir," he says, indicating the direction.

"Right," Sam says, "crack on." He turns to go, but then turns back. "By the by, Staffero, some armor will be joining you shortly." Then he turns to follow the Corporal, his aides trailing behind.

"Thank you, sir," she tells the retreating back, wondering how the tanks will get through the trees. *'Guess they'll just knock them down,'* she thinks.

A crashing behind her soon provides the answer. Three bulldozers in a line clear a path for the platoon of tanks and platoon of armored personnel vehicles coming up in support.

"Brilliant," she says to no one in particular.

<hr>

The smell of rotting human flesh, overpowering all the other foul odors from the battlefield, reaches Sam before he can see the scene. The Corporal leads them from the shattered trees into an area left mostly untouched by the shelling since it was outside the camp proper.

As they emerge into a small clearing, Sam sees the source of the stench—under a large canvas cover, half a dozen human torsos, minus arms, legs and heads, split open and gutted hang from hooks. On four tables are parts of bodies cut into chunks of meat. A short way to the left is a pile of discarded heads, feet, hands, intestines, and other internal organs. To the right is a small stockade open to the air. Inside sit seven emaciated and terrified Enemy Soldiers, clothed in the ragged remnants of uniforms.

"See to those poor buggers," Sam says quietly to one of his aides, who heads off to get them sent to the rear holding area for treatment and food.

"Sergeant Major," Sam says as he comes up to Haroldson.

"Sir!" the Sergeant Major responds, coming to attention.

"Stand easy," Sam says, surveying the scene. More than a dozen Enemy Soldiers, wearing heavy, blood-stained aprons, lie scattered about, shot multiple times. None seem to be armed. The torsos hanging from hooks also have been hit multiple times.

"Poor fire discipline," Sam comments dryly as he gazes at the torsos.

"Sir," Haroldson says. "When my blokes came across this," he says, motioning to what is before them, "they found heavily armed Enemy. So they just cut lose. I'll talk to them about fire discipline."

"Heavily armed?" Sam says quizzically, his eyebrows raised, doubt in his voice since he doesn't see any firearms in evidence.

"Yes, sir," Haroldson says emphatically. "You should of seen them heavy meat cleavers those wankers was armed with. They were something frightful. A whack from one of them would of split one of my blokes in two. We weren't taking no chances, sir. If you get my meaning, sir."

"Yes, Sergeant Major," Sam says, looking at the small man next to him, "I think I do." Turning to another aide, Sam orders him to document the scene and then either burn or bury the human remains.

Sam walks away, wondering when he will ever feel like eating again. Maybe he'll become a vegetarian.

CHAPTER 21

Absentmindedly snuggling deeper into his coat against the February chill, Sam stands contemplating a map of southern Norway pinned to the side of the canvas wall. The heaters scattered around the large square command tent do little to fight off the bone-chilling cold for anyone more than a meter away.

"Here, sir," a Lance Corporal says, moving one of the heaters closer to Sam.

"Thank you," he replies, only realizing what had happened a few seconds later as he wrenches his mind away from the map, showing the last stronghold of The Enemy in Scandinavia.

He had feared what the bitter cold in the mountainous terrain would do to his Marines. It turns out the cold and snow became allies. Outside of some scattered cases of frostbite, his Royal Marines and the Irish Soldiers fared well, making swift progress with the help of the Norwegians and Swedes who swept down from the north, joining forces with the two allies. Even the short days did not slow the advance as much as Sam had feared.

What the frigid temperatures did do was decimate The Enemy's ranks. Thousands of frozen corpses were found, and even more starving and freezing POWs were captured as the allies swept south, clearing all of Sweden and pinning the remaining Enemy Troops into a perimeter on the southern Norwegian coast, from Kristansand east to Mandal in an arc, stretching nearly fifty kilometers through the rugged countryside.

The short days also prevented The Enemy from forming any coherent formations since runners frequently got lost in the dark, resulting in the capture of many found wandering around, frequently stumbling into the allies' lines or patrols. The Enemy resorted to runners because the mountainous terrain frequently blocked their short-range radios, they only ones they had.

The allies also found plentiful evidence of cannibalism: gnawed and charred bones around fires, severed heads, hands and feet often in evidence. The Enemy was eating itself.

Those sights hardened all of Sam's Marines as well as the Irish and Scandinavians. They give no quarter to anyone they find with such evidence, especially when they are in the act of eating another human, which occurs at times.

Sam shudders at the thought. He has seen enough of those sites to more than last the rest of his life, and to refrain from ordering his forces to try to take those Enemies as prisoners. He knows it is an order many, even officers, will not follow. *'Some may consider my lack of action criminal,'* he thought, *'but I can do nothing else.'*

Walking outside the tent set up on top of a ridge overlooking a large section of The Enemy's last defensive works, Sam studies them for the hundredth time through a powerful pair of binoculars. He can see Enemy soldiers building up the simple earthworks. They look emaciated and move sluggishly. Even the Sergeants look in bad shape. They have two lines stretching the entire length of the front they have been squeezed into as the allies have pushed them in from both sides as well as the front.

Intelligence estimates that more than twenty thousand Soldiers are inside those lines. How many were being used for food is anyone's guess. Sam has contemplated establishing a siege until The Enemy has literally eaten itself to death, but his Marines and the Irish Soldiers all want to go home. They are deeply tired of the cold and snow. They miss their families and/or girlfriends and boyfriends. Though if the rate of pregnancies is any indication not all of them are missing home that much.

One last push is in the offing.

"Sir, the Marine and Irish commanders are assembled," Lieutenant Jason Whitebread, one of his staff officers, reports.

"Very good," Sam says, lowering his binoculars and turning to go into the tent.

"Sir, that," Whitebread says indicating The Enemy's defensive works, "should be a nice stroll in the park."

Sam turns back around, looks at The Enemy position and then fixes Whitebread with a hard stare. "That attitude, Leftenant, is dangerous; it could get a lot of our Bootnecks killed," he says of their Marines.

"Sir?" Whitebread says, confused and taken aback.

"Never go into an operation thinking it will be easy. That is an excellent way of being unprepared to react to changing circumstances. Plan well and train hard as if your enemy is as good or better than you," Sam says. "That way, you will be much better prepared for any surprises The Enemy might throw at you. And surprises there will be."

"Yes, sir," the chastised Lieutenant says. "I understand."

"Do you?" Sam replies, breaking his stare and turning to walk back into the tent.

"Brigadier on deck!" Codrington orders, bringing everyone but the two Irish Brigadier Generals to attention.

"Stand easy, ladies and gentlemen," Sam says, nodding a greeting to the Irish commanders. The tent is full of the command staffs of the Marines and Irish Brigades, as well as the four Commando leaders and their executive officers, and the Irish Battalion commanders and their execs, along with the Norwegian and Swedish commanders.

"Sir," Codrington says, coming up beside Sam to speak quietly to him, "the Irish Brigadiers would like a word."

"They would, would they," Sam responds thoughtfully in an equally quiet voice. "Is it what I think it's about?"

"I believe so," Tom says.

Sam thinks a bit. "We'll meet in my office. Invite their chiefs of staff to come along. I want you there as well."

"Sir," Codrington says, turning to carry out his mission as Sam heads to the canvas walled-off area of the command tent that serves as his office. Inside is a desk with a chair, and some chairs scattered around. On one wall is another map of the battle area that also shows the disposition of the forces.

As Codrington ushers in the Irish officers, Sam shakes each hand as the four men and women come in.

"May I offer some tea?" Sam asks as he walks near the map, making it a point not to go behind his desk.

"That would be brilliant," Brigadier General Leary says.

Sam nods to Codrington who steps out, has an orderly fetch tea, then returns.

"Well, gentlemen," Sam says with a smile to the two Brigadier Generals, "this is your party."

"Brigadier," Gerard says, "we would like the honor of leading the attack on the last enemy bastion."

"We believe," Leary says before Sam has a chance to respond, "that our lads and lassies have proven themselves. Frankly, they feel like they are being treated as second-class soldiers."

"I assure you, sir," Sam says, thinking to himself that the two top Irish officers were the main ones whose morale is suffering, "we do not harbor those feelings. Your Soldiers have acquitted themselves admirably."

"Thank you, sir," Gerard replies formally with a slight bow of his head.

"What do you propose?" Sam asks, wanting to get past this awkward moment.

"We propose for our two Brigades to attack side by side," Leary says as two orderlies enter with trays carrying tea, milk, and sugar. Codrington has them put the trays on a table set against the canvas wall opposite the map.

"Please," Sam says with a sweep of his arm, indicating his fellow officers should help themselves.

After they have all served themselves, they move back toward the map.

"Colonel," Gerard says to his Chief of Staff, "lay out our plans for the Brigadier and the Colonel."

"Yes, sir," Siobhan Doyle says, heading toward the map. She puts her tea cup down on Sam's desk and takes a collapsible pointer from her right pocket, extending it out to its full length.

"What we propose is for each Brigade to send in two Battalions side by side presenting a four-battalion front with the other four battalions behind, striking here," she says as she points to a spot in front of Kristiansand. Once we break through, the four trailing battalions will advance through the battalions to their front, wheeling to their right and attacking down the length of The Enemy's works. Three of the four original Battalions will extend the line to the coast and provide support for the attackers. The fourth will be held in reserve."

Doyle looks around at Sam and Codrington, and receiving understanding nods from them, continues.

"We request the Royal Marines provide supporting pressure along the rest of the front to fix Enemy forces in place until our Soldiers can deal with them and to provide protection for what will become our rear as we wheel toward the west."

"I see," Sam says, nodding thoughtfully. "Colonel Codrington, any thoughts?" he asks.

"A couple, if I may, sir," he says, looking at Gerard.

"Please," the Irish Brigadier General says.

"May I suggest we request the Norwegians and Swedes to guard your rear. I believe they are capable of that task. That would free our Marines to provide additional support for your Soldiers, especially along the coast where you may be stretched thin. That would allow you to keep your formations more concentrated."

"I see," Gerard says. "And your other thought?"

"Yes, sir. As your Battalions advance driving The Enemy back, they will uncover our Marines. I would propose we have the Marines fall in behind your formations to secure any prisoners that you may collect, deal with any stragglers, and strengthen that coastal flank."

"Sean?" Gerard says, turning to Leary.

"I believe those are brilliant suggestions."

"Excellent," Gerard says. "Shall we invite the Scandinavian commanders in?" he says to Sam.

"I have taken the liberty of alerting them to the possibility that they may be participating in this attack. They have both indicated that they will perform any role given them."

Gerard contemplates him for a moment. "You suspected we would request this?"

"I thought it was a possibility," Sam says, smiling a bit. "I like to be prepared for all eventualities."

"I suppose we should not be surprised," Leary says, smiling as well. "Careful preparation is your reputation."

"Speaking of preparation," Sam says, hurrying past what was quickly becoming an awkward moment, "may I offer the support of our armor units, as well as artillery and air support?"

"That would be brilliant," Leary says.

"And what we hoped for," Gerard adds.

"I believe we can support you with eight tank companies," Codrington says. "Your blokes have been working with our armor already so there should not be a problem."

"No, there should not," Gerard agrees.

"I would also propose," Sam says, "that we begin with an artillery attack along the entire line starting four hours before the infantry goes in so as not to alert The Enemy unduly to the point of attack. After sunrise, we will also have air attacks along all concentrations of Enemy forces."

"Agreed," Leary says.

"One hour before the attack, the main artillery strikes will be at the point of the attack, along with air attacks being concentrated in that area. We will also request the Royal Navy to shell the point of attack. Those big guns can do a lot of damage."

"Indeed," Gerard says. "I have seen what they can do."

"So now the question is: When do we launch this attack?" Sam asks, looking around the room.

"The Irish are ready to go tomorrow," Leary says, pride showing in his voice.

"That's brilliant," Sam replies, almost laughing, "but a bit too quick for us to coordinate with the Navy and Air Force and to get our armor into position and our artillery set up and supplied with enough ammunition to do the job. And our Marines and the Scandinavians will have to be briefed and moved into position."

"Seventy-two hours," Codrington says. "We will commence the artillery fire at that time and continue through the night. Those buggers won't get any sleep," he says, almost triumphantly.

"Shortly after dawn," Sam says, taking over from Codrington, "we will shift the bulk of our artillery, air, and naval fire onto the point of attack," he tells the Irish officers.

"Will you be able to provide a rolling barrage?" Gerard asks.

"Without a doubt," Codrington replies. "Our artillery liaison officers will be embedded with you to control fire."

"My goal," Sam says, "is to finish off these sods with as few casualties as possible. We have been able to build up our supplies, especially of artillery shells. I want to use them liberally. Hopefully, this will be our last battle before we go home. I don't know about your blokes," Sam says to the Irish officers, "but ours need a rest and are anxious to get home."

"So are ours," Leary says.

"That is settled then," Sam says. "Please have your detailed plans to us by the morning so we can cut our orders and make detailed requests to the Navy and Air Force," Sam tells the Irish. "For our part, we will alert all our guys and set things in motion."

"Thank you," Gerard says.

"And on that note, I think we are done." Sam announces.

After the Irish leave, Codrington turns to Sam, "What do you think?"

"I think the Irish will be do a brilliant job. I also think our Marines will get a much deserved pass on leading an attack. Now, let's go face all those people we left standing around and tell them what is going on." Sam then leads Codrington back out to the main room.

CHAPTER 22

Shortly before zero six hundred, Sam and Codrington stand outside the command tent huddled in their coats against the cold. The sporadic artillery fire had gone on for the last three days, as have patrols probing for weaknesses and prisoners. Sam ordered those continued so The Enemy would not expect the coming attack. Several Enemy attacks launched against his lines were easily turned back with only a few casualties and no deaths. For the last six hours the volume of artillery fire has increased all along the line and held steady with just over half the tubes engaged at any one time.

"Any moment now," Codrington says quietly.

Before Sam can respond, every artillery tube the Marines and Irish have opens fire, raining a variety of calibers on The Enemy's two lines. The sound is tremendous, the individual cannon shots merging into a general roar. Even at this distance, the two officers can feel the vibrations in the ground from the exploding shells.

"Sam, why don't we go inside where it is warm?" Codrington asks. "We can monitor things better in there. Besides, these old bones can't take the cold like they used to."

Sam just smiles at his friend, then turns to lead the way back into the command tent.

<hr />

"Bloody cold out here, Major, ma'am," a Corporal says to Judy as she joins two Marines in their fighting hole.

"Bloody right," she responds as she uses night-vision binoculars to study The Enemy's line.

The roar of artillery shells passing overhead is nearly deafening. She quickly gives up trying to see what damage is being done. The whole line of earthworks has disappeared in clouds of smoke and dirt being thrown up by the explosions. She has read about the shelling of German lines in World War I in the early twentieth century, which didn't do much good. But the Germans were motivated, well-armed, and in excellent trenches with well-constructed dugouts. She hopes this Enemy is not as prepared.

If they are, this attack could turn into a bloodbath for the Irish and the Marines.

Whatever the case, she plans to be with the first wave. The Commando's Mortar Section will start dropping smoke rounds just in front of The Enemy's works as the Marines advance. That should help reduce casualties.

At least, that's the plan.

Staffero has Judy going in with the left-wing of the attack, taking in the first two companies as the Irish sweep—they hope—across The Enemy's lines.

"When do we go in, ma'am?" the Private in the fighting hole asks.

"Sometime after dawn," Judy replies. "It depends on how quickly the Irish advance. Dawn, by the by, is just after zero eight hundred. They will go in about zero eight thirty. Forty will be the first to go in. We're next."

"Yes, ma'am," she replies.

"Do you two understand what we will be doing?" Judy asks.

"Ma'am," the Corporal says, "we move in behind the Irish and swing down to the coast to strengthen that flank and lengthen Forty's line, picking up any prisoners we find along the way."

"Brilliant," Judy says as she starts to get out of the hole. As she leaves, the artillery fire in their front abruptly slackens, while the fire on the assault area crescendos as most of the artillery shifts targets and the Navy's big guns join in pounding the area in front of the Irish Brigades. Overhead, Air Force fighter bombers and Marine attack helicopters hit areas toward The Enemy's rear where Troop concentrations have been identified.

"Major," the Corporal says, arresting her motion, and yelling to be heard over the noise, "will the MPs take the prisoners off our hands?"

"That's the plan," Judy says, with a bit of a laugh. "We will sort anything we have to as we go along."

"Yes, ma'am. Thank you, ma'am," the Corporal replies, her voice none too happy.

Without another word, Judy hoists herself out of the hole and heads down the line, checking on some of fighting holes, spending a few minutes with each pair to reassure them and make sure they know the plan. She sees the commanders of the two Companies she is responsible for checking in with each hole. While she finds that reassuring, some of the Marines think having two officers quiz them one after the other them is irritating.

As she nears the end of the line, Staffero summons her over the Commando radio network. Judy quickly reverses course and heads toward their command post set up about fifty meters behind and slightly to the right of their line on a small hillock that provides a good view of their entire line and The Enemy works they face.

As Judy nears the CP, most of the artillery and naval gunfire abruptly cease, along with the bombing. Only artillery hitting the attack area continues, providing a rolling barrage as the Irish advance. Judy shakes her head, wondering if she's gone deaf. Then the sound of small arms and tank fire filters in. It seems almost silent after the massive artillery barrage.

"Leftenant Colonel," Judy nearly yells as she approaches Staffero, who holds up a hand for her to wait as she finishes with a radio call. Putting down the handset, she moves to Judy.

"I don't think we have to shout anymore," she says, smiling.

"So it would seem," Judy replies sheepishly.

"We have a change of orders." Judy just nods in response. "It seems," Staffero says, "the Irish are moving a lot quicker than anyone thought. The whole Enemy line just collapsed. They're meeting minimal resistance. Just a few hot spots. Resistance is not organized."

Judy smiles in satisfaction and nods.

"We are going in early," Staffero continues. "Command believes the lines in front of us are either deserted or lightly held by dispirited Soldiers. In about thirty minutes, we're to lay down a smoke screen and then go in with Forty on our left. Four Six will come in as soon as we are over The Enemy works."

"Understood," Judy replies.

"Also," Staffero says, "we will not be going to the water. We will be swinging in on Forty's left flank. They will be advancing along the earthworks. We will extend the line. Your Troops will be on the Commando's left. Four Six will tie in on your left. Watch your flank when you get out there. Four Five will hold position, extending to their left to prevent escapes. Our major objective is to secure prisoners and clean up any stragglers who elude the Irish."

"Ma'am?"

"They don't need us on the coast," Staffero says. "Thirty reports no resistance. Just masses of Enemy Soldiers anxious to surrender. They are also finding the bodies of numerous Sergeants. Fresh kills. Apparently, their Soldiers turned on them as we attacked. They also report finding evidence of cannibalism. And most of the prisoners are suffering from starvation and hypothermia."

"Yes, ma'am."

"Judy, you better head back to brief your Troop commanders and spread the word on our new assignment. Time is short."

"Ma'am," Judy says as she turns to go.

"Judy!" Staffero calls after her. "Take care of yourself."

Judy smiles over her shoulder, "You do the same, Michelle." She's soon back on the line, briefing the commanders of A and D Troops, who pass the word onto their Color Sergeants and Sergeants.

Shortly after zero-nine-fifteen, the Commando's mortar Section lays down a smoke barrage in front of what's left of The Enemy's works. Staffero issues the go command to the entire Commando. The Marines immediately leave their fighting holes and start running in a crouch toward The Enemy lines. All of them are ready to hit the deck should they encounter any fire.

They don't.

The Marines scramble over the earthworks and through the holes left by the shelling. They find a few stunned survivors who are no longer armed, along with many shredded bodies and body parts. A few bodies show no marks at all, having been killed by concussions from shells that exploded nearby.

A Section from D Troop is detailed to collect and guard the prisoners—the number quickly growing to more than five hundred–until they can be turned over to the MPs. Four Two holds their position as Forty's line passes by. Then the Four Two Marines quickly fill the line on that Commando's left. Judy has A Troop on the extreme left with one Section as flank guard until Four Six comes up.

At their front, Judy hears sporadic gun fire, at times heavy sustained firing along with the bark of tank guns and the deep-throated sound of heavy machine guns as the Irish Brigades sweep forward. Her Marines don't fire a shot the entire day. They collect about six hundred more cowering Enemy Soldiers. They are dressed in rags, some with just shreds of uniforms left. Few have boots, their feet wrapped in rags. All are skin and bones, with sunken cheeks and ribs protruding from their bodies. Many are losing hair, and even more have lost teeth. They have no protection from the cold. Those who have blankets are wrapped in the scraps. Judy finds herself stepping over the bodies of men and women who have either starved or frozen to death. She can't tell which. Possibly both.

"Poor buggers," she hears one Marine mutter as he stands looking down at half a dozen cowering prisoners.

Judy, as well as the other Marines, are beginning to take pity on what used to be Enemy Soldiers but are now just pathetic remnants of human beings.

"You bloody sod!" A Marine's yell draws her attention. She quickly covers the ten meters between them. When she gets there, she finds a Sergeant restraining a Lance Corporal who has trained her weapon on an Enemy Soldier who seems to have been knocked to the ground and is holding the side of his face. Blood is coming out of a new wound on his cheek. Next to him is a fire that has gone out and piles of human bones around it.

"Don't!" the Sergeant is telling the Lance Corporal.

"Sarge, the bloody sod doesn't deserve to live!" she says, nearly crying. "Look how bloody fat he is! You know what he's been eating! The bloody fucking sod!"

"Alright, lass, I understand," the Sergeant replies. Judy has stopped two meters away watching. The Sergeant seems to be dealing with the situation well. "But we have our orders," the Sergeant continues. "We can't kill the unarmed, even sods like this who deserve killing if anyone did."

"Then he just gets away with it?" the Lance Corporal says, frustration and anger in her voice. But she lowers her weapon, relaxing her shoulders.

"Nay," comes the reply, almost dismissively. "Wankers like him will be brought up on charges."

"And what? This sod gets some cushy time in prison?"

"Tell you what," the Sergeant says. "You sort this one. Put him with the other prisoners."

"Sarge?"

"He should be fine. And if he ain't, well, I don't think anyone will give it a second thought."

"Yes, Sarge," the Lance Corporal says, almost happy, definitely relieved. She turns to her prisoner, prods him to his feet and heads for the POW collection point.

The Sergeant watches her go and then turns to move, coming to an abrupt halt when he sees Judy watching. She just nods at him and heads toward the advancing line.

The fighting is over by sixteen hundred as the Irish reach the end of the earthworks. The trailing Marine units have gathered the prisoners and are moving them into collection points where medical personnel are caring for them. Sam has had his supply and medical people preparing for this. Tents have been set up with heaters inside. Food and water are being provided, as are blankets. Cots are in short supply, but the prisoners don't seem to mind. MPs are constantly patrolling to ensure that no one steals food or blankets from others.

⊰━◈━◇━◈━⊱

As the sun starts to set about seventeen hundred, Sam and Codrington tour the POW area, entering one of the dozen hospital tents.

"How are things going?" Sam asks one of the doctors who is nearly running from one patient to another, ordering nurses and orderlies to do various tasks.

"As well as can be expected, Brigadier," replies the doctor, who looks tired and frustrated.

"Oh, I'm sorry," Sam says quickly, holding out his hand. "I don't seem to know your name. Are you new?"

"Yes, sir, sort of," comes the reply as he takes Sam's hand. "I joined the unit a fortnight ago, although I was with the medical unit when the

Brigade was in France. I am a reservist. Part-time Bootneck, I believe is the term. Except I'm Navy," he says with a shrug. "I am Doctor Josh Evans, or Leftenant Commander Josh Evans, if you prefer."

"Right," Sam says. "We're happy to have you, even if it is only occasionally. We certainly need all the help we can get. I'm, by the by, Brigadier Hope. This is Colonel Codrington, my Chief of Staff."

"Good to meet you, sirs," Evans says shaking the Colonel's hand.

"And you, Leftenant Commander," Codrington says.

"Now," Sam says, sweeping his hand around toward the POWs, "what's the prognosis for these people?"

"Not good, I'm afraid," Evans replies. "We have already had several deaths. Some of these poor devils are just too far gone to save, although we will keep trying. You never know when you'll get a miracle."

"Right," Sam says. "If you need anything, let us know and we'll see what we can do."

"Thank you, sir," Evans says, then as he starts to hurry to his patients, he turns back. "Brigadier, there is one thing you could help us with right now."

"And that is?"

"Translators," Evans says. "None of us speak Norwegian or Swedish. We are having the devil's own time communicating with these poor buggers."

"Right," Sam says, then turning to an aide, orders: "Find the Norwegian and Swedish commanders. Ask them to send as many translators as they can."

"Sir," the aide says and then hurries off.

Sam turns back to the doctor, only to find he has gone back to his patients.

"How many POWs?" Sam asks Codrington as he looks around the hospital tent.

"At last count, 12,742," comes the reply.

"I thought Intelligence estimated at least twenty thousand and as many as thirty thousand."

"They did," Codrington replies, satisfaction in his voice. "Our artillery, along with the Navy and Air Force did a bang-up job."

"So it would seem," Sam says. "Well, not much more to be seen in the dark. Let's return to HQ. We can finish the tour in the morning."

"Good idea," Codrington says as the two officers head out and back to their quarters.

⤜⟪⟫⟩⟨⟫⟩⟨⟫⟩⟫⟳

Zero six hundred the next day. Sam makes another visit to the hospital tents for his Marines and the Irish Soldiers. He chats with a few of the wounded and asks the doctors if they have everything they need. He sends the list to his supply officer with an aide.

Amazingly, at least for him, his Brigade has suffered only two fatalities during yesterday's sporadic fighting. Most of the wounded have not suffered serious injury, with only a few being permanently disabled, mainly because of loss of limbs.

He walks out into the cold morning air as the sun begins to rise. Half a dozen well-armed Marines provide security. He has three aides and a radio operator with him. He takes a deep breath of the cold air. It stings his lungs a bit, but he also finds it invigorating. He also enjoys the quiet. Especially the absence of gunfire, both small arms and artillery. He can see patrols checking the battlefield, but it is too early in the morning for the work of cleaning up to begin. That will be the job for the Royal Engineer regiment which has accompanied his Marines, though he knows a large number of his Bootnecks, especially the Engineers, will be pressed into service.

"Well, Colors," he says to the Color Sergeant in charge of his security detail, "shall we take a walk on this fine morning?"

"Yes, sir," the Color Sergeant replies, never stopping his scan of the area, looking for trouble.

Sam glances at him, smiles to himself and steps off at a rapid pace. Walking is not easy. Craters from shells and bombs litter the entire area. Bodies and body parts of Enemy Soldiers are still lying about. Sam steps carefully to avoid stepping into intestines scattered around or onto severed arms and legs. He is thankful the cold temperatures have retarded decomposition. The air smells fresh and clean since a brisk wind has blown away the smell of cordite.

As he crosses the battlefield, he comes upon a Marine sitting on the top of a bomb crater, his legs dangle down the side, his eyes fixed on something in the hole.

Sam walks up behind him. He looks over his head to what the Private is staring at. It's a head. No body. A helmet is firmly fixed on the head, long blond hair splayed on the ground around what used to be a woman.

"Are you alright?" Sam asks.

The reply comes after a moment. "It's creepy. She's staring at me. Like this is my fault. I didn't want to kill her. I didn't want to kill anyone. All they had to do was stop their killing. So why is she blaming me?"

Sam kneels down next to the distraught young man. He can see tears rolling down the Private's face. He puts his hand on the Marine's shoulder. "Son," he says softly, "it's not your fault. None of us wanted to kill these people." He pauses for a moment. "It's the price we pay for protecting our families, our loved ones, for saving those we can." Sam looks at disembodied head. "She paid the price of being in the way of that. God knows, I didn't want to see her dead. Or anyone else for that matter. Saving our families comes first, and those people would surely have killed them. That is the only way I can justify to myself for being part of this slaughter."

The Private finally manages to take his eyes off the head and look at the man who's been talking to him. His eyes open wide in horror. "Sir, Brigadier, sir ..." he stammers out and he starts to rise.

"Take it easy, son," Sam says, squeezing his shoulder. "You've been through a hell of a lot. And I'm glad you are asking these questions."

"You are, sir?" comes the puzzled response.

"It means you are a moral person. Just the kind of Marine I need. Now, just take it easy for a bit and then rejoin your mob."

"Yes, sir, thank you. I'm alright now," the Private says as he gets up. He comes to attention and salutes, holding it until Sam returns it.

"Be careful. Protect yourself," Sam says.

"Sir!" the Private replies in a strong voice, before doing an about-face and heading off to find his Troop.

Sam watches him go before resuming his tour. He pauses atop a small hill where he can get a good view of this area of the battle field. Shattered tents and other kit litter the area. At the bottom of the hill are the remains of a Sergeant. His stomach has been torn open, probably by shrapnel, his eyes are staring unseeingly at the sky. Sam feels only contempt for him, and satisfaction at his death. He just hopes it wasn't too quick.

"Sir," his radio operator says, coming up to him and breaking into his thoughts.

"Yes?" Sam responds, turning around to see the proffered handset.

"It's the Colonel, sir."

"Right," he says, taking the handset and keying it. "Good morning, Tom. What's cracking?"

"Good morning to you, too," comes the reply. "The Engineers are just about ready to start. They plan to bulldoze the entire area, putting the bodies into mass graves along with the destroyed kit."

"Sounds like a good plan."

"Also," Codrington continues, "the Army just landed two Battalions to take charge of the prisoners, along with their own medical staff and supply."

"Brilliant," Sam says. "What's the bad news?"

"Bad news?"

"You've only given me good news so far. The bad news has to be coming soon."

"Not really," Codrington says. "The Norwegians and Scandinavians want to get home. They don't see where they are needed here anymore."

"True. Let them go, but ask them if we can give them a formal send off. Also ask them if they can leave some interpreters with us."

"And what about the Irish? Formal send off for them as well?"

"What? They want to leave as well?"

"Not exactly. Their government wants them back now the fighting is done."

"Oh, very well," Sam says a bit exasperated. "We could have used their help making sure we haven't missed anyone."

"Sorry, that does not seem to be in the cards."

"Ask the Brigadier Generals to come to lunch. Perhaps we can get them to drag their feet a bit."

"Will do."

"Anything else?"

"Isn't that enough?" Codrington quips, humor in his voice.

"More than enough for this early in the morning," Sam says, almost laughing. "And I haven't had breakfast yet."

"Come on back and I'll have the table laid."

"Brilliant. Just make sure there is enough for the six combat Marines as well as three aides, and the radio operator with me."

"Consider it done."

"Thanks," Sam says, handing the handset back to the operator.

Sam gives another look around. "Well, ladies, gentlemen," he says to no one in particular, "let's go have some breakfast."

With that, he turns and heads back to Brigade HQ.

⁂

The Marine Brigade spends the next thirty-two days cleaning up the battlefield and patrolling throughout southern Scandinavia, accompanied by Norwegian and Swedish interpreters. The two Royal Army Battalions, fresh from fighting in Poland, also help. They find the bodies of several freshly killed Sergeants and more than three thousand Enemy Soldiers, who are tired, cold, hungry, and more than ready to surrender. Rarely do they meet resistance.

Finally, the day comes the entire Brigade has been waiting for. They pack their kit and board transports for home. As they sail out of the harbor, Staffero and Judy are standing at the railing watching the Norwegian coast fall behind them. Their Commando's members have all been given quarters and fed. Now the two senior officers are relaxing, bundled in cold-weather gear to enjoy the clean air and quiet.

"Do you think we missed any?" Staffero asks, a wistful tone in her voice.

"If we did, warmer weather will certainly tell the Norwegians where they are," Judy replies, her voice sounding contented.

"Judy, you can be really ghoulish sometimes," Staffero says, laughing.

"Can't help it," she replies with a sharp laugh. "I don't think any of The Enemy Soldiers who are alive now will survive much longer unless they surrender. If they don't, they will either be claimed by starvation or the cold. Or shot. And since there are not enough wolves to take care of the carcasses, the warm weather will."

1m pas

"You are such an optimist," Staffero says, the sarcasm dripping from her voice.

"Bloody right," Judy replies happily. "I'm just happy we won't be there to smell them. I'm ready to go home."

"As I am," Staffero says. "I miss Aleck and the kids. I need hugs and to get laid."

The two officers stare across the water in silence for a few moments.

"You have anyone waiting for you?" Staffero asks.

"Not exactly," comes the deadpan reply.

"Not exactly?" Staferro says, turning to the younger woman. "What does that mean?"

"Josh is on the hospital ship. He should land a day ahead of us."

"Josh?"

"Leftenant Commander Joshua Evans. He's a reservist doctor."

"Serious?"

"It's getting there."

"Good for you. I hope it works out."

"Me, too." Judy falls silent for a moment. "I'm getting cold. I think I'll get some sleep."

"I won't be far behind you," Staffero says. "We both have a lot of sleep to catch up on."

"Good night."

"Good night."

CHAPTER 23

T om," Sam says as his Chief of Staff enters his office, parking himself
in a comfortable chair in front of the Brigadier's desk, "they promised
us six months before we got a new assignment. And they kept their
word. Just."

"What is it?" Codrington ask, looking at his Brigadier with interest.

"We are going to America," Sam says matter-of-factly.

"Across the Pond, is it. When?"

"Two years or so," Sam says. "Our assignment is to land on a place
called Long Island, just off the coast of New York, or what used to be New
York. Gather intelligence and help the people there start to reclaim the
mainland, if possible. That should give us ample time to plan and train,
especially since so many of our blokes are leaving. It's a shame, but given
what they've been through, I can sympathize with their desire for a quiet
life."

Codrington stares out the window of the spacious office, with its
subdued painted walls, bookshelves lining one wall. A couch and some
chairs are set in one corner. A small conference table inhabits another
corner. Sam's desk faces away from the windows, his chair facing into the
room. If he faced the windows, he says, he would spend too much time
staring out of them.

"Tom," Sam says gently, "what are you thinking?"

"I won't be going with you," Codrington says, as he keeps his gazed
fixed on two birds in a tree just outside.

Sam is silent, waiting for him to continue.

Finally, Codrington looks at him. "My Abigail is sick." Sam nods,
since he has known this from the start of her battle with cancer seven
months ago.

"She may not have much time left." Codrington sighs deeply, looking out the window again. "I want to spend as much time as possible with her and take care of her. I owe her that, God knows. She has put up with my, really our, thirty-seven years in the Marines. She raised our children almost as if she was a single mother." Codrington pauses again. "She never complained. She never made me feel guilty about my absences. She always told me it was in a good cause, keeping her and the children safe." He shifts his gaze back to Sam. "Sir, I intend to put in my papers next week. I will retire as soon as my replacement is named and brought up to speed."

Sam leans back in his chair, contemplating his friend and partner. "You'll be missed. Sorely missed by me," Sam finally says. "You are my alter ego. You have excellent tactical and strategic sense. You can, and do, take command whenever needed, such as in Italy. You could easily replace me, and the Corps would probably be the better for it." Sam holds up a hand to forestall the objection that was about to come. "Having said all that, I completely understand. And I will help you in any way I can. I will miss you, and, frankly, wish you weren't in a position you feel you have to take this step. But," Sam says, reaching down to a bottom drawer in his desk, retrieving a bottle of scotch and two small glasses, "I must admit that if our positions were reversed, I would be doing the same thing." As he talks, he pours two drinks and hands one to Codrington, who reaches across the desk to get it.

"Thank you, sir," Codrington replies.

"Sam. It's Sam now and always. Hell, Tom, you're almost a civilian."

"Yes, yes I am," Codrington replies, a rueful smile crossing his face as he sits back in his chair, taking a sip of the liquor, then looking at the glass. "I will really miss this good scotch. This is difficult to get it in the civilian world."

"No worries," Sam replies. "I will ensure you have a steady supply."

"For that, I will forever be in your debt."

Sam just looks at him and shakes his head. "Now, since you are abandoning ship, have you given any thought about your replacement."

"That I have." Codrington stops talking and just looks at Sam, expectantly.

Sam snorts finally and says, "Alright, since you are clearly going to make me ask: Who?"

"Michelle Staffero."

Sam sits up erect. "Who?"

"Leftenant Colonel Michelle Staffero," Codrington quietly replies, enjoying the surprise he has just sprung.

"She's an outstanding officer," Sam says, sitting back in his chair, "but she's new to her command. And she's junior to the other Leftenant Colonels."

"They'll be alright. You will support her, and they'll come around."

"I know, but …"

"Sir, Sam," Codrington says, correcting him. "I have talked to McBride and he's in full agreement that she is the most qualified officer to take the position,"

Sam leans back, contemplating the other man and what he has said. "By the by, Geoffrey is now a Colonel."

"Indeed," replies Codrington, who already knew.

"He's been posted as head of Intelligence Operations for the entire Corps," Sam says. "I'm glad a worthy use was found for his talents." Sam pauses. "You know, he would have made a brilliant Chief of Staff or Brigadier if it hadn't been for that bloody awful wound."

"Which is why I went to him. He is the one who put forward Staffero. He believes her leadership and organization abilities are among the best in the Corps. Us excepted, of course," Codrington says, smiling.

"Of course," Sam says. "Have you thought about who will replace her at Four Two?"

"I have a candidate in mind, but I should like to confer with her first."

"Of course," Sam says. "When do you want this change to take place?"

"By Friday next."

"That's awfully fast."

"Oh, I'll be around for a bit as an adviser, but she will need all the time she can get to settle into her new job, as will the new Four Two commander."

Sam just nods. "In that case, we should tell her now." Sam reaches for the phone and asks the Color Sergeant to find Staffero and have her come to his office. "I guess we'll need a third glass," he says, reaching down to retrieve another glass.

"Excuse me?" Sam blurts out, sitting bolt upright, as his former Chief of Staff and new Chief of Staff sit comfortably in the two chairs in front of his desk two weeks after Staffero's promotion. "She's a junior major who has been an executive officer for but a brief moment. Now you want to make her a Leftenant Colonel in command of Four Two?"

"Exactly," Codrington says.

"Major Hope is more than qualified," Staffero adds. "She has led several attacks, organized defenses, and shown she can bolster morale and keep it high. She is well respected by both the officers and ranks. And she does not shrink from making the hard decisions. In the last attack, she led her Sections of Four Two over The Enemy's works without hesitation."

"Brilliant," Sam says, sounding unhappy at the same time. "It only took you both two weeks to cook up this plot? This is the problem," he says leaning forward, "Judy is just 30. She has moved up very quickly, and no matter how warranted that may be, the stench of nepotism will adhere to her with this promotion. And don't tell me blokes won't suspect that I have my fingers on the scale, that she was promoted not because of her achievements but because of me. I don't like it. Not one bit." He sits back heavily in his chair, looking frustrated, upset and defeated.

"Sam," Codrington says, putting his hand on Staffero's forearm to forestall the rebuttal she was about to make, "do you really want to hold back a talented officer who deserves a promotion simply because of her connection to you?"

Sam looks up at Codrington, a look of profound sadness on his face.

"Sir," Staffero says, "I have had some quiet conversations with Four Two's senior officers and some of the senior NCOs. When I asked who should replace me, all but one mentioned Major Hope. I did not suggest a name at all."

"And the one who held back?" Sam asks with a look of curiosity. "If you feel comfortable telling me."

Staffero greets the question with a big grin. "Major Hope, sir."

"Who did she suggest?"

"She said the decision was above her pay grade."

"Did she now."

"Yes, sir. Brigadier," Staffero continues, "Major Hope will be completely and happily accepted by Four Two, from the senior leaders right down through the ranks. They all trust her judgment and leadership. When the other Commandos see how well accepted she is, they will quickly come around."

"Sam," Codrington says, "what the Colonel and I would like to do is have a promotion ceremony with you absent."

"Absent?" Sam says, a bit bewildered since the practice is for the Brigadier to present new Lieutenant Colonels with their insignia of rank.

"Everyone will wonder where you are," Codrington continues. "It will raise some eyebrows. We," he says, indicating himself and Staffero, "will make it abundantly clear that we made this call, not you. That will go a long way to scotching any rumors. Everyone knows and respects the Colonel and her abilities, and her accomplishments. She has been completely accepted as the Chief of Staff. And they all know me and our relationship. Besides," he adds, smiling, "I'm retired. There is nothing you could do to me even if you wanted to."

"Don't tempt me into trying," Sam says, still looking sour. He turns and stares out the window for a moment before turning around. "Okay. I'm still not sure I like it, but I will defer to your judgment. And, Colonel, understand that if there is adverse reaction, you, Judy and I will all be paying a price," he says, leaning forward, his elbows on the desk, a finger on his right hand pointing at Staffero.

"Yes, sir," Staffero replies. "This was not a quick and simple decision. The Colonel and I considered many candidates but kept coming back to Major Hope. And as I pointed out, she will be happily accepted at Four Two. The other Commandos will come around. And, if someone doesn't, I will deal with that."

"Lovely," Sam says, still not sure of the wisdom of Judy's promotion, but at the same time proud of her. "Now," he says, "the reason I asked you two to come, before you ambushed me." He glances at them, seeing both smile back. "Yes, right," he says. "Our orders just came through." He looks at the other two, both of whom sit up straighter. "We sail next year, now, in April, on a date still to be determined. The entire Brigade will go, along with all our heavy weapons and helicopters. A Navy task force will accompany us to provide gunnery and air support. We also will be carrying heavy weapons and small arms along with ammunition to the Americans. Accompanying us, will be a Royal Engineer regiment and an

Irish Brigade, which one has not been designated by the Irish government yet, but I presume it will one of the two we fought with in Scandinavia. At least, that is my fervent prayer."

"Amen to that," Staffero says.

"Indeed," Sam says, handing packets of information and intelligence assessments across the desk. "As you will see from that," he says, pointing to the paperwork, "we have had an ongoing relationship with the people on Long Island, off the coast of New York and Connecticut. They apparently have maintained a high level of civilization, using wind, solar, and ocean power to provide electricity. They are self-supporting in food. And, it seems, they have a small, rudimentary military and are eager to return to the mainland and take back their country."

"Brilliant," Codrington says.

"Colonel," Sam says, turning to Staffero, "I would suggest we plan to land in three waves, spaced several days apart, so we don't overwhelm the Yanks with a mass invasion. The pacing will depend on how quickly the Engineers can prepare camps. You will need to contact Colonel Hope of the Royal Engineers to work out that schedule."

"Your wife is coming?" Codrington asks.

"Yes, Tom, she is. When I requested Royal Engineers, it seems the powers-that-be decided to send Sarah and her Regiment. They seem to think that because we were both born in North America, we will be more readily accepted. That is also the reason the Irish were asked to send a Brigade. We'll find out if either is true."

"Sir?" Staffero says.

"It seems people in our government are worried the Americans may still harbor some animosity from their rebellion when they broke away from Britain. I don't see why they should since it happened in the late eighteenth century. But there you are."

"Yes, sir," she says. "How would you like the three waves to be organized?"

Sam contemplates her for a moment. Glancing at Codrington, Sam looks back at Staffero, saying, "What would you suggest, Colonel?"

Staffero sits back in her chair thinking for several minutes. "Well, sir, I should think the first wave should include Brigade command staff, along with Engineers to prepare our camps. Thirty should also come along to start reconnaissance of the mainland." She pauses for a moment. "We should also land the Americans' weaponry and start training them."

"And?" Sam says prompting her.

"Yes, sir," she quickly goes on, "the second wave should include the rest of the Brigade and all their kit. The Irish will come in the third wave. As for the Navy," she hurries on before Sam can ask her, "they should have their aircraft carrier and some of their surface ships with the first wave to support Thirty when they go ashore. The rest can come along with the second and third waves. My concern is that we are landing a lot of blokes, a lot of young blokes, on an island that, I presume, has not had much contact with us or anyone else."

"That is true," Sam says. "How would you deal with it?"

Staffero thinks for a moment. "By making it clear that anyone who steps out of line will pay a heavy price. And having an obvious presence of officers and MPs. Our relations with the Americans will be fragile, so we must set boundaries for our blokes and ensure they stay within those bounds."

"And make sure our guys get the proper beer rations, and nothing more," Codrington says.

"Of course," Staffero replies, smiling.

"It seems you have things well in hand," Sam says to her. "Get with the staff and start planning the details: Amount of kit and food we will need, number of ships and the like."

"Sir," Staffero says, gathering up the paperwork and heading out of the office.

Watching the door shut behind her, Sam turns to Codrington, "You were spot on about her. She's a keeper."

"Told you," Codrington says.

"So you did."

"By the way," Codrington says, "do you still have any of that excellent scotch?"

Without a word, Sam pulls the bottle and two glasses from the desk drawer.

CHAPTER 24

have reservations for three at 1 p.m. under Brigadier Hope," Sam tells the greeter at the door of the restaurant in the Dorset Hotel.

"Ah, yes, sir," the greeter says, checking his name off the list before picking up three menus and looking around the large room.

"By the front windows, if you please," Sarah says.

"Yes, ma'am," the greeter says, leading the way to a table with four chairs set by the large bay windows overlooking the harbor.

"Thank you," Sarah says as the server holds a chair out for her. She and Sam, both in uniform as they prepare their commands to sail for America, sit opposite each other so they can look out at the harbor and survey the room, waiting for Judy to join them.

"Will the third member of your party be joining you?" the server asks, putting a third menu down in front of the chair facing the window.

"Yes," Sam says, "she should be along presently."

"Would you like to order drinks while you wait?"

"Tea would be nice, if you have any," Sarah says.

"Yes, ma'am. And you sir?"

"The same," he says. "Would you," Sam says interrupting the server's departure, "please tell your executive chef we would like a word with him."

"Well, yes, sir, I can do that," the server says. "But I don't think he will come out. He doesn't like leaving the kitchen."

"Just tell him two old friends from his sailing days are here," Sarah says.

The server looks puzzled. "Yes, ma'am," he says walking away toward the kitchen.

"Liverpool seems like it hasn't changed since we were here last," she says, gazing out the window.

"I wouldn't be too sure of that," Sam says. "We never saw much of it while we were here. And that was nearly thirty years ago. Judy was just two."

"And Frank wasn't even born when we arrived," Sarah adds, sadness in her voice about the son they lost in the fighting in France. "Our boy was born here."

Sam silently reaches across the table, taking her hand and gently squeezing it.

"Well, I'll be knackered," George calls out as he strides across the dining room, clothed in a white shirt, pants with a crazy design, a white apron, and a tall chef's hat. "I haven't seen you two in thirty years."

"More like twenty-six. But who's counting?" Sam says as he and Sarah rise to greet one of the people who fled from The Enemy in America with them on a sailing vessel of questionable safety.

"How have you been?" George responds, a big grin on his face as the two men shake hands. "Sarah, you are as beautiful as ever."

"And you are arguably the most famous chef in the United Kingdom," she responds, giving him a hug, "How's Jessica?"

"Still teaching third grade and loving it," comes the happy reply. "We have three children, two at university, both in the Royal Army Reserve, and the third is in the kitchen, learning how to be a chef."

"I understand," Sam says, "you opened another restaurant?"

"Two, but who's counting," George says with a wink as he repeats Sam's phrase. "They aren't white-table places like this, but the food is great, if I do say so myself," he says, some shyness of his earlier years creeping back in.

"And what about you two? More children? Careers? I hear you are a Brigadier in the Marines these days," he says to Sam, getting a nod in acknowledgement, "and you," turning to Sarah, "are some kind of engineer?"

"I'm a Colonel in command of a Regiment in the Royal Engineers."

"Brilliant. And your kids?"

"Judy will be here at any moment. She's a Leftenant Colonel in command of Four Two Commando. Her sister, Emily, graduated medical school and is now doing her residency in a Glasgow hospital, specializing in general surgery, and our son, Samuel, is an electrical engineer. He's just been called up by the Royal Air Force."

"Brilliant," George says, then the smile disappears from his face. "Wait. Didn't you have another one? Frank, wasn't it? Wasn't he born just after we landed here?"

"We lost him in the fighting in France," Sam says. "He was a Staff Sergeant in the Royal Army infantry."

"I am so sorry," George says.

"Thank you," Sarah responds, while Sam just nods in acknowledgement.

"Look," George says, breaking the awkward silence, "I have to get back to the kitchen. But you order anything you want. It's on the house. And come back for dinner tonight. I'll get Jessica here and we can have a proper visit."

"Thank you, and we will," Sam says.

"Oh, yes," George says, turning around as he is about to leave and Sam and Sarah are sitting back down, "I'm going to send out a bottle of excellent wine. It may be a bit early in the day, but this is a day to celebrate old friends."

"Thank you," Sarah says.

"Thanks," comes from Sam.

"He looks good. Happy," Sarah observes.

"Yes, he does that," Sam agrees. "She's here," Sam says as Judy, wearing a knee-length blue dress with flower patterns on it, enters the restaurant and heads for the table.

"You two are no good at camouflage," she quips. "Sitting right in front of that big window."

"We like the view," Sarah says, smiling at her daughter.

Judy exchanges kisses with her parents and sits in the chair facing the harbor filled with ships, mostly freighters, some at quays being loaded, others waiting their turn or having been loaded, waiting for the order to sail.

"Shall we order? I'm famished," Judy says, picking up a menu.

"You always were a big eater," Sarah observers.

"The Marines help me keep my girlish figure," Judy says as she peruses the menu. "What's good here?"

"I suspect just about everything," Sam says. "The executive chef is George. You probably don't remember him. He was one of the people on the ship with us when we came here."

"The Hope," Judy says, sitting back. "I have vague memories of that lot. I've only really kept in touch with Adam."

"How's he doing?" Sam asks.

"He's a mechanic. Married with two kids," Judy says, somewhat wistfully as she slides her left hand up and down the side of the menu, occasionally running it over the top.

Sam and Sarah just exchange glances.

"How does it feel to be the youngest Leftenant Colonel in the Royal Marines?" Sarah asks.

"I'm getting a handle on it," Judy says, shaking the reverie out of her head. "Michelle, the Colonel, has been a Godsend. I don't know where I would be without her advice and guidance. And my officers and ranks have been really supportive."

"Brilliant," Sam says, relieved to hear that. He has purposefully distanced himself from Four Two so it would not look like he was showing favoritism to his daughter.

The server arrives and takes their orders.

"And I thought being an Executive Officer was complicated," Judy says with a laugh and a shake of her head. "Now, I am responsible for everything that goes on in Four Two, from leading them into battle to making sure the food is tasty and everyone has the proper kit."

"Your new exec isn't helping?" Sam asks.

"No, no, don't get me wrong. Without him, I would have drowned long ago. But he's new to the job, too, so we are both learning. Michelle is teaching me and I am teaching him."

"Lovely," Sam says, a hint of sarcasm in his voice, as their food and the promised bottle of wine arrives, and they begin to eat. Judy is impressed with food, but only takes the smallest of sips of the wine, which she also finds impressive.

"George was always a great cook," Sam says.

"Emily and Samuel couldn't make it," Sarah says. "They both send their regrets."

"Sorry they couldn't be here. I haven't seen them in a while," Judy responds.

"Your sister is in Europe with her members of her hospital's staff helping deal with the effects of starvation and disease," Sam says. "As for Samuel, he's in hospital with Joyce. She is in labor with their second. Everything looks good and he promised to call us once the baby girl is born."

"Brilliant," Judy says.

The trio eat in silence for a while, exchanging glances, but no one talking.

"We sail the day after tomorrow," Sam finally tells Judy. "You'll be five days behind us."

"Yes, I've seen the orders."

"Excuse me," their server says as another employee clears the dishes, "the Chef has asked me to offer you coffee or tea and a special dessert he has prepared."

"Excellent," Sam says. "Tea and dessert, please."

"And for me," Sarah adds.

"I'll have the dessert, but coffee instead, if you please," Judy says.

"Yes, of course," the server says and heads off.

"Remind me to recommend George for a medal," Sam jokes. "I think the passage back to America will be a lot more pleasant than how we got here," he says, changing the subject.

"That wouldn't be hard," Sarah observers.

As the custard dessert, tea, and coffee arrive, they fall into talk about the coming operation and what might happen when they enter the mainland.

As they are finishing, Judy gives her parents a hard look. "You two may be the most unobservant senior officers in His Majesty's service."

"Excuse me," Sarah blurts out. Sam just stares at his dessert.

"I've waving this thing," she says, holding up her left hand, "in front of your faces this whole time and neither one of you has noticed."

They both stare at the ring finger.

"You're engaged?" Sarah blurts out.

Sam gags on the sip of tea he had just taken.

"When? Who?" Sam finally manages to get out.

"Two days ago," Judy says, triumphantly.

"Have we met this person? And is that why you are wearing that dress instead of uniform?" Sarah asks.

"Yes, I'm going to meet him after I leave here, and Dad has met him."

"I have?" Sam says, perplexed. "Who?"

"Josh Evans," Judy responds. Realizing that has not cleared up the mystery for her father, she adds, "Commander Joshua Evans of the Royal Navy Medical Corps, Reserve. He was a Leftenant Commander, I believe, when you met him."

Sam thinks for a moment, staring at nothing in particular. "Yes, I did meet a Dr. Evans. He was caring for The Enemy Soldiers we captured in the final battle in Norway. But where did you meet him?" he asks, looking up at Judy.

"In France. He looked after me in hospital when I was wounded. We stayed in touch, and when we got back to England, we started seeing each other. One thing led to another, and here we are."

"When is the wedding?" her mother asks.

"Sometime after we get back," Judy says, with a shrug.

"I see," Sam says.

"Oh, yes, and one other thing," Judy says.

"There's more?" an exasperated Sam says.

"By the end of the year, you'll have five grandchildren."

"You're pregnant?" a surprised Sarah nearly shrieks.

"About four weeks," Judy says.

"And you plan to lead Four Two on this operation?" her father challenges her.

"Yes, I do. Regulations do not prohibit senior officers, which I am now one, from performing their duties while pregnant. I do not have to go into combat. If, for some reason, I cannot carry on for a time, my exec will be more than prepared to take over my duties."

"I won't permit it," Sarah says. "It's too dangerous."

"Mum," Judy says softly, taking her mother's hand, "I am doing this. You can't stop me; neither can Dad, even if he wanted to."

"How could you be so careless?" Sam asks.

"Who said I was careless?" Judy challenges him. "I want a career, but I also want a family, like you have, like Emily and Samuel have."

"Who will take care of the baby?" Sarah asks.

"After the baby is born, Josh will take a leave of absence from the Medical Corps and return to England to care for our child. It's the same thing you two did, only the father will be the one with primary duties."

"Does the Colonel know?" Sam asks.

"Yes, I talked to her just before coming here. That's why I was a bit late."

Sam nods. "And she's on board with this?"

Judy snorts a laugh. "She congratulated me, warned me about the downsides, but ultimately agreed nothing in regulations prohibits me from carrying on. So, here we are."

"Well," Sam finally says, "since we have no choice, we will be fully supportive of you."

"Thank you," Judy says, a bit sarcastically.

"Understand this, though," he says, "as your Brigadier, if I detect any slacking in performance, I will relieve you in a heartbeat."

"Brigadier," Judy replies formally, "I wouldn't have it any other way."

CHAPTER 25

never thought we would ever come back here," Sarah says as she and Sam watch the approaching Long Island coast while leaning on the railing on the main deck of the HMS Bristol. The cruiser is serving as the command ship for the initial deployment of British and Irish forces in America.

"Me either," Sam agrees as they watch the land grow larger in the early morning light, "but we are returning as liberators instead of fleeing for our lives."

"And our daughter's," Sarah adds.

"And our daughter's," Sam agrees. "And our other kids who weren't born yet."

"We've had a good life," Sarah says, contemplatively as the coastline rapidly expands.

"Now, wait," Sam says, "we are having a good life. It isn't over yet."

"No, it isn't," she replies, slipping her arm through Sam's and resting her head against his shoulder as they feel the ship turning to approach the harbor. The plan is to land in Brooklyn, where port facilities are in good shape. The following waves of Marines and Irish Soldiers have the ability to land over the beaches, which will speed things up, especially if they off-load on the mainland. With that possibility in mind, the cargo was combat loaded, a more inefficient use of space, but necessary if a landing is made on a hostile shore.

"Sir, ma'am," a Navy Lieutenant says, coming up to them. "The Admiral sends his respects and requests you meet him on the bridge."

"Right away," Sarah says, unwinding from Sam. "Lead on."

"Ma'am," the Lieutenant says, turning and heading for the ladder leading up to the bridge level.

"Sir, you wanted to see us?" Sam says as they enter the bridge where the Admiral and the ship's Captain are quietly talking.

"Ah, there you are," the Admiral says. "Brigadier, Colonel, we have just had a communication from the Americans. They are requesting that you helicopter ashore to confer about the landing, etc."

"We are preparing a helicopter at the moment," the Captain says. "It should be ready in about thirty minutes."

"We were to land in Brooklyn," Sam says.

"Yes," the Captain responds, "but now they want you to come in further east in a more open area. They have sent GPS coordinates for the landing site."

"They have satellite access?" a surprised Sarah asks.

"Yes, these Americans have built quite an impressive operation given their lack of access to raw materials and the like," the Captain answers. "How they did that, I do not know. In any case," he says, changing the subject, "how many in our landing party?"

"Twelve," Sam says, after a moment's thought. "Six senior officers, two aides and four ranks. Will the Navy be sending anyone?"

"The Flag Chief of Staff and two aides," the Admiral answers.

"Sir," a Lieutenant says, "the helicopter is ready for launch."

"Very good," the Captain says. "Leftenant, please show these officers the way."

"Sir," that officer responds and ushers the party out, leading them aft to where the helicopter is waiting on the pad, its rotors turning.

When the passengers are in and buckled, the helicopter takes off, heading for the landing zone. The ride is taken in silence, everyone straining to get a look at this island they are about to land on. As they come in, they see a welcoming party waiting for them. Before the rotors have stopped, the doors are open and the passengers get out, walking toward the three people approaching them.

"Welcome, welcome," a tall man in civilian clothes says, holding out a hand, which Sam, as the senior officer present takes, "I'm Kibwe Magnus, Administrator of Long Island."

"Sam Hope, Brigadier commanding the Royal Marine Brigade. May I introduce my fellow officers?"

"Yes, please, do."

"This is Captain Michael Johnston, Flag Executive Officer for the Royal Navy fleet that is coming. Colonel Sarah Hope, commanding officer of the Fifth Royal Engineer Regiment. Leftenant Colonel Jack Griffith, commanding officer of Thirty Commando. Leftenant Colonel Pierre De Castellano, head of Brigade intelligence. And Leftenant Colonel Tilly Evans, Brigade Supply Officers."

"Welcome, welcome," Magnus says, bowing slightly to each one. "And may I present Chloe Kim, the head of our intelligence operation, and Colonel Lawrence Petrakis, our military commander."

After greetings are exchanged all around, Magnus leads the group into a nearby house. "We can talk comfortably here," he explains.

"So, ladies, gentlemen," Magnus says, opening the talks when they are all comfortably seated on plush chairs and a couch in the living room, "we are grateful for your assistance, although I must admit, I am not sure how far that can take us."

"Sir," Johnston says, "I most urgently need to talk to your harbor master about landing our people and unloading our freighters."

"She is in Brooklyn, I am afraid," Magnus says. He turns to an assistant, saying, "Please arrange immediate transportation for the Captain. Will that be satisfactory?" he says, turning back to Johnston.

"Yes, quite," comes the reply.

"Captain," the assistant says, "there is a car outside which can take you right away."

"Brilliant," the Captain says as he and his aide get up and follow the assistant out the door.

"We are supplying you with heavy weapons," Sam says, leaning forward in his chair. "Obviously, they are for your defense, but we are also hoping you will join us in entering the mainland. My Marine Brigade and the Irish Brigade are veteran fighting forces, but we are entering a continent that will dwarf the numbers we can bring to bear."

"We cannot add much to those numbers," Petrakis says. "Most of our strength is in our reserves, men and women who are vital to the survival of our people in civilian endeavors. Our active military is only five thousand strong. So, what can we really accomplish?"

"More than you might expect," Sam says, leaning back. "From the intelligence reports we have received from you, we suspect we will find much the same conditions we found in Europe. Once we break through the hard shell, we expect to find a hollow interior. We are rapidly on our way to retaking Europe, Africa and Asia. Much of the military and even civilian strength to do that has come from captured Enemy soldiers. Once they realize we are there to help them, they are eager to turn on their former masters. We expect the same will hold true here. That means an army can be built to retake your country."

"Despite the brutality they have suffered? You have no idea how they have been treated," Kim says.

"Actually, we know exactly how they've been treated," Sarah interjects. "The Brigadier and I, along with some others, escaped from one of their camps south of here. Ultimately, we built a small sailing ship and managed to escape to England."

"You're from America?" a surprised Magnus says.

"Yes, we are," Sarah answers him. "And we would love to liberate this continent of our birth."

"You must have quite a story to tell," Kim says after a pause in which the Long Islanders digest what has just been said. "And you accent doesn't sound American."

"We have been living in England for decades now," Sarah responds.

"On our side," Magnus joins in, bringing the topic back to liberation, "we have a long history of struggle ourselves, and would like to reclaim our land."

"You're not planning on staying forever?" Petrakis says.

Sam, Sarah and Griffith look confused. Evans laughs.

"Don't worry, Colonel," Evans says. "We know you colonists will never rejoin the Empire. Which by the by, no longer exists anyway. We just want our world back, to live in peace and safety. That's all this is about."

"I was just joking," Petrakis says defensively.

"And once you Americans can take over," Sam adds, shaking his head at such a question, "we will happily go home. England is now our home," he says indicating Sarah. "That is where our children and grandchildren live. That is where all our families are. So, don't worry on that score. We will leave as soon as you are able to stand on your own."

"I understand," Magnus says, "that your government will send over two to three divisions of your Army for up to two years."

"Correct," Sam says, "if you request it and there is the potential for progress. We won't know that until we have landed on the mainland."

"And when do you plan to do that?" Petrakis asks.

"That depends on what Leftenant Colonel Griffith and his Marines find."

"You are planning to explore the mainland?" Petrakis asks, surprised.

"Yes," Griffith answers. "The main mission of Thirty Commando is reconnaissance."

"I will have some of my people go with you."

"With all due respect, I am sure your people are very good," Griffith says, "but my blokes have been doing this for a long time. I believe it would be safer for everyone if you just place on a map the location of The Enemy encampments."

"Colonel," Sam says, "please do not take offense. I'll tell you a story. When we were in France, I went ahead of the front lines to take a look at The Enemy's position. As I was about to raise my binoculars, a whispered voice came up from right at my feet. 'Get down, you bloody fool, before get your bloody fool head blown off.' I was startled but immediately dropped to the deck and found myself face to face with one of Jack's Lance Corporals. She," Sam says, chuckling a bit at the memory of incident, "was horrified at whom she had just called a bloody fool. I told her she was quite right to do that, and then belly crawled back until I was a safe distance away." He pauses for a moment. "The point of the story is that Jack's blokes are nearly invisible when on a mission."

"Nearly?" Griffith asks, humor in his voice.

"Right," Sam says, laughing, "they are invisible."

"We would be happy to train some of yours in our techniques," Griffith tells Petrakis.

"That would be great. Thank you."

"Shall we have lunch?" Magnus asks, after an assistant comes in to indicate the food is ready. They all get up and head for the dining room.

They sit down at a large, rectangular mahogany table to a meal of baked tuna steaks, baked potatoes and salad, with water and milk to drink.

"Would you tell us how you managed to survive?" Sarah asks the three Long Islanders sitting opposite her.

"It all happened before we were born," Kim says. "Our parents and grandparents fought off the attackers."

"How did they manage that?" Sam asks. "We know The Enemy attacks in mass waves, ignoring casualties, until they overwhelm the opposition. They just keep coming," he says, his voice dropping down as he recalls the battles he has fought. "Sorry," he says, regaining his composure.

"The attacks came in just that way, but our folks had the advantage of being on an island," Petrakis says. "Army and National Guard units fought rear guard actions as they retreated into the city. They destroyed the bridges and tunnels, except for one bridge going to the mainland. They wanted to keep that open as a way back. But the attackers swarmed over the defenses, so in the end they were forced to blow that bridge as well, cutting off all contact to the mainland. They prepared for the attackers to come by boat, but that never happened. So eventually, they were able to relax their guard."

"The problem was food, water, power, just about everything," Magnus says, picking up the story. "The islands of Long Island, Manhattan, and Staten Island had ten million people. Everything was brought in from the mainland. Chaos and looting soon broke out. So martial law was imposed. Private cars were banned from the streets and electricity was strictly rationed. All food was collected in central storehouses and rationing was strictly enforced."

"Was there a black market?" Sarah asks.

"Black market activities were punished by expulsion to the mainland," Petrakis says.

"Harsh," Evans says.

"Perhaps," Magnus replies, "but necessary to save lives." He takes a sip of water. "But even with rationing, millions starved. There just wasn't enough food and rations were repeatedly cut to stretch supplies. We tried sending foraging parties to the mainland, but most of them did not come back. And then medicine ran short and water stopped flowing in many areas because the pumps lost power. Sewage backed up and could not be treated. Lack of food weakened millions, then diseases took them. Bodies began piling up, too many to bury. So they were burned."

He pauses, looking out the window. Kim and Petrakis looked at their plates. None of the British break the silence.

Finally, Magnus looks up. "Everyone probably would have died, but some leaders emerged who organized things. Politicians, scientists, and just ordinary people, especially the few farmers we had. They turned every available green space into gardens and food crops. Central Park in Manhattan, and every other park in the city and on the island, along with all athletic fields and most backyards, and even front yards, were soon planted with food crops. It was back-breaking work, but eventually the food situation was resolved. Potable water and sanitation were bigger problems, but they managed to create enough solar and wind power to solve most of those problems."

"You seem," Evans observes, "to have plentiful electric power now."

"That came later," Kim says, picking up the story. "Our scientists and engineers built a system of windmills and solar panels, along with ways to store power to provide electricity for most of our needs. And they managed to used the tides to help generate electricity. We still have some blackouts, but those are in the small hours of the morning when few people are up anyway. Developing a barter trade relationship with Britain helped a great deal."

"Yes, I understand much of our solar technology came from your scientists," Evans says.

"Where did you get the materials?" Sarah asks, before Kim can respond to Evans.

"By salvaging material, mostly from Manhattan, but also from Staten Island and parts of Queens and Brooklyn," Kim answers. "Those all used to be part of New York City. Most of the people who live there now are the guards who watch for attackers. Many of them have their families with them now since attacks never came. We stripped wire out of buildings, took chips from every place we could find them, such as cars, laptops, computers, you name it. We have a group of talented metal workers and dye makers who fashioned windmills out of all kinds of metals. They built smelters to reduce the metal to a molten state and then fabricated the parts they needed to build windmills and other things."

"And we were fortunate that a large number of fishing boats escaped from the Northeast and found their way here. They have supplied us with fish ever since," Magnus adds.

"Where did they get the fuel?" Sam asks.

"At first, they were given priority for gas," Magnus says. "Eventually, they converted to electric motors that will run for up to five days, three in heavy seas."

"Amazing," Sarah says.

"You and your people are to be congratulated not only on your survival but for what you have built here," Sam says.

"Thank you," Magnus responds. "But when it is a question of survival, you become very resourceful. And we were lucky to have the vast majority of our people pulling together."

CHAPTER 26

As he enters the map room for their briefing on The Enemy the next day, Sam tells Griffith, "Your blokes will be camping out for a bit. The engineers need a few days to get sorted and build the camp."

"Not a problem," Griffith responds. "We're used to roughing it."

"Indeed," Sam says, then looking at Petrakis, "Sorry, I'm late. Some logistical problems needed to be sorted."

"No worries," he says.

"Sir, we haven't really begun yet. Just getting acquainted," Griffith says. The medium-sized rectangular room has maps pinned to the wall on one long side. Sitting and standing around the large table in the center are all the officers of Thirty Commando, the Brigade staff, Long Island intelligence officers, and a collection of Long Island Defense Forces officers.

"Very good," Sam replies. "Shall we start?"

"Yes, sir," Petrakis says, picking up a pointer and indicating a map of New York State and the surrounding area. "We have identified two major camps, each holding at least twenty thousand, perhaps as many as thirty thousand," he says, pointing to two squares drawn in red, one in the Hudson Valley just north of New York City and the other a few kilometers inland from the Connecticut shore. A few other camps of less than a thousand have been found, but those move continuously, so we're not sure where they are or even what their function is.

"Also," he says, putting the pointer down, "we don't understand their command structure. All we have been able to identify are Sergeants who seem to be running things."

"We also have never been able to find a definite command structure," De Castellano says. "We identified several of what appeared to be command and control centers in Europe, but when we took them out, nothing seemed to change. We are at a loss to explain how this military organization is run."

"I'm glad we're not the only ones in the dark," Kim says, her sarcasm mixed with frustration drawing laughter from around the room.

"Precisely," De Castellano says, chuckling.

"Anyway," Petrakis says, "the camps are not well guarded. Our people got up to almost shouting distance before being spotted. They have roving patrols around the perimeter, but they do not appear to worry about an attack."

"Weapons? Food?" De Castellano asks.

"We only saw rifles and machine guns," he answers. "As for food, we are not certain about their supplies, but with the exception of the Sergeants, everyone we saw appeared to be in need of a meal."

"Any fighting holes? Berms? Trenches?" Griffith asks.

"None that we observed," Petrakis says. "The last time we got close to the camps was nearly six weeks ago," he says, anticipating the question. "Both camps seem to be run in identical manner with well laid out streets of tents, and a field for exercise as well as a rifle range. I should add that it has been, oh, say, two months since we heard any gunfire. That could mean they are low on ammunition."

"Do you have anyone over there right now?" Sam asks.

"No, sir," Petrakis says. "We send over patrols about once a week and try to get close to the camps monthly, but we haven't been very successful recently because of their patrols."

"Right," Sam says, looking at De Castellano and Griffith, "anything else?"

"Yes," Griffith says. Turning to Petrakis, he says, "Sir, I will need tide charts and secluded landing areas."

"I believe we can accommodate you on that."

"Brilliant," Sam says. "Jack, can you be ready in a week?"

"Give us three days and we'll be ready," he said, more than hint of pride in his voice.

"Take a week," Sam says. "Don't rush this. Besides, I want the Navy in position to back you up in case anything untoward happens."

"Yes, sir," Griffith reponds, a bit deflated.

"Well, then, ladies and gentlemen, let's get cracking," Sam says. He leaves, followed by the other officers who disperse to get their Marines sorted and start gathering information and making plans.

CHAPTER 27

aptain Bev Whitehouse sits near the stern of the lead twenty-person black boat as it cruises up the Hudson River north of New York City. The fifteen boats run past the city with their powerful gas engines on, but once moving north on the Hudson, they switch to electric motors. That drops their speed from sixty knots to about fifteen, but the motors are silent. Ten to fifteen Marines and all their kit are in each boat. Two Long Islanders are in Whitehouse's boat to serve as guides. Each boat has a thirty-caliber machine gun mounted in the bow, but otherwise, A Company's weapons consist of the rifles, grenades, and individually operated machine guns they carry.

The moonless night is black, the shore barely discernable without the night-vision gear they all wear. No one says a word, except as necessary and then in whispered voices.

"There," the guide whispers to Whitehouse as he points toward shore.

"Right," she whispers back. "Turn west," she says over the radio as her coxswain steers the boat to shore, cutting speed to about five knots. The trailing boats, traveling in a column of two, conform silently to the movement, although two nearly collide when the boat on the outside turns earlier than its partner. The boats silently pull up to the shore, where the Marines get out and pull the craft onto the land.

Leaving a Section of Marines and the two Long Islanders with the boats, Whitehouse leads the rest of her company into the forested hills. They know where to find The Enemy encampment, about a kilometer from the river. About half a kilometer from the suspected site, the column halts.

Whitehouse, Lieutenant Jack Armstrong, and six Marines from his Two Troop go forward to scout the camp.

W.R. Blocher

An hour later, Whitehouse and her patrol are back. She gathers her Troop leaders in what has been set up at the command post, although it doesn't look like one from a meter away.

"The camp is laid out exactly as the Americans described it," she says, looking around the tight circle. "One, Three and Four Troops will take this side and the short sides to the north and south, in that order. Mike," she says to Lieutenant Michael Mort, "since you are a Section short, you will take the center on a constricted front. Jack, you will take the west side," she tells Lieutenant Jack Armstrong, commander of Two Troop. Each of you is to hold back a Section in reserve in case this whole project goes to shit. Any questions?"

"If this does go balls up, we use standard exfil procedure?" Armstrong asks.

"Yes, brilliant," she replies. "Shoot and move your asses." The comment draws dry chuckles from the officers. "We have three hours of darkness left, so we need to be in position in that time. Jack, you have the furthest to go, so you better move your guys now."

"Ma'am," he says and immediately heads off to organize his Troop and get them moving. The others quietly disperse. Soon the entire company is moving silently into position.

⁂

'What the bloody hell is that stench from?' Color Sergeant Henry Fielding thinks to himself as he settles in for the day. He recognizes the nearly overwhelming smell of decaying human bodies. Carefully, he looks around in the gathering light of dawn. He has charge of the two Sections on the extreme right of the line. He almost hopes the odor is coming from his left.

But it isn't.

He messages Lance Corporal Marsha Owens to check it out since she seems to be the closest to it. Her Sergeant also picks up the message since it comes over the company net in morse code, which can only be heard through their headsets. It's a messaging system using a modified Q and Z code system from the Navy that is unique to Thirty Commando among the Royal Marines, allowing them to maintain complete silence while

236

communicating. They will break vocal radio silence only in the case of emergency.

Fielding receives an understood and settles back to watch and wait. The Marines are close enough to watch the camp and gather intelligence, while far enough away to avoid easy detection.

A bit more than an hour later, Owens reports: "Bodies. Hundreds. Sergeants. Shot. Wood brought. More coming. Expect fire."

Fielding acknowledges receipt and begins to wonder what is going on: Are The Enemy Soldiers rebelling? It would be a relief if they didn't have to fight them. Or maybe someone else is taking over? Could that make matters worse? Fielding shakes his head to clear it and settles back to watch and wait. What he sees and hears puzzles him.

"More wood in pit," Owen messages.

Fielding acknowledges. The soldiers in the camp seem almost to be on holiday. They are wandering around, chatting, some are just relaxing. A bell rings a number of times and everyone walks over to … where? He can't see. In less than half an hour, they come wandering back, most still eating their breakfast.

This is completely different from the camps they surveilled in Europe. There, when the meal bell rang, there was a mad rush toward the food, with people being pushed out of the way and even trampled. The Brigadier had told them the Sergeants never had enough rations for everyone. The weakest starved. Here, now, no rush. No panic to get to the food. He watches as work details form and set off.

A flame of light and smoke to his right draws his attention.

"Burning bodies," Owens messages.

<hr>

"Couple coming," Four Troop commander Lieutenant Sean Daughtry hears over the Company net from Private Harvey Sturges in mid-afternoon.

A few minutes later: "They're going to shag."

"Say again," Color Sergeant Mary Waters messages back.

"Getting naked to do the deed," Sturges replies. "Half a meter from me. Good view."

Whitehouse shakes her head at that then joins the conversation. "Let them finish. Then take them prisoner."

Daughtry messages three other Marines to move into position to strike.

Twenty minutes later: "Done."

"Move," Daughtry messages. She doesn't hear anything for a few minutes. Then, from Sergeant Sean McDougal: "Two taken."

"Hold them there until pull back, if practical," Whitebread messages.

"They're naked," McDougal messages.

"Cover them," she replies, emitting a little laugh.

⁓⁓⁓⁓◇⁓⁓⁓

After full dark has fallen, Whitebread orders everyone to rally at the Company CP. She is startled as two pale bodies emerge out of the dark. A man and a woman. Both naked except for shirts draped around their shoulders and boots on their feet. Their mouths taped shut. Their hands bound. She motions for them to be sat down a short distance away. They look terrified. No one has spoken to them or even in their presence.

"We didn't think it a good idea to free their hands," Daughtry says as way of explanation.

"Brilliant," Whitebread says. She goes over to the two prisoners. Kneeling down in front of them, she says, "Do you speak English?"

They nod yes in response. Tentative nods, but nods just the same.

"If we remove your gags will stay quiet?"

They nod more enthusiastically.

Whitebread nods to the guards who pull the tape from their mouths, none too gently.

"What are your names?" Whitebread asks.

After a moments silence, the woman speaks, "He's DeWayne. I'm Margarita."

"Right. Here's the deal: If we free your hands and let you get dressed, will you stay quiet and not start any trouble?"

"Yes," they both say.

"Lovely," the Captain says. Looking at one of the guards, "Free them and get them their clothes. And get them some rations and water." As she stands up, she says quietly, "Keep a close watch."

"Ma'am," the guard says.

"Hey, lady," Margarita says in a low voice. "How come you sound funny when you talk?"

"What?" Whitebread responds, perplexed by the question. "What do you mean?"

"You sound funny when you speak," Margarita says.

It takes a moment from Whitebread to realize what is going on. "You mean my accent?"

"I guess," comes the reply.

"I'm from England."

"Where's that?" DeWayne.

"Where's?" Whitebread says, a bit confused by his lack of geography. "Never mind. We'll talk about that later." As she turns to walk away she nearly runs into another prisoner. This one is fully dressed and looking just as terrified as the other two.

"Look what we found," Color Sergeant Tomas Rodriquez says quietly but triumphantly. "This bloke was out for an evening stroll when he walked right up to us as we were pulling out."

"Brilliant," the Captain says. "Tell him if he stays quiet and does not make any trouble, his gag and binders will be removed, and he'll be fed."

"Do you think he speaks English?" Rodriquez asks.

"Those two do," she responds, nodding to the couple who are just getting dressed.

Rodriquez looks over at the two who are getting dressed. His eyebrows arch at the sight.

"That's how they were captured," she says, anticipating his question. "I'm sure the Four Troop guys will be more than happy to fill you in."

"Ma'am," Rodriquez says, knowing when not to pursue a conversation. He leads his captive over to the other two.

Chuckling quietly, Whitebread goes about the business of organizing her Company's withdrawal.

"This is the hard part. Waiting to find out how the mission fared," Sam says, staring out into the dark, as he, Sarah, De Castellano, Magnus, Kim, and Petrakis sit on comfortable chairs on the veranda of a house overlooking Long Island Sound. With them for dinner and now on the porch are a married couple, two academics, biologist Marisol Gonzalez and agronomist John Kelly. They have just finished dinner and are sipping some port De Castellano brought along.

Sitting in the chair next to Sam, Sarah reaches out and gives a reassuring squeeze to his hand. He gives a light squeeze back.

"Lieutenant Colonel," Kim says to De Castellano, changing the subject, "you were asking earlier about what we know about the rest of the country."

"Yes, yes, indeed," he says, sitting up in his chair. Sam and Sarah also perk up, listening intently.

"Some we know. Some we just hope. Mostly we don't know," Kim says. "What we do know is that some groups survived in the Rocky Mountains and in the remote areas of Alaska and northern Canada. We don't know anything about the middle of the continent. Perhaps some have survived in the Appalachians. We just don't know. We don't see how anyone could have survived in the plains. We also hope that some have survived in the mountains of Mexico and South America, perhaps in the Amazon. But, again, we just don't know."

"What do you know about the survivors in the west?" Sam asks.

"In Alaska and northwestern Canada, they are hunkered down in mountain valleys, hoping not to be noticed. Although the Canadians say they have ventured a bit to the south and found it deserted. They are not willing to go too far south, though, for fear of running into trouble."

"Understood," De Castellano says.

"And people in the Rockies?" Sam asks.

"Well," Kim says, "we have good radio contact with them. They are in remote valleys and have rigged wind turbines for electricity and have managed to manufacture rifles, pistols, ammunition, and even some bombs."

"Has there been fighting?" Sam asks.

"Not in quite some time," comes the reply. "They have pushed out all the way to the Pacific. A few areas have large concentrations of Soldiers, but most are deserted. Where they have found Soldiers, they have also found evidence of cannibalism and fighting among various groups."

"Same as in Scandinavia," Sam observes.

"Indeed," Magnus says, joining the conversation. Then looking at the two scientists, "that fits into your theory."

"It's not exactly a theory," Gonzalez says.

"Just speculation," Kelly adds.

"What speculation?" Sarah asks, looking back and forth at the two.

Kelly and Gonzalez look at each other for a long moment. He gives a bit of shrug with his head and shoulders. She nods in response.

"Ever heard of lemmings?" she asks, looking at the three Marines, all of whom shake their heads. "Well it's myth, but it bears repeating in a way. Lemmings are small rodents that inhabit Canada and Norway among other places. The myth is that lemmings commit mass suicide when their population gets too big. The reality is that when their population in one area becomes too large for the food supply, they embark on a mass migration."

"Now, what if," Kelly says, picking up the story, "there was no place for them to migrate to?"

"I suppose they would starve," Sarah says.

"Yes, but what if they didn't starve? What if they found a way to keep getting food while their population continued to expand, even explode? What then?"

"I don't know?" Sarah answers, as both Sam and De Castellano nod in agreement.

"We think," Gonzalez says, "nature would intervene and find a way to reduce the population to a sustainable number."

Silence prevails for a few moments.

"You think that is what has happened to us?" Sam asks.

"We don't really know," Gonzalez says with a sigh. "But until, and unless, someone comes up with a better explanation, I guess this can work. I mean, we always don't get answers to why things happen," she says, throwing up her hands. "Why did this person get hit by lightning while the person three meters away didn't? Why is there even life on this planet? Some people believe in God, while others look to science, chance or even aliens. Brigadier, I suppose you and your Marines have wondered why one dies and one lives."

Sam nods yes, thinking about the survivor's guilt he and others have had when dealing with that very question.

"We may," Gonzalez says, "never have satisfactory answers about why this happened, which is a shame since we can only guess how to avoid having it happening every again."

"It's just the best speculation we can come up with," Kelly says about their suggestion of overpopulation. "We can find no other rhyme or reason for the catastrophe that has gripped humanity. And we have no clue where they keep getting Soldiers. They always seem to have younger people. What happens to the older ones? We have no answer for that."

"And we may never now how these bloody armies are organized and controlled, fed and armed," De Castellano says.

"We just hope we learn from this and don't repeat the mistakes of the past," Gonzalez says, sighing and sitting back in her chair.

"Let's hope," Sarah says as the group falls silent, each caught up in her or his own thoughts, all just staring out into the dark toward the sound of waves against lapping the shore.

CHAPTER 28

Attention!" barks Lieutenant Colonel Clyde Lee, commander of Four Six Commando and the senior officer in the large pale-white meeting room furnished with institutional chairs as the Brigadier enters followed by Staffero, then De Castellano, and Kim.

"Rest," Sam says as he reaches the center of the low stage with a huge map of the area directly across from Long Island. "Take your seats," he says as he surveys the room. In the first row are Brigadier General Sean Leary, commander of the First Irish Brigade, and his senior officers, the five commanders of the Commandos and their executive officers, along with Petrakis. Behind them are the commanders of the Companies, with the exception of two Thirty Commando companies who are deployed. The next group is the Troop commanders who have not been deployed, and last, their senior NCOs. The Thirty Commando companies are keeping watch on the two encampments nearest Long Island, while some of the other Troops are scouting further inland and along the coast in both directions.

"Ladies and gentlemen," Sam says, quietly but firmly, "we are about to launch the first of two operations." He pauses to let that sink in. "Leftenant Colonel de Castellano, please continue the briefing."

"Sir," De Castellano says sharply, stepping forward. In his right hand is a long pointer. "The first operation will be here," he says, tapping a large rectangle in an area just west of the Hudson River. "The second operation will be here," he says, pointing to another rectangle about one kilometer from the Connecticut coast. He walks to the front of the stage.

"The first operation will involve most of Thirty and the other Brigade Commandos," he says. "The First Irish Brigade will sit this one out for two reasons. The first is that we plan to launch this operation in three days

243

and much of that Brigade's kit is either still being unloaded or is at sea. A storm has delayed its arrival." He pauses.

"And the second reason?" Lieutenant Colonel Blair Fraiser of Forty asks in a stage whisper.

"The second reason," De Castellano hurries on, "is that we believe we can win them over without a fight."

"Brilliant," Lieutenant Colonel Aurora McLaren of Four Five says, the sarcasm obvious in her voice. "They will just happily surrender."

At that, Sam advances from the back of the stage where he has been standing. "We will not ask them to surrender." He looks over the room at the confused and questioning faces. "The intelligence Thirty brought back is that this group has killed their Sergeants. We are not sure who is running the camp, but it appears to be organized and functioning reasonably well, although we think their food supply is in question. The Soldiers have maintained discipline of a much more relaxed variety."

"Then what, sir?" Fraiser asks.

"I want to ask them to join us," Sam says, holding up a hand to stop any questions. "From what Leftenant Colonel Griffith's blokes tell us, and from what we have gleaned from the Soldiers they brought in, this group may be willing to throw in its lot with us. As we did in Europe, we will ask them to join us. Those who do will receive rations and medical care. When the Army arrives, they will be trained and formed into units. As in Europe, the goal is to create a large force that can eventually rid this continent of The Enemy. A major thing we have going for us is that the disintergration we found in Europe seems to be going on here as well. Any questions?"

"What of those who do not join us?" Judy asks.

"As long as they are not hostile, they will be allowed to leave and go anywhere they wish. We will allow them to take their weapons, which they could well need for self-defense should they run into any of their former companions, and we will supply them with seven days' rations and water. We are hoping they will stay in the area and start farming and other constructive activities."

When no one raises any more questions, Sam turns to De Castellano. "Continue, Leftenant Colonel."

"Yes, sir," he says, walking to the front of the stage again. "The plan calls for Thirty to deploy on the west, north, and south of the encampment.

Their mission will be to warn the rest of the Brigade of any threatening movements. Four Two and then Forty will land and deploy in battle formation one half kilometer inland. That will put those two Commandos within less than a kilometer from the encampment. The landing craft will then return for Four Five and Four Six.

"With the Commandos will be light artillery, mortars, and heavy machine guns. The tanks and heavy artillery will stay afloat to be landed as needed. We will also have available air assets, both fighter jets and attack helicopters. They also will be held back to be used as needed.

"After Four Five and Four Six have landed, the Brigade will hold position. A party of officers from the Brigade and the Long Island Defense Forces along with our three new recruits," he says of the three Soldiers Thirty brought in, "who have decided to join us, will then advance to the camp to talk to the leadership."

He pauses to let his audience digest that. "If all goes well, most of the Brigade will withdraw. Four Two will remain behind, along with medical and supply people to see to our new recruits' needs. We estimate this encampment holds up to twenty-five thousand but is leaking people every day. We have not determined where they are going, except not to another encampment within twenty-five kilometers. That is the extent of Thirty's reconnaissance. Once the camp is stabilized and deemed safe, the bulk of Four Two will be withdrawn in preparation for the second op."

"And if it doesn't go well?" Lee asks.

"Then," Sam says, stepping forward, "the Brigade will do what the Brigade does." His comment is greeted with some sarcastic chuckles and deep sighs from his audience. "Continue," he says to De Castellano.

"Sir," he replies.

"Leftenant Colonel," says Captain Ivan Handly of D Company, the Four Six, "what do we know about who is running this camp?"

"From what our new recruits tell us, a group of undetermined size, but at least forty, led the revolt against the Sergeants and now run the camp. They rule through persuasion not coercion. The Soldiers are free to leave the camp if they desire, and apparently some have, both in groups of three or four and groups of up to one hundred. What seems to be holding the bulk of soldiers together is fear of the Sergeants returning. Periodically, patrols are sent out for up to ten kilometers to warn of such an event. On the plus side for us, they know an attack will not come over the river, so they do not patrol in that direction. We believe that fear, along with food, clothing, and medical benefits, will prompt the majority to join us."

"Not to mention revenge," Handly says.

"Yes, quite," De Castellano says. "Now, the second operation will begin two weeks later, if all goes as we hope with the first. This one will be a combat operation. The Sergeants are still in control of this camp so we expect a fight. The Brigade—the Marine Brigade," he quickly corrects himself, "will land here," pointing to an area south of The Enemy camp, "while the Irish Brigade lands here," pointing to an area north of the camp. Thirty will maintain a cordon around the encampment to warn of any movement. We will land heavy artillery and armor with both Brigades. The Navy will stand off the coast as near The Enemy as possible to provide gunnery support."

"They will hear us coming, won't they?" Judy asks.

"We expect they will since this area is lightly wooded," De Castellano replies. "But it is also relatively flat as opposed to the hilly terrain in the first operation, so our armor should be able to bull its way through. As soon as Thirty detects any movement, they will pull back and we will hit the camp with air and naval guns. The two Brigades will advance as rapidly as possible to catch any fleeing enemy. They will leave blocking units on the north and south, joining forces to the east of the camp and then driving west. The goal is to overrun the camp and destroy any opposition as quickly as possible, taking as many prisoners as practicable. We believe the key to this operation will be close communication between the two Brigades to avoid friendly fire."

"You don't say," one of the Irish Colonels comments dryly.

De Castellano just looks at him and smiles. "To do that, both Brigades will be equipped with radios to communicate with each other and with the Navy, as well as Navy and Marine air. We also have established a unit boundary here," he says pointing to the Connecticut River.

"That will make the boundary easy to spot. Both Brigades will have bridging equipment and Royal Engineer detachments to throw the spans across the river. As you can see, The Enemy camp lies on both sides of the river, with slightly more than half to the south. Our drones have photographed a number of wooden bridges. We do not believe the bridges are sturdy enough to hold armor or other heavy equipment. The Engineers will remedy that problem as quickly as possible."

"The two Brigades will be fighting independently?" Leary asks.

"Yes and no, Brigadier General," De Castellano replies. "While they will be on opposite sides of the river, they will be mutually supporting with infantry and, possibly light artillery, and able to cross."

"Thank you," Leary says.

"Sir," he replies.

"Ladies and gentlemen," Sam says, stepping forward, "those are the broad outlines of the plan. For my Commando commanders, you will receive your detailed orders as you leave. Any questions or concerns you may have, contact Colonel Staffero.

"Brigadier General Leary," Sam says, turning to the Irish commander, "I will provide you with a set of plans immediately we adjourn. If you have any objections or concerns, please contact me within the next few days. Changes can and will be made as needed. I apologize for not having consulted you earlier."

"That's quite all right," Leary replies, "We just landed today and time is of the essence. I and my staff will review the plans and be in touch within the next two days."

"Thank you for your understanding, sir," Sam says. "Then, ladies and gentlemen, thank you, good hunting and stay alert," Sam says, turning to leave.

"Attention!" Staffero commands, bringing everyone to their feet as Sam and the other senior officers walk out, leaving behind an excited room. De Castellano goes down to the floor and hands Leary a detailed copy of the plans, offering to provide any assistance needed during the review process.

⬦⬦⬦⬦◯⬦⬦⬦⬦

"Which company will be landing with us?" Sam asks Staffero as they sit in a room that has been turned into his office in the small two-story wood-framed house he has been given to use as a headquarters next to the area the Brigade is camped in. His and Staffero's sleeping quarters are upstairs. He shares his bedroom with Sarah, whose Regiment is camped nearby as well. The house had been empty for a number of years, but Sarah's Engineers quickly rehabilitated it.

"B of Four Two," Staffero says.

"Right. How are our recruits doing?"

"They are settling in nicely," Staffero says. "The B Company guys have taken them in and cared for them well. They are certainly enjoying regular food, showers, and new clothes."

Sam just nods. "Now …" The buzzing intercom interrupts him. He raises a finger to indicate a pause and reaches for the receiver. "Yes?"

"The Commandos wish to see you and the Colonel, sir," the Sergeant on the desk outside his office says.

Sam looks quizzically at Staffero, who returns the look with a shrug thrown in. "Have them enter," Sam says, putting down the receiver.

Both he and Staffero stand to greet the five Lieutenant Colonels, who march in with the senior in the lead and the junior, Judy, at the end of the line, indicating this is a formal meeting. They come to attention in front of his desk and all salute.

A bit startled by this formality, it takes Sam a moment to respond before returning the salute.

"Stand easy," he says. "I would invite you to sit, but I am afraid I do not have enough chairs."

"Quite alright, sir," Lee, the senior Lieutenant Colonel, says.

"Then," Sam says, his eyebrows raised, "you may all speak freely."

"Sir," Lee continues, "we were wondering who would be leading the contact party."

"I will, of course," Sam says, a bit taken aback by the question.

"Sir," Griffith, the second senior Commando officer, says, "We respectfully request that you stand down and allow one of us to take that assignment."

The question takes Sam both by surprise and irritates him. "And why should I do that?" he barks out.

"Sir," McLaren, number three in seniority, replies, "you are the heart and soul of this Brigade. We cannot afford to lose you should this initial contact go awry."

"You're saying one of you is expendable?" he shoots back. "We are on the eve of a major operation and losing any one of my Commando leaders would be devastating, not to mention bloody inconvenient."

"Sir, with all due respect," Fraiser, the fourth senior, says, "we are all more expendable than you."

"Bloody hell," Sam nearly shouts back. "None of my Marines are expendable and I'll be bloody damned if I will let any of you take a risk I myself am not willing to take."

Sam stands there glaring at his top Commando officers, all of whom are just looking straight ahead.

"If I may," Staffero says, breaking the standoff and the uncomfortable silence. "I will lead the contact party."

Sam furrows his brow, then glances over at the Colonel. "I can't spare you," he says quietly.

"You can't spare anyone, it seems," Staffero says, keeping her voice as neutral as possible. "However, my elimination would be the least disruptive for this operation. Therefore, I am the most, if you pardon the expression, expendable."

Her statement is greeted with silence, but everyone is now looking at her, although no one is talking. All that can be heard are the waves hitting the shore and the distant sound of training coming in through the office's open windows.

"Brilliant," Staffero finally says, again breaking the silence. "It's settled."

"I have not agreed to this, Colonel," Sam says slowly and emphatically.

"Brigadier," she replies patiently, "you have all made excellent points. The solution is obvious. Besides," she says, hurrying along before Sam can interrupt her, her tone light, "it will get me out from behind a desk and back into the field. I need the exercise. And with all due respect, sir, you're pushing well past fifty." She smiles broadly at Sam, leaving unsaid the obvious that he is past his physical prime and could be more of a liability than a help in case of a fight.

"Oh, bloody hell," he says, reaching down to his bottom desk drawer and pulling out a bottle of single-malt scotch and seven glasses.

As he starts pouring, Judy says, "None for me, sir."

Sam stops for a moment, looking at his daughter. He smiles and finishes pouring six glasses of scotch and one of water. He passes them around, then lifts his glass, a motion they all mimic.

"Ladies and gentlemen," he says, "here is to a successful operation."

CHAPTER 29

S taffero sits in the middle of the third boat—the initial landing party is in boats with silent electric motors—as they approach the Hudson River shore. With her are the three recruits, as the Marines now think of them, plus two officers of the Long Island Defense Forces. Elements of Thirty Commando are already in place around the camp's perimeter. The report: All is quiet; no one within half a kilometer to the shore.

When the two lead boats hit the riverbank, the Marines pour out and deploy without a sound, pulling the boats up on shore as they go. Staffero's boat lands a few seconds later, quickly followed by the other B Company boats. The rest of the Four Two is down river in front-ramp landing craft with the engines idling, waiting for the signal to land.

The three recruits have been told not to speak until they are sent forward into the camp. While they assured the Marines they would be welcomed, Staffero is taking no chances, deploying the company in combat formation with the rest of Four Two approaching as quietly as possible, also to deploy in combat formation.

Staffero and her contingent walk relatively quickly through the forest, not trying to conceal their presence but making sure not to outpace the Marines on either side. She worries the three recruits will blurt out the news Marines are quietly approaching the camp, ready for a fight. They have assured her they will not do that—now that assurance will be put to the test.

As they emerge from the woods—security is lax, with no sentries posted around the perimeter—a soldier spots them and sounds the alarm. Quickly, armed soldiers are taking positions facing them. They remind her of pictures she's seen of eighteenth-century soldiers all lined up shoulder to shoulder.

"Bloody beautiful target," she says under her breath. "Alright, you three," says to the trio from the camp, "you're on. Just try not to get shot as you approach."

"Thanks for the confidence," DeWayne says, giving her a weak grin as the three walk slowly forward, their arms and hands up as they call out to their comrades.

A woman steps out of the ranks, her hand on the stock of her rifle resting on her shoulder, the barrel pointing up. She looks at them intently, then motions them to come into the camp. When they reach the line, a quick intense conversation ensues. Soon, the quartet disappears into the camp. The Soldiers in the firing line relax, some sitting on the ground, with their rifles no longer pointing at the Marines.

Staffero quickly gets on the command net, telling Sam and the Commando leaders what is going on. She orders the rest of Four Two to deploy, but stay within half a kilometer of the river. She leaves the other Commandos afloat.

Sam, who is aboard an old ferry he is using as a command post, briefly wonders whether that is a good move. He's tempted to ask her but restrains himself. His Colonel is the senior officer on the spot, so he will defer to her judgment. He's just frustrated by not being there.

"You know," Sarah says, walking up to him with two cups of tea as he stands on the top weather deck looking toward where his Marines are deployed, "you should relax. Michelle is an outstanding officer, that's why Tom recommended her, and the others have accepted her so readily despite her lack of seniority." Sarah decided to join Sam at the last minute on the excuse she needed to evaluate what her Engineers will required to do. A good rationale, but the underlying reason is she and Staffero wanted to make sure Sam didn't make a last-minute switch and replace the Colonel with himself.

"I know all that," Sam says, taking the cup and leaning against the railing. "But I should be there. I need to know what is happening in case we need to act quickly."

"Oh, bollocks," Sarah snorts. "You just want to be where the action is. You always do. And I and the kids are bloody damn lucky you haven't gotten yourself killed. We've been together too long for me to lose you now over some silly adventure. It's time to let the younger folks take care of things."

Sam reaches out and squeezes her hand, "Like Judy?"

"Shut up!" Sarah snaps. "The silly girl is just like you: All piss and vinegar. Never a thought about her personal safety. Not even a pregnancy gets in her way. Maybe having a child will change her attitude."

"Do you really believe that?" Sam asks, looking over at his wife.

"No," Sarah replies, dejectedly. "I just hope Josh can take care of her."

"He will," Sam says. "Just like you've taken care of me." He pulls up her hand and kisses it. She returns the kiss. They both look toward the forest, appreciating the silence. And wondering what is going on.

Staffero is wondering the same thing.

Finally, nine people come back through the lines toward them. None are armed. She recognizes the three recruits, DeWayne, Margarita, and Ahmed. The other six, she assumes, are some of the camp's leaders.

The party stops just a meter in front of the Marines.

"They tell us," one of the women says, indicating the three recruits, "that you will help us and you want us to join you."

"That's true," Staffero says. "I am Colonel Michelle Staffero, the Chief of Staff of the British Royal Marine Brigade. We are hoping that you will join us in the fight against our common Enemy. Whether you do is completely up to you. We are ready to provide you with food, clothing, medical care, proper military training, and weapons."

"And if we don't wish to join you?" one of the men asks.

Staffero just shrugs. "Then we will leave, and you are free to go on doing whatever it is you do."

"You won't attack us?" another woman asks.

"Only if you attack first," Staffero says.

"How can we trust you?" the first woman asks.

"Two reasons," the Colonel replies. "First, we haven't attacked you, and second, we are offering to help you reclaim your country and your lives. We know you have been through a horrendous experience ..."

"You have no idea what we have been through," a second man says.

"No, I don't," she admits. "But our Brigadier, our commanding officer, does. He and his wife escaped from this land about thirty years ago. He has been fighting our common Enemy ever since."

"We've been told you're from England, which is why your accent is funny," a third man says.

"True," she says, "but we all speak English, and our Brigade, along with a Brigade from Ireland, is on Long Island. We are working with them to enter the continent."

The six leaders look at each other, then move back out of earshot as they huddle in a conference. Arms fly, and they repeatedly glance at Staffero. The three recruits stay with the Marines, looking nervous and uncertain.

Finally, the six return.

"We want to meet your Brigadier. We want him to come here," says the first man, "and we want to send someone to Long Island to find out what is going on."

Staffero nods. "Give me a moment." Now it is her turn to retreat out of earshot. She calls Sam, explaining the situation to him.

"Sounds like they want a hostage in case we do something nasty to their people," Sam says, chuckling.

"Yes, sir. I am not sure it is a good idea. They are very suspicious," Staffero says.

"Don't blame them." Sam thinks a moment. "Right, tell them I'm on my way and they can send their delegation to Long Island as soon as I arrive."

"Yes, sir," she replies, not sure it is a safe move, but realizing it is probably the only one that can win these people over. She goes back to the leaders, telling them Brigadier Samuel Hope is on the way. "How many do you want to send to Long Island?"

"Three," one of the women says. "Myself, Kyle, and Jahne."

"Brilliant," Staffero replies, knowing enough from Sam not to ask for surnames. "And you are?"

"Mary Sue."

"Excellent. If it meets your approval, these two officers from the Long Island Defense Force will accompany you. They can tell you about their people and what kind of life they are living."

"That is acceptable," Mary Sue says.

"When will your Brigadier arrive?" one of the men asks. "I'm Patrick."

"He should be here within thirty minutes," she says, feeling reassured by the leaders giving their names.

"Where is he coming from? I'm RaShonda," another of the women asks.

"He's down river on a ferry we are using as a command post."

"So, you were ready for a fight?" the last man challenges her.

"We were hoping it would not come to that," Staffero says. "But we had to be prepared in case you attacked us."

The man nods, accepting the answer as logical. "Stanley. My name is Stanley."

"Yes, thank you. I'm Michelle," Staffero says.

An awkward silence falls on the group.

"Tell me about England," RaShonda says. "How did you beat off the attack?"

"England is on the island of Britain we share with Scotland and Wales. It's all one country actually. Ireland is another island to our west."

"You were never attacked?" RaShonda asks.

"No, not directly," she replies. "In the early days, we lost all our food and energy imports from Europe. There was mass starvation and hopelessness, so I am told."

"You were told?"

"It was before I was born," she says. "Our people pulled together, just like the blokes on Long Island did, and managed to muddle through. Now we have a decent standard of living and are safe. A few years ago we went back to the Continent ..."

"Continent?"

"Europe. With the help of Soldiers, Soldiers like you, who came over to our side and people like those on Long Island who had managed to survive, we are liberating the Continent and helping them rebuild their lives."

RaShonda nods as she contemplates what she has been told. "Where is Europe?"

After dealing with the recruits, Staffero is not surprised by the question. "It's across the Atlantic Ocean to the east," she says pointing in that direction, "about five thousand seven hundred kilometers."

"What's a kilometer?" Patrick asks.

That question throws Staffero who has to think of way to explain it. "It's a measurement of distance," she says, unable to come up with a better definition. "We'll get into that later," she says reassuringly, hoping that will put the matter to rest for now.

The silence that resumes is soon broken by a loud crashing of people walking through the woods. As the noise comes closer, everyone turns in that direction. Sam and Sarah soon emerge from the woods, accompanied by four aides.

"Noisy," Staffero comments, a small smile across her lips.

"Didn't want to surprise anyone," Sam replies. "As for my wife being here," he says, anticipating the question, "she wouldn't stay behind. I pulled military rank. She countered with marital rank. And logic. You can see who won."

"Bloody right I did. I have to make sure he stays out of trouble," Sarah announces with glee.

"Indeed," Staffero says, smiling. "Let me introduce you."

The introductions are quickly made, then Staffero turns to the three recruits. "Would you please accompany the Brigadier and the Colonel?"

"Yeah, no problem," Ahmed replies.

"Good," Staffero says. Then turning to Mary Sue, Kyle and Jahne, she says, "Are you ready?"

"Yes, we are," Kyle says, a bit nervously.

Staffero then turns to the Long Island officers. "Please show them the way."

One of the officers nods, then leads the way toward the river, accompanied by one of Sam's aides.

"If you are ready," Patrick says to Sam and Sarah.

"It's after noon," Sarah observes. "We should plan on the two groups spending the night. If that is agreeable?" she asks the six from the camp.

They quickly confer.

"Agreed," Kyle announces.

"Now, lead on," Sam says, as he and Sarah, followed by three aides, begin to head to the camp.

"Not them!" RaShonda says sharply, indicating the aides.

Sam holds up a hand to forestall Staffero's protest. "As you wish," he says, then tells the aides to accompany the Colonel. He and Sarah, with the three leaders and the three recruits, then head into the camp.

"And no radios," RaShonda orders pointing to the headsets Sarah and Sam are wearing.

"We need to keep those," Sam replies quietly.

"Why?" RaShonda challenges him.

"If our Marines worry about our safety, they are likely to come fast and hard," Sam says. "Neither of us want that. We want to resolve this peacefully. Staying in contact will go a long way to preventing an attack."

RaShonda studies him for a moment. "How do we know you can do that?"

Sam keys his radio, ordering a flyby of fighter jets followed by attack helicopters. Within three minutes, a flight of four jets screams low over the camp, followed two minutes later by half a dozen helicopters swooping by. That catches the attention not only of the six leaders but of the entire camp.

After they pass, RaShonda looks at Sam. "Keep your radios."

"Thank you," Sam says as he and Sarah follow the three leaders into the camp. The three recruits stay close to them.

As she watches them go, Staffero is not happy with the situation, but resigned to accepting it.

"They bloody well better not hurt them," she mutters under her breath. Despite the demonstration, she doubts these people know the kind of pain that will descend on them if anything happens to the Brigadier or his wife.

⟫━┈━⟪⟫━┈━○━┈━⟫⟫━┈━⟪

The Soldiers in the camp stand and stare as Sarah and Sam walk in after the trio of leaders. DeWayne, Margarita and Ahmed try to form a protective shield on each side and behind them. They also draw stares from the other Soldiers, many of whom recognize them but wonder at the new

uniforms and boots they are wearing and their bathed appearance as well
as their well-fed look.

Deep into the camp, the party comes to an open area with a large
group of Soldiers standing in a circle. RaShonda and Stanley stand aside
as Patrick leads Sarah and Sam into the middle. Their escort stops at the
edge of the ring.

Sam and Sarah feel exposed and vulnerable, feelings they keep well
hidden, as several hundred pairs of eyes stare at them. They hear muttered
conversations but can't tell what is being said.

Finally, Patrick speaks. "Listen up! These are the leaders of the people
we've been told about."

"Where are the others?" someone calls out.

"They are going to take a look at the camps these people," Patrick
says, indicating Sarah and Sam, "have set up on Long Island. They will
report back to us."

"Where is Long Island?" someone else calls out.

"Down river," Patrick responds.

"What's there?" someone else asks.

"These people's camp and they say a community of people who never
fell to the Sergeants."

"Bullshit!" someone yells, provoking derisive laughter.

"It's true!" Sarah says, stepping forward and looking around the circle.
"You know The Enemy does not cross water. Long Island is off the coast,
surrounded by water. Our Enemy, your Enemy, never could get there.
They have survived and we are helping each other free this land."

"Why? Why do you care?" a voice in the crowd yells.

"Because," Sam says, joining Sarah, "we are all better off when we are
free to live our own lives. To do what we want, when we want, as long as
we're not hurting anyone else. To work together, to help each other to raise
our children and to build our societies."

"The Sergeants wanted to dominate us," Sarah says, looking around at
the people who have now grown quiet. "They told us what to do with our
bodies and minds. They wanted to control us. To dominate us."

"Where we live," Sam says, "we elect the people who run our
government. If we don't like what they do, we can kick them out of office.
We live in a place governed by laws designed to protect everyone."

"We know what you've been through ..." Sarah starts to say.

"No way you can know!" someone yells.

"We do because we came from the same kind of camp you are in!" Sam says.

"Many years ago," Sarah says, "my husband and I were in this kind of camp far south of here." She and Sam take turns telling the story of their escape, the battles, friends they lost, then how they and their companions built a ship, and sailed north. How they were rescued by a British fishing trawler. How they built new lives in England. And how they have been fighting The Enemy ever since. How their daughter fights with them. And how they lost a son in the battles in Europe. They had to explain where Britain and Europe are.

"How do we know any of this is true?" someone yells.

Sarah and Sam look at each other.

Sam shrugs.

"You don't," Sarah says. "The only way we can prove any of this is by you joining us and helping to defeat The Enemy."

"If you join us," Sam says, "we will provide food, clothing, medical care, and training, as well as helping you build proper buildings."

"You personally?" someone asks.

"Actually, no," Sam replies. "I am commander of the Royal Marine Brigade. Sarah is the commander of a Royal Engineer Regiment. We will provide the initial help. That will be taken over by the Royal Army Troops who will be with you long-term."

"If we don't join you?" someone yells.

"Then you don't join us," Sam shrugs. "You go your way, and we will let you alone provided you do not attack us. We will not make you fight with us and we will never punish or hurt anyone for not joining us."

The questions stop as quiet but animated conversations break out throughout the entire circle. Voices rise and fall. Sarah and Sam catch a word here and there, but not enough to know what is being said.

Finally, the conversations start to die out.

"How do we know you can do what you say you can?" asks Patrick, who has been quiet this whole time.

"I can have food and clothing here by the morning," Sam says. "We also can have doctors come to provide care."

"I can have my Engineers here in the morning to work with you about improving conditions here, if you wish to stay," Sarah says. "Or we can scout out other locations and build a camp there."

"But you say you can beat the Sergeants," RaShonda says, stepping into the middle. "How do we know you can do that?"

"Tell you what," Sam says, "there is a camp on the other side of the river that is run by the Sergeants. We can't approach them the way we did here. We have no choice but to attack. You are welcome to send observers to watch what happens and how we do it. I think that will show you that we can do what we say."

RaShonda looks contemplatively at the couple.

Stanley steps forward, "I think we've heard enough for now." Turning to DeWayne, Ahmed, and Margarita, he says, "Why don't you show them around the camp. Let them see how we live and what we are like."

"Okay," Ahmed says. "Should we go?" he asks Sam and Sarah.

"Sweetheart," Sarah says as an aside to Sam, "I do believe we have been dismissed."

"It would seem so," Sam says, smiling. "Well, guys, lead on," he tells their escorts.

They follow their three guides out of the circle. Looking back over his shoulder, Sam sees the circle collapse into ever changing groups, presumably to discuss what they have just heard.

As Sam and Sarah walk through the camp, amused by the stares their presence provokes, bothered by the fear they see in some eyes, they are confronted by the memories of their own experiences in a camp such as this. The well-ordered streets with eight-person tents neatly lining either side. Everyone looks hungry, dressed in rags. Many have no boots. Few have coats. The smell of unwashed bodies assails their senses. They see a few women in various stages of pregnancy, uniforms straining as stomachs expand. The couple stop to chat with some of the Soldiers. Some are willing to talk; others just stare at them or move away. To the ones who will talk to them, they compare their experiences with what these Soldiers have endured.

In the distance, a gong starts sounding.

"Dinner," Margarita says. "This way." The trio leads them to an open area where people are queuing for food. The lines are orderly and calm. No pushing. No shoving. None of the fighting Sam and Sarah experienced in their time in such a camp. Here, everyone expects to get their share of the food. It may not be a lot, but it is doled out fairly.

"This is good," Sarah says.

"Yes," Sam says. "We can work with these people."

As they reach the head of the line, they are handed a tin plate and fork, as well as a cup with water. The food plopped onto their plates is a simple stew.

"I'd love to know what the meat is," Sarah whispers to Sam.

"Don't ask," Sam replies, his voice faux serious.

"Right," she says.

Ahmed leads them back to the area where the circle was. The five of them join the group there, sitting on the ground.

"I do miss George's cooking," Sarah says, her face screwed up at the taste of the food.

"Not everyone can be a magician," Sam says as he forces himself to swallow the questionable concoction.

"May I ask what this meat is?" Sarah asks those around them.

"Squirrel or rat," Margarita says nonchalantly. "Maybe both."

"Oh," Sarah replies, hesitating before taking another bite.

After they are done eating, DeWayne takes their plates and cups away. Sam and Sarah stand, wondering what is coming next.

What's next is revealed by Stanley, Patrick, and RaShonda, who walk up to them in the growing darkness. Fires are being lit throughout the camp, providing light and some warmth that is eagerly sought by the people there.

"We've decided to take you up on your offer," Patrick says.

"All of you?" Sam asks.

"All of us who wish to," Stanley responds. "We will know in the morning how many will join."

"Our decision is tentative," ReShonda adds. "It depends on whether you do what you say you can."

"And we want to send observers when you attack the other camp," Patrick says.

"Fair enough," Sam says. "We'll start making arrangements right away."

"Good," Patrick says. "Then, until morning. RaShonda will show you to your tent."

"Thank you," Sarah responds.

"This way," RaShonda says, leading them a short way to an eight-person tent they will have to themselves.

Once inside, Sam contacts Staffero, briefing her on their day and hearing about what the three from the camp did. He then orders her to have one hundred thousand rations delivered in the morning, as well as many uniforms, boots, and coats she can manage.

"By the by," he says, "we also need a medical team. There are some sick here and a number of pregnant women. Tell the medics to plan on being here a while. And see if the Long Island blokes can provide any maternity clothes."

"Yes, sir," Staffero answers. "I'm glad you and the Colonel are safe and well."

"We're fine. We have a tent to ourselves and are bedding down for the night. Talk to you in the morning."

"Yes, sir."

<hr />

Just after dawn, the camp is stirring with Soldiers heading toward the mess area for breakfast. Many are in line, while a few already have their meals and are sitting on the ground.

Sam and Sarah wander out of their tent, yawning and blinking in the early light, listening to the muffled sounds of a camp just beginning to stir, watching Soldiers wandering toward the chow line.

"Where are our minders?" Sarah asks.

"Minding something else?" Sam manages to get out during a yawn.

The roar of diesel engines, the crashing of trees falling shatters the morning calm. Everyone freezes, staring off to the east.

"We're being attacked!" a man screams, breaking the shock that has descended on the camp. Everyone scatters, grabbing weapons. Soldiers who are apparently in command issue orders, forming companies. Everyone is casting worried glances toward the advancing noise. Hard stares are directed at Sam and Sarah.

"Oh, bollocks!" Sarah exclaims. "They started early."

"We better get things under control fast," Sam says.

"No kidding," she responds.

"What the fuck is going on?" Stanley yells at them as he runs up, his rifle at the ready, followed by Patrick, RaShonda and others. "You promised not to attack us! We will fight back!"

"Take them prisoner!" RaShonda orders. "They will not get away with this!"

"Wait a bloody minute!" Sarah yells over the loud, angry voices surrounding them. "This is not an attack!"

"Then what is it?" Stanley demands.

"My Engineers started earlier than I told them to. They are cutting a road from the river to the camp so we can move supplies."

"Sarah," Sam says, "order them to stand down. Now."

She nods and keys her radio. The noise quickly fades to a low rumble of idling engines.

"I bloody apologize for this," Sarah tells the angry and bewildered faces around them. "They weren't supposed to start work for a couple of more hours."

"Then why did they?" RaShonda demands.

"I have some over-eager Battalion commanders," she says. "I suppose they thought they were doing the right thing to cut the road as early as possible."

"Why?" RaShonda asks.

"The road will be used to truck in supplies," Sam says. "I have ordered one hundred thousand rations and as many clothes and boots as possible to be delivered today. The most efficient way of doing that is to bring them in by trucks. And those trucks need roads."

"How do we know you are telling the truth?' Stanley demands.

"Tell you what," Sarah says, "why don't you come with me, and I will show you what is happening."

The people around them look at each other questioningly. They do not trust Sarah.

"I'll stay here," Sam finally says.

RaShonda nods to Patrick.

"Okay," he says. "Me and RaShonda will go with you."

"Brilliant," Sarah replies. "Let's go." She quickly leads the pair off toward the river.

"You might have your people stand down," Sam tells Stanley.

He stares at Sam for a moment. "When they get back." He then tells those around him to have everyone hold in place. As they scatter, he glares at Sam for a moment, then stalks off.

Sam just sighs, resigning himself to an uncomfortable wait, and hoping no one gets trigger happy.

❧

The rumbling of engines grows louder as Sarah leads the other two through the woods outside of the camp. As they emerge from the trees, they find four bulldozers abreast, followed by four more about one hundred meters behind them.

Sarah quickly walks up to a Lieutenant Colonel for a quick conversation. Then she returns to Patrick and RaShonda. "What they are doing is knocking down the trees and leveling the ground as much as they can with the front bulldozers. The ones behind move the trees off to the side."

"The stumps are still there," Patrick observes, looking down the wide swatch the bulldozers cut.

"Yes," Sarah replies. "That will be alright for now. The trucks have high ground clearance so they will be able to make it through. Later on we will build a proper road. It will be dirt but usable except in heavy rains."

Patrick and RaShonda walk off a few meters. They talk quietly, glancing at the bulldozers.

When they walk back, RaShonda looks hard at Sarah. "You could use this road to attack us."

The comment startles Sarah. "We could, but we would have no need to use a road."

The two look at each other, still doubting.

"Give me a moment," Sarah says, keying her radio.

A few minutes later, Staffero and Judy come striding past the bulldozers. Both are armed with pistols and rifles slung over their shoulders. Patrick and RaShonda look surprised and worried.

"This is Colonel Staffero, the Brigade's Chief of Staff, and Leftenant Colonel Hope, commander of Four Two Commando, and my daughter. Ladies, this is RaShonda and Patrick, two of the leaders in the camp."

"Hello," the two Marines say, offering to shake hands—hands that are tentatively taken.

"RaShonda and Patrick are worried this road could be used to launch an attack against them," Sarah says. "Is that right?" she asks them.

"Yes," RaShonda spits out, defiance returning to her voice.

"Color Sergeant Farley!" Judy calls.

"Ma'am," he says, standing up from where he was concealed two meters to the right of the road, taking both Soldiers by surprise.

"What are you orders?" Judy asks, her gaze fixed on RaShonda.

"To protect the bulldozers."

"Under what conditions are you allowed to fire your weapon?"

"Only if fired upon first," comes the brisk reply.

"Very good," Judy says. "As you were."

The Color Sergeant resumes his concealed position, feeling a bit foolish since he has revealed it to a potential enemy.

"If we wanted to attack you," Staffero says, "you would never see us coming. We do not need a road. We would hit your camp with air and artillery, pounding it into pieces. We would then launch a coordinated ground attack behind a rolling artillery barrage, mopping up what was left."

Patrick and RaShonda are left in shock by the confident tone in which their potential destruction is outlined.

"But," Staffero says, after giving them a moment to digest what they have just heard, "we have no desire to attack you. As the Color Sergeant said, we will only fire if fired upon. We have our Marines protecting our engineers as a precaution. Nothing more. We are here to help you, if you want us to."

Looking at Sarah, Patrick says, "Let us return to camp to tell everyone what is going on before you start your road building."

"Brilliant," Sarah says, then thanking Staffero and Judy, she follows the pair back to the camp.

When they get back, Patrick and RaShonda call a meeting of leaders, describing what they have learned, but leaving out Staffero's description of what an attack would look like.

"How do we know they're telling the truth?" someone asks.

"They are," Patrick says. "They don't need that road to attack us."

"We can fight them off!" someone else announces.

"No, we can't," Patrick says. "We've seen their aircraft. And we are convinced that if they wanted to attack, we wouldn't stand a chance."

"They are offering us food and other supplies," RaShonda adds. "Patrick and I believe we can trust them."

Conversations break out among those gathered. The consensus is to accept RaShonda and Patrick's evaluation. At that, RaShonda turns to Sarah, telling her Engineers' work can resume.

Soon, the roar of engines and the sound of trees falling resumes. Soldiers straggle back into camp, many looking over the shoulders, worry on their faces.

After two hours, the first bulldozers break through the last trees. They are soon followed by the trailing dozers, clearing more of the ground. As soon as the heavy equipment is out of the way, fifty heavy duty trucks roll into camp, loaded with rations. With the help of the Soldiers, the trucks are quickly unloaded. They then turn around to bring in more supplies.

"Thank you," Stanley tells Sarah and Sam.

"Our pleasure," Sam replies.

"This doesn't mean we will fight with you," Stanley says.

"Of course not," Sam replies. "That is not why we are doing this. We just want to help you survive and rebuild your lives. If you do join us, that would just be grand, but it is not required and no one will be forced to do anything against their will."

"In any case," Sarah says, "we must be getting back to our commands."

"Yes, yes, course." Stanley says. "We will stay in touch."

"Brilliant," Sam says, then he and Sarah head off. As they leave, they see Jahne, Mary Sue, and Kyle getting out of a truck and hurrying off to talk to their counterparts.

"Wait! Brigadier!" Jahne yells at Sam's retreating back. He turns around and walks to the group of now six leaders, while Sarah continues on her way to her command, stopping by the Engineers to talk to them about the progress they are making.

"Yes?" he says as he walks up.

"One minute," Kyle says, holding up a hand as the six huddle together in hushed conversation.

Sam stops abruptly, his eyebrows raised in surprise and annoyance. Sam forces himself to remain at least looking calm as he awaits the results.

Five minutes go by as arms fly around in gestures and the volume goes up and down. When it goes up, furtive glances are cast his way. He retreats a few more steps because it is obvious they do not want him to hear what they are saying.

Finally, the conclave breaks up and all six walk to him.

"We would like to send observers when you attack the other camp," RaShonda says.

"That will help us decide whether to recommend to our people about joining you," Mary Sue adds.

"Brilliant," Sam says, ignoring the fact he had already agreed to that. He turns to gesture to an aide to join him. Turning back to the group, he says, "Choose your observation party and this officer will escort you to my HQ. You will be privy to the final planning and preparations for the attack as well as the attack itself."

"May we join a front-line unit?" Mary Sue asks.

"Hmmm," Sam says, thinking a moment, "we'll have to have that decision later. It wouldn't do to have one of yours killed, or one of mine killed trying to protect you. We will try to get you as close to the front as possible consistent with those parameters. No promises for now."

An unhappy Mary Sue nods, not exactly sure what is being said.

"Leftenant," Sam says, "see that our guests are well taken care of and provide them transportation, quarters, rations, and new uniforms."

"Sir," she says in affirmation.

"If that is acceptable," Sam says, "then I must be on my way. I have a great deal of work to attend to."

"Thank you, Brigadier," Patrick says.

Sam nods and heads toward the river, striding as quickly as he can while taking in what is going on around him.

CHAPTER 30

S ir," one of Sam's aides says, interrupting a conversation among the top commanders of the two Brigades and the top Long Island commander, "the representatives of the New York encampment have arrived."

"Show them in," Sam says.

"Sean," he says turning to Brigadier General Sean Leary, "these are the people I've been telling you about."

"Ah, yes," comes the reply as six people in new Marine uniforms, but lacking any markings of rank, are ushered in.

"Welcome," Sam says to the six arrivals. "You've come just in time. We launch the attack in the morning. Allow me to introduce," he continues without interruption, "Brigadier General Sean Leary, commander of the One Irish Brigade, and his Chief of Staff, Colonel Kellen Byrne. You already know Colonel Staffero, Colonel Petrakis, and Leftenant Colonel de Castellano."

"Thanks," Jahne says as the six shake hands all around. "What are you plans for us?" she asks Sam, also looking around at the others.

"We regret that we cannot incorporate you with front-line units as you requested," Sam says. "Quite honestly, your training does not mesh well with ours, and our Marines and Irish Soldiers are battle-tested and have formed cohesive units. I fear adding an unknown factor could end badly."

"I see," Kyle says, obviously disappointed, "so what will we be able to observe?"

"We would like you," Staffero says, "to send two observers to two of our Commandos and two others to the Irish Brigade's Battalions. Two of you would also be with our Brigades' HQs. We would like you to make those assignments."

"What will we be able to see at those places?" Patrick asks.

"You will be able," Leary says, "to follow the course of the battle, and when the field commanders go toward the front, you will accompany us."

"May I ask a question?" RaShonda says.

"Please," Sam replies.

"Your accent," she says pointing at Sam, "is different than ours. And yours," now pointing at Leary, "is different from both of ours, yet I can understand what you are both saying."

"Many years ago, before all this happened," Sam says with a bit of a laugh, "there was an old saying the English and Americans were peoples separated by a common language. We can add the Irish in there as well. I suppose the fact that all three peoples developed somewhat independently of each other included how we speak our common language."

"Don't forget the Scots and the Welsh," Staffero adds, a hint of her Scottish brogue still evident despite years of living with mostly English people.

"Them, too," he says, nodding to her. "We all speak English, but sound different based on where we live," Sam says, smiling. "Getting back to the matter at hand, you," he says indicting the six Americans, "will be going in with the two Commandos leading the attack, and I believe Brigadier General Leary has similar plans?"

"That is correct," he says. "And as a point of history," he said, pride showing in his voice, "the English conquered Ireland, which is on a separate island, centuries ago. We finally drove them out in the twentieth century, regaining our independence."

"You fight with them now?" Kyle asks.

"Yes," Leary concedes, "because we have a common enemy and because our differences with the English are in the past. We have gotten past that, especially with the world in the poor condition it is now. America, by the by," he goes on, "was a refuge from many million of Irish fleeing English oppression."

"Good," Sam says, interrupting the history lesson, "we are all set for the morrow now. The Leftenant," he says, turning to the six former Enemy Soldiers and indicating one of his aides, "will show you to your quarters, and we hope you will join us for dinner at nineteen hundred hours, two hours from now. We will leave this base at zero one hundred hours. The attack forces will already be aboard and heading toward their assault beaches. Those you choose to go with them will join the Commandos and Battalions directly after dinner."

"Thanks," Jahne says as the group is ushered out. The Marine and Irish officers disperse right after them.

⊱——┼—◆≫━◦━❍━━◦━◅≪◆—┼——⊰

As her landing craft approaches the shore in the pre-dawn dark on this moonless night, Lieutenant Colonel McLaren sweeps the beach and the woods behind it with her nightvision binoculars. She sees and hears the small arms fire being exchanged between her Four Five Commando's first wave and the defenders.

"Crap! Bloody buggering crap!" she curses under her breath. "Radio!"

"Ma'am!" the operator responds.

"Pass on to Brigade and other Commandos that the initial wave has met moderate resistance from small arms."

"Ma'am," and the operator passes on the information.

⊱——┼—◆≫━◦━❍━━◦━◅≪◆—┼——⊰

"Sir," a Marine communications officer says, coming onto the weather deck and handing the message to Sam, who is outside HMS Northampton's command center.

Sam frowns as he reads it, then passes it to Leary.

"It seems," Sam says for the benefit of Staffero and Byrne, "The Enemy knows we have landed." Sam goes into the command center for a few minutes, then comes back out.

"I have asked the Navy to commence bombardment and air strikes on the preset coordinates," he barely gets the word out when the roar of the cruiser's twelve-inch guns blots out all other sound.

Studying the shoreline with powerful binoculars, Sam can see the flashing of small arms fire as well as the larger weapons on the landing craft opening fire. They can hear the low rumbling of exploding naval shells in the distance. The Navy's guns stop firing as attack jets drop napalm on The Enemy's camp. As soon as the jets are clear, the ship's guns resume firing on targets three kilometers inland.

<hr />

"Ma'am," the radio operator says, "Four Six is reporting moderate to heavy opposition to their landing."

"Right," McLaren says. "Any word from the Irish?"

"Light opposition," the operator says. "And ma'am, Brigade is releasing the armor. They should be landing ten minutes after us. Artillery will land as soon as we are half a klick in."

"Brilliant," McLaren says as she finishes putting on her kit for battle. Turning to Jahne, she says, "You are about to get a closer look at battle than Brigade planned. I don't lead from the rear."

"Good," comes the reply as the landing hovercraft moves up onto the shore. The front ramp falls, allowing the Troop inside to pour out and deploy in battle formation.

"Percival," McLaren orders, "bring the portable along. Stay on the Brigade net and attached to my hip."

"Ma'am," the Corporal says, grabbing the radio, his rifle and other kit, and following the Lieutenant Colonel onto the shore and into the forest. McLaren then orders the two armor companies to deploy with her two reserve companies and prepare for an immediate attack.

"Stevens," she calls on the Commando net, "are you aligned with Four Six?"

"Closer than I am to my wife," responds Captain Michael Stevens, C Company commander.

"Keep it that way," she orders. "Let me know if it changes." The woods are not thick, but still, vision is limited, and McLaren can only see about fifty meters of the line in either direction.

"Ma'am."

"Grant, report," McLaren says, as she follows D Company toward the firing.

"We have overcome the opposition," Captain Hamish Grant, commander of A Company, reports. "Staying aligned with Stevens' mob," he adds, knowing McLaren was going to ask.

"Keep it that way," she says. Turning to Percival, "Any word about the Irish?"

"They are past the mouth of the river and are waiting for us to catch up."

"Bloody brilliant," she says. Then ordering B and D Companies to hold position, she moves past their lines to see how the fight is going. Her Marines are slowly pushing The Enemy back, despite the additional numbers of Soldiers joining the battle by entering their firing line.

She finds Stevens crouching about three meters behind his firing line. "How's it going?" McLaren asks as she kneels beside Grant.

He glances over and then looks up at Jahne, who is standing behind her. "Get down, you bloody fool," he barks at her. "Are you looking to get shot?" Jahne quickly drops down. He then looks back at the firing line.

"It's a slaughter. The bloody sods think this is the eighteenth century," he says. "They come marching up in parade formation and then form a firing line standing up. If they didn't keep sending more and more people in, it would be a cakewalk."

"It's the way we are trained," Jayne says, a look of horror on her face as she sees the bodies piling up as close as forty meters away among the trees.

"Right," McLaren says, looking at her, too preoccupied with battle to feel any sympathy for her. "We'll see how they deal with tanks," she says, turning her attention back to Grant. "Hold position here. How's your ammo holding?"

"We bloody well could use more," he says, exasperation in his voice.

"Right," McLaren says, then calls back to order an immediate resupply. She then heads off to find Grant's HQ. Keeping low, she works her way down the line to the left company, finding Grant just past the middle of his line. He's on the radio calling for an emergency resupply of ammo.

"How goes it?" she asks. This time, Jahne drops immediately to the ground.

"That depends on our ammo resupply. We are critically low. They," he says, waving toward The Enemy, "have launched four wave attacks at us. We have beaten them back but we're expending ammo at a ruinous level."

"Right," she says. She gets on the radio and finds the armor has just about moved into position with the two reserve Companies. "I want the attack launched in five. Understood? Five." She gets positive response. "Hold position," she tells Grant.

"Bloody glad to," he says.

In less than five minutes, the crashing of tanks moving through trees breaks through the sound of small arms fire and the not-too-distant naval guns being controlled by Navy fire control officers with the Marines.

⊱─━⊱──✦──⊰━─⊰

"Lee, status," Staffero says over the Brigade net.

"We are critically low on ammunition," he says, yelling into the handset so he can be heard over the noise of battle. "They keep launching human wave attacks. Each one gets closer. We need ammo and water. I need to call up my two reserve companies if we are to hold the line."

"Understood," she replies. "Armor is moving into position. You will soon have a company of tanks plus APVs loaded with ammo. Water, I will have to see about."

"What's their ETA?"

Staffero quickly consults with an aide. "About ten."

"Bloody well better be here fast."

"McLaren has her armor and reserve companies online now. She is holding until you are ready to attack."

"What about our flank?" the worried Commando leader asks.

"Fraiser has two Troops south of you, including patrols that should have made contact with your left."

"They did but I haven't heard if they are having problems."

"None. They are just picking up stragglers. No, I repeat, no indication that your flank is in danger."

"Thanks. We … Wait. I can hear the tanks moving up now. A and B Companies will come up with them."

"Brilliant. Coordinate with McLaren. I want this attack launched together, and as soon as possible."

"Ma'am," Fraiser says, signing off.

Staffero radios Sam, who is on his way to shore, bringing him up to speed. She understands his desire to get closer to the fighting, but at the same time is jealous. Someone had to stay at the command center and he pulled rank. Although, she also appreciates the confidence he has shown her by leaving her to coordinate the attack.

⟫⊶⊷⟫⊷❬❍❭⊶⟪⊶⟪

"When do we go in?" Captain Jules Parrish, B Company's commander, asks McLaren as they stand behind one of the two tanks guarding a road running straight through their position.

Before she can answer, one of the tanks fires its main gun. The two officers quickly look down the road. What they see are pieces of a pickup truck landing on both sides of the road. Behind it, another pickup is coming toward them at high speed, a machine gun mounted over the cab firing. The second tank's main gun fires, destroying that threat. The six following pickups come to screeching halts, then reverse up the road, firing as they go. The two tanks take turns firing, destroying all six.

"We'll go in as soon as Four Six is ready," McLaren tells Parrish. "Make sure you Bootnecks are ready to go."

"Yes, ma'am," he says and heads off.

McLaren checks in with Lee, who tells her he'll be ready in about five minutes. Then she makes sure the ammo and water brought in by the armored personnel vehicles are being distributed.

"Aurora," Sam says as he walks up, using her first name, "report."

"It's brilliant, sir," she says, turning at the sound of his voice. "We are ready to go in as soon as Four Six gets in line."

"Very good," he says. "Have you had any human wave attacks?"

"No, sir, but Four Six reports they have."

"I am aware," he responds. "That is an old tactic of The Enemy, going back to when all this started."

"Here, they just march up, form a firing line standing up. My blokes just mow them down. Only the trees get in the way. The problem is ammo and the resupply has solved that, along with the tanks. I am moving the APVs up to join the fight."

"Casualties?" Sam asks.

"Amazingly light for the amount of firing coming our way. Three dead and fourteen wounded. They've been evacuated to the rear."

"Alright," Sam says.

"Sir, what I don't understand is where all these people are coming from. The Navy is plastering the area between the camp and here and the attack craft is hammering the camp."

"I suspect we will find a lot of dead when we advance."

"Yes, sir. That would be preferable to getting shot at."

"Yes, it would. Well, crack on," Sam says as he heads toward Four Six to find Lee, trailed by a radio operator and three aides. Two of Sam's four-member security detail are on either side of him, with one a bit further back and one in front. Before he reaches Lee's HQ, he hears the roar of tank and APV engines, and a crescendo of fire from the Marine lines as the attack kicks off. When he reaches the Commando HQ, he finds the executive officer, Major Jon Stoneman, there.

"Where is Leftenant Colonel Lee?" Sam asks the Four Six exec.

"He went up to the line, sir," the Major answers.

"Brilliant. What's your status?"

"We are moving out to attack with Four Five. The Navy has shifted most of its fire to the Irish front. They are reporting heavy human wave attacks. They are sending their attack planes over there as well. The Irish say they are hard pressed. Sir, those human wave attacks were bloody horrific. They just kept coming and coming. You can see the piles of dead and wounded stretching back into the forest," the Major says, pointing to the bodies strewn among the trees, at places piled onto each other. "The sods nearly broke through. It was a bloody close thing."

"You did a brilliant job," Sam says, putting a hand on the Major's shoulder. "I think the worst is over. We are on the attack now."

"Thank you, sir," the Major says, then returning to organizing resupply and making sure the reserve companies are ready to go.

"Corporal!" Sam says to one of the Commando's HQ personnel. "Do you have any idea where the Leftenant Colonel is?"

"Yes, sir. He said he was going up to B Company. I'll take you there if you wish, sir."

"Crack on," Sam says, waving a hand toward the firing. He and his party follow the Corporal toward the firing line.

They find Lee crouched down, yelling into his headset to be heard over the noise of battle. A and B Companies are advancing with the tanks and half the APVs through the trees. The fire of rifles and machine guns, both heavy and light, is periodically punctuated with the tanks' main guns and the 40mm guns on the APVs.

"Status," Sam yells, kneeling beside Lee.

"The Enemy line melted away when the armor moved forward," Lee yells back. "Guess they had no stomach for that."

"Brilliant," Sam says. "Four Two is landing now and the rest of Forty is moving onto your flank. They will be sweeping up any hostiles headed that way."

"Thank you, sir."

"I'm off to the left to see how they are doing," Sam says.

"That's A Company. Captain Jamison."

"Yes, thanks," Sam says, as he heads off. He knows who commands each company but appreciates the reminder, in case battle has forced a change. He's happy it hasn't. Sam heads down the line just in front of C Company, which is awaiting orders to advance. He stops to allow six wounded Marines to pass in front of him on their way to the rear. He speaks briefly with some of the Marines waiting to attack and then heads off to find the advancing A Company, following the clearing made by a tank, stepping over and around the bodies of Enemy Soldiers. The roar of battle rises as he nears the front line, but then it drops off suddenly. He stops and listens. Firing is still going on but sporadically. Wondering what happened, he starts moving forward again.

After about 100 meters he finds the front line and the reason for the drop in fighting. Jamison is standing just inside the tree line. The forest in front of her has disappeared for the most part, its trees blasted by heavy Navy guns and burned by napalm all the way to The Enemy's encampment, about two hundred meters away. Her Company and the tanks have stopped at the ragged edge of the forest. Marines are firing at the few Enemy soldiers trying to make a stand. A tank's main gun barks. A pickup truck in the camp goes flying into the air before landing upside down.

"Captain," Sam says as he walks up beside her.

"Sir," she says, looking around at his voice, surprised to see the Brigadier standing next to her in the front line.

"Status."

"I have patrols probing forward before we attack in force. One problem is finding a good route for the armor. Those big Navy guns left holes too deep for them to readily navigate. Not that I'm complaining, sir," she hurriedly adds.

"No, of course, not," Sam says, smiling. Sam can still hear the naval guns, but their shells are landing far to the north, he assumes in the Irish sector.

"Sir, should I be doing something differently?" she asks, nervous about having her Brigadier watching.

"Captain, I'm not here to run your Company or to second-guess you," Sam says, as reassuringly as he can. "I just want to know what's going on."

"Yes, sir," she replies, relief in her voice.

"But if you need anything, I'm here."

"Yes, sir. Thank you, sir," she says.

"Boss," a Color Sergeant says, as he comes running up, so focused on the Captain, he doesn't notice the Brigadier, "patrols report The Enemy has fallen back to and through the camp. Corporal Gottering says they've taken a thousand or more POWs. Seems like the bloody bastards are falling all over themselves to surrender. He says they need help."

"Colors, I can still hear some fighting," Sam comments dryly.

The Color Sergeant freezes for a moment, becoming aware of the Brigadier for the first time.

"Sir, sorry, sir," he stammers out. "I, I didn't see you …"

"Never mind that, Colors," Sam says. "I'm just here observing."

As he talks, Jamison is ordering the rest of the Company to advance, holding one Troop back as a reserve. She then reports to Lee.

As she moves forward with her Company and armor, which is picking its way carefully around the deep shell and bomb craters, Sam steps into the open. Looking to his right, he sees Marines and armor pouring out of the woods, rapidly advancing on the camp. Firing is sporadic, with occasional heavy bursts. Any check in the advance is quickly dealt with by the tanks' main guns or their heavy machine guns.

Sam motions for his radio operator. Picking up the handset, he contacts Staffero for an update. With the help of naval air and gun support, and Marine armor, the Irish have beaten off the human wave attacks and are advancing with armor support.

"Have Forty move into The Enemy camp's flank," he tells Staffero. "What's Four Two's status?"

"They have landed and are awaiting orders."

"Excellent," Sam says. "Use them as you need to."

"Yes, sir. And you?"

"I'm going to take a closer look at The Enemy's camp."

"Sir, I would not recommend that. It's not secure yet."

"Thank you for your concern, Colonel," he says, signing off and handing the handset to the radio operator. Sam has two purposes in crossing with this Company. One is his need, or desire, to see what is happening. He has never been happy watching from the sidelines. The other is that he wants Staffero to gain command experience and confidence in her own abilities.

Sam follows the Marines of Four Five and Four Six across the open space and into The Enemy's camp.

"Brigadier," the radio operator says, holding out the handset, "the Colonel."

"Staffero?" Sam says as he keys it.

"Thirty reports up to two thousand Enemy fleeing west in a body about two kilometers off. I have ordered Four Five in pursuit, with Four Two moving to support as soon as they are able. Air is tracking with heat sensors. Attack choppers will strike as soon as we confirm their position and Thirty is out of the way."

"Armor?"

"Moving in support but their pace will be slowed going through the forest. I have ordered Four Five to engage as quickly as possible with choppers providing fire support. Three Thirty Troops will be in support."

"Well done, Colonel."

"And sir, we are moving Brigade HQ onto shore."

"Have it set up in The Enemy's Camp. We will take it over as our base for now."

"Yes, Boss."

Sam hands the receiver back to the operator. He watches as Four Five Commando quickly reorganizes and sets off in combat formation. A company each of tanks and APVs follow, each in a column of twos, but, as Staffero pointed out, cutting paths through the trees slows them down. Four Six's Marines spread out.

About ten minutes later, the Marines of Forty and Four Two arrive. Four Two does not break its march route, heading off through the path cut by the armor. Sam watches as Judy strides along with her Marines, watching to make sure they keep moving in good order.

Forty's commanding officer, Lieutenant Colonel Blair Fraiser, finds Lee. The two quickly make a plan with Forty taking over guarding the camp and POWs while Four Six's Marines stand down. They gather inside the camp to rest, eat, and replenish supplies of ammo and water.

Standing in the middle of the wreckage of what used to be the Enemy camp, Sam watches as a squadron of attack helicopters sweep overhead, heading west.

"They must have found The Enemy," he says to no one in particular. He soon hears the muffled sounds of distant rocket and chain-gun fire. "That should slow them down."

"Sir," an aide says to Sam, coming up and saluting.

"Second Leftentant!" a Color Sergeant barks at the aide, "you never salute the Brigadier in a combat zone! You could draw fire on him!"

The aide stops short, his mouth moving but no words coming out as his face flushes bright red.

"Thank you, Colors," Sam says, a small smile crossing his lips.

"Sir!" the Color Sergeant says, then backs off, watching the new officer closely.

"I'm sorry, sir," the Second Lieutenant finally manages to stammer out. "I, I didn't think."

"That's alright, son. What is it you want to tell me?"

"Sir," he says, regaining some composure, "where would you like HQ established?"

"I think this spot will do just brilliantly."

"Yes, sir," comes the aide's dubious reply as he surveys the scene of scattered bodies and wrecked tents. He realizes someone will have to organize a cleanup detail before HQ tents can be set up. Then he realizes that someone is him. Sighing, he sets off to find HQ personnel to start the work.

The attack helicopters peel off as the leading elements of Four Five Commando make contact with The Enemy. D Company is in the lead. Quickly, A and C Companies come up, forming a line that overlaps The Enemy by a bit.

In the blasted area in front of them, trees have been shredded by the rocket and chain-gun fire. Bodies and parts of bodies are strewn around the ground. Sergeants are driving the shell-shocked survivors into a ragged line to fight the Marines. The Sergeants shoot down any soldier who tries to flee. But the increasing volume of fire from the Marines prompts an increasing number of Soldiers to make the attempt. Some succeed.

Four Two Commando nearly runs to catch up to the fighting, outpacing the armor.

"Where do you want us?" Judy asks McLaren when she finds her fellow commander kneeling behind the line, directing the fight.

"Deploy to attack through us as soon as the armor is up. My blokes are fagged out," the senior commander on the scene says. "We will have your flanks."

"Will do. The tanks are no more than ten minutes behind us," Judy says.

"So I hear," McLaren says, smiling a bit. "By the way, how are you doing?" she asks, looking at Judy's growing stomach. Both duck as bullets fly just over their heads.

"I'm fine," Judy replies, looking toward the battle line. "I'll make it through this operation easily."

"Excellent," McLaren says as they both duck again.

"Best get moving," Judy says as she heads off to deploy her Commando. Three Companies form the line, each with a Troop in reserve. The fourth company is the Commando reserve. A few minutes after the Marines deploy, the tanks come crashing up through the trees, already deployed in attack formation, with the APVs deployed in a line behind them covering the gaps between tanks. Judy had contacted their commander with the plan, including the width of the attack line.

As the Marines and armor surge forward with machine guns and rifle fire blasting the line in front of them, the remaining Enemy Soldiers panic. Some head for the rear, killing the Sergeants who try to stop them, while others drop their weapons. The few who stand trying to surrender are hit by the fuselade of fire coming from the armor and the Marines. The rest either drop to the ground or run for the rear, many of those being hit.

It takes Judy and her officers and Color Sergeants a few minutes to get the firing stopped. The armor stops a few meters in front of what had been The Enemy's firing line. The dead and wounded, some screaming in pain and calling for help, are scattered on the ground.

Two companies move in to secure the battle ground. Judy sends the other two companies after the fleeing Enemy. She calls in helicopters with infrared to track the fugitives and attack helicopters to support her two Companies.

Medics from both Commandos move in to treat the wounded, first tending the fourteen Marines who were hit before turning their attention to the Enemy casualties, while other Marines collect the prisoners, making sure they are not armed and collecting the weapons in piles. They will be destroyed later. Among the prisoners are four Sergeants, prized captives Intelligence hopes can provide some insight into The Enemy's command structure. But before they can be separated from the other POWs, one Soldier pulls out a large hunting knife and slits the throats of two of them. A Marine saves the other two by knocking the attacker to the ground with the butt of his rifle, then taking the knife away.

"You didn't waste the bloke?" another Marine says, looking at the dazed prisoner as the surviving Sergeants are led away.

"Nah," the first Marine says, "if it was up to me, I'd let him gut all of those bloody sods."

The prisoners are docile and scared. They calm down when they realize they are not going to be killed by these fighters with funny accents. They calm down further when the Marines hand out water to them. They stare at an obviously pregnant officer who walks up to look at them and issues orders to their captors. They are taken aback when they realize she is in command.

McLaren has two of her Companies come up to help guard the nearly seven hundred POWs who were in the area that was blasted by the helicopters. A burst of firing to the west captures the attention of the two commanders. They listen intently as it rises and then abruptly ends.

"That's a good sign," McLaren says.

"Yes," Judy responds. "Casualties?"

"Eight wounded, one seriously," she replies. "Good thing these blokes can't shoot worth a bloody damn. You?"

"If nothing changes," Judy says, waving a hand toward the west, "Six, all light. It seems your guys took the fight out of them."

"I think the armor had something to do with that," McLaren observes.

"No doubt," Judy responds with a bit of a laugh. "Grant, report," Judy says in her radio headset to the senior Company commander of the pursuing force.

"A few got away," he reports. "Nearly a hundred KIA. About two hundred POWs, including the wounded. We're policing the weapons and then will head back."

"Casualties?"

"One. You-know-who stood up to see what was going on. He took a through-and-through in his right leg. He won't be walking for a bit."

"Right," Judy says shaking her head. "Do you need medical?"

"We'll be back in ten. Wounded are being loaded into the APVs."

"Brilliant," Judy says, signing off.

CHAPTER 31

S arge, how much longer we gonna be out here?" Private Horace McVey asks.

"Until the Boss says we bloody well don't have to be. Got that?" an irritated Sergeant Michael Standard snaps at his chronic complainer.

"Yes, Sarge," comes the reply as the Marines put their kit together after their third night on patrol. They cautiously cover about ten kilometers a day, looking for signs of The Enemy. So far, they've come up empty.

"Everything alright?" Lieutenant Stan Franklin asks Standard as he walks by.

"Brilliant, Boss. No problems," comes the grumpy reply.

Franklin smiles and just keeps walking. "Colors!" he says to Color Sergeant Mikey Garrity. "We need to move quickly."

"Ten minutes, Boss. What's up?"

"We have a sighting. Don't know how large, just a sizeable blip on the infrared. About three klicks north of here."

"Are they moving?"

"Appears they're stationary for now. Hence the need to move."

"Yes, Boss," Garrity responds, then sets off to make sure the Marines in Nine Troop, D Company, Forty, are moving quickly.

"Sergeant," Franklin says to another Sergeant, "your lot have point. Get started."

"Right now, Boss," she replies. "Okay, you blokes, move your asses! George, you're on point!"

Without another word, the Marines start heading north, carrying nothing that can make a sound as they move as silently as possible through the forest, alert to any out-of-place sounds. They've gone about half a kilometer when George signals the column to stop and drops to one knee. Franklin quickly moves to the head of the column.

"What?" he says in a whisper.

George points to her ear then down the path. A second later, the movement continues. People moving through the woods, and not too quietly. Using hand signals, Franklin has his Troop go to ground.

Two women in ragged uniforms come half-running, half-walking through the forest. They pass George and Franklin without seeing them. When they are two meters down the path, Franklin stands up, bringing the rest of the Marines to their feet, weapons pointed at the two fugitives.

The two women scream and look for a way out. They are surrounded. One drops to the ground, crying, her head buried in her hands. The other stands defiantly but fear is written across her face. They don't know who these people pointing guns at them are.

"Sergeant," the defiant one says, the words flowing quickly as Franklin walks up, "we weren't deserting. Just looking for our unit. We got separated when the attack began…"

Franklin holds up his hand to stop her tirade. "I am not one of your Sergeants. I am a Leftenant. Leftenant Franklin with the British Royal Marines. You may address me as Leftenant. You are our prisoners. If you do not resist, you will not be hurt. Do you understand?"

"Yes," the defiant one says cautiously, a look of suspicion on her face. The other just looks up, hope on her face.

"Sergeant," Franklin says, "take charge of the prisoners."

"Yes, Boss," Standard says.

Franklin then leads the rest of the Troop north.

"Sarge, do you want me to pat down the prisoners?" Private Herman Percival asks.

"Stand down, you bloody pervert," Standard growls. "Corporal Davies, take charge of the prisoners. I don't want no surprises."

"Yeah, Sarge," she responds. Turning to the two women, she tells the one on the ground to stand. She gets shakily to her feet. "Here's the deal, you lot: If you behave, you get treated well. We'll give you food and water. We'll take care of you. If you try to escape or attack us or try to warn your mates …"

"Our what?" the defiant one asks.

Davies is confused for a moment. "Your friends, the blokes you were with."

"What are blokes?" the nervous one asks in a weak voice.

"Oh, for the bloody love of God," Davies says in exasperation. "Just don't try to make any noise and don't let anyone know where we are. Got that?"

"Yes," they reply.

"I'm Corporal Janice Davies. What are your names?"

"You sound funny," the defiant one says.

"What … and you sound funny to me. It's called an accent. Now what're your names?" comes the irritated demand.

"I'm Yolanda," the defiant one says.

"I'm Maryanne."

"Brilliant," Davies says. "Hold your arms out like this," she says, stretching her arms out straight from her body. Yolanda and Maryanne follow her example. Davies then runs her hands over their bodies checking for weapons or other dangerous items. She finds a hunting knife tucked into Yolanda's pants.

"You're not allowed to have this," Davies says, holding it up.

"Can I get it back?"

"We'll see. I'll hold on to it for now," she replies. "Let's go," she says, indicating for the two women to walk in front of her, about in the middle of the Marines. The Section then heads off after the rest of the Troop. They walk quietly through the woods, hearing a few birds and the sound of small animals scurrying through the brush and the trees.

Standard holds up a hand, stopping the column. He looks back at Davies, who nods in understanding. She gets her two charges to sit on the forest floor, while the rest of the Section catches up to the Troop.

When Standard finds Garrity, the Color Sergeant uses hand signals to indicate The Enemy is near and he is to hold his Section in reserve. Standard nods in understanding, then has his Marines deploy in a compact line, lying down.

The rest of the Troop is quietly approaching The Enemy camp. About fifty soldiers are there, with at least four Sergeants in command.

Franklin surveys the scene again. Then, when he is sure everyone is in place, he quietly orders the attack over the Troop's radio net. The Marines on the firing line, open up on The Enemy, aiming particularly for the Sergeants. Nearly everyone standing in The Enemy camp is hit, with a few able to dive for cover. The rest are either sitting or lying down, so they are able to avoid the fusillade coming in. A weak, ineffective fire is returned, but quickly ends. In takes a few minutes, but Franklin orders a ceasefire as soon as he realizes resistance has ended.

Quiet descends on the forest.

"Please, don't shoot!" a plaintive voice comes from The Enemy camp after a few minutes. "We won't shoot back! We quit!"

Franklin pauses for a moment before replying. "If you wish to surrender, stand up with your hands in the air and no weapons!" he orders.

One person stands with his hands raised over his head. When he is not shot, another stands. Then another. Then three more. Finally, nearly thirty soldiers are standing with hands over their heads. A few only have one arm up, the other apparently injured. No weapons in sight.

"Slowly walk forward!" Franklin calls. Four with leg wounds can stand but can't walk. They stay in place, obviously worried about what will happen to them.

"Colors," Franklin says over the radio net, "secure the camp and those four."

"Yes, Boss," he replies, leading two Sections into the camp. One of the wounded has dropped to the ground, unable to stand any longer. The bodies of fifteen dead and seven severely wounded are spread around. Two Sergeants are among the dead. Another is lying badly wounded with a gut shot, frothy blood coming from his mouth. The Marines look at him, then move on, sweeping the camp, securing weapons, checking the bodies, and providing first aid.

"Hey, Colors," a Marine calls, "you need to look at this."

Garrity returns to where the injured Sergeant lays. The wounded man is now dead, a sharp stick rammed through his throat. Garrity and the Marine look down at the corpse, then at the three wounded Soldiers around him. All are suffering. None seem to be interested in the Sergeant.

"He's done for," the Marine says dryly.

"No loss," Garrity says.

"Hey, you! Stop!" a Marine yells from the where the POWs are being searched. Garrity starts to move but sees Franklin is already there.

"What the bloody hell happened?" the Lieutenant asks the Corporal, who is standing over a barefoot, ragged POW sprawled on the ground, his eyes wide in fear of the rifle pointed at his chest.

"This silly sod pulled that bloody big knife," pointing to the blood-covered weapon lying a short distance away, "and ripped that bloke's head just about clean off," the Corporal responds. "Done him in proper."

"Where in the hell did he get the bloody knife?"

"Sorry, Boss, they were in the back and we hadn't quite got to them yet."

"Understood," Franklin says, studying the body that still has blood flowing from the horrific wound to the neck. "See those stripes? He's one of those Sergeants. I suppose that's what provoked the attack."

"What do you want us to do, Boss?" the Corporal asks.

"I want you to make sure no one else has any weapons."

"I mean about him?" the Corporal says, indicating the man lying on the ground.

Franklin looks at the man for a moment. "Get him back with the others. But check for more weapons first."

"Yes, Boss," the Corporal says. "Alright, you silly sod, on your feet," he says to the man, who gets slowly, warily up. "Check him," the Corporal tells another Marine. The POW gets patted down, then put with the others. The dead Sergeant is left where he was killed.

Franklin contacts his Company commander, updating him on the situation. A few moments later, he gets his orders.

"Colors," he says, walking up Garrity, "we are to move this lot to a clearing about half a klick to the west. The clearing's wide enough for our big choppers to land. I'm going to take two Sections to secure the LZ. You organize this lot to get everyone there."

"Right, Boss," Garrity says.

Franklin takes two Sections and heads off toward the landing zone. Garrity has his Marines create stretchers out of the few tents in The Enemy camp, using the tent poles and M-1 rifles, ammo removed. The POWs are formed into a column of twos with stretcher bearers in the middle, four to a stretcher, and the walking wounded helped along by their fellow POWs.

The Marines form a security guard on both flanks and the rear, with half a Section leading the way. Two of the stretcher cases die on the way. The Color Sergeant wants to leave their bodies in the forest, but gives in to the protests of their fellow POWs who want to bury them. They bring the bodies along.

As they work their way toward the landing site, they are met by four Marines sent back to show them the way. When they reach the clearing, two large helicopters are waiting for them. The POWs are loaded aboard, then they and the Marines are flown to Long Island.

When they land, the wounded are taken to hospital while the rest are put in a stockade built next to the Brigade's home base. About four thousand POWs are being held for processing. The dead are buried in a graveyard that has been created nearby, their names and date of death scratched on the boards serving as temporary head stones.

The POWs will be released when they are deemed no longer a threat and when they have decided whether to join a fighting force that is being formed or move into some kind of civilian life.

The few Sergeants who have survived long enough to be taken prisoner are held separately for their own safety. No one knows what to do with them. Interrogation provides little useful information. The Sergeants seem to know nothing about the command and control of their organization, not even how or from where their orders come, or why it is breaking down.

The members of the Troop are assigned quarters until they return to their Commando on the mainland.

"Thank you for coming," Sam tells Fraiser as she enters his office in the Brigade's permanent HQ on Long Island and comes to attention. "Oh, stand easy. We're alone," he says, sitting back in his chair.

"Thank you, Brigadier," she replies relaxing a bit.

"Have a seat, Blair," Sam says, waving toward a chair in front of his desk as he pulls a bottle of Scotch and two glasses from the bottom drawer of his desk. "Drink?"

"Yes, sir," she says appreciatively. "That would be nice."

Sam pours two drinks, passing one over to her. She reaches to pick it up, then sits back, taking a sip.

"How are things going?"

"Very well, sir," Fraiser answers. "We have the area secure and have started basic training. All the POWs seem anxious to get back at their captors."

"How many will join the military?"

"Perhaps a bit more than half. Say, eighteen thousand."

"And the rest?"

"The blokes from here are interviewing them. As soon as they are done, they will be given jobs. Some of those people are quite talented. They have already identified engineers, teachers, medical types, you know, doctors and nurses, and a few dentists. Some mechanics, electricians, and plumbers. And apparently there are a number of farmers, who the Long Islanders really seem interested in."

"When do you anticipate advanced training for the military will begin?"

"Perhaps in two months," she replies thoughtfully.

"Brilliant," Sam says. "The Army is scheduled to be here in four months. I would like these blokes to be properly trained before they get here. They won't be Marines but they will be proper Soldiers."

"Yes, sir. We can do that."

"Right," Sam says. "Now for the real reason I asked you here. I want to keep Nine Troop here to help train the Long Islanders and any of those in the stockade who are going to join the military. The Long Islanders can decide what to do with the others. The Colonel has organized a number of training sessions in both camps, so we can send them to a beginning one."

"Yes, sir," Fraiser says, a bit unhappy about losing one of her best Troops.

"I'm sorry to do this to you, but I am trying to speed things up so they are finished by the time we shove off for home. And I think the Long Islanders will take to training better if they do it here."

"Won't they have to join with the forces on the mainland?"

"They haven't decided what they will do. I hope they will, but in any case, I want them prepared.

"Yes, sir."

"Thanks for understanding," Sam says in a way that she knows he appreciates her sacrifice and acknowledges her being unhappy with the situation. "Before you head back," he says, "see the Colonel about anything you need. And here, take this with you," he says, handing her an unopened bottle of twelve-year-old single malt.

"Thank you, sir," she enthusiastically responds, as she reaches across the desk for the scotch.

❦

"Did you enjoy some R and R this week?" Sams asks the three Marines standing at ease in front of his desk.

"Yes, sir," Franklin, Standard, and Davies reply in unison.

"Brilliant," he says, looking at each of them, dressed in new uniforms and looking rested. "I apologize for separating you from your Company, but I need you here to train these blokes on Long Island."

"Yes, sir." Again in unison.

Sam looks down, smiling to himself. Looking back up, he says, "The three of you have each compiled excellent combat records, both on the Continent and here." He holds up a hand to prevent them from saying anything. "Sergeant Standard, you are promoted Color Sergeant. Corporal Davies you are promoted Sergeant." Turning to the officer, he says, "Leftenant Franklin, you have earned a Capitancy." Sam pauses, then rushes on, "But if I do that, I would have to transfer you to staff duty. You are, quite honestly, too valuable in the field. Once we are back home, you may have your pick of assignments that go with higher rank. As soon as one of those slots open up, it's yours."

"Yes, sir. Thank you, sir." He looks appreciatively at Sam. "I wouldn't want to leave my guys until this is over, so again, thank you, sir."

"Brilliant," Sam says. "Now, Color Sergeant, Sergeant, if you will excuse us, I have some things to discuss with the Leftenant."

"Sir," both say, coming to attention and saluting. Sam stands to return the salute, then watches them leave before sitting down.

"Leftenant, please," Sam says, waving a hand toward a chair.

"Thank you, sir," Franklin says, sitting down.

"A drink?" Sam says, retrieving his Scotch bottle and two glasses from the bottom desk drawer.

"Thank you, sir," Franklin says, taking the offered glass.

Sam takes a sip of the whiskey. "I want you to cull out any of your guys who won't be a good fit as trainers. I want these people properly trained, without leaving any bad tastes behind."

"Yes, sir. And what should I do with them?"

"Your call. Either detail them to other duties here or send them off with the Company as replacements for any shortages in the other Troops."

Franklin laughs a bit. "That, sir, could raise a bit of stink with my fellow Troop commanders."

Sam laughs in his turn. "I am well aware of that, Leftenant. That is why I am dumping this decision on you."

"Thank you, sir. I appreciate that. I think," he answers, a dubious tone in his voice.

Sam just laughs. "The Colonel is handling the operation on the mainland. You'll report to me. I want a training plan by the day after tomorrow. Doable?"

"Yes, sir. Quite."

"Good," Sam says, indicating by his body language that the meeting is over. Franklin quickly drains his glass, stands, comes to attention, salutes, and leaves.

Sam turns his swivel chair around, facing the French doors along the back wall of his office. He looks out at the water and the camp sprawling along the shore. Thinking.

CHAPTER 32

A lright, sweetheart," Sarah says over the dinner table at their quarters between their HQs, "you've been ducking this conversation for four months now. It has to stop. You've been, not moody exactly, but withdrawn. A bit," she hurries on as Sam starts to protest, "just a bit. I want to know why."

"We ship out in two days," he says, playing with the beef and vegetables on his plate, then taking a sip of wine.

Sarah says nothing, just looks across the table at her husband, waiting for him to continue.

"You know, my senior officers think I'm well past fifty," he says with a shrug, looking up at her.

"Well," she replies, "since we don't know your birthday, we don't really know how old you are."

"The docs tell me that physically I have the body of a man close to his sixties." He pauses for a moment. "I don't have the stamina I used to have. I can't run as far or as long. My knees hurt if I push too hard."

"Your mind is still in prime form," Sarah protests. "That is what a commander, a Brigadier, needs above all else."

Sam shrugs. "You know before we went onto the mainland, my senior commanders told me I am too old to take the lead in the field."

"They didn't!" Sarah says, shocked.

"Not in so many words, but that was the gist of what they were saying. They were worried that I would be a burden on the ranks, that some Marines might get injured trying to protect me in a firefight."

"Those bloody sods," Sarah blurts out. "Was Judy a part of this mutiny?"

"That's pretty harsh," Sam says softly. "It wasn't a mutiny. They were concerned for my safety and the safety of the ranks should I be involved in a firefight. And, yes, Judy was a part of this. I would have been disappointed if she hadn't been supportive of her fellow officers in this. And for all I know, she may agree with them."

"You never asked her?"

"No," Sam says, sighing. "I would not put her on the spot like that. It wouldn't be fair. Perhaps someday. After we return home," he says wistfully.

"What does all this mean then?" Sarah asks, leaning forward and taking his hand that is lying on the table.

"It means," Sam says, reaching across the table to take her other hand, "that I will step down as Brigadier after we get home. Michelle will capably fill the slot. Who she picks as her Chief of Staff is not my problem."

"You're putting in your papers?" Sarah says, a bit shocked at the thought of Sam retiring.

"Ah, no," he says. "I have been offered a Major Generalcy responsible for operational planning and readiness."

"That's in London, isn't it?" Sarah asks, worried that they may have to leave the home they have lived in for more than thirty years, and what he expects her to do about her career.

"No, that was part of the deal," Sam says, a bit triumphantly. "I can set up my HQ anywhere I like. We will stay in our home and you can do anything you bloody well please."

Sarah sits back and looks at Sam. "Why now? It's not just the physical thing is it?"

"No," Sam says, a bit ruefully. "I, even more than you, have spent a great deal of time away from home." He looks out the window for as moment before turning back to Sarah, his voice wistful. "Away from our children and grandchildren. I missed a lot of our children's childhood. I can't make up the time I lost with Frank," he says, the sorrow evident in his voice, "but perhaps I can to some extent with the others. I want to be there for them. You know, take care of our grandchildren when their parents are busy or away. Go on proper holidays with our family. My new job will have some travel, but not a great deal. And I'll be off most weekends and holidays."

"And what would you like me to do?"

"My love, you will do whatever you like. All I ask is that you accept my decision to step back from active operations."

"Of course, I accept your decision," she says. She looks out the windows at the growing dark. "I am not going to let you have all the fun," she says, forcefully, looking back at Sam, giving his hands a squeeze before sitting back in her chair.

Sam looks at her quizzically.

"It will take two of us to handle all those grandkids," she says, smiling. "I have twelve years of active duty and more than twenty in the reserves. That's more than enough time."

"You're going to retire?"

"Not exactly," she replies, "I'll go on inactive reserve status. You know, break glass only in the case of an emergency."

"And?" Sam asks, knowing his wife is not just going to tend the grandchildren and their garden.

"And I will become a consulting engineer," she says, a bit of pride in her voice. "I have the reputation that will keep jobs coming my way until I say stop."

"And when will that be?"

"When I bloody well feel like it!" she says sharply.

"You've been thinking about this, too, haven't you?" Sam asks, looking at her quizzically.

"Yes, a bit," Sarah admits. "Now and again. I've just been waiting for you to call it a day. As long as I stayed on active duty, I could still be with you in the field. But now that you are no longer going to be there, I would much prefer to stay home."

Sam laughs a bit. "So we are closing a door."

"Only to open another."

Printed in the United States
by Baker & Taylor Publisher Services